Debra Hurford Brown

About the Author

LOUISE WENER, author of a second novel *The Perfect Play*, was born and raised in Ilford, East London. In the mid-1990s, after years of singing into hair brushes and working in dead-end jobs, she found fame as lead singer with the pop band Sleeper and went on to record three top-ten albums and eight top-forty singles. She lives in London.

Goodnight Steve McQueen

Goodnight Steve McQueen

A NOVEL

Louise Wener

Perennial
An Imprint of HarperCollins*Publishers*

Thanks for permission to quote "Bad Harmony," written by Frank Black, published by Spime Songs (BMI).

This book was originally published in Great Britain in 2002 by Hodder and Stoughton, a division of Hodder Headline.

HarperCollins books may be purchased for educational, business, or sales promotional use. For information please write: Special Markets Department, HarperCollins Publishers Inc., 10 East 53rd Street, New York, NY 10022.

First Perennial edition published 2005.

Designed by Nancy Singer Olaguera

Library of Congress Cataloging-in-Publication Data

ISBN 0-06-072563-X

05 06 07 08 09 ❖/RRD 10 9 8 7 6 5 4 3 2 1

For Andy

Goodnight Steve McQueen

1

Do you remember the quiz show *Winner Takes All*? It had a top prize of one thousand pounds. They kept it in a Perspex display case. A thousand crisp green notes. Right there. Right under your nose, and it was real money as well, not like those cheques they wave about on *Who Wants to be a Millionaire?*

I can't remember anyone winning it, though. Not ever. Most of the contestants seemed happy with fifty quid and a slap on the back from Liza Tarbuck's dad: a weekend for two in Blackpool if they were lucky. And you knew it would rain the whole time they were there. And you knew Peter from Wilmslow was secretly gay so he'd have to take Beryl, his arthritic nan, instead of Rita, his imaginary wife. And you knew he wouldn't be able to go backstage and have his picture taken with the Nolan Sisters after all, because he'd have to be back at the Grand Palace B&B before the ten o'clock curfew.

Thanks, Tarby. Thanks very much.

I mean, what a con. Talk about massaging the truth. It should have been called *Loser Takes All*. It should have been called *No-*

Hope-Rubbish-Hair-Crap-Job-No-Prospects-Lousy-Boyfriend-Loser Takes All.

I can't help thinking I would have done rather well.

My name is Steve McQueen and I'm a very bitter man. What on earth were they thinking of, calling me Steve? Didn't they realise it would ruin me? Didn't they know I'd be tortured? Didn't they understand it would be impossible for me to live up to? Did they hell. It was my mum's fault, of course, she was obsessed with him. The only reason she married my dad in the first place was because of the name. It didn't matter that he was a geography teacher. It didn't matter that he was bald at the age of eighteen, fat at the age of twenty-two, and dead at the age of thirty-three and a half. Mum had what she'd always wanted. She'd married herself a genuine McQueen.

I was three years old when my father died—he had a heart attack on a field trip to an ox-bow lake—and for a long time I actually thought Steve McQueen was my real dad. I remember my mum sitting me down to watch *The Towering Inferno* when I was five—spooning down my second helping of Heinz spaghetti hoops—and feeling really proud. We both clapped at the end. What a guy. He'd even managed to save Fred Astaire and the cat. What a guy. What a dad.

There were pictures of him all over the house. Steve driving his Porsche 917 from *Le Mans*, Steve flying through the air in his 1968 Mustang from *Bullitt*, Steve being chased by Nazis in *The Great Escape*, and a giant scrapbook filled with press cuttings that she kept in a bruised leather suitcase under her bed.

"Who's this?" I said, flicking through her scrapbook one afternoon. "Who is this?"

"It's Ali MacGraw, the lady out of *Love Story*."

"What's *Love Story*?"

"Oh, it's so sad. Oh, I don't think I can talk about it. Not without crying."

And off she went, off to fetch a hankie from the dressing-table drawer, and all I could think was, Why is Dad doing that? What is Dad doing kissing Ali MacGraw?

I suppose things were okay to begin with. I was a great-looking child. I looked like the Milky Bar Kid only cuter: white blond hair, wire-rimmed spectacles, and the cheekiest, wide-mouthed, gap-toothed grin you've ever seen.

She was dead proud of me. I could tell she thought there was hope: that I might grow up to be a movie star or a Formula 1 driver or a teenage multimillionaire, and for a few precious years (apart from finding out that my dad was a dead geography teacher instead of an A-list Hollywood star) I was blissfully happy.

I brought home crayon drawings of racing cars and Mum stuck them on the fridge next to her collection of Steve McQueen quotes. I built models of doomed Apollo rockets out of cornflake packets and Mum put them on the sideboard next to her picture of Steve McQueen's house: 27 Oakmont Drive, Brentwood, California—we knew the address by heart. I collected model motorcycles, built planes out of balsa wood and elastic bands, and I even went to martial arts classes on account of my namesake being a third-dan black belt in karate. I was rather good at it. I won the club's under-tens trophy in 1979. It was a great year. The same year I won a *Blue Peter* badge for my papier-mâché Shep.

And then it all went wrong.

"What's this?" I said, pointing to an angry red lump on my forehead. "What *is* this?"

"Acne."

"What's acne?"

"Oh. It's so awful. I don't think I can talk about it. Have you been masturbating, Steve McQueen?"

Of course I'd been masturbating. I was thirteen years old. My life was one long shower. I was the cleanest teenager in the whole of Woodford Wells. I masturbated so much I worried that my cock would spontaneously combust from all the friction (spontaneous combustion was very big in the eighties), and anyway it was supposed to make you go blind, not cover your face in deep-pile *acne vulgaris*. I didn't wank again for almost three years. I didn't dare.

I tried everything I could think of. I gave up chocolate, stopped drinking milk, painted my skin with foul-smelling potions that made my skin peel like a sun-baked onion, but nothing did any good. Every morning I'd wake up in a pool of nocturnal emissions, half my face stuck to the brushed-nylon pillowcase, desperate for a wank and a bowl of Coco Pops, hoping against hope that nothing had grown in the night, but it always had. There they were, regular as clockwork: a brand-new crop of festering, pus-laden fumaroles, steaming on the side of my once perfect cheeks.

She thought they were disgusting. My own mother. I can still remember the look on her face when she realised I'd have scars. It's the same look she had when I told her they were remaking *The Thomas Crown Affair* with Pierce Brosnan and Rene Russo.

"It won't be the same," she said quietly. "It just won't be the same."

Needless to say my teenage years were hell. My friends called me Moony on account of my lunar-landscaped face and my enemies—of which there were many—called me twat. I did have a girlfriend, though: Vivian Ducksford. She was fifteen years old with eyes the colour of sucked Black Jacks, and it was common knowledge that she let boys finger her for chips in the local swimming baths. It was only a matter of time before I plucked up the courage and took my turn.

"You shouldn't be doing this, Vivian," I said, eyes half closed from a crop of particularly livid styes. "Everyone thinks you're a slag."

"I'm not a slag. I'm mature for my age."

This was true. She had bigger tits than my mum.

"Yeah, but, erm . . . everyone *thinks* you're a slag."

"Are you going to have a go or what? I want chips afterwards, though. You got enough money for chips, right?"

I certainly did. I had fifty pence stuffed tightly into the toes of my changing room socks. I even had enough for an ice cream if she'd wanted one.

"No ice cream, just *chips*. Get it? Just chips."

"Right then, chips you say. Best get on with it, then."

For as long as I live I'll never know what possessed me to try and do it underwater. I mean, what was I thinking of? Maybe it was because I could hold my breath for a full minute and a half (Houdini was a very big influence on me in those days). Maybe I thought I'd get a better view. Either way it was a complete disaster. I couldn't find my way into her Speedo. I remember tugging and tugging at the elastic round her leg but it just wouldn't give. I think I must have touched something hairy at one point, but by then my lungs were about to explode and all I can remember is surfacing in a fit of panic; light-headed from the lack of oxygen, mouth filled with water and bits of old plasters, right thigh cramping from the giant stiffy between my legs, and it was all I could do not to pass out there and then.

It was a good job I didn't. Not only would I have quite likely drowned, I'd also have missed out on Vivian's kind words of encouragement:

"What are you doing, you wanker?"

"Sorry, sorry, I didn't . . . I couldn't . . . I can't breathe."

"What were you trying to touch me arse for? Fuckin' poofter, are you? Wait till I tell everyone what you done."

"Vivian . . . wait, I got lost . . . I got . . . I'm *not* a poofter."

Vivian wasn't listening. She'd already hoisted herself on to the side of the pool: belly flat to the wall, long arms dripping water on to the verruca-ridden tiles, contempt pouring from the back of her shiny, seal-haired head. And then she mumbled something under her breath. It took me almost five minutes to work out what it was.

"Loser," she said. "You're a loser, Steve McQueen."

2

Alison calls me at 2:30.

"You're up, then?"

"Of course I'm up. What do you mean, 'You're up, then?' I'm up!"

"Yeah, wouldn't want to miss any of *Supermarket Sweep*, would you?"

"I'm not watching *Supermarket Sweep*. I'm writing a song."

"Well listen, I'm going to be home a bit later than I thought, so go without me. I'll try and catch you at the pub later. All Bar One, right?"

"No, Harringay Arms. We're all going to the Harringay Arms."

I hear her sigh at the end of the line.

"All right then," I say, "you win, we'll go to All Bar One."

"Right, I'll see you there, some time after nine."

"Great, see you there."

"Oh, and don't drink all of my Bacardi Breezers. I'll want one when I get home."

I finish my lime Bacardi Breezer, put down my cornflakes and mute Dale Winton for a moment. Even with the sound off I can tell that Jane from the Midlands doesn't realise the crème fraîche is more expensive than the Blu Loo, and I'd usually shout something pithy and incisive at the screen at this point, but Alison's call has me worried.

Alison and I have been together almost five years now and it's probably fair to say that things aren't going as well as they might be. She's always working late, at least a couple of times a week, and she seems distant, you know, a bit distracted. Maybe it's because I've never had a proper job, maybe it's because I'm a waste-of-space musician. Maybe it's because I get up at midday, eat my breakfast in front of *Supermarket Sweep* and drink all of her Bacardi Breezers before she gets home. Maybe she's just gone off me.

"Maybe she's having an affair."

"She is not having an affair. Jesus, what makes you say that? I mean, what do you want to go and say a thing like that for? We're just going through a bad patch, that's all."

Vince sips his Staropramen. Bad patch. That's what he said before Liz left him. Just going through a bit of a bad patch, mate. Haven't had sex for three months. Haven't had sex for six months. Haven't had a blow job for the best part of a year. She's left you, hasn't she Vince? Yes mate, she's left me.

"So . . . how long since you last . . . you know . . . had a bunk-up?"

I knew he was going to ask me this.

"Yesterday, if you must know. I mean, our sex life's fine. That's not the problem. Regular as clockwork. Three times a week, twice on Sundays. Once we've read the papers, after we've boiled the eggs, after we've caught up with the *EastEnders* omnibus and taken in a bit of Formula One. If she's not too tired."

"You're lying."

"No I'm not."

"Yeah you are, you've torn the label off your Budvar."

"Right, you're right. Once a week, then . . . once a week. If I'm lucky."

Vince mulls this over for a while and then he says:

"Still, not bad though, considering you've been living together for four years."

"Exactly. That's what I thought."

"Probably just a bad patch, then."

"Yeah, bad patch. D'you fancy another drink?"

Too right he does.

I'm at the bar waiting for our beers and it strikes me (not for the first time) how much I hate All Bar One. All Bar One is a girl's boozer. It's a place girls go to talk about cellulite and makeup and blokes like me and Vince. It's the Starbucks of pubs: a pub by numbers. It's even got CCTV cameras on the walls. What the fuck for? What do they think they're going to find? Probably scanning the room for anyone who doesn't look like they work in marketing or media sales. And they always give you your change on a poncy silver tray, like you're actually going to tip them or something. Fat chance.

By the time I get back to the table Kate and Matty have turned up and everyone's planning new ways to murder Jamie Oliver. Oliver is our long-term hate figure on account of him being a wanker and having a great life and, I have to say, I'm quite taken by Vince's idea of gutting him and stuffing him with his own entrails mixed with some lemon and parsley to "bring it all together."

"Of course, the thing you have to understand is he's only half a gene away from being a retard."

"What d'you mean?"

"Well, he's got a lisp, hasn't he, and one of them tongues that are too big for his mouth. It's like Downies are one chromosome off normal and Oliver's only a half. He got lucky. He's only half a chromosome out." I love Vince. You can always count on him to lower the tone.

"So where's Alison tonight, then?"

Trust Kate to ask me this. A bloke would know better than to ask you where your girlfriend was. He'd know it might be a touchy subject. I've a fair idea Kate knows this as well but she can't resist having a pop, can't resist putting me on the spot.

"She's working late," I say. "She should be here a bit later." I glance at my watch. It's already ten o'clock.

"She's just busy at the moment, you know, lots going on."

Kate is about to say something else but Vince gives her a look and she lets it go. Alison hasn't been out with us for over a month.

It's starting to get late; the bar staff are twiddling their aprons and hassling us to leave; Matty is on the verge of asking us if we fancy going for a Chinese and I decide it's probably time to make a move. I tell Vince and Matty that I'll see them at rehearsals on Friday and I stop at the 7-Eleven for a couple of cans of Stella on the way home.

Alison is watching TV when I get in. She's stretched out across the sofa in her work clothes and she's halfway through a bottle of cheap white wine. I fancy Alison in her work clothes. Something about the black tights and the short skirt and the fitted blouse and I get the overwhelming urge to go over and run my hands up and down her nylon-covered thighs. Alison says the only reason I find office clothes attractive is because I've never worked in one. She's right, of course.

"Where were you?" I say, bending down to give her a kiss on the cheek. "Everyone was asking where you were."

"Shhh, I'm watching *Ally McBeal*. It's a John Cage episode."

"You should have come out," I say, cracking open a beer and sitting down next to her. "Vince had a brand-new way of killing Jamie Oliver."

"Shhh, I'm watching."

"Yeah, we're going to gut him like a guppy . . ."

"SHHHHH!"

"We're gonna make tartar sauce out of his own . . ."

"Danny, please. You know I like this programme. Can't you just shut the fuck up for five minutes?"

I don't say another word. I go to the kitchen, switch on the radio and sulk. I'm half hoping that she'll come after me but she doesn't. It's not what she does.

I'm in the middle of fixing myself a tasty snack of cream crackers dipped in yesterday's Bolognese sauce when I hear Vonda Shephard belting out one of her nauseating covers from the living room. I'm guessing *McBeal* has almost finished. It has.

Alison pads into the kitchen, squeezes my arm and heads over towards the fridge.

"Sorry," she says, "I didn't mean to shout at you like that. Long day at the mill."

"Yeah, well, you didn't have to bite my head off, I was only asking why you didn't come out."

"You drank all my Breezers again, didn't you?" she says, peering into the fridge.

"Y'what?"

"My Bacardi Breezers. There were two left this morning. What happened to them?"

"Shit, Alison. Sorry. I meant to buy you some more."

"But you didn't, though, did you? You never do."

"I do, I got you some on Sunday."

"You didn't, Danny. I bought them."

"Right, you're right, I'll go now. I'll go down the 7-Eleven and get you a couple."

"It's too late. It's too late to buy booze now, and anyway I've still got some wine left."

And then she starts to cry.

"What's the matter?" I say, putting my arm round her. "Did something happen at work?"

"No."

"Well what then, what's wrong?" I can't believe she's getting this worked up over a couple of alcopops.

"It's everything."

"Everything? Everything like what? Everything like us everything?" She pulls away and reaches for her wineglass.

"We've got to talk, Danny."

"Fine, let's talk then. I mean, I've been trying to talk to you for the last hour but you couldn't take your eyes off the TV set. I've been trying to talk to you since I came in."

She looks exasperated. She looks tired.

"I don't mean like that. I don't mean sitting on the sofa listening to your bloody pub anecdotes that I've heard a hundred thousand times. I mean properly. You and me. You and me, Danny. We really have to talk."

And I'm not stupid. Even I know what that means.

3

"I've been offered a new job."

"Well . . . that's good . . . *isn't it?*"

"It's in Bruges."

"Bruges?"

"It's in Belgium."

"I know where it is. It's thousands of bloody miles away."

"Four and a half hours on the Eurostar."

"Four and a half hours? What do you mean? You're not thinking of taking it, are you?"

She starts to pick her nails.

"I've been asked to work as a marketing consultant for Thorstans. They make posh chocolates, you know, the ones with all the cream in the middle."

I'm about to say something fantastically lurid about fondant fancies but I decide this probably isn't the time.

"They're planning to launch over here at the end of the year and they want someone with experience of UK markets to oversee the initial campaign. It'll be six months tops. It's really good money."

"But you can't," I say. "It'll be full of Belgians. They put mayonnaise on their chips."

"I think it would be a good idea, Danny. Give us some space from one another. I'll be home at weekends."

"I can't believe it. I can't believe you're actually thinking of taking it. When did they offer you this job exactly?"

"Last Wednesday."

"You've known about this for a week? Why the hell didn't you tell me?"

"I wanted to decide by myself. On my own."

"You've decided, then? Already? Without even speaking to me. Your boyfriend."

"Yes. And there's something else."

My heart actually stops beating. I'm so wound up I think she's said *someone* else instead of something else and I'm already imagining Alison having anal sex with a donkey-knobbed, moustachioed Belgian when she says:

"I want you to get a job."

I can barely hide the relief on my face.

*

The first time I saw Alison I knew I loved her. Granted, she was a pixie-nosed blonde with fantastic tits and legs the length of the M1, but I like to tell myself it wasn't just her looks. I flatter myself I'm a better man than that.

"Hey, Vince, take a look at her . . . stacked or what?"

It was in the Camden Falcon. The headline act had just come offstage and Alison was over by the bar chatting to her mates. I couldn't take my eyes off her. She was wearing a tight track suit top with Adidas stripes, a suede miniskirt that showed off her tanned legs, and a pair of ten-hole Doctor Marten boots that looked way too big for her feet. She wore her hair short in those days, cropped like a boy's. She looked like Mia Farrow. Only with tits.

"Go on, mate, I reckon you're on. She was watching you the whole time you were packing away the amps."

I didn't need telling twice.

"Can I buy you a drink?" I say, wondering if I still look sweaty from the gig.

She stares at me for a long second, checking me out up close, making up her mind. "Yeah, go on, then," she says. "Why not? I'll have a pint of Caffrey's."

We ended up talking for the rest of the night. Or rather she talked and I listened. I was happy just to listen. Happy that she thought I was someone worth talking to. When I ask Alison about it now, though, she just says, "Yeah, I thought you were okay, but you must have been really nervous or something because you wouldn't shut up."

"Did you enjoy the band?"

"Not much really. The singer was pretty awful."

"I was in the support band. We're called Yossarian."

"After the character in *Catch-22*?"

"Exactly. Did you see us?"

"No. I must have got here too late. We went for a curry first."

This was good. A curry-eating, pint-swilling goddess who'd even managed to miss the worst gig Yossarian had ever done. What am I saying? Every gig was the worst gig Yossarian had ever done. We were awful. My Bloody Valentine meets Nirvana meets The Smiths. Or was that The Smurfs?

"What music do you like?" (Nice one, McQueen, what a skilled conversationalist you truly are.)

"Oh, I dunno, Blur, I suppose, and Radiohead. I quite like Frank Sinatra, and Wham! when I'm pissed. Oh, and I used to like Spandau Ballet. I was in love with Gary Kemp when I was little."

I remember feeling irrationally jealous of Gary Kemp at this point.

"So what do you do in the band?"

"I'm the guitarist. I play lead—vintage Stratocaster, 1968 limited edition with classic sunburst finish."

"Hmmmm." She mulls this over for a while and then she says, "You know what's always confused me?"

"What?"

"Well, why is it that some guitars are so much bigger than the other ones? I mean why do some of them only have four strings?"

Thank God Vince wasn't listening to this. He'd have had a blue fit.

To be honest, I wasn't that bothered by Alison's lack of musical knowledge. I'm not exactly an expert myself, not like Vince—he's a walking encyclopedia. He knows everything there is to know, especially about Dylan. Dylan, Costello, and Dexy's Midnight Runners. Vince is obsessed with Dexy's Midnight Runners.

"So, what made you want to be a musician?" said Alison after I'd taken her through the rudiments of the bass guitar.

"I didn't really. I wanted to be a racing driver, or a karate champion, or a film star, or . . ."

She laughs. Her blue eyes crinkle at the edges and a crooked smile lights up her whole face. She tells me later that she thought I was unusual. She'd never met anyone who'd said they wanted to be a film star before. Not out loud.

"So what happened?"

"Well, we weren't rich enough for racing cars and I could never keep up with the karate and . . ."

"The acting?"

I shake my head. "Oh, you know, couldn't act for toffee. It's a bit crap really, you know when you find out you're no good at the one thing you always wanted to be . . ."

Alison smiles at me like she knows exactly what I mean.

*

"So what happens now? Where will I live? Who'll pay the rent?"

"I'll still pay the rent."

"But you won't be living here. You'll be shacked up with Donkey-schlong in Bruges."

"What did you say . . . ? Look, I will still be living here. I'll be home every other weekend."

"You said every weekend, now it's every other weekend . . . you see the way this is going, don't you?"

"It's only six months, Danny. It's perfect. It'll give us time to sort our lives out."

"What d'you mean? Our lives are sorted out. What's wrong with our lives?"

"We can't carry on like this. You can't carry on like this. You can't work in a video shop for the rest of your life."

"It's just until we get signed. You know I'm only doing it until we get signed."

"You're twenty-nine, Danny, you've got to be realistic. It's time you thought about doing something else."

*

"Yeah, so my uncle bought me my first guitar when I was fourteen. I'd had a nasty incident with a girl at the local swimming baths and he was trying to cheer me up, and anyway, the moment I started playing I couldn't imagine doing anything else."

"Wow, I think that's so great. I mean, I think it's really cool that you didn't go to university or anything. My parents would have had a fit if I'd told them I was dropping out of my A-levels to join a band."

We're back at Alison's shared house in Tufnell Park and we're smoking a joint and drinking neat vodka in her boxroom. She's made it nice, though, not like my hovel in Finsbury Park. It's amazing what girls can do with a lava lamp and a couple of cushions. It felt like we were in a harem.

"Well, they did go mad, at least my mum did. My dad died when I was a kid."

"Oh, I'm sorry." She says this like she really is sorry.

"I mean, it's not my mum's fault," I say, not wanting to get into my dead dad story just yet. "She had big plans for me. Wanted me to go to uni or film school or something. I think she was scared I'd end up a drug-addled waster."

"Bet she won't be saying that when you're on *Top of the Pops*."

"Exactly. Take tonight—there were three record companies down there tonight."

"To see you?"

"Well . . . no, they were there for the headline band. But they might have seen us as well. You never know."

"So have any record companies ever been down to see you?"

"Yeah, a few. I mean, we've had a lot of interest. My last band nearly got a deal with Polydor. It's just a matter of time really."

"That's so cool. How much money do you think they'll give you when you get signed?"

"Dunno, really, depends on the advances and the points and all that."

"What's points?"

I'm not entirely sure I like the way the conversation is going so I decide it's time to turn things round a bit.

"What about you?" I say, handing her the half-bottle of Absolut. "What did you want to be when you were a kid?"

"Honestly?"

"Honestly."

"Oh, I can't say it. It's too embarrassing."

"No, go on, I won't laugh, I promise."

"It's stupid really," she says. "I wanted to write detective novels. I wanted to be Agatha Christie. I mean, imagine that, how unrealistic is that?"

And she takes a long swig of vodka and gazes out of the open window onto the street.

4

"But that's your favourite thing about me. The fact that I haven't given up, that I haven't been sucked in. The fact that I haven't succumbed to the whole fast car, porcini mushroom, power suit, Arena Homme, designer bog roll *thing*."

"Like me, you mean?"

"No, not like you. I mean, you wouldn't get in Arena Homme. You're not a Homme."

"I'm serious. That's what you think of me, isn't it, that I've copped out, joined the rat race, gone over to the other side?"

"Of course not. You're different."

"How am I different, Danny? How?"

Because you're Alison.

She thinks we should go to bed. She doesn't think we're getting anywhere. She thinks we're both too tired and too drunk to say anything sensible and she doesn't want us to get things out of proportion. We can talk in the morning, she says. She'll go in late. Everything will make more sense in the morning.

You know you're in trouble when your girlfriend starts saying things like it'll make more sense in the morning.

21

*

"How you feeling?"

"Great," I say, hoping she can't smell my breath from her side of the bed.

"Not too hung over?"

"No, not too bad, really."

"You're lucky. I feel like an elephant took a dump in my head. I'm gonna make some coffee. You want some?"

"Yeah, coffee, that'll be great."

The sun is streaming through the net curtains, there's a warm breeze wafting in from the road, and I'm smoking my first Marlboro Light of the day in Alison Poole's bed. I can't believe my luck. I can't believe how great she is. I feel like I already know everything about her, everything I'll ever need to know:

"What is this, *Twenty Questions?*"

"Come on, I want to know everything about you—where you grew up, what your parents did, who makes you laugh, what clubs you used to go to on a Saturday night."

"Oh God, it's really boring. My parents are both doctors, Dad's in orthopaedics . . ."

"Bones, right?"

"Yeah, bones, and Mum's a psychiatrist."

"Shit. Does that mean you've been shrinking me out all night?"

"No way. I don't know the first thing about it. I reckon most of it's bullshit anyway. I mean, why is it always your parents' fault? Why is it every bloke who's even remotely fucked up always blames it on having an overbearing mother or something?"

I nod sagely at this point.

"I mean, I think you make your own life. You can't go on blaming your parents forever, can you?"

"No," I say. "Certainly not."

• • •

"So where did you grow up, then?"

"Epingham."

"Epingham?"

"It's near Lincoln. More of a village really. Farms, cottages, church fêtes, everyone know's everyone else's business—you know the sort of thing."

"No, not as such . . ."

"Well, I couldn't wait to get out. Sometimes I think my life only started when I moved down to London. There's only so many weekends you can spend drinking Snakebite and getting chatted up by pig farmers in Mustang Sally's before you start to go a bit mental."

"Mustang Sally's?"

"Yeah, Lincoln's finest—it's either that or the Ritzy."

"Sounds like a riot."

"Well, it wasn't, believe me. They're not as idyllic as you think, these small towns. There's all this pent-up aggression everywhere. Honestly, I saw more pub fights on a single Saturday night in Lincoln than I did the whole time I was living in King's Cross."

"So where did you study, then?"

"North London Uni. I did English. I'm just finishing a postgrad in marketing and information technology."

"Wow, that's er . . . that's . . ."

"Yeah, I know, pretty dull stuff."

"No, no, it's very . . . interesting."

"Well, I did think about doing journalism for a while but . . . I don't know, this seemed more practical, I suppose. And I'm quite into the computing side of things, especially all the Internet stuff. I reckon the Web is going to be pretty huge."

The only thing I know about the Web at this point is that spiders make them so I say:

"What about medicine? You didn't fancy being a quack like your old man?"

"No way," she says, grimacing at the thought. "I practically faint at the sight of blood. It used to drive my parents completely mad. I remember sneaking into my dad's study when I was little and having a look at some of his medical books, really gory stuff, you know—people with half their heads hanging off, kids with the skin peeled back off their arms and legs. I almost threw up on his desk. Honestly, I don't know how people cope with it. And anyway," she says, "I've had enough of hospitals to last a lifetime."

"Why, you're not ill, are you?"

"No, not me, it's my younger brother. He's schizophrenic."

"What, like two personalities?"

"No, nothing like that. But he was sick a lot of the time, just used to disappear somewhere into his head, he'd go quiet and untouchable and there was absolutely no way of reaching him, and other times he'd be totally manic, he'd stay awake for days on end, couldn't get him to go to sleep, and he'd start obsessing about things. He became convinced there were aliens in Mum's rose bushes once, and another time he thought Dad was making a nuclear bomb in the shed."

"I'm sorry," I say. "That must have been pretty rough."

"Yeah, well, he's been a lot better lately, they've pretty much got his drugs sorted out."

"Was he ever violent or anything?"

"Violent? God, no, Rufus wouldn't hurt a fly."

She looks vulnerable suddenly. She's hugging her knees to her chest and I can see where the summer sun has brought out the freckles on the bridge of her nose. She suddenly looks very young.

"So," I say, changing the subject, "did you have a pony, then?"

"*No*! No, I didn't. Shit, I did not have a bloody pony."

"I bet you did. Girls like you always had ponies."

"What do you mean girls like me? You cheeky fucker."

"You did, didn't you, and one of those hats and the tight trousers."

"They're called jodhpurs, idiot."

"I was right, ha, I knew it . . . I was right . . ."

She's hitting me now. Hitting me with a cushion like she wants to kill me, but she's laughing as much as she's shouting and she finally runs out of steam and comes over to sit next to me. She smells of perfume and tobacco and fresh sweat.

"My turn, my turn now."

"Go on then, ask me anything you like."

"I'm thinking. I'm thinking. Oh, I know, what was the name of the first girl you kissed?"

"Vivian."

"What was the name of the last girl you kissed?"

"Joanne."

"What sign are you?"

"No idea. What sign is November?"

"Not sure. Aquarius, I think, or is it Cancer? I don't know. It's bollocks really, isn't it?"

I smile and pass her the remains of the joint.

"Come on then, what else?"

"Oh, I don't know, erm . . . what's your middle name?"

"Danny."

"*Danny?* Isn't that your first name as well?"

"It's a long story," I say.

*

Alison undresses quickly and gets into bed. She plugs in her mobile, turns off her laptop and rolls over to switch out the bed-side light. I can hear the soft shoop-shoop of her breathing as she starts to drift off to sleep. I wait for her to say it. It's one of those stupid codes we have: one of those things she does to let me know that she's not cross with me any more. And then she says it: quietly, sleepily, under her breath.

"Goodnight," she says. "Goodnight, Steve McQueen."

*

"Wow! Why did you change it? God, I wish I was called something like that. I think you should use it all the time. I would."

"Trust me, it only sounds good when you're stoned."

"Yeah, but it would be great when you were booking flights and restaurants or stuff, wouldn't it? Imagine their faces. They'd be bound to give you the best table, and there's nothing they could do because it really is your name."

It's not true. I tell her about the night me and Vince took magic mushrooms and tried to blag our way into the première of *Highlander II*, and nearly got ourselves arrested:

"So I'm shouting at Sean Connery at the top of my voice, 'Sean, Sean, it's me, don't you recognise me? It's me, Steve McQueen, back from the dead. Sean, turn round. Turn round, and get them to let me in, or I'll tell the whole world you were always a fucking baldy bastard.'"

We're in fits now, we're corpsing from the dope and the vodka and the mountain of sexual tension, and suddenly she just reaches over and kisses me. Typical that it was Alison who made the first move.

It wasn't the best sex either of us had ever had but it was pretty spectacular nonetheless. She was perfect: confident and sexy and uninhibited, and I remember lying next to her as we fell into a hazy post-coital sleep, and that was the very first time she said it.

"Goodnight," she said. "Goodnight, Steve McQueen."

5

"You're late."

"Sorry, Kostas, I'll make up the time."

"Well, you'd better had, I got *A Fistful of Dollars*, *A Fistful of Fingers*, *The Good the Bads and the Ugly* and *A Town Called Bastard* and I don't know if they is supposed to go in Kongfoo or Porn."

"Westerns, Kostas, they're all westerns."

"What, even *A Town Called Bastard*?"

"Yeah, Kostas, especially *A Town Called Bastard*. You might like it, actually. Telly Savalas is in it."

"Telly Savalas is a very nice actor. There's nothing wrong to say about Telly Savalas. Why you don't like Telly Savalas?"

I give up. Sometimes you just can't win.

I've worked in Kostas Videos in Crouch End for about five years now and it suits me fine. I do three days a week, alternate evenings and the odd weekend, and it gives me all the time I need for the band.

There have been quite a few changes since I started. It used to be that we were the only video shop for miles, and then they opened a pair of Blockbusters—one in Muswell Hill, one on the other side of the Broadway—and if it hadn't been for me, Kostas would probably have gone out of business there and then.

It was a total mess. He never had enough new releases, he never remembered to check if the rentals had been returned on the right day or not, and he was forever sending people home with the wrong film in the right box. It made them furious—the only reason they put up with it was because there was nowhere else to go. And then the Blockbusters came along.

He tried everything: lowering the cost of the films, offering two for one, giving away free popcorn and crisps, but nothing worked. When his halloumi kebab promotional night failed to pull in the punters Kostas finally held up his hands. And then I had a brilliant idea.

"We're going to go specialist, Kostas."

"What you mean, like porns?"

"No, not porns. I mean, yes, some porn, but the good stuff—Russ Meyer, sixties sexploitation, stuff like that. We'll do rare stuff, stuff people can't get hold of anywhere else. Art movies and old classics, foreign films and black-and-whites, Indian cinema, Frank Capra, John Waters, Charlie Chaplin . . . I don't know. What do you think?"

"Will it keep the shop open?"

"It might."

"Then we give it a go."

It took a while to catch on but within six months people were coming from all over North London. We could get anything they wanted in forty-eight hours, and by the end of the year we'd built up a library of rare and interesting films that kept most of the punters happy without having to order in at all. The business was saved. Kostas was saved. He even came up with a brand-new logo for the front of the shop:

KOSTAS VIDEOS, NOT JUST THE SAME OLD CRAPS.

People seemed to like it.

We've built up a fiercely loyal clientèle over the years. Most of them I know by name, but out of everyone Sheila is probably my all-time favourite. She must be eighty if she's a day, but she's completely mad for martial arts movies. She's seen every one we've got (twice) but she still comes in three times a week to choose herself another tape. Regular as clockwork, right after she's had her second cup of tea at Hot Pepper Jelly. We let her take them out for twenty pence a day.

"Afternoon, Daniel. How are you today? I missed you yesterday, didn't I?"

"Yeah, I wasn't working yesterday, Sheila. What can I do you for?"

"Oh, I didn't like this one much," she says, handing me back a copy of *Young and Dangerous 3*. "Not nearly as good as *Enter the Dragon*."

"Well, nothing's as good as *Enter the Dragon*."

"Quite so, but perhaps you have something a little more . . . feisty. This one had much too much talking in it. Not enough fighting, you see. I like the fighting bits the best."

"I'll see what I can do."

I head off to the kung fu section to find her a copy of *The Bruce Lee Story* and she decides to follow me. She seems bothered about something.

"Now then," she says, searching for her glasses at the bottom of her Budgens carrier bag, "you don't seem quite your usual self today. You seem a little off colour to me. Am I right?"

I know there's no point in lying to her so I say, "Yeah, you're right, Sheila, I've had a bit of an argument with my girlfriend."

"Nothing too serious, I hope?"

"I'm not really sure. She's sort of given me an ultimatum."

"Oh, Daniel, you've not been seeing a fancy woman, have you?"

"No, nothing like that, not apart from you, of course."

She giggles and her face creases up like a wet paper bag.

"You see, she wants me to get a job."

"Well, you have a job, don't you? I mean, you work here."

"I know, but Alison thinks I should get something a bit better, something more like a career. I am nearly thirty."

"Tush, you're no more than a child. Wait until you get to be my age, then you'll see what life's made of."

"Right. I mean, I'm sure you're right . . . but anyway she's only given me until Christmas to sort it out."

"Well, what about your music? I thought you still played in that little band of yours. I thought that song you played me the other day was rather lovely."

"Well, see . . . the thing is she wants to see something concrete. She wants to see something on paper, a record deal or a job—one or the other, by the end of the year."

"Well, that doesn't seem like very much time to me."

"I know, but she's just been given this job in Bruges and . . ."

"Bruges?"

"It's in Belgium."

"My dear boy, I know where it is. I'm not senile, you know."

"No, of course not, I didn't mean . . ."

"In fact my husband and I spent some time in Antwerp before the war. Lovely city, Antwerp. Beautiful cathedral.

"Still," she says, taking my arm and beckoning me close to hear her secret. "They're a funny lot, you know . . . the Belgians."

"How so, Sheila?"

She looks both ways to check no one's listening.

"They put mayonnaise on their chips."

"You hear about all this ridiculousness, Sheila?" says Kostas, coming to join us from the stockroom. "This boy let his girlfriend tell him what's to do. Have you ever heard such ridiculous thing as this? The girlfriend telling the boyfriend what's to do?"

"Oh, I don't know," says Sheila, picking up a copy of *Best of the Best,* "she sounds like quite a young lady to me."

"She is," I say. "That's the problem."

"Tsk. You ought to behave like a man, Danny. You wants to tell her what's to do. A man should be kings of his own castle."

"Well . . . it's more Alison's castle really. She does pay almost all of the rent."

Kostas looks faintly disgusted and then Sheila taps me on the hand with her bony finger and gets me off the hook.

"You are still coming to mow my lawn for me on Saturday, aren't you?"

"Yes, of course I am. We said some time around four, didn't we?"

"Yes, because my daughter's visiting with my grandson on Sunday and I'd hate for the lawn to be overgrown. I don't want her thinking I can't take care of myself."

"Don't worry, Sheila. I'll definitely be there."

It's funny what old people worry about. She can barely afford to clothe herself on her pension but she still wants to make sure she's got a neat lawn when the grandchildren come round.

6

"Hi, how was work?"

"Fine," I say, heading over to the fridge and helping myself to a Snapple. "Kostas made a list of his top-ten Telly Savalas films of all time and that guy from the post office came in to rent *House of Whipcord* again."

"That's nice. I've made us something to eat—turkey mince chilli okay?"

Alison is starting to freak me out. Ever since she said she was leaving she's started behaving like the wife in a fifties American sitcom. She's home by six, she's tidied the house, and she's always got something to eat waiting in the oven when I get home. I know, freaky, and the only thing that gives it away is that Alison can't cook. I mean, she's brilliant at almost everything else but somehow she's utterly incapable of following a recipe. When I cook, I follow the recipe like it's a mathematical formula; when Alison cooks, she's always convinced the recipe could do with a little improving.

"Well," I say, taking a butcher's at the pile of steaming grey matter in the saucepan, "that looks . . . er, lovely, but I thought I'd just grab a burger on the way."

"On the way where?"

"Rehearsals. I'm supposed to be meeting Vince and Matty at seven."

"Oh . . ." she says, digging at the rice with the back of her spoon.

"What? . . . You thought I wasn't going, didn't you?"

"Well, I just thought . . ."

"That's it, isn't it? You thought I wasn't going to go any more."

"No, that's not it at—"

"That's why you're being so nice to me, isn't it, all this cooking and cleaning and . . . you thought you only had to utter the words and I'd dump the music straight away, just like that, that I wouldn't even want to give it another chance."

"No, Danny, that's not—"

"I mean, I haven't even had a chance to tell Matty and Vince what you said yet, I haven't—"

"Listen to me. It's not like that, I wasn't expecting you to give up overnight, I just thought that since I'm leaving for Bruges on Monday you might want us to spend a few evenings together. I just wanted to spend some extra time with you before I go."

I feel so guilty I have two and a half helpings of the turkey mince chilli.

"I spoke to my brother today," she says, spooning the last of the chilli on to my plate.

"Did you?" I say, picking a piece of gizzard out of my teeth. "How did he seem?"

"Fine. You know, he seems pretty settled in his new flat. I think he's a bit worried about me going away, though."

"Yeah, well, that's no problem, I've got loads of free time, I don't mind checking in on him while you're away."

"Would you?"

"Yeah, of course. As long as he promises to let me win a chess game once in a while."

"No chance," she says, grinning at me. "You can't even beat Sheila."

"Yeah, well, that's as may be, but I'm learning, aren't I? And I killed Matty at draughts in the pub yesterday. He didn't stand a chance."

"Thanks, Danny," she says, reaching over and giving me a kiss, "I'd really appreciate it. I know Rufus would love to see you."

Alison brings out a Marks and Spencer's raspberry trifle and I attempt to capitalise on my newly won brownie points by telling her all about my conversation with Sheila.

"I told Sheila about you today," I say, dividing the trifle into two (fairly) even pieces. "I told her that you'd given me an ultimatum."

"Oh my God, you didn't. What did she say?"

"She said I ought to wait until I got to be her age then I'd know what was what."

"Did she say what she thought you should do?"

"Well, um . . . not really . . . I think she thought you were being a bit unreasonable . . . with the whole six-months thing."

"Danny, we talked about it. I just don't want this thing dragging on."

"So that's it, then. If I don't sort myself out by Christmas you're going to leave me?"

"No, of course I'm not, I told you, I just want us to have made some decisions by then, that's all."

I don't know why I'm pushing her like this. She's already explained herself a hundred thousand times and she looks like she's starting to get upset again so I say:

"Sheila said something else about you as well."

"Really? What did she say?"

"She said you sounded like quite a young lady."

"Hey, have you seen this?" she says, handing me an article from the *North London Herald*. 'The local health authority have stopped offering IVF treatment to women over thirty-three. It's awful, isn't it? Most women don't decide to have children until they're in their thirties these days, so they won't even know they're infertile until it's too late."

"Yeah," I say, looking at my watch, "but they have to draw the line somewhere, don't they? I mean, it's harder to get pregnant when you're in your thirties, isn't it, so they probably think it's a waste of money or something."

Bad answer.

"But what if it was us? What if it was us, Danny, and we found out we couldn't have any kids? How would we pay for it?"

"It's not going to happen to us. Look at you, you're the picture of health."

"It doesn't work like that. You can't just look at a person and know whether they're going to be able to have children or not. Look at Ruth. You wouldn't think Ruth would be the one to end up with blocked fallopian tubes, would you? God, she spends more time in the gym than she does at work."

"Well, no, but I don't know what you're worried about, you're only just thirty, you've got years yet, you've got buckets of time."

She walks over to the kitchen and starts doing the washing up.

"See you later then," I say to the back of her head. "I won't be too late."

"Right."

"No later than ten."

"Okay."

"We won't bother going to the pub then."

"Fine."

"I'll come straight home."

"Whatever. Oh, and don't forget to tell Vince and Matty about Saturday."

"What's happening on Saturday?"

"I told you, I've organised a leaving do with some people from work. Ruth and Shelley are coming. We're going to The Medicine Bar. I told you."

Great, exactly what I need right now, a night out in a poncy bar with Alison's friends.

7

Things left to do before Alison leaves on Monday:

- Buy present (something personal that will make her think about me while she's away).
- Get haircut and buy new shirt from Ted Baker (so Alison will spend journey to Bruges thinking how good I looked at leaving party).
- Try to lose some of beer gut. Tricky since just consumed two and a half helpings of turkey mince chilli and a whole raspberry trifle.
- Buy champagne for last night.
- Cancel that. Champagne might look like I'm celebrating her going.
- Buy bottle of that expensive Sancerre that she likes instead.
- Buy ingredients for romantic dinner for two. Maybe try making that duck pancake thing again.
- Cancel that. Last time tried to make duck pancake thing it was a disaster on account of leaving the giblets in. Buy M&S duck à l'orange instead.
- Go to rehearsal.
- Play set.
- Find way of telling Vince and Matty that we've only got six months left to become household names.

8

Vince and Matty are waiting for me outside the rehearsal room when I finally turn up.

"What are you doing outside?"

"Never mind that. Where have you been? We've been trying to get hold of you at the shop."

"I popped home first. Alison cooked. What could I do? I had to stay and eat it."

Vince nods sympathetically and Matty asks me if I want a bite of his doner kebab. They both have limited experience of Alison's cooking—including her famous pilchard and sweet corn curry—so they immediately assume I'm still hungry.

"So anyway, the rehearsal's off," says Vince. "There's been a power cut. Some plank went and overloaded the circuits."

"Shit. So what shall we do?" I say through a small mouthful of Matty's kebab.

"Not much we can do, I suppose. Reckon we should just go next door for a couple of jars and see if they have any luck fixing it in the next hour or so."

Fat chance. Vince knows full well it'll be one excuse after another until at least the beginning of next week:

"Sorry, mate, the PA's blown up now."

"Sorry, mate, the rats have gnawed through the wires again."

"Sorry, mate, I know I said I'd have it done by Monday but

our in-house engineer is laid up with a nasty dose of athlete's foot, smells to high heaven . . . yeah, even if he does keep his trainers on. We'll definitely have it done by the weekend, though. No problem."

For "in-house engineer" read local spliff dealer with an HND in household electronics. For "athlete's foot" read . . . well, athlete's foot. For "done by the weekend" read some time before August 2004.

It's a pity: a dose of hardcore rehearsal-room tinnitus is exactly what I need to take my mind off things.

*

I can still remember the first rehearsal room I ever went into. It was part of a desolate industrial estate somewhere off the Mile End Road, and I remember that you had to trek across half a mile of waste ground and ride up five floors in an open-sided lift before you reached the practice rooms. It was called Broken Lives.

I was shitting myself. I'd finally plucked up the courage to phone one of the "Guitarist Wanted" ads in the back of the *Melody Maker* and I was on my way to audition for a band called Code Red. Vince was the lead singer. He'd written the ad himself:

BAND WITH RECORD COMPANY INTEREST SEEKS
SHIT HOT GUITARIST WITH OWN GEAR.
INFLUENCES: DEVO, DYLAN, THE DOORS AND DEXY'S

(He was very keen on bands beginning with the letter D.)

ABSOLUTELY NO TIME WASTERS.
(WE MEAN IT MAN.)
EAST LONDON.

Melody Maker comes out on a Wednesday but I didn't summon up the nerve to call Vince until the following Sunday afternoon. His first words to me were:

"What kind of a wank-stained pillock phones up in the middle of the football . . . West Ham are two nil up, for fuck's sake."

I swallowed hard and told him I was calling about his ad.

"Oh . . . really?" he said, sounding somewhat surprised. "Right then, where you from?"

"Woodford," I said, wondering if he knew where it was.

"Oh yeah, I know it, me and the lads are up Leytonstone way. We've got our own squat."

"Cool," I said, wondering if this would be a good time to mention that I still lived with my mum. "Sounds nice."

"So . . . what kind of guitar d'you play?"

"Erm . . . a Squire."

"Hmmmmn."

"It's got its own hard case," I added, hoping that this might help chivvy things along.

"Well, what amp you got?"

"A Peavy, fifteen watt . . . it's more of a practice amp really."

He didn't sound too convinced.

"So, who are your influences, then?"

I wanted to say The Smiths and New Order but I decided to plump for a couple of the bands that Vince had mentioned in his ad.

"Well, Devo, I like Devo and, er . . . yeah, I really like Dexy's Midnight Runners. They're practically my favourite band of all time."

Bingo.

It turned out that the band were holding auditions on Tuesday night and Vince asked me if I wanted to come along.

"Yeah, we rehearse at Broken Lives. Buster Bloodvessel used to rehearse there, as it goes. You know where it is, right?"

I had no idea.

"Yeah, 'course I do. I mean, who doesn't? See you Tuesday, then."

"Nice one, mate, see you Tuesday."

Vince went back to the West Ham game—they'd conceded three goals to Tottenham Hotspur in the time we'd been on the phone—and I spent the rest of the weekend learning all the songs off *Searching for the Young Soul Rebels* and desperately trying to find someone, anyone, who'd actually heard of Broken Lives.

The thing that struck me most when I first walked in was the smell. The whole place stank of damp and rot and blokes that didn't wash and I remember a thin stream of condensation running down the back wall which was collecting in a small puddle on the carpet under the sound desk. Actually, that's not strictly true. You couldn't really call what was on those floors carpet. It looked like someone had been down to the local PDSA, collected up all the dead hamsters, beaten their corpses to a bloody pulp and brought back the resulting mess and flattened it out into a sort of a rug. Code Red were sitting on it. Vince was rolling a gigantic spliff.

"You must be Danny, right?"

"Yeah. You Vince?"

"'S right. This is Woolfy and Allen, bass and drums. I'm lead and vocals. I write all the songs."

I looked at Woolfy and Allen. They looked hard. They were wearing exactly the same clothes as Vince: black donkey jacket, second-hand Levi's and monkey boots, and even though it was sweatier than Big Daddy's underpants in there, they all had woollen hats pulled down low over their eyes.

The whole of Code Red were staring at me by now, and it was becoming clear that I'd got my own outfit very wrong indeed. After lengthy consideration—including a rather fetching dungaree, beret moment—I'd finally gone with my favourite Saturday night ensemble: flouncy Mr Byrite shirt, loose jeans held up with a red nylon soul-boy belt, and a secondhand army jacket that I'd bought in Camden Market that was my absolute pride and joy. The whole outfit was nicely topped off with a pair of black Adidas trainers, white socks and a ludicrous Phil Oakey-style fringe that hung down to my chin in a vain attempt to cover my dreadful acne. It's a wonder they didn't decide to beat the crap out of me there and then.

"Nice haircut," said Vince, passing me the spliff. "Very Flock of fucking Seagulls."

And then he suggested that we all have a jam.

Not having ever jammed before I was a little unsure what I was supposed to do. Vince said I could plug into his spare amp and Woolfy said I should just join in when I felt comfortable. I soon got the hang of it. It turned out jamming just meant playing pretty much anything you wanted with no regard whatsoever for what anyone else in the room was doing. It was brutal, Allen whacking the heads of the rehearsal room drum kit like he was the bastard seed of John Bonham, Woolfy playing slap bass on his fretless five-string and Vince squeezing ear-splitting feedback out of his Marshall amp and grunting unintelligibly into the battered mike.

I loved it.

Every once in a while Vince would bark some chord change or other over the PA and every fifteen minutes or so the jam would inexplicably break down and this would be the cue to spark up another spliff and hold a detailed debrief about the jam.

"Yeah, nice one, Woolfy, liked what you was doing in the middle eight there, when you was sliding up the neck and hitting the G to my D. Nice one. Rockin'."

And then it would start all over again: everyone turning his own instrument up so that it was louder than everyone else's, everyone lost in some private reverie of his own, and it wasn't until Flob, the rehearsal room manager, stuck his head round the door and told us that we only had half an hour left that I realised no one had actually spoken to me for the last hour and a half.

"Does anyone fancy playing a song?" I said when it was time for the next spliff break.

"What, like a cover, you mean?" said Allen, itching his balls with his drumstick.

"Yeah, we could do something off *Searching for the Young Soul Rebels*. I mean, we could do 'Geno' or something."

And so we did. We played "Geno" and "Burn It Down" and "Love Part One" and before we knew it Flob's bald head was back round the door telling us it was time to sling our hook.

"And don't forget," he said, laying down some fresh mousetraps next to the wall, "that's fifty quid you lot owe me. You're gonna have to settle up next time . . . I ain't letting you in here again unless you settle your tab."

And that was that. The moment I mentioned my Saturday job savings (66 pounds and 72 pence) I was in. The moment I agreed to cut my hair, buy a donkey jacket, wear a bobble hat (sans bobble), lend Code Red fifty quid and split the cost of rehearsals four ways, I was in.

Vince didn't seem to care that I was only sixteen, and I didn't care that Code Red were the worst band I'd heard in my entire life. I'd passed my first ever audition. I was over the moon.

Vince told me later I was the only one who'd bothered replying to the ad.

9

"Hey, Vince," I say, reaching out for Matty's packet of cheese and onion, "do you ever wonder what happened to Woolfy and Allen from Code Red?"

"No."

"No?"

"No, don't have to, I know what happened to them."

"What?" I say, suddenly fascinated. "I mean, how come?"

"I thought I told you, I ran into Woolfy at The Monarch a couple of Christmases ago. He works there now, he does front-of-house sound, does a bit of touring as well."

"Really? What about Allen?"

"Not sure. Last thing Woolfy heard he was driving a minicab somewhere over in Elephant and Castle."

Of course he was. What else would he be doing?

By rights, Vince and I should both be driving minicabs by now. It's what failed musicians do. They hang up their guitars, go to work on their bum crack and hightail it to the nearest illegal cab rank that will have them. They might not have completely given up on their dreams of making it—no musician completely gives up on his dreams of making it—but most are savvy enough to know when it's time to give up and call it quits.

For instance: a decade and a half of serial failure is a good time to call it quits; realising that you're ten years older than most of the people who'd want to buy your records is a good time to call it quits; finding out that the bass player from your very first band is ferrying Special Brew drunks up and down the Old Kent Road in a clapped-out, C-reg, champagne Vauxhall Nova is a very good time indeed to call it quits.

Alison is right. We should have given up years ago. And if it hadn't been for another band stealing our record deal from underneath our very noses, we probably would have.

*

Vince and I share a dream that dates back a long way: Christmas 1987 to be specific. It was a Friday night. Code Red had long since bitten the dust and one year and two line-up changes later we'd finally discovered what we thought was the winning formula and christened it Agent Orange.

Everything was falling into place: my acne had given up trying to eat its way through my cheeks, Vince had begun writing songs with actual choruses and, spurred on by our first positive review in the national music press, his voice had blossomed like a newly watered cactus.

We were breaking our backs in those days, humping our gear up and down the country in Vince's white Escort van, playing in small venues to smaller crowds, but the gigs were filling up with every new one we did. We began to get ourselves a following. Out of nowhere, people began comparing us (favourably) to the Wonder Stuff, and we suddenly had managers queuing round the block to represent us.

More and more people were coming down to the shows. We were being offered bigger fees and better slots and the whole thing finally came to a head with one infamous gig at the Town and Country Club in Kentish Town.

It was packed to the rafters. The whole place was heaving

with punters and publishers and record company A 'n' Rs, and I remember Vince saying to me before we went on that he thought this was it, that this was going to be the one. We all did.

The band played out of its skin that night. The crowd were with us the whole way, pogoing and body-surfing and cheering us on like some kind of returning army, and I can still remember every word from the NME review that ran the following week. It was so gushing I was almost too embarrassed to read it. Almost.

I've never been able to work out exactly what went wrong. I just remember the guy from Polydor coming backstage and telling us that we were the best band he'd seen all year. The following week we heard he'd signed the Wonder Stuff.

After that it was like we were damaged goods. Everybody had been down to see us but nobody had taken the bait. Every time our manager phoned up another company or sent out another demo the response was always the same. Our moment had passed. We were yesterday's news.

We ran into the Polydor bloke at the Camden Palace a couple of months later and he told us it had been a very close call. Fifty-fifty, he'd said. Between them and us. I'll never know if he was telling the truth, but I sometimes think it was coming so close that ruined us. We never got over it. I remember me and Vince sitting on a burnt-out car in the middle of Wanstead Flats, pissed out of our skulls on Jack and Coke and me telling him that we had to go on, that it was just bad luck, that we'd still make it one way or another. It was our right, I said.

Twelve years on and there's still a small part of us that believes it.

*

"I drove past Wanstead Flats the other day," I say, as if this is some kind of an accomplishment.

"That's nice for you," says Vince, indicating that it isn't. "What d'you want to go out there for anyway? It's a shithole."

"I was on the way to my mum's. I just fancied it, I suppose. Don't you ever get the urge to go back and take a look around?"

"No, mate," he says, getting up and heading off to buy the next round of drinks. "I can't honestly say that I do."

Vince shares none of the nostalgia I do for the stomping grounds of our youth. He thinks suburbia has been romanticised to death. If you watched any of those seventies retrospectives on TV you'd imagine it was a place where everyone was forever listening to Slade and riding around on Space Hoppers and where the worst thing that could possibly happen to you was burning your tongue on the mince in your Findus Crispy Pancake.

Vince remembers it differently—maybe because he's a few years older than me. He remembers the power cuts and the three-day weeks; the "Love Thy" neighbours with their "tut tut" curtains; and the boredom and the conservatism and the feeling that the worst thing you could possibly do was stand out from the crowd. And Vince did: with his punk ethics and his natty clothes and his very own novelty disease that no one (least of all him) knew how to spell.

Vince is mildly dyslexic. He had enormous difficulty learning to read, and despite the fact that he was sharper than a Wilkinson's sword, his classmates always treated him like he was a moron. They teased the crap out of him—much like they did with me and my acne—and by the time everyone finally realised why he was having so much trouble with his schoolwork it was too late.

"I didn't stand a chance," said Vince, pulling his copy of *Don't Stand Me Down* out of its pristine sleeve and slipping it on to the turntable.

"What . . . you mean they didn't even leave you alone once they'd found out what you had?"

"No, it was 'orrible. Rob Hollings stuffed me head down the bogs and flushed it and when I comes up for air he says: 'I want you to remember something, Vince Parker, jus coz you is dyslexic don't meen you ain't still a thick cunt.'"

Vince got out as soon as he could. He bought himself a guitar, grew himself a six-inch, navy blue Mohican and left school on the eve of his sixteenth birthday without a single qualification to his name.

He always claims the dyslexia isn't the real reason they bullied him, though. I remember sitting in his bedroom just after he'd told me about it: listening to Dexy's and dabbing my gums with cheap speed and Vince insisting that my zits weren't the real reason they picked on me either. They picked on us because we were ambitious; because we wanted out, because we had the vaguest suspicion that we might actually be better than everyone else instead of just being different from them. Vince says the moment you dare to show ambition in a place like that they turn you into an outsider.

Strange, really. Before I met Vince I'd always supposed it was the other way round.

10

"Oi," says Vince, slopping another round of drinks on to the table and shooting me a wink. "Did any of you see that programme last night?"

"Which one?"

"The one about them tsunamis, them giant tidal waves that are going to take out the whole of the east coast of America."

"Wow," says Matty. "When's that, then? When is it going to happen?"

"Thursday week, they reckon, somewhere around teatime, I think it was."

"Christ, I mean shit . . . God, they must be shitting themselves. Fuck. What are they going to do?"

Vince starts to laugh, a deep guttural chuckle worthy of the late, great Sid James, and then he reaches over and starts patting Matty on the back.

"Only joking, mate. Only joking. It might not happen for thousands of years yet, might not even happen at all."

Matty looks momentarily confused.

"Oh, right, I get it, you're having me on again, aren't you?"

"Yes, mate, I am. I am most definitely having you on."

• • •

Matt Starky is the baby of our group. He's only twenty-four and he's one of the most gullible people I've ever met. You can convince him of anything. Vince once told him that Lemmy from Motorhead had been born a girl and for a whole year, whenever Lemmy came up in some passing conversation, Matty would shake his head and say: "Poor Lemmy, what he must have been through, and you'd never guess, I mean, you'd never think it to look at him, would you?"

He wasn't even that bothered when he found out we'd been winding him up. He just sort of smiled and said: "Yeah, I always thought there was something fishy about that, what with him having those moles and everything. I mean, you don't see many women with moles like that, do you?" After that we had a hell of a job persuading him that my real name was Steve McQueen.

The other thing I like about Matty is that he's enthusiastic. About everything. He's never been in a proper band before and he's the perfect foil to me and Vince. If you sliced Vince or me in half you'd probably find the word "cynic" stencilled right through us like a stick of rock. If you cut Matty in half you'd probably find the word "mega." Everything is mega to Matty: one of our gigs mentioned in the listings pages of *Time Out*; someone from an obscure fanzine in Rhyl giving us a rave review; someone offering us free recording time in their demo studio; it's all "wicked" or "awesome" or "blinding" or "sorted." It's also incredibly infectious. It's part of the reason we keep him around, that and the fact that he's handsome enough to make all three of us look good.

"So, when did Agent Orange call it a day?" says Matty, tucking into his fourth vodka and Red Bull.

"End of '88," says Vince, rubbing his chin. "You was probably still in nappies."

Matty does a quick(ish) bit of maths on his fingers.

"No I wasn't, I was thirteen years old in 1988."

"Great," says Vince. "We were slogging our guts out in the collective pissholes of England and Baby Face here was still waiting for his first wetty."

"Wetty?"

"Wet dream, mate. Don't tell me . . . you're still waiting."

"Oh, right, I get you . . . but no, I'd already, well, you know . . . lost it by then."

"What, had sex?"

"Yeah."

"At thirteen?"

"Yeah, with my little brother's baby-sitter. I think she was Brazilian or something . . . or was it Puerto Rican? Actually she might just have been Italian . . . I don't know. Anyway, she was definitely my benchmark arse."

"Benchmark arse?"

"Yeah, you know, your first truly great one. The benchmark. The arse against which you judge all future arses."

We take a short pause.

"So," says Vince, sounding a little agitated, "let me get this straight. You're saying that you lost your virginity with your little brother's horny Brazilian baby-sitter when you were only barely out of short trousers?"

"Yeah, pretty much," says Matty, breaking into a slight shrug. "Hey, do either of you fancy a pickled egg?"

I knew it. I just knew it. If he wasn't such a great drummer I think I might have to have him killed.

*

We were definitely floundering until Matty came along. Agent Orange split up shortly after the Town and Country Club fiasco and Vince and I had gone our separate ways for a while. Vince went off to tour Germany with some rockabilly band that he hated but paid him actual money and I loitered around Camden with the shoe-gazers, getting more and more despondent. We re-formed eighteen months later (Vince got sick of oiling his quiff and living on sauerkraut) and spent the next five years trying (and failing) to restake our claim. We could never seem to get it right, though: the timing was always wrong. We were just mastering baggy when grunge hit. We were finally mastering grunge (around the time I met Alison) when Britpop was getting into full swing, and we were just getting comfortable in our Fred Perrys when Matty came along and saved us.

Matty auditioned for us in 1998. He bounded into rehearsals wearing his Maharishi combats and his silver Nikes and one of his two thousand different Duffer of St George T-shirts and he said:

"I'm Matt Starkey. We spoke on the phone."

Vince wanted him in immediately.

"He's called Starkey, like as in Ringo. He's bound to be brilliant." And it turned out he was.

Not only is Matty a great drummer, he also knows his way around a sampler, and he's entirely responsible for updating our sound. He grew up listening to a completely different set of music to me and Vince and if it wasn't for him the whole techno revolution might have passed us by for good.

Matty changed all that. The first week we met him he had us listening to the Propellerheads and Moby and the Chemicals and Air and Vince was secretly blown away. It struck him that if we just managed to absorb some small part of this stuff into the guitar music that we were already making we might still stand a chance. Matty definitely thought so. He thought the stuff we were doing was mega. That's why Vince likes to wind Matty up as much as he does. It's a power thing. He doesn't like to admit that Matty's quite as important to us as he is.

For form's sake, we decided to rename the band after Matty joined us. I suggested that we call it Chief after the character in *One Flew Over the Cuckoo's Nest* but Alison pointed out that if you didn't hear it right it sounded like we were called Cheese, so we changed it to Dakota after the Dakota building instead. We also slimmed the whole thing down to a three-piece: Vince on bass and vocals, me on lead and Matty doing all the programming and triggering all the samples off the drums. It worked really well. When we were offered our first gig at the Water Rats Matty was running around like a kid who'd just been given his first skateboard. He couldn't believe it. He still listens to stories of our Agent Orange days with a look of wonder on his irritatingly youthful face. It makes us feel good.

Sometimes I think giving up will hurt Matty even more than it will Vince.

*

"So, did you give any thought to what we were talking about the other day?"

"What?" I say, suddenly convinced Vince has been reading my thoughts.

"You know, about the shoes. That whole thing about finding a decent transitional shoe."

Vince has a thing about shoes. Apart from a minor obsession with hair products (he's paranoid about going bald) he's convinced that it's shoes that maketh the man. He also thinks it's a little unseemly to still be wearing trainers at the age of thirty-three.

"Yeah, because you can only wear trainers until you're thirty and then you start to look like a bit of a ponce. By the time you're thirty you want to be on the lookout for a whole different kind of shoe altogether, something to bridge the gap between trainers and dad shoes. Then what you have is this long hiatus until the age of, say, seventy-five or so, and then it's okay to start wearing them again. I mean, a bloke expects to be wearing trainers by the time he's seventy-five, that's if he can still stand up. It goes with his twenty-four-hour clothes. Yeah, they actually 'ave 'em, twenty-four-hour clothes that you can eat in, sleep in and quite possibly shit yourself in. My granddad buys his from John Lewis.

"So anyway, what a bloke really needs is a transitional shoe for the middle years. Not exactly a slip-on, not exactly a lace-up. More of your desert boot but less hippyish. Not exactly a work shoe but not quite as casual as your plimsoll neither."

Last week Matty suggested a clumpy leather arrangement with Velcro straps that he'd seen in Camper but Vince pointed out (quite astutely, I thought) that they would make him look like he was mentally handicapped. It's definitely been worrying him, this whole transitional shoe thing.

We carry on like this for the rest of the night: arguing the toss about bands that we hate, defending the honour of records we love, drinking and shouting and winding Matty up as far as we dare.

"Have either of you ever used nose-hair trimmers?" I say, wondering if it's worth buying the ones I've just seen in this month's Innovations catalogue.

"Yeah, they're great . . . saves you pulling them out with your fingers. They do your ears as well."

"What . . . you've got hair in your *ears?*"

Vince rubs his chin, takes out a Rizla and begins another roll-up.

"Just a matter of time," he says gravely. "My old man's got more ear hairs than pubes these days, and he reckons most of them have gone grey."

Matty stares at his beer glass for a moment. He looks perplexed, and then he starts to laugh.

"Ha, ha . . . *ear* hairs. Right. Good one. Blimey, I thought you were serious there for a second. Fuck me. Ear hairs. Phew . . . Anyone want another drink?"

Too right we do.

I'm enjoying it. I'm enjoying the lager and the banter and the chance to reminisce and it's a relief not to have to think about Alison and the job and the ultimatum and the whole damn thing. I decide to tell them later. I decide to discuss the whole six-month thing after Alison has gone. It'll be easier then. I'll have a clearer mind. It'll make more sense after Alison has gone.

"So how's things shaping up with Alison's job, then?" says Vince.

"Oh, not bad, y'know, just about getting my head round it, I suppose."

"Still, it's not for long, though, is it?"

"No," I say, and then I remember something. "Yeah, she asked me to see if you wanted to come to her leaving do on Saturday."

"Where's she having it?"

"The Medicine Bar in Islington."

"Nice one. Can I bring Kate?"

Kate is Matty's girlfriend and for some reason I've never been able to work out Alison has always seemed to have it in for her.

"Of course you can," I say. "You're all invited."

And then it's last orders and we decide to make a move and head for home.

11

Bollocks! Why did I say I'd do it? Why did I promise Sheila that I'd mow her lawn this afternoon?

It's Saturday, it's almost noon, and I still haven't done any of the things I meant to do before Alison leaves on Monday. I haven't bought her present. I haven't organised a haircut or picked up the food or bought a new shirt, and now I've only got three hours to get all the way into town, buy everything I need and make it all the way back up to Hornsey Lane to do Sheila's garden before four o'clock.

I could cancel. I could do it next week. I could phone her now. Fuck it. Can't cancel—she said her daughter was coming over tomorrow. I'll grab some breakfast then I'll just have to shoot.

"Morning, Dog Breath, I just made coffee, there's some left if you want it. We're out of milk, though."

"I know," I say through a mouthful of dry cornflakes. "What you watching?"

Alison is watching the end of *CD:UK* with Ant and Dec. She harbours some kind of kinky fantasy involving both Ant and Dec that she doesn't think I know about, but I overheard her discussing it with her friend Shelly one night when they were both pissed, so I like to wind her up about it.

"Hmmmm . . . what? Oh, nothing, I just turned over. Some kids' music show I think."

"Isn't that Ant and Dec?"

"Erm . . . yeah, I think so. Not sure what their names are really."

"They're a right pair of tossers, though, aren't they? Don't you reckon?"

"Dunno, they seem all right."

"They've definitely got to be shagging each other, haven't they? Which one of them d'you think's the daddy?"

"Neither of them. They're not. I mean, I think they're straight."

"Yeah, but look at that one's hair, what's going on with that dark one's hair?"

"Ant?"

"Ha! . . . I thought you said you didn't know what they were called. You even know which one's which."

"I don't. It was a guess."

"You fancy them, don't you? You fancy Ant and Dec. You want to have a double bunk-up with Ant and Dec and then you want them to have sexy homo love games with each other while you watch."

"Danny, shut up. Don't be disgusting. God, you're so filthy sometimes."

Alison loves it when I'm filthy.

"So d'you fancy going out for breakfast? We could go to the World Café or something."

"I can't," I say, indicating the cornflakes. "I've got to run into town for a couple of things and then I said I'd go over to Sheila's and mow her lawn for her."

"Today?"

"I know, I'm really sorry, but I sort of promised her and she's counting on me now. I'll be as quick as I can."

"You're too nice, Danny McQueen, too nice for your own good, that's your trouble."

And then she taps her lips, indicating that she wants me to come over and give her a snog. Her mouth tastes sweet, sweet and warm from the coffee, and I notice her passport lying on the sofa as I bend down to give her a kiss. It suddenly strikes me as weird: knowing that she's going away somewhere and knowing that I'm not going with her.

1 p.m. What is it with hairdressers? Why do they all keep telling me which day of the week it is? *It's Saturday, sir.* I know it's Saturday. I've known Saturday was the day that comes after Friday since I was three years old. *Well, you have to book sir. It's our busiest day of the week, and it is August.* August? So what? So friggin' what it's August? What fucking difference does it make if it's August? *Well, a lot of people go on holiday in August. A lot of people like to have their hair cut before they go away on holiday. And it is Saturday.* Bastard!

No one will give me a haircut. I only want the whole thing tidied up a bit. Just so as I look a bit more presentable, a little less like a mature sociology student and a bit more like Phil Daniels in *Quadrophenia.* Who am I kidding? Phil Daniels was about twenty when he made *Quadrophenia.* Maybe I should be going for more of a sixties Terence Stamp sort of a vibe. Sod it, I'll just have to go to the barber's in Crouch End when I've finished up here.

• • •

2 p.m. Have just wasted half an hour looking at transitional shoes in Neal Street and now they've run out of duck à l'orange in Marks and Spencer. I just missed the last one. I saw the bloke that got it, some git in a suit with a great haircut, and now he'll be eating mine and Alison's duck à l'orange and it'll be him getting his knob felt instead of me. Wanker. They've got Sancerre, though. Excellent. What else goes with Sancerre? *Fuck. Fuck.* Can't decide what to get. Dressed lobster? What's a dressed lobster, then? What's it got on, fucking trench coat or something? Can't get lobster. Looks like I'm trying too hard. Can't get two Lincolnshire sausages in onion gravy—looks like I'm not trying hard enough. What's this Malaysian curry with lemon-grass and coconut rice? Shit, no good—it's low calorie.

Suddenly notice extremely attractive-looking woman in short skirt buying Honey Chicken with Balsamic Potatoes and decide to plump for that. And a cake. A Thomas the Tank Engine cake. Don't ask me why.

2:30 p.m. There are no shirts in Ted Baker. No shirts. At all. Well, there are shirts, but none of them are blue. Black's no good and I'm fucked if they're getting me in something with a sodding pattern on the front.

2:35 p.m. In desperation have tried on something black and shiny with pattern on the front. Look like Robbie Williams's dad. Robbie Williams is the new David Essex. I am David Essex's dad. I am David Essex's *dad*. Decide to forget whole new shirt thing and stick with navy blue Carhartt hooded top instead. Alison likes me in my navy blue Carhartt hooded top.

That's it, then. Just have to pick up some flowers on the way home and then I can head over to Sheila's. Everything going well. Everything under control. Better than expected. Maybe go for quick pint in the Lamb and Flag before I head off.

3:15 p.m. *Shit!* Forgotten to buy Alison's present. Have forgotten the whole reason I came up here in the first place. Got all the way down to the Piccadilly Line platform and was busy reading a fascinating advert about haemorrhoid cream when suddenly felt like I'd forgotten something important. Fought my way back to the lifts, realised I didn't have time to queue and decided to run up the stairs.

3:20 p.m. Have had heart attack. Well, it feels like I've had a heart attack. There are 193 stairs at Covent Garden station. That's the equivalent of fifteen flights. Am definitely going to pass out. Why did I try and run up? What am I trying to prove? Why do I feel like David Essex's dad?

3:25 p.m. Looking good, feeling good. Am in great shape for a bloke my age. Pulse rate back down to sixty in less than ten minutes. Fitness is all about recovery time anyway. I read that on a Tube ad somewhere.

So, what to get for Alison? What does Alison like? She likes things that smell nice. She likes those expensive candles that are supposed to smell of autumn leaves and chocolate but actually smell like your nan's sock drawer. Fine. I know where to get those. Scented candles and maybe a book I can write something nice in, a guide to Bruges maybe.

Hang on. Hang *on*. Alison will put the candles in her hotel room. She'll invite some of her new workmates up for a drink. The women will all go home and Alison will be left alone with Donkey-schlong. She'll light the candles. He'll try to suck up by saying how nice they smell and Alison will say, *Thanks, they were a present from my boyfr— Oh, it doesn't matter, come over here and have a sniff. Has anyone ever told you that you look a little bit like Ant and Dec?*

BASTARD!

It's gone 5:30 by the time I make it over to Sheila's and at first I'm convinced I'm at the wrong house. Sheila doesn't even have a lawn. What she does have is a jungle. The grass is up to my knees. It probably hasn't been mowed since they stopped rationing. It's going to take me hours, and I'm actually considering running away when Sheila spots me from the window, sees me with Alison's flowers and says, "Oh, Daniel, lilies. Goodness me, you shouldn't have."

It takes forever. Sheila's lawnmower is more blunt than Vince when he's being very bloody blunt, and I end up hacking at some of the weeds with one of her kitchen knives. I'm showered in grass and soil and bits of snails that I've accidentally trodden on and I'm getting quite used to the sickening crunch they make when I stand on them now. It's almost seven before I'm finished.

"Oh, that looks very good. Now, you must let me make you a cup of tea."

"I can't, Sheila, honestly, I'm really late, it's Alison's leaving party tonight. I've really got to go."

"Nonsense. I've bought you some Mr Kipling's Bakewell Slices. I went to Budgens specially."

The thought of Sheila making a special trip to Budgens and fishing about in her purse for a few spare coppers is more than I can bear. I sit down and have a cup of tea and a cake with her. I need it, actually. I haven't had anything but a few dry cornflakes all day.

Sheila wants to chat. She wants to tell me everything she's

found out about Bruce Lee (which thankfully isn't very much) and she's fished out some pictures that she wants to show me of her and her late husband when they were in Antwerp together before the war. Antwerp looks nice. Sheila looks nice, about a foot taller than she is now with dark hair ironed into neat curls, and wide, smiling eyes that look full of hope. She must be about twenty. Her husband looks like a film star, Ronald Colman or someone like that: tall with black hair and a rakish moustache, and he's got one hand on his pipe and the other resting on the small of Sheila's back. They look very happy. They look very much in love. They were married for the best part of fifty years.

"Sheila, do you mind if I ring Alison and tell her that I'm going to be a bit late?"

"No, of course not, and tell her from me what a very lucky girl she is to have you."

"Where the hell have you been? It's almost eight o'clock. I was about to leave without you."

"I'm sorry, I didn't realise it had got so late. I've been held up at Sheila's. You wouldn't believe the state her garden was in. I'm leaving right now."

"Well, I can't wait for you. I told everyone I'd meet them at half past. It's my party. I can't turn up late."

"Okay, okay, I'll meet you there, then. I'll come home, grab a quick shower, have a quick shave, phone Vince and Matty to remind them where they're going, and I'll meet you there."

"Danny, I can't believe this. Shit, I can't . . . look, I've got to go. I'll see you when you get there."

And then she puts down the phone.

I go as fast as I can. I run home, jump in the shower, slap on some Black and White, change into my Levi's and my Carharrt hoody all in twenty minutes flat. I just have to wrap Alison's presents then I'm done. I just have to find where she keeps the Sellotape then I'm done. It's not in the drawer with all the take-away menus in it. It's not in the toolbox with the screwdriver set her dad bought us that we've never used. It's not with her office stuff. It's in the food cupboard. Behind the pickled onions. Of course. Stupid of me.

I'm done. I ended up buying Alison a silver bracelet that I can't really afford but I know she'll really like because she pointed it out to me a couple of weeks ago when we were out shopping for hooded tops. It's a bit crap, I suppose, getting her something that she's already seen, but it'll have to do. I can't do anything about the flowers now either, but there's always the guide to Bruges. And the Thomas the Tank Engine cake.

I leave the presents on the kitchen table and head off to the Medicine Bar. It's almost nine o'clock.

Something tells me it's going to be a long night.

12

The second I arrive at the Medicine Bar I have the overwhelming urge to run away. It hits me in the stomach like a bad prawn, and it's all I can do not to turn on my heels and scarper. I can just make out Alison through the window. She's sat on a long leather sofa at the back of the room and she's surrounded by a dozen or so people, most of whom I don't know. The table in front of them is littered with empty bottles: champagne bottles, beer bottles, wine bottles, and towers of sticky shot glasses, and it's clear that there's been some serious drinking going on. Alison likes places like this, places you can order a martini dry enough to make your toes curl.

It looks to me like she's been holding court. The girls are fussing round her like mother hens, and a slick-looking bloke in a beige Smedley is offering her a smoke and trying to look down the front of her party dress. I want to punch his face in. I want to punch him for wearing beige and ogling my girlfriend's breasts but mostly I just want to run away.

"What are you doing?"

"Watching."

"Watching?"

"Yeah, take a look. I'm an hour and a half late for Alison's party. I think she wants to stab me. What do you think?"

Vince gets to work. He doesn't bother asking me why I'm an hour and a half late for my own girlfriend's party—I doubt the question even crosses his mind—he doesn't bother asking me why I'm stood outside spying on her from the pavement, he just recognises that I'm in the shit and sets about giving my predicament his full attention.

We make an odd tableau, the pair of us: hands in pockets, noses pressed up against the plate glass, immune to the scornful looks from the polenta posse making their Upper Street *passeggiata* behind us, immune to the braying trendies who flicker in and out of focus in front of us, immune to everything but the problem in hand.

After a while Vince turns back to me and shakes his head. He takes a short, sharp breath through his nostrils and he says:

"You're dead meat. Everyone knows what you done: the girls think you're a bastard; the blokes think you're a tosser, and the git in the beige is trying to take advantage of your girlfriend's weakened emotional state."

"That's what I thought," I say, rolling up my sleeves and heading for the door. "That's exactly what I thought."

It's hot inside. The bar is heaving with lumped-up twentysomethings doing the Saturday night shuffle, and I can feel tiny beads of sweat beginning to break out across my forehead. I feel dizzy, dizzy from the heat and the adrenalin, and I'm quite relieved when Vince steps in and advises me not to bother with the whole punch-up thing.

"It's not like I wouldn't be right behind you, mate," he says, offering me a roll-up. "It's just that you might end up making things worse."

"How could it be any worse?" I say, wiping my forehead on

my sleeve. "And anyway, Alison would love it if I got into a fight over her. Women love that kind of thing."

"Come off it, you'd just embarrass her."

What he really means is that I'd just embarrass myself, but he's too loyal to say so.

"All right," I say, noticing Kate and Matty over by the bar, "we'll have a couple of beers and then I'll go over and make the peace. After I've calmed down a bit."

Vince thinks this is a good idea.

"Danny! Where've you been? Come over here and give me a big sloppy snog!"

Matty's girlfriend is your classic squealer; the kind of girl who makes you wonder what she sounds like when she comes. She's short and thin and pretty—if you like that no bra, pierced navel, glittery make-up kind of thing—and she's one of those overly affectionate people who always insist on greeting everyone they meet by kissing them full on the mouth. It doesn't matter if she knows you or not: a moment's hesitation and you're over; a second's indecision and she's lunging at you with her pouty red lips and smearing make-up all over your evening stubble.

Just my luck: the moment our lips meet and she starts to wind her skinny arms round my neck I suddenly notice Beige Jumper Man pointing me out from across the room. He knows exactly what he's doing. He times it perfectly: holds out his finger like a dagger and waits for Alison to turn round and clock me. Our eyes meet. She holds my gaze for a split second and then she turns away.

Vince was right. I'm a dead man.

"I'm sorry," I say, squeezing in next to her. "I completely screwed up."

"So what's new?" she says, draining her glass.

"That's a bit harsh," I say. "I mean, things just got away from me, that's all."

"How could you do this?" she says, reaching for my beer. "Where have you been all this time?"

"Look, don't make a scene, Okay. I'm sorry, everything just got out of—"

"Don't make a *scene*? Fuck you," she says quietly. And then she gets up and says she needs to take a piss.

"Woof, woof."

"You what?"

"Woof, woof. Still in the dog-house, then?"

This is Ruth. Of all Alison's friends I like her the least. She's tight and pushy and mean spirited and there's only so long you can forgive someone for being a cow just because they've got wonky fallopian tubes.

"Well, I'm sure we'll work it out," I say. "More of a misunderstanding than anything."

"Oh, I'm sure you will," she says, breathing smoke at me across the table. "Alison's been in such a rut lately but she's so much happier now you've decided to give up the music and get yourself a job. She's so relieved. We all knew you had to come to your senses sooner or later. I mean, it's not like your band is actually going anywhere, is it?"

I don't know what to say. I notice that the right side of her mouth moves up and down as she talks and that the left side always stays perfectly still. I notice that Vince has been listening to every word she's said.

"And anyway," she continues, "I know some people in telesales who might be prepared to give you a go if you fancy it. Call me next week and I'll pass on the numbers."

• • •

I know the kind of job Ruth is talking about: fifteen grand a year and two weeks' holiday that you're too scared to take; free membership to Commuters Anonymous and a lifetime subscription to the "team." That's the kind of person they want: someone who'll put up with any old shit and let everyone else take all the credit. Someone who's prepared to whoop and holler and suck up and cold-sell and wear the company logo like a tattoo where their individuality used to be.

I don't care how bad things get. I don't care that I'm not actually qualified to do anything else. The day I take a job which advertises for team players is the day I set fire to my own small intestines with lighter fluid.

Vince has fucked off somewhere with Kate and Matty and I'm starting to wonder where Alison has got to. I've been making polite conversation about house prices and car prices and trekking holidays to Vietnam for almost an hour now, and it feels like my head is about to explode. No one wants to talk about anything interesting like James Caan in *Rollerball* or new ways to kill Jamie Oliver. If they mention a film it's only because they've read about it in the *Guardian* and they're still wondering what they're supposed to think. If they mention music it's only to say how it's all gone downhill over the last couple of years, and you know it's only a matter of time before one of them wants to talk about Coldplay or Travis or Badly Drawn Boy.

"Hey, here's an interesting piece of pop trivia," I say, addressing the table in general. "Did you know it was Joe Dolce's 'Shaddap You Face' that kept Ultravox from having a number-one single with 'Vienna' in 1981 . . . I mean, imagine that."

No one seems to know what I'm talking about, and for some insane reason I suddenly decide this would be a good time to start singing.

"You know, it went like this: 'What's a madda you, HEY! Godda no respect, HEY! Whadda you think you do? It's a nice a place, HEY! It's a nice a face. *AHHHhhh . . . shudupa yer . . . faaace*.'"

Everyone is looking at me like I've just farted. Maybe I should have left out the "heys." Maybe this is a good time to go and see what's happened to Alison.

I look everywhere. I comb the bar from top to bottom (including a very informative diversion to the girls' bogs) and I eventually find her sitting outside on the pavement. She's crouched up against the window with her knees to her chest; smoking a cigarette and calmly watching the world go by.

People are beginning to make their way home: singles clutching early editions of the Sunday papers, couples stopping to window-shop in estate agents' for flats they can't afford, gangs of pissed-up girlies tottering home in their high heels and flimsy skirts and gangs of lairy men in their best white shirts chasing hopelessly after them.

There's a full moon. It's warm and muggy and close and some of the nearby restaurants have spread their tables out on to the street: a few stragglers are drinking liqueurs and pretending to be continental while the waiters pace about in circles wondering if they're ever going to leave.

"I've been sick," she says matter-of-factly.

"Thought you might have," I say, sitting down next to her.

"I think I'd like to go home now."

"No problem," I say. "I'll nip back inside and tell everyone that you're not feeling well."

"You ruined my night," she says, stubbing her cigarette out on the kerb.

"I know. I didn't mean to. I'm sorry."

"So where were you, then?" she says, trying to meet my gaze. "Coz, you know, even you couldn't make mowing a lawn take that long."

"I went into town," I say. "I wanted to buy you a leaving present but it all took much longer than it should have on account of the Ant and Dec question, and then Sheila turned out to live in the Amazonian rain forest and then she wanted to show me her photos of Antwerp and then . . ."

"You're a very weird person," she says, softening slightly. "You're a very weird person, Danny McQueen."

And then she throws up again, spilling her multicoloured guts all over the parched summer pavement and clearing the last stragglers away from their tables. The waiters are grateful. And I lift her up, hail us a taxi and carry her back home to bed.

13

Alison has gone without me. The reason I know she's gone without me is because she's left me a note.

"Dear Danny," it says,

I've gone without you. You looked so peaceful I didn't want to wake you up. I'll call as soon as I get in. Love you lots Al x.

Well, that's a lie for a start. I never look peaceful when I'm asleep. I honk and fidget and dribble and snore and I quite often get woken up in the middle of the night by Alison digging me in the ribs and telling me to shut the hell up. I wanted to go with her. It was going to be great. I was going to wave at her from the platform like Trevor Howard in *Brief Encounter*. I was going to kiss her on the forehead and wish her luck and she was going to cry her eyes out and tell me how much she was going to miss me. I was going to buy myself a stale chicken tikka baguette and wait around with her bags while she went to look at lacy pants in Knicker Box.

Alison loves shopping at departure points. Airports are her all-time favourite, but I know she'll be indulging in some quality retail activity at the Eurostar terminal. I can see her now: nipping into Smith's for a copy of *Hello!* (she only reads *Hello!* when she thinks no one will see her), ordering a cappuccino from Costa Coffee, popping into Body Shop for kumquat-flavoured toiletries and wandering into Knicker Box to eye up the rails of skimpy underwear.

Under normal circumstances I might spend some quality time imagining Alison in skimpy underwear at this point, but I'm not really in the mood. Why didn't she bother to wake me up? We agreed last night that I'd drive her to Waterloo. It's not like I can't get up early when I have to, it's not like I have to stay in bed all morning, it's just that I tend to go to bed late. It's just that daytime telly doesn't really kick in until after the Jerry Springer show comes on. Not unless you count the *Columbo* reruns on BBC Choice. I love *Columbo* reruns, I love how everyone thinks Columbo is a complete numbskull when actually he's a super-cunning detective genius.

I look at Alison's note again. There's a clear subtext hidden between the lines. She may still love me but she's definitely beginning to lose respect for me.

The living room is a mess; pieces of crumpled wrapping paper all over the floor and yesterday's food spread out across the dinner table in a deep greasy pile: the M&S ready meal that we were too hung over to eat, the bottle of Sancerre that we were too hung over to drink, and the decimated Thomas the Tank Engine cake that was all either of us could face. Alison liked her cake. She liked her cake and her guidebook and her silver bracelet and when I explained that her flowers were currently languishing on the windowsill in Sheila's front room she didn't seem to mind.

She put the bracelet on her wrist and kissed me gently on the cheek. I kissed her back. I kissed her mouth and her neck and her fabulous tits and then the hangover horn kicked in with a vengeance and we ended up screwing right there on the sofa.

She looked incredible. Even with her hair all messed up and smelling ever so faintly of puke, even with mascara clotted in filthy black rings round her eyes, even with cake icing smeared across the edges of her beautiful mouth. I love Alison's mouth. I love her mouth and her legs and the taste of her cunt and the way her whole body tenses up like a bullet when she comes.

We stayed on the sofa for a long while after that: curled up in a duvet, sipping hot tea and polishing off the rest of Thomas's bright green funnel with our hands. She said she forgave me. She said it would have been a crap party anyway because she didn't like most of the people who were there. She made me sit in the damp patch on the duvet by way of a punishment. She made me realise just how much I'm going to miss her.

I spent the rest of the afternoon watching her pack, avoiding the washing up and drip-feeding her Coke and cupfuls of soluble aspirin. At one point I came up with a unique hangover treatment consisting of aspirin, fresh orange juice, Pepto-Bismol and a whole raw egg but, oddly enough, she didn't seem overly impressed. I told her what Ruth had said to me the night before. She told me it was all bullshit.

"I didn't tell her anything," she said, rolling her T-shirts between tissue paper so they wouldn't get creased on the journey. "Ruth just presumed. I only said you were thinking of doing something else, not that you were definitely going to."

"So you didn't ask her to find me a job in telesales, then?"

"Jesus, no. Are you kidding? I'd rather you spent the rest of your life in a bar mitzvah band than got a job in telesales."

Thank God for that.

"So, how about I take you to Waterloo in the morning?" I said when we'd finished forcing her suitcase shut.

"Bit early for you, isn't it?" she said carefully. "I've got to be there by half nine."

"No problem. I'll get up and drive you. You don't want to lay out fifteen quid for a taxi when you've got me to take you. I mean, there's no point, is there?"

"But I've already ordered one, for eight thirty, it's all arranged."

"So cancel it," I said. "They won't care."

"Okay," she said. "I'll go and do it now."

I'm ninety-nine and a half per cent sure she never cancelled that cab.

My second mug of coffee is going down nicely and I'm beginning to feel a bit more positive. If Alison is losing respect for me then it's up to me to win it back. It's up to me to prove that I can do it: that all those years in damp rehearsal rooms and piss-stained dressing rooms haven't been a complete and utter waste of time.

We've got to pull ourselves together. We've got to start taking this thing more seriously. We've got to give the band one more Atlantic City-style spin of the dice.

It's about time I called Vince and told him about my plan.

14

Vince is in a mood with me. I can tell he's in a mood with me because he won't give me any of his chips.

"Come on."

"No."

"Come on, give us a chip."

"No, and they're not chips anyway, they're curly fries."

"I don't care what they're called, just give us one."

"No, get your own."

"Can *I* have some?"

" 'Course you can, mate . . . D'you want ketchup on 'em?"

"Yeah, nice one."

"How come *he* gets to have some?"

"Because he's not a wanker."

"And *I* am?"

"You said it."

The emergency band meeting isn't going quite as well as I'd hoped. Not only has Vince refused to give me any of his chips, he's also made it quite clear that he doesn't think very much of my plan.

"It's a rubbish plan."

"Why is it rubbish?"

"Because it's exactly the same plan we've been having for the last ten years, that's why."

"It's not," I say, pulling a neatly folded sheet of A4 out of my pocket. "Look, I've made a list of things to do. Just wait until you see this."

I have to say that I'm particularly pleased with the way my "to do" list has turned out. I've used a different colour felt-tip pen for each new suggestion, and I've also underlined what I consider to be the key points in lime-green Magic Marker. It took me the entire length of *This Morning* to get it just right.

"Blimey," says Vince, biting into his cheeseburger and splattering my "to do" list with globs of chilli sauce, "it gets worse. Oi, Matty, listen to this."

Matty spears another forkful of chips on to his plate and Vince clears his throat and begins to read aloud.

"Ehem . . .. point number one," he says, tapping the paper on the table like a pretend newsreader, "*get decent* . . . what does that word say? Right, manager, yeah . . . *get decent manager with office in Camden town or similar.*

"Point number two: *get some decent live dates instead of just playing for beer at friends' parties.*

"Point number three: *record new demo and send it to various A 'n' R departments instead of relying on Sheila at the video shop to tell us if the new songs are any good or not.*

"Point number four: *get matching poodle haircuts in the manner of early Bon Jovi videos so that the three of us start to look more like a proper band.*

"Point number five . . ."

"Fuck off," I say, snatching the list off Vince and folding it back into my pocket. "You're just taking the piss now. It doesn't say that at all. I was only saying that we should make an effort to look more like a cohesive unit. *What?* What are you both laughing at? What the *fuck* is so funny all of a sudden?"

"You are," says Vince, wiping his eyes with his serviette. "You with your felt-tip pens and your Magic Markers and your emergency ten-point plans. I mean, when was you actually going to get around to telling us?"

"Telling you what?"

Matty makes a violent whipping motion with his arm.

"About Alison."

"What about Alison?"

"About what she said. About the ultimatum. About the whole six-month thing."

"*Whoopah!*" says Matty, cracking his arm in the air and slapping his middle finger into his palm with a sharp, neat crack: "*Whooopahhh!!*" he says again.

"What are you doing? *What is he doing?* Are you doing what I *think* you're doing?"

"Pussy-whipped," says Matty. "It's the sign for pussy-whipped, *whoop—*"

"Matty, do that again and you're a fucking dead man . . ."

"All right, calm down," says Vince, pulling me back into my seat and offering me his plate. "I think you'd better have one of my curly fries."

"I suppose Ruth told you, then?" I say, chewing sulkily on my chip.

"Yeah, at the Medicine Bar. We came back just after you'd taken Alison home and she told us the whole thing. It was pretty obvious, Danny, all that guff about finding you a job in telesales and Ruth saying that we were shit and you not even bothering to stick up for us."

"I know, you're right, I should have told her where to go."

"So it's not true, then? You haven't told Alison that you're giving up?"

"Of course not."

"But you have agreed to it, though, the six-month limit?"

"Yeah," I say solemnly, "I suppose I have."

"Right then."

"What do you mean, 'right then,' what does 'right then' mean?"

"It means at least we know where we stand."

Vince stares at his coffee, I stare at my emergency ten-point plan, and Matty looks from Vince to me and back again. No one says anything.

"Guys, *guys*," says Matty finally, "I mean, come on, we can sort this out, right?"

"Ask him," says Vince, looking over at me.

"*Danny?*"

"Ask him," I say, looking back across the table at Vince.

"Right, I'm off to the newsagent to see if the new NME's in yet. You've got exactly five minutes. If you've not sorted things out by the time I get back I'm calling up the first wanted ad that I see. Got it?"

"Yeah, suppose so."

"Good. I mean it, guys, five minutes, or I'm off."

We watch Matty get up and march purposefully towards the door. Neither of us is quite sure what to say.

"Blimey," says Vince after a while, "old Nappy Rash can be quite firm when he wants to be, can't he?"

"Yeah," I say, breaking into a smile. "Who knew he had it in him?"

• • •

By the time Matty gets back with his paper Vince has almost decided to forgive me.

"I didn't appreciate having to hear it from someone else, that's all," he says, reaching over for my packet of cigarettes and helping himself.

"I know," I say, "it was out of order. I suppose I thought it would be easier once Alison had left."

"Well, I don't see why," he says, taking Matty's Zippo out of his pocket and flicking it alight. "And I'll tell you something else for nothing. Your missus has got rotten taste in mates."

"I know . . . I don't think Alison's friends like me very much."

"No, mate, they don't, especially that Ruth one. She's a nightmare."

"Yeah, well, she's infertile or something," I say by way of an explanation.

"Thank Christ for that," says Vince.

"Well, that's more like it," says Matty, slapping us both on the back. "That's what I like to see, the two of you taking the piss out of each other agai—*Hey,* isn't that my Zippo? I've been looking for that Zippo for ages. How long have you had it?"

"Sorry, Matt, I borrowed it off you the other day. I was just about to give it back to you, as it goes."

"Well, I suppose that's Okay, then. But don't borrow it without telling me next time, Okay?"

"No problem," says Vince, putting the Zippo back in his pocket and taking a wheezy suck on his fag. "Who fancies some more coffee, then?"

We all do.

"So, what happens now?" I say, beckoning the waitress over to take our order. "What do you think we should do?"

"Well, there's not much we can do, really. If six months is all we've got, then six months is all we've got."

"Not very long, though, is it?"

"What d'you mean? Of course it is," says Matty enthusiastically. "Six months is loads of time."

"No, mate, it's not. I mean, how are we going to do it? How are we going to find a manager, record a demo, and sign, seal, and deliver ourselves a record deal all by the end of the year? It can't be done."

Vince looks down at the table and begins to play absent-mindedly with his hairline. Matty looks disgusted with the pair of us.

"I can't believe what I'm hearing," he says. "I can't believe you're both being so defeatist. What about all the new material we've been working on? What about that new song Danny wrote last week? It's great stuff. It's way up there. Christmas is loads of time. It is. We can do it, guys. We can find a live agent and get some decent gigs and if we all pitch in we can definitely afford some more demo time . . . I mean, we just need to be more positive. We can do this. I *know* we can."

"Yeah . . ." says Vince, banging his chair leg on the floor for emphasis. "And right here is where we start payin' . . . *in sweat*."

"Y'what?"

"*Kids from Fame*," I say, explaining Vince's ludicrous American accent to Matty. "Bit before your time."

"Well, I don't get it. I'm going to read my paper. Let me know when you've decided you want to do something constructive instead of sitting about moaning like a couple of old grannies."

The waitress arrives with our coffee and I spend a quality moment checking her out to take my mind off things. She's very sexy. Cute and dark and curvy with one of those very short fringes that only look good on seriously attractive women. I notice the way she looks at Matty as she puts down his cup. All women look at Matty like that: like they're not quite sure if they want to mother him or fuck his brains out.

"Fuck me," says Matty, lifting his nose out of the NME and almost causing the waitress to spill Vince's drink. "Look who's in here."

"Who?"

"Scarface. You remember. You said you used to go to school with their lead singer."

"Yeah, complete prat. His band are awful, never make it in a million years."

"Well, according to this they already have. Says here that they signed a huge deal in America at the end of last year."

"No . . . they can't have. Are you *serious*?"

"Yeah, they've been touring the States for the last nine months. NME reckons they've sold close to a million records."

"How can they . . . I mean, how did it happen? Why hasn't there been any news about them over here?"

"Well," says Matty, reading out excerpts from their centre-page spread, "it says here that they're coming over in a couple of months to do a British tour. Their record company wants to break them in the UK before they start work on their next album in LA. Wow. I can't believe you know their lead singer, man. That's amazing."

I need to see for myself. I reach over, grab the paper off Matty and start scanning the article for information. I take in a hundred facts a second: their chart positions; their front covers; their designer dishevelled clothes; the stupid, squinty, mock-moody grins on their faces that say they still can't quite believe their own good fortune. Scarface. Bastards. Talentless, witless, sub–Kurt Cobain copyist bastards. How could this have happened? How could Ike Kavanagh have turned into a millionaire big-cheese rock star without me knowing it? How could he be recording his next album in Los Angeles and going out to dinner with Mick and Keith while I'm still working for Kostas in a specialist video shop in Crouch End? I can't take it in. I can't seem to breathe.

And then I notice it: a small but perfectly formed sentence lurking at the bottom of the page. Right next to the picture of their shiny silver tour bus; curled up underneath the venue listings for their "major UK tour."

SUPPORT ACTS STILL TO BE ANNOUNCED.

Support acts *still* to be announced. I have an idea. I lift up the article and beckon Vince and Matty across the table.

"Now that," says Vince, screwing up my "to do" list and flicking it into the ashtray, "is what I *call* a plan."

15

"It's genius."

"I know."

"Sheer genius."

"I know."

"It means we can bypass the whole thing. We can go straight to the next level. We'll get press coverage and huge exposure and we'll play to thousands of people and if there's a shred of justice left in the world we'll blow them off-stage and get ourselves the record deal of the fucking century."

"Too right."

"Too right."

"And this time next year . . ."

". . . We'll all be millionaires."

"I'll drink to that."

We've walked the fifty yards from the World Café to the Harringay Arms and we're celebrating the birth of our first good idea in years. It's perfect. All I have to do is call in a favour from an old school friend and the tour is as good as ours. No matter that Ike Kavanagh hated my guts at school, no matter that he's the sort of bloke who still wears a hammer-and-sickle badge on his lapel and peppers his sentences with the word "dude." No matter that he thinks Scarface is an acceptable name for a rock band and that I haven't actually spoken to him for the best part of two and a half years.

"So when did you last see him, then?" says Vince, taking a sip of his lager.

"I ran into him in Camden Town a couple of years ago. He was on his way to post a Jiffy bag to some guy at the *Melody Maker* who'd given him a bad review."

"A Jiffy bag?"

"Yeah, a padded envelope. With a turd in it."

"You're kidding."

"No. He did it all the time. He got a lot of bad reviews in those days."

"I suppose that's why they went off to America, then."

"I guess so."

"Still, must be nice for him now, though, everyone in this country saying he was shite and him getting to come back over here as a bona fide pop star."

"Yeah," I say, "it must be fantastic."

"Wow," says Matty. "How did he manage to poo in the bag? I mean you'd need a pretty good aim, wouldn't you? And what if the bag was too small? What if you'd chosen one of those small ones and forgotten that you'd been out for a super-hot curry the night before and then when you got your arse to the edge of the envelope it started to fill up too fast and come over the edges and . . ."

"Matty?"

"Yes."

"Why don't you ask him when you see him . . . Okay?"

"Okay, good idea."

"So, what makes you think he'll give us the support slot? It's not like we've got a deal or a press profile or anything like that."

"Simple. I'll blackmail him."

"Blackmail him?"

"Yeah. I mean, look at this," I say, spreading the NME article across the bar. "It says here that his favourite bands when he was growing up were the Clash and the Beatles and the Stooges and the Smiths."

"What's wrong with that?"

"Nothing, it's just that it's not true. Ike Kavanagh was a Nick Kershaw fan. He liked Level 42 and Haircut 100 and, get this, his all-time favourite song was 'Total Eclipse of the Heart' by Bonnie Tyler."

Vince shoots me a look. We both know I was a bit of a Howard Jones fan myself until Vince got hold of me and forced me to spend a whole weekend listening to *The White Album* and *Blood on the Tracks*, but it's not the kind of thing he'd ever bring up in front of Matty.

"I mean, he didn't go to his first proper gig until he was almost twenty," I say, ignoring Vince and folding the paper away. "The nearest he got was his big sister taking him up the West End to see *Cats*. He saw it five times. I tell you, we could destroy his street cred overnight."

Vince looks concerned.

"I don't know, mate," he says, flicking his cigarette into the ashtray. "Sounds to me like you're the last person he'd want to have around. He's not going to want to hang out with someone who remembers every gory detail about his naff adolescence, is he?"

"Well," I say, "that's where you're wrong. The other thing about Ike is that he's a bit of a sadist. He won't be able to resist it. He won't be able to resist taking us on tour and showing us everything that he's got and rubbing our noses right in it."

"Sounds like a nice guy."

"Yeah," I say. "Ike's the best."

• • •

I leave Vince and Matty in the pub plotting world domination and make my way home along Mount View Road; Alison promised she'd phone me when she got to Bruges and I want to make sure I'm there to take the call. It's a perfect afternoon—the trees are thick with leaves and I can feel the sun burning a small red patch into the back of my neck as I walk. I wonder if the whole of August is going to be like this. I wonder if it's as hot in Belgium as it is over here.

"Danny, it's me."

"Hey, how is it?"

"It's great. It's *great*. The apartment they're putting me up in isn't ready yet so I'm staying in this ridiculously swanky hotel for a few nights. It's got a phone in the bog and a view across the whole city and—"

"Has it got a minibar?"

"Yeah. D'you want to know what's in it?"

"Definitely."

"Okay, wait a minute . . . right, it's got Belgian lager . . ."

"Obviously."

"Er . . . assorted miniatures including two schnapps and three cherry brandy . . . two packets of M & M's, a bottle of Cabernet Sauvignon, a quarter-bottle of champagne and . . . let's see, what else . . . ? Oh yeah, three packets of Pom Bars. Assorted flavours."

"What the hell are Pom Bars?"

"Some sort of crisps, I think. Yeah, crisps shaped like little bears . . . *uhmm*, they sort of stick to the roof of your mouth . . . a little bit like Wotsits, but not quite as cheesy."

"It's no good," I say. "It's still not a proper minibar."

"Why not?"

"No Toblerone," I say. "Every minibar worth its salt has to have a bar of Toblerone, everybody knows that."

"Bugger," she says. "I'll have to ask them to move me somewhere else now."

It's good to talk to her. I know she's only been gone a few hours but it's still nice to hear her voice. I like talking to Alison on the phone. We used to have these conversations that went on for hours before we moved in together, and to be honest there's always been a part of me that's sort of missed them.

"So, how was the journey?"

"Good. It's really easy. I was going to start reading *Captain Corelli* again but I just ended up reading *Heat* and *Hello!* and your Let's Go guide to Bruges instead."

"Who was in it?"

"*Heat* or *Hello!*?"

"*Hello!*"

"Oh my God, it was priceless. They had a whole article on Hale and Pace enjoying themselves on a day out with a pub lunch."

"Fantastic. What did Hale have?"

"Hale had steak and chips and Pace had the fish. Honestly, Danny, I was laughing so much I thought I was going to puke."

"What did *you* have?"

"Oh, it was brilliant, I was in first class so you get these mock-gourmet meals that taste a bit like the stuff you get on a plane, and a glass of champagne and a packet of nut truffles . . . oh, and a tiny bit of smoked salmon with a caper on the top. It was ace."

She sounds on top form, like she's really enjoying herself. Come to think of it I'm not sure I can remember her sounding this animated for months.

"So what's Bruges like?" I say, flicking the kettle on for a Pot Noodle.

"It looks nice. I haven't seen that much of it yet but, you know, it looks pretty, loads of canals and stuff."

"Great. So are you going to go out and have a look around?"

"Yeah, Didier's taking me out for a meal later on. He's going to recommend some good places to go."

"Didier?"

"My new boss. Like a welcome dinner. You know, welcome to Thorstans, here's some free chocolate . . . that sort of thing. I haven't met him yet but he sounded like a bit of a dick on the phone."

"Good," I say without thinking.

"So anyway," she says gently, "how are you?"

"Not bad," I say. "I was a bit pissed off that you left without waking me up, though."

"Yeah, sorry about that, but I know how much you hate getting up in the morning and it just seemed easier . . . I'll let you take me to the station next time. I promise."

"No chance," I say, peeling back the lid of my noodle and searching around for the Tabasco. "You can walk next time for all I care."

She laughs.

"Look, Danny, I can't stay on for too long . . . I've got to take a shower and unpack my stuff . . . I'll phone you again tomorrow . . . same sort of time, Okay?"

"You sure you don't want me to call you?"

"No. I get my calls on expenses so I might as well phone you from here. They're fixing me up with a free mobile account as well, so my old number might be out of order for a couple of days."

"Okay, I'll wait for you to ring me, then. Speak to you tomorrow."

"Okay, take care . . . I love you."

"Yeah. I love you too."

It's only after I put down the phone that I realise she hasn't even told me the name of her hotel. It's the first time in almost five years that I haven't known exactly where she is.

16

"Kostas, is that you?"

"Yes, is me, Kostas. Let me ins, I have somethings for you."

"But it's nine o'clock in the morning."

"Yes, but I have present for you . . . from Mrs. Kostas."

I shut the bedroom window, put on some pants and head downstairs to open the door for Kostas.

"What is it?"

"Dinner."

"Dinner?"

"Yes. Mrs. Kostas is worried you don't have girlfriend to cook you dinner no more so she want you to have this. Is very nice. Is kleftiko."

I take the lid off the Pyrex dish Kostas is holding and take a look inside. It looks good. A huge shin of lamb melting off the bone into a pool of thick, herby gravy. It smells fantastic.

"Thanks," I say, "but she really shouldn't have gone to all this trouble. I usually cook for myself anyway."

"So I see," says Kostas, eyeing up the empty Pot Noodles by the sink.

"Still," he says, "really is no problem. You bring back dish when you finished and, if you like, Mrs. Kostas can make you something else next week."

"Do you want to stay for some coffee?" I say, searching through the cupboard to see if we've got anything besides instant.

"No thank you, must get on. Have delivery of John Woos coming for Sheila in half an hour. I see you at the shop laters, Okay."

"Okay, Kostas. Thanks again."

This is nice. This is really nice. Sitting in my kitchen, waiting for the kettle, listening to *The Moral Maze* on Radio 4 and eating cold kleftiko for breakfast. I wonder if caramelised onions are a good idea first thing in the morning. I wonder if the braised chillies might be pushing things a bit too far. I wonder if *Columbo* is on yet.

"Danny?"

"Yeah. Who's that?"

"It's me, Kate."

"*Kate?*"

"Yeah. I'm not disturbing you, am I? It's just that I wanted to make sure I got hold of you before I went into college."

She is, actually. I was just about to take a shower. I was right in the middle of a delicate and highly complex operation. Our shower is evil. It's old and cranky and glazed with rust and the pipes shake like an epileptic with a strobe light every time you try to turn it on. It's very temperamental. There's less than a millimetre of dial between freezing cold and boiling hot and I very nearly had it. I was almost there. I only bothered answering the phone in the first place because I thought it might be Alison.

"No, it's fine," I say, reaching for a towel and wrapping it round my waist. "I was just about to take a shower, that's all."

"Really?"

"Yeah . . . you know, most people take them in the morning."

"Yeah, of course, I do too . . . take a shower, I mean."

"Good."

"Good."

"So, Kate, was there something that I could help you with?"

"Oh, right, of course, the gig."

"The gig?"

"Yeah. Matty said you were going to try and blag yourself on to this Scarface tour, which is *way* cool, by the way, and I thought, hey, you guys are going to need some warm-up dates to get yourselves back into shape, so why don't I ask the events officer at my art college if he can fix you up with something."

"*Really?* Could you do that? I mean, do you think he'd be up for it?"

"Sure, no problem. I thought I'd try and get hold of him this afternoon. Maybe I could pop over later and let you know what he says."

"All right then, thanks. That's really good of you."

"Okay, wicked."

"So . . . then."

"So . . ."

We take a short pause. I'm not used to speaking to Kate on the phone. I only ever see her when she comes out with Matty, and I'm suddenly not quite sure what to say.

"Er . . . how's your sculpture class going?" I ask finally.

"Good," she says, "I'm really enjoying it. I've just finished my first installation. It's a giant wingless bird made out of scrap metal and pubic hair. I've modelled parts of it on my own body. Not the beak, though . . . obviously."

"Right," I say. "Sounds . . . fascinating."

"Well listen, if you're interested you should come down and see it sometime. The exhibition's on for another couple of weeks yet."

"Yeah . . . er, nice one . . . I'll see if I can make it down."

"Great," she says, "and it's definitely okay if I call round later and let you know about the gig?"

"Sure, absolutely, no problem."

What a nice thing for her to do. A gig at her art college is exactly what the band needs to warm up for the tour. Alison is completely wrong about her. She might be a bit over the top but deep down she's a really good kid. Things are definitely looking up. All I have to do now is convince the shower not to boil me alive, find myself some semi-clean clothes from under the bed, and try to work out how the hell I'm going to get hold of Ike.

17

For a very brief period —spring 1983 to the summer of 1985—there was a chance that Ike Kavanagh and I might be friends. We were both equally hated. Me for being spotty and bearing a ridiculous name and him for being overweight and rich. He was the richest kid in our school: the first one to get an Atari, the first one to get a pocket calculator, the first one to get Kickers and a Kappa track-suit top. His dad owned an aerosol factory in Dagenham and he used to collect Ike from school in an olive-green Rolls-Royce with hand-stitched cream leather seats. Everybody wanted to take a ride in it. Almost as much as they wanted to kick Ike in the head.

So we both kind of bonded for a while: the class losers, the school spanners, the two kids who were always last to be picked for games and first to be picked on for ritual humiliation. We used to sit together in maths and music. I used to go round to his house and he'd show me his swimming pool and his snooker table and the Sinclair C5 that his dad had bought him for his thirteenth birthday. He never let me have a go on it, though, not once.

And then, one day, midway through our mock O-level exams, I came in to find the whole class holding a séance and pretending that they were trying to contact the spirit of my dead dad. That happened quite a lot. People were always giving me shit for having no dad and no mates and a crazy mother who insisted on wearing kaftans and ostrich-feather mules to sports days and parents' night. It was their idea of fun. They were always trying to spook me and wind me up and they'd often pretend that they'd just seen my father giving a ghostly geography lesson at the back of the class.

And there was Ike. Right in the middle of it: puppy fat rippling round his stomach as he laughed, pupils shining like burnt chocolate, lips shrunk back into his face like a snorting horse.

"Hey, Moony," he said, carving an extra pentangle into the desk with his penknife, "when you off to Hollywood, then? When's your old man coming back to fetch you? Yeah, didn't you know? Moony's dad was a famous actor. He faked his own heart attack, didn't he, Moony? Ran away to America just so as he could get away from your loony mum."

Everyone collapsed and I hardly ever spoke to Ike again. That's the thing about kids who are bullied—the second you give them the chance to cross over to the other side they jump at it with both sweaty hands. Arsehole. The only reason he got into a band in the first place is because it was the one thing I ever managed to do before him. If I'd had any sense I would have decked him there and then.

*

"Yes, I'm a *very* close friend of his. We go way back."

"Well, I don't know. We don't usually give out contact numbers for our artistes, sir."

"But he'd be happy to hear from me, honestly, he'll be really pissed off if you don't give me his number."

"Well, if you'd just like to hold for a moment . . ."

Hold? Doesn't she realise how much this is costing me?

Doesn't she realise that I've already waited five hours for the lazy bastards in New York to get up out of bed and come into work? Doesn't she understand that if Alison comes home and finds twenty million calls to the States on our next phone bill she's going to lynch me?

"Sorry to keep you waiting, sir . . . but like I said, it's really not Geffen's policy to give out contact numbers over the phone. Perhaps you could try somewhere else."

"I already have. I've tried his management office and his publishers and the snivelling little shit-bag in Pasadena that does all of his West Coast press."

"There's no need to get abusive, sir . . ."

"But it's not fair. What's wrong with you people? I mean, Ike Kavanagh . . . he's hardly a threat to national security, is he?"

"Sir . . . *sir* . . . you are going to have to try and calm down . . ."

"How about his mobile?"

"No."

"His girlfriend's number, then?"

"No."

"The hotel he's staying at, the house that he's renting, the number at his million-quid condo on Malibu Beach."

"Ike doesn't live near the beach, sir . . . he doesn't like sand. Now if you'll excuse me I'm going to have to terminate you . . ." *Click*.

Sod it. I'm not sure who else to try. His parents moved away years ago and his father's factory got closed down on account of the ozone layer. Fuck it, fuck global warming. Fuck Ike Kavanagh and his money and his attitude and his Jiffy bags full of hot steamy turds. There must be someone else. There must be some other way of getting hold of him. His live agent. I haven't tried his live agent yet—the name's at the bottom of the tour ad in the NME. They're called ICN. I'll try them. I'll try a completely different tack.

• • •

"Good morning. Brad Pearlman speaking . . . how may I help you today?"

"Er . . . yes . . . thank you, Brad . . . my name is Terry Stamp, I'm the front-of-house manager at the Shepherd's Bush Empire in London, England."

"I see."

"Yes . . . er, and of course we are expecting Scarface over to play at our esteemed venue in October and I have a couple of queries regarding the band's rider."

"You do?"

"Yes. It says on our fax here that Mr Kavanagh will be expecting a range of stationery to be supplied backstage along with the usual supplies of beer, spirits, and hot-and-cold running buffet for twenty."

"Well, yes, as you know, the band will be expecting a wide selection of beverages, spirits, and cold cuts . . . but *stationery*, you say?"

"Yes, stationery, and I just wondered what kind of thing Mr. Kavanagh would be expecting . . . plain white, padded brown, W. H. Smith's notelets with kittens on the front or regular plain old Basildon Bond?"

"Baiziledon Bond?"

"Oh yes, Brad, a gentleman knows exactly where he is with Basildon Bond."

"Hmmmmn . . . well, perhaps I should give you his tour manager's cell phone number, then. He's English so he'll probably have more of an idea of what it is that you're actually talking about."

"Okay, that's very kind of you."

"No problem, Terry."

"Thanks, Brad."

"You're very welcome, Terry."

Bingo.

The number is engaged so I stand in front of the hall mirror for a while practising what I'm going to say. His tour manager isn't going to be fooled by bogus queries about padded envelopes, so I'm going to have to try to convince him that Ike and I really were friends. Maybe I'd sound more convincing if I was wearing a different T-shirt. I wonder what I'd look like if I gelled my hair up into one of those shark's-fin styles that everyone was wearing last year. Yeah, my yellow Pixies T-shirt, my second-hand Levi's jacket and a bit of a sharky haircut. Excellent.

It hasn't worked. My Pixies T-shirt has a huge stain on the front. It's so faded you can barely read the words any more and the stain makes it read "This monkey's gone to *heave*" instead of "heaven." And my hair is a complete disaster. I've used nearly a whole pot of Black and White and something of Alison's called Perfume Fudgey Whip. I smell like a rent boy. I look like I've just had my hair cut by someone called Giovanni. It's gone all high. I have dome-head. I have third-degree hat hair and I haven't even been wearing a hat.

"Hi," I say, trying to pat my hair down with the heel of my hand, "my name's Danny McQueen."

"YOU WHAT!?"

"Danny McQueen."

"You'll have to speak *up*! Hold on, I'll just take you outside."

There's a tremendous amount of noise on the other end of the line: drums and guitars and piercing feedback squalls and a thin, reedy voice darting in and out of range through the middle of it. It sounds like the tour manager is standing dead centre on the main stage at Glastonbury. And then it all goes quiet.

"Right then . . . who did you say you were?"

"Danny McQueen. I'm an old school-friend of Ike's. I've been trying to get in touch with him. You wouldn't happen to know where he is, would you?"

"Yeah, he's right next door. In the rehearsal room. I'll just see if he wants to speak to you . . . Hey, Nathan, tell Ike there's someone called Sammy McQueen on the phone for him, will you . . ."

"Danny . . . not *Sammy* . . ."

He isn't listening. I hear a door open and the music turns from a dull pulse back to a violent, cacophonous wave. Someone is shouting above the noise. I hear the band stop playing. I feel a bit anxious. He probably won't even remember who I am.

"Sammy?"

"No, no, it's Danny . . . Danny Mc*Queen*."

He pauses for a second. I'm not sure if this is because he can't place me or because he's just trying to make me think that he can't.

"Moony?"

"Erm . . . yeah . . ."

"Moony . . . *Moony McQueen* . . . no shit . . . how you doing?"

"Fine . . . fine," I say. "What about you, though. Looks like you've finally cracked it."

"Yeah, well . . . you know . . . success brings its own hassles."

What a twat. What an almighty twat.

"So what are you up to these days, Moony . . . ?"

"Well, I'm still playing in the band . . . we're called Dakota now."

"You've got a *band*?"

"Yeah . . . you know I have . . . I've always been in a band . . . I—"

"Oh yeah, right, right, I remember, you used to play the guitar or something?"

"Yes . . . look, Ike, I know this is out of the blue and you probably have a lot of people asking you for favours and stuff these days but . . ."

"Yeah, I do . . . everyone I've ever said more than two words to in my life is suddenly crawling out of the woodwork and claiming to be my best-ever friend."

"Well . . . I'm sure . . . but the thing is I was wondering if—"

"Hey, why don't we catch up for a drink?"

"Sure," I say, surprised. "I mean, that would be great but I think LA might be a bit far to go for a pint of lager."

"No, I'm in London . . . King's Cross. We're rehearsing here while we do all of our European promotion. We're finishing up about four. You should pop down and say hello."

I look at my watch. It's almost 3:30. No time to change out of my Pixies T-shirt or to get the half-pound of scented wax out of my bouffant. Vince had better appreciate this.

18

This is unlike any rehearsal room I've ever been in. It's huge. It's got a reception. It's got a receptio*nist*. It's got windows and daylight and cheese plants and chairs and a polished wooden floor with spotlights running right through the middle of it. The receptionist clocks my hair as I walk in and stifles a smirk. She looks like she works for *Razzle* on her days off: dark brown hair bleached with an Addams Family streak and a Barbara Windsor bosom that spills over the top of her blouse as she speaks.

"Can I help you?" she says, twirling her pen lid round her collagen.

"Yeah," I say, "I'm here to see Ike Kavanagh . . . from Scarface."

"One moment, I'll just phone down to the studio and let his tour manager know that you're here . . . Hi, yes, this is Kelly from reception, I've got someone here to see Ike."

This isn't right. This is all wrong. I wonder if Kelly has ever had athlete's foot. I wonder if Ike has shagged her yet.

"Okay, that's fine," she says, smiling at me with a mouthful of expensively whitened tooth enamel. "Someone will be up to collect you in a minute."

I sink into a long leather sofa and flick through one of a pile of

Music Week magazines that are stacked up on the table next to me. I feel like I'm in the waiting room of a millionaire music mogul turned evil suburban dentist: Brian Epstein meets David Geffen meets Laurence Olivier in *Marathon Man*. I think about pretending to be Dustin Hoffman by stuffing some tissue paper in my cheeks, and asking Kelly if it's "safe," but I don't think she'd get it. It's at least ten minutes before anyone bothers to come up and collect me.

The practice room itself is the size of a small aircraft hangar. It's got a raised wooden stage at one end and an overhead lighting rig illuminating piles of amps and guitars and drum cases at the other. Scarface are still on stage. Ike is throwing messy rock poses with his guitar while his tour manager barks a complicated series of instructions at his team of roadies and press officers and assistants and glorified hangers-on. One of the road crew—fat gut, stocky limbs, scrappy dragon tattoos etched into his freshly shaven head—is crouched over at the side of the stage making a tray of joints for the band. He's like a machine: rolling them up, licking their seams, rolling them up, licking their seams, rolling them up, licking their seams, fitting them with roaches and dotting them about on the band's equipment like sweets.

Ike sees me come in and gives me a quick nod. He leans over, selects the fattest joint he can find, jumps down off the stage and strolls over to slap me on the back. Hard.

"Moony, duuuude . . . long time no see. Long fucking time."

"Hi, Ike," I say, "you're looking well."

"Cheers, yeah . . . but look at you, man . . . look at *you* . . . still exactly the same . . . I mean, really, Moon, you haven't changed a bit since school. Not one little bit."

"Well . . . I've seen you a few times since then, Ike. Remember when you were off to post that Jiffy bag to the *Melody Maker* that time?"

"No. Not sure what you mean. Was it a demo tape or something?"

"No, it was a turd."

"Oh yeah," he says, taking a long toke on his spliff. "I remember. That was cool, man. That was one stinky fucking turd."

Ike lifts the spliff back to his lips and inhales deeply. I notice that he holds the smoke in his lungs for as long as he can. I notice that he plucks his eyebrows and that he wears chipped black varnish on his fingernails. I notice that his hand shakes a little as he pulls the butt from his mouth and passes it back to his roadie.

"Right then," he says, "that's better. Now we can go up to the cafe for a bit of a chat."

Ike has a severe case of the munchies so we head over to the serving hatch and join the food queue. Ike orders shepherd's pie and peas. And a plate of spotted dick and custard for dessert. I'm not feeling that hungry so I settle for a mug of tea. And a packet of Hula Hoops. And a small slice of pie.

We spend the next half hour making idle music-business banter and pretending that we're both interested in what each other has been up to for the last five years. He's exactly how I expected him to be: full of himself. He's got a skewed mid-Atlantic accent that keeps lurching into "dudes" and "mans" and "sure things" and then crashing back into comedy Dick Van Dyke mockney. He can't stop bragging: the places he's been to, the people he's met, and he's sipping his tea and stirring his custard and spilling their names like party wine and waste paper.

"Of course, Madonna," he says, leaning in low over his mince, "has got fantastic tits . . . for her age . . . I mean, she's a bit long in the tooth, yeah? But she's definitely a nice bit of old.

Came down to our gig at the Whiskey last month . . . amazing. Remember that sex book she did . . . ? *Man*, I must have worn my dick away bashing off over that book . . . especially that picture of her and that model, you know, the one where it looks like Naomi Campbell is sniffing her crack or something."

I have the feeling Ike was more likely to be found masturbating over his souvenir *Cats* programmes than dirty pictures of Madonna, but I let him carry on regardless.

"And Kate Moss, dude. Sooo cool. Came to our album launch at Chateau Marmont. Really fit. *Really* fit. I like 'em skinny. Anything over a size eight and you just feel like you're dipping your prick into a bucket of lard . . . know what I mean?"

I don't say anything.

"So what about you, eh . . . ? Making up for lost time, no doubt?"

"Lost time?"

"Yeah . . . I mean, let's face it, Moon, no one was gonna let you anywhere near them with those zits of yours, were they?"

"Well, I'm living with someone now . . . her name's Alison. We've been together about five years."

"Right, right . . . so you don't get bored, then?"

"No, she's great . . . she's just landed this job in—"

"Yeah, whatever," he says, stubbing a cigarette into his beans and reaching over for his dessert. "Couldn't do it myself, though. So much pussy, man. *So* much pussy, so little time."

I finish my Hula Hoops and watch while Ike spoons pudding into his mouth and splatters custard down the front of his shirt. He chews with his mouth open, breathing through his food like an asthmatic weasel, stuffing more in before he's even finished with his last mouthful. There's an awkward silence developing. He's looking at me like he can't be bothered to think of anything else to say, like he can't believe he ever knew me.

• • •

And then I come straight out with it.

"Hey, I'd love to help you . . ." he says, wiping up a spot of custard with his sleeve, "you know I would, but it's not really up to me who we take. We usually leave that sort of thing to our live agent."

"Right."

"I mean, if it was up to me . . ."

"If it was up to you . . . ?"

"Yeah, if it was my shout . . ."

You'd do fuck all about it.

Ike finishes his food and gets up to leave. It's clear that I've outstayed my welcome. He's got what he wanted. He's shown me a slice of the kind of life he's living now and he's seen just enough to get the measure of mine. He takes his thousand-dollar leather jacket off the back of his chair and flings it across his shoulder like it's made out of recycled cotton. He takes in my disastrous haircut and my stained Pixies T-shirt and runs his fingers idly over his bleached blond crop.

"So . . . take care then, Moony . . . give our tour manager a bell some time and we'll see if he can get you and a mate into the London gig. Maybe we'll give you a couple of after-show passes or something."

"Thanks very much."

"No problem. No problem at all."

And then he's gone.

I feel poisoned to the core.

19

The evening rush hour is in full swing: afternoon shoppers fat with carrier bags, out-of-town tourists thin with confusion, and waves of commuters spreading out across the concourse like tides of muddy water. They look tired: suits creased from the summer heat; faces crumpled with boredom; eyes fixed dead ahead so as not to attract anyone's attention.

I sit down on the floor and watch them spill past me. I know that I'm watching myself. What was I thinking of? What made me think I could avoid it? Why did my lunatic mother convince me I was going to grow up to be rich and famous when the truth is I was destined to spend thirty-five years strap-hanging to work with another commuter's brown leatherette briefcase jammed hard into the crease of my arse cheeks?

It's not right. If me and Alison ever have kids I'm going to make sure I tell them the truth right away. I'm going to lock them in their bedrooms and beat them with a stick until they've finished all their homework. I'm going to ban them from listening to music and watching the telly. I'm going to take them to work with me and show them the crappy office where their dad sits locked away from daylight for 363 days of the year. I'm going to show them the rented flat in Crouch End that is all they'll ever be able to afford to live in, and if one of them even so much as hints at wanting to learn how to play a musical instrument I'll send them for a course of electroconvulsive therapy that will fry their brains into submission and turn them into wannabe lawyers or crawly chartered accountants.

Ambition is the worst thing you can give a kid. They'll always be disappointed.

I buy myself a ham-and-cheese croissant and wander around King's Cross feeling sorry for myself. It's almost 5:30. I'm not due at the video shop until seven and there's not much point in going home because I've probably already missed Alison calling me from Bruges. I wonder if she'll have left the name of her hotel on the answerphone. I wonder if she had a nice time with Didier last night. I wonder if the travel agent's next to W.H. Smith is still open. It is.

The travel agent is busy with a young couple looking at beach holidays, and I amuse myself with a top-quality EuroDisney brochure while I'm waiting. He's giving them the big sell. He's pressing figures into his pocket calculator and running his tongue round the roof of his mouth, and he's just about to lean in for the kill.

"Well, yes, it is rather expensive," he says, focusing his attention on the woman and smacking his lips together, "but of course, you're buying more than just a holiday when you select a trip like this. You're buying the holiday"—he pauses for effect—"of a *lifetime*."

I can feel myself getting agitated. "Holiday of a lifetime" is one of the most depressing phrases in the English language. Everyone uses it. Every piss-poor perma-tanned travel show presenter, every greasy-haired, white-shirted travel agent; every moronic quiz show host that has ever had the temerity to live and draw breath. It's insulting. The idea that you might only be able to take one great holiday in your life. That you should only *expect* to take one great holiday in your life. That two weeks swanning about in an upmarket Novotel with palm trees and piped music might constitute the highlight of your entire life's leisure.

Still, it did look nice, though. I wonder if Alison would fancy a trip to Bali.

The couple leave without buying anything and I slide up the banquette and take my seat in front of Darren. I know he's called Darren because he has his name pinned carefully to his left lapel.

"Right then, Darren," I say, rubbing my hands together noisily, "let's go somewhere fabulous."

"Excuse me?"

"Fabulous . . . you know, yachts and models and movie stars and coconuts and a host of pre-paid excursions suitable for myself and my lovely wife Audrey."

"Erm, were you thinking long-haul, sir?"

"Oh yes, very long, the longest."

"Far East perhaps?" he says, reaching for his Kuoni luxury breaks brochure.

"Not sure," I say. "Has it got coconuts?"

"Of course. There's an abundance of coconuts in the Far East. Perhaps you might like to think about Thailand."

"Too Leonardo DiCaprio."

"Malaysia?"

"Too harsh on drugs."

"Singapore?"

"Too harsh on chewing gum."

"Well, perhaps sir might like to think about the Caribbean."

"Is it nice?"

"Oh yes, it's very nice indeed."

"Really? What's nice about it?"

"Well, the beaches are excellent and the hotels are first class and there're some very pleasant excursions to places of local colour and interest."

"How d'you know?"

"Well, it's all here . . . in the brochure."

"Yes, but how d'you know? I mean, have you actually been there?"

"No."

"There we go, then. Not sure I can take a recommendation from you unless you've actually been there. Perhaps we should try somewhere a little bit closer to home."

"The Gambia?"

"Too many mosquitoes."

"Egypt?"

"Too many pyramids."

"The Canaries?"

"Not enough coconuts."

"Well, sir, I'm not sure what else I can sugges—"

"How about Bruges?"

"*Bruges?*"

"Yes. How about some city breaks brochures that include a wide and varied selection of hotels in and around the medieval city of Bruges?"

Darren loads me down with shiny brochures and sends me on my way. He thinks about it but in the end he doesn't bother to tell me that coconuts are not, as far as he knows, indigenous to Belgium.

"Just look at this," I say, opening the World Choice city breaks brochure and offering it to Sheila and Kostas in disgust.

"Look at this hotel. Look at these pictures."

Sheila lifts her glasses out of her bag and moves forward to take a closer look.

"Oh, how lovely," she says, eyeing up the soft-focus photography and reading aloud from the blurb. "*Hotel Romantic, every bedroom individually decorated with exclusive fabrics and antiques.* And what a nice idea to have flowers and champagne in the room on arrival."

"Exactly," I say, pulling the brochure back across the counter and flicking to the next page. "I mean, look at this one, this one is even worse."

"*Hotel Barrone, built by a seventeenth-century count. Intimate hotel full of charm and character in peaceful setting overlooking the 'Lake of Love.'*"

"See, see what I mean? Look at those cushions. Look at the size of that bed. Look at the lace curtains and the silk eiderdown and the free mints on the pillow. I mean, just think about that for a second. Not one mint. Two. *Two* mints. Who is eating it? Who is eating Alison's other mint? She's shacked up with the Count of Monte Cristo in the 'Lake of Love.' *Already*. She's only been gone two days. I can't believe it."

"Maybe is not so bads," says Kostas, reaching for the brochure and flicking back to the cheaper hotels. "Maybe she is only staying here, in Hotel Sleeuwebrugghe. Very bad furnitures. '*Cosy hotel decorated in typical Flemishes style. Radio in room and free bike for hires.*' Maybe she is too busy for mints because she is riding round Bruges on a bikes."

I consider the bike option for a moment. "No," I say, "I don't think so, Kostas. Alison's not really a bike sort of person."

"You sure? Maybe she went to take ride round the Grotty Market."

"*Grote*, Kostas," says Sheila knowledgeably. "I think you'll find that it's actually pronounced Grote."

• • •

I spend the rest of the evening moaning and sighing and haranguing every customer that wanders into the shop to come over to the counter and take a look at my brochures. The pillow-mint issue divides them fifty-fifty. The women think Alison will just eat the second pillow mint herself. The men think she'll definitely be sharing it. Especially when I show them a picture of her. Especially when I show them a picture of her and hold it up next to me. Especially when I show them a picture of her, hold it up next to me and tell them all about her new boss Didier taking her out for a romantic champagne-and-oyster dinner. (Even some of the women begin to look a bit doubtful at this point.)

It doesn't seem fair. I bet Didier could afford to take Alison on a holiday of a lifetime. I bet Didier isn't planning a winter break in Larnaca at one of Kostas's cousin's apartments. I bet Didier's never been stuck on a rush-hour train with a leatherette briefcase shoved up his arse crack. He probably has a bigger dick than me. And bigger balls. And one of those greasy Hercule Poirot moustaches that curl up like a fork at both ends.

For some reason Kostas thinks it might be a good idea if I knock off early for the night. I tell him that I'm more than happy to stay and help him lock up the shop, but he seems quite insistent that I go. He thinks I seem depressed. He thinks I'm scaring off the customers. If I promise to cheer up he thinks Mrs. Kostas might make me some more hot dinners at the weekend.

I do as I'm told. I leave the shop around ten, pop into the 7-Eleven for a newspaper and a can of Diet Coke and walk home to a flashing answerphone and the silence of an empty flat.

20

This morning's kleftiko has a waxy film of fat right across the top of it. I crack the surface with the back of my spoon, part the layer of dripping from the layer of meat and begin eating straight from the Pyrex. The gravy has turned to jelly: burnt peppercorns stuck to the surface like trapped flies and chunks of red and green pepper dotted through the middle like pieces of candied fruit. I spoon some into my mouth, swallow hard and hit the message button on the answerphone. It blinks at me crossly. I have five new messages.

> Hi, Danny, it's me . . . are you there? . . . come on, Columbo can't be that interesting . . . it always ends the same way . . . Danny? . . . Okay, I'll try you a bit later on . . . *beeeep*.

> Yeah, Danny, it's Kate. Looks like the gig's all set. Will three weeks be long enough to get yourselves ready? I'll try you again this evening. Maybe I'll pop round later to see if you're in. If that's okay. Right, but you can't tell me if that's okay or not because you're not actually there . . . shit, I hate answerphones . . . they totally stress me out . . . *beeeep*—

Danny . . . Vince . . . just checking to see how you got on with finding that toss-wipe from Scarface. Give us a bell. Laters . . . *beeeep—*

Steve . . . it's your mother. Perhaps you could give me a ring when you have a moment . . . *beeeep—*

Hey, you, it's me . . . I guess—

A piece of chilli hits the back of my throat and makes me cough. I can't hear what Alison is saying so I rewind her and start the message over again.

"Hey, you, it's me . . . I guess you're still at work. I'm feeling a bit tired so I'm going to get an early night. I'll try and give you a bell tomorrow. Everything's going really well. Give my love to Sheila and Kostas . . . Miss you . . . big kiss . . . bye . . . *beeeep*."

I sit down on the sofa, put down the empty Pyrex and pour myself a very large drink. There's no wine or beer or Bacardi Breezers in the house but there is a bottle of Galliano that my mum brought us for Christmas a couple of years ago. I wrench open the sticky lid and pour some of the thick yellow liquid into a glass. It's disgusting. But it is alcohol.

I toss my Bruges brochures onto the floor and flick over to BBC2. The Learning Zone hasn't started yet and *Newsnight* has just finished. ITV is showing *Renegade*, Channel 4 has got something about clitorises and BBC1 is showing a made-for-TV film about incest that's based on a true story. I sip my drink and flick between the clitorises and the incest.

I feel stupid. Like I've let everybody down. Why did I tell Vince and Matty that I could pull this thing off? What made me think Ike would be prepared to do me a favour after all this time? Why is my girlfriend so fed up with me that she feels the need to go and live in a whole other country? I wonder what my mum wanted. I wonder if Kate will mind cancelling the gig at her art college. I wonder if Galliano tastes any better if you put some ice in it and mix it with Diet Coke.

Fuck me. Galliano is excellent. It really is. I mean, once you get over the sickliness, once you get over the taste, once you get over halfway through the bottle. It's great. I feel fantastic. Maybe I should phone Vince and see if he fancies coming over for a quick game of Fifa '98. Maybe I should do 1471 and see if I can find out what hotel Alison is staying at. Well, what's the good of that, then? What's the good of 1471 if it doesn't work on international calls? Useless fuckers. Maybe I should phone Matty; he's bound to be up late. I love Matty. He's a top bloke. I love him almost as much as I love Vince. And I *really* love Vince. A lot. Bollocks, he's DJing tonight. He'll be at Bar Vinyl till two. Maybe I could go up there. I could have a couple of beers and chill out to his set of sexy seventies Lounge Core.

Wait a minute, I know who'll still be up. I know who I can phone. Why didn't I think of it before? What have I possibly got to lose?

I turn off the PlayStation, slam down the dregs of my Galliano and try as hard as I can to remember the international direct dialling code for Los Angeles.

"Brad Pearlman speaking. How may I help you this afternoon?"

"*Brad,* thank God I caught you . . . it's me . . . Terry!"

"*Terry* . . . the stationery man, right?"

"Right . . ."

"From the Sheep Herd's Bush."

"Right again."

"Great, great . . . so how did you get on . . . did you manage to finalise all of Ike Kavanagh's requests?"

"Well, we certainly did, and what a lovely chap he turned out to be, very polite, very easygoing. He plumped for a mixture in the end. Half a dozen padded, half a dozen plain."

"Good, good, so glad you managed to tie things up there."

"Yes, and I just wanted to thank you for all of your help."

"No problem, Terry, any time at all."

"And the thing is, I wondered . . . I mean I was wonder*ing* if I might do you a small favour in return."

"Sure, go right ahead."

"Well, I happen to know that you're still looking for support acts for the Scarface tour in October and I thought I might be able to recommend someone. We get a lot of excellent new bands coming through our doors here at the Empire and there was one recently that particularly caught my eye."

"Oh, really?"

"Oh yes. They're called Dakota. Guitar three-piece from North London. One of the best live acts I've seen on these shores in some quite considerable time."

"Well, Terry, coming from you I'd say that was some recommendation. Who are they signed to?"

"Well, that's the best part, Brad. They're not even signed yet. It's going to happen for them, though. Very soon. They're going to be huge. Massive. The hugest. And the thing is, I know how concerned you are with making Scarface appear credible to the British media and I just thought how cool would it be if they were seen to take an unknown band out on tour with them? An unknown band that are inches away from being the next big thing. If you timed it right it would look like Scarface had had a direct hand in discovering them."

"You don't say . . . well, Terry, we should get on to this right away . . . perhaps you could send me a press pack and a band résumé and a sample of some of their recent work."

"Yes, well, I could do that, certainly, but the thing is—and I'm letting you in on a little bit of inside information here, Brad—I happen to know that a major UK act are looking at taking them out on tour at precisely the same time."

"Really? Who?"

I take a short pause.

"I don't think I'm at liberty to divulge that, Brad, it's a little, how can I put this . . . hush-hush."

"That big, huh?"

"Yes, Brad, that big."

"Okay, then, let's move on this one, Terry. Let's get it done. Let's be the first frogmen into the talent pool. Let's knock this thing out of the ballpark."

"Okay, Brad, now you're talking my language. I'll just give you the number of the band's manager. Lovely chap. His name's Vincent."

"Vincent . . . got it . . . I'll call him right away."

Shit. Unbelievable cock-up. Cannot believe what I have just done. Cannot believe I have just phoned one of the biggest live agencies in the world and tried to blag my own band on to the Scarface tour. Cannot believe Galliano has made me too pissed to dial Vince's number. It's too late. Vince is already engaged. To Brad.

"Danny, what the hell's going on?"

"Vince! Mate, *tell* me that you didn't fuck it up."

"Of course I didn't."

"So what happened?"

"Well, I don't know really, some Yank just called me up while I was watching this programme about clitorises and started talking about frogmen and talent pools and knocking things out of ballparks."

"But what did he say . . . I mean what did he mean? . . . I mean did he give us the gig or not?"

"Well, yeah, I think he did. I think he just offered us the October support slot with Scarface."

"You're kidding me."

"No. He said he'd heard fantastic things about us. Says to keep it all hush-hush until he's released it to the press. Wished me good luck with negotiating the record deal and told me he'd fax the contract and all the tour details over to our live agent by the morning."

"Shit, we don't have a live agent. What did you say?"

"Said his name was Kostas and gave him the fax number at the video shop."

"Vince . . . you fucking star."

"So, are you going to explain what's going on or what? I'm missing some quality telly here. There's a bird on the screen looks like she's got some sort of a miniature penis or something."

I give Vince a brief rundown of the last twelve hours, stagger towards the bedroom and collapse on to the bed like a sick giraffe. My head hits the pillow like a wax brick. My clothes lie in a crumpled pile on the floor along with the empty bottle of Galliano that I've sucked dry. I have crystals of dried alcohol all over my mouth. And my chin. I still have my underpants on. And my shoes.

I rule.

21

Kostas is loving every minute of it.

"So this man, right, he comes on the phones and he say to me, *What you want for the band's riders?* I say to him 'champagnes,' he say to me, *We give you one bottle of white wines*. Then he say to me, *What food you want?* I say 'smoke salmons and caviares.' He say *No caviares, just fish pastes sandwich*. Then he say to me, *How long you can play for?* I say to him you very good group, you much better than Scab Face, you can play for the whole night long. He say to me, *You can play for half an hours only*."

"Thanks, Kostas," I say, picking up the contracts and folding them into my pocket. "You don't mind if people keep phoning you like this and sending more faxes through to the shop?"

"No, is very good. I play hard balls. I get you the very best deal in the whole musics business."

I leave Kostas contemplating his new role in band mismanagement and shuffle out on to the Broadway. I don't feel very well. I spent half the night with my head hanging over the toilet bowl—breathing in the heady fumes of puke and Toilet Duck—and I've been left with the kind of indigestion that makes your whole chest feel sore and knotted and tight. It feels like I'm wearing a corset.

When did this happen? When did I become the kind of bloke who has to get up in the middle of the night and search through the kitchen drawers for a packet of broken Rennies? Five years ago I could have eaten a vindaloo, munched my way through a jar of pickled onions, polished off a barrel of home-brewed lager and not so much as raised a fart. Now I have to take spearmint-flavoured Remegel before I go to sleep. And an Alka Seltzer. And a Zantac. A mouthful of cold lamb and a few glasses of liqueur and I have the kind of acid indigestion that feels like my own stomach is trying to eat itself from the inside out.

And then there's the hangover. The kind of hangover that you know is going to last all day. The kind of hangover that hits you in the nuts and the temples and makes you feel like you're about to vomit every time you make a sudden movement. I'm only twenty-nine. Christ only knows how Vince feels after a night out on the lash.

I'm waiting for Vince in one of the greasy spoons on Park Road and the scent of hot pig fat is filling up my nostrils and making me heave. I order tea and a couple of slices of dry white toast, wash down a couple of aspirin with a slug of Pepto-Bismol and try to make some sense out of the tour contracts I've picked up from Kostas.

It turns out Brad Pearlman is a much smarter cookie than I thought he was. He's not going to pay us a penny. In fact, he wants us to pay him: one thousand dollars. He's checked us out. Nobody has heard of us. He's doing us a massive favour, he says.

I take a quick look at the tour itinerary: twelve dates. A dozen cities. Two full weeks on the road. Ike wants a long turn-around between bands and we're only going to have time to perform a thirty-minute set. Maximum. Eight to eight thirty. Sharp. Vince isn't going to like this one bit.

Vince strolls into the cafe, orders himself breakfast A with extra fried bread, nicks one of my Marlboro Lights and sits down opposite me with a big grin on his face. He's looking particularly dapper this afternoon: two-tone suede leather belt; beige wide-collared shirt with palm trees on the front; and a giant pair of charity-shop sunglasses that he picked up from the local Oxfam for fifty pence. He looks slightly demented: part rock star, part retard, part cheapskate *Miami Vice* pimp.

"You look like shit," he says, unbuttoning his cuffs and rolling up his sleeves.

"Thanks very much," I say, pushing away my toast and taking a small mouthful of tea. "You look like an Australian bag lady."

"Well, you've got to make the effort, haven't you?" he says, straightening the collar on his shirt. "I mean, I don't want to be outdone by that cockhead from Scumface, do I? . . . So come on, then, did our man Bradley send the contracts over to Kostas or what?"

"Yeah," I say, offering the sheets of curled-up fax paper to Vince. "Take a look for yourself."

Vince picks up the contracts and reads through them without taking off his shades. It takes him a while to get the gist.

"They're asking us to *buy* on to the tour?"

"Yeah, a grand. They want us to pay a thousand dollars for the privilege of supporting Scarface."

"And we're first on?"

"Eight o'clock sharp."

"Bollocks," says Vince, taking off his sunglasses and stubbing out his fag. "The *Brookside* slot."

Eight o'clock is a particularly duff time to go onstage. It's still light out, the venue is still filling up, and if you're playing at a university union most of the students will still be sat in the pub or standing in their rooms wanking over the sink and watching the end credits of their favourite soap while you're just about to run through the last of your unrequested encores. No one's pissed up yet so they're not quite ready to start enjoying themselves. They're still waiting for their girlfriends to turn up and their beards to start growing and they're usually too busy adjusting their hair gel and picking their spots to bother with watching the support band. You're the musical equivalent of Polyfilla: plugging the gaps until the headline act can be bothered to take the stage.

Vince wipes a piece of fried bread round the pool of egg yolk that's spilled out on to his plate. It repulses me and makes me feel hungry at the same time.

"Well then," he says, mid-wipe, "I think we should just get on with it."

"You don't mind going on at eight o'clock?" I say, amazed that he's taking it so well.

"Well," he says, "these are big venues, Danny, they'll be at least a third full by the time we go on. That means we'll be playing to nearly six hundred people every night. It's more than we've ever played to before. And anyway . . ." He pauses to put some bread into his mouth. "It's probably going to be our last chance."

I can't help feeling guilty. Vince has invested more than a decade in this band. In me. Why should I be forcing his hand just because my relationship with Alison is going through some kind of a five-and-a-half-year crisis?

"Maybe I'll have a word with Alison," I say, taking a small bite of my toast. "See if she's prepared to extend the deadline a bit. A year maybe, or eighteen months. A little while longer isn't going to make any real difference to her."

"No, mate," he says, "I've made up my mind. Alison is right, six months is long enough. If we don't end up with a result by the end of the year we should bite the bullet and jack it in. I've had a word with my uncle and he says there's enough plumbing work for me to join the firm full time if I want to."

"But you hate plumbing," I say, pouring some extra sugar into my tea. "You said the sweaty hair balls in the U-bends make you want to puke."

"Yeah, well, there's worse ways to make a living."

"But what about the sewage factor? You can't tell me that you aren't put off by the sewage factor?"

"Look, give it a rest, will you, Danny. I'm trying to eat my breakfast here."

"Sorry," I say. "I just didn't think you were that keen on plumbing, that's all."

Vince stares down at his plate and starts digging into a piece of bacon like it's still alive. It makes me uncomfortable to hear him talk like this. I've never heard him talk seriously about giving up before, and it feels like a turning point. It makes it seem real. It makes me feel unbelievably maudlin.

"Cheer up, you wanker," he says, noticing the look on my face. "You never know, it might still work out for us. We should at least try and make the best of it."

"Yeah, you're right," I say, dipping my toast into Vince's beans and taking a small bite. "It's a good opportunity."

"Exactly, and anyway," he says, pushing away his plate and lighting himself another cigarette, "you're gonna be a busy boy."

"Why, what d'you mean?"

"Well, one of us has got to work out how we're going to raise the money for the buy-on fee and the wonga for the hotels and then there's the van hire and the sound guy and a roadie and—"

"What about you? How come I've got to do it all?"

"Come off it," he says, exhaling a thick plume of cigarette exhaust, "where am I going to find the time? I've got less than six weeks to organise what we're all going to wear onstage and, more importantly, I've got two weeks' worth of compilation tapes to make. You can't expect us to go out on tour without a top-notch set of vintage-Vince compilation tapes, can you?"

"No," I say, waving the smoke from Vince's cigarette away from my face. "I suppose not."

22

I wonder if I could get away with wearing flared trousers like Vince's. I have a feeling that my legs may be too short to carry it off. It's not like I'm a short-arse—I'm five foot ten and a half—but I've always thought that flares look much better on you if you're over six foot. I had a pair of cream corduroys with sixteen-inch bottoms once. Alison liked them because they were really tight around the crotch but I had to stop wearing them in the end because I kept getting my left bollock caught in the material when I sat down. I wonder if I've still got them somewhere.

I'm almost at the flat and I'm just wondering whether we should go all out for seventies psychedelia with paisley shirts and fake Afros or stick to basic indie-issue black when I notice someone sitting outside on the wall. It's Kate. She's got her hair in bunches and she's wearing a low-cut summer dress over a pair of cotton Indian-style trousers. The whole effect is quite flimsy, and as I draw nearer I can see her nipples sticking through the fabric of her dress like a pair of pink, fleshy wheel nuts. Kate has big nipples and small breasts. They point upwards and outwards like miniature winter Olympic ski jumps.

Maybe it's the remnants of my Galliano hangover or the humidity of the afternoon sun but something about the whole combination—pert tits, flimsy cotton, the gash of red lipstick on her fat, smiley lips—gives me an instant semi. Well, not quite a semi, more like a quarteri. This is exactly what I'm talking about, though. This is exactly the kind of moment when you want to make sure you're wearing baggy combats instead of tight-crotch corduroy flares.

"Danny, hi."

"All right, Kate," I say, holding my 7-Eleven bag in front of me so she can't get a look at my quarteri. "What's up?"

"I just popped over for a chat. I wanted to talk to you about the gig. You don't mind, do you?"

"No, no, not at all. Come on up, I'll make us some coffee."

The flat is a bit of a state: dirty clothes piled up in front of the washing machine, yesterday's Pyrex stuck to the coffee table and a range of glasses and mugs and cutlery and PlayStation games scattered all over the living-room floor. Kate doesn't seem to notice. She asks if I've got any herbal tea, flops down in the middle of the sofa—narrowly avoiding a three-pronged fish fork—and starts rooting through her bag for details of the warm-up gig that she's organised at her art college.

She keeps all her college notes in a large satchel decorated with sequins and mirrors and bits of old ribbon, and I can't help noticing the beads of sweat nestled in her cleavage as she reaches over to belt it shut. The bunches and the satchel give her whole look a sort of teenage Britney Spears effect, and something about the way she twirls her hair with her fingers and crosses and uncrosses her legs makes me feel a little bit like a dirty uncle. Plus she's Matty's girlfriend. It's not on. It may be the height of summer, but I shouldn't really be checking out Matty's girlfriend's cleavage. Or her tits.

"Right then," she says, kicking off her sandals and wriggling back into the cushions. "Here it is. I think I've asked all the right questions."

I take her sheet of notes and sit down next to her. There's not much to it, really. Fifty quid for an hour-and-a-half set. Three weeks' time. Union bar. Guaranteed audience of about a hundred people. She could easily have sorted it out with me over the phone.

"Yeah," I say, "seems okay to me. It's exactly what we need, actually. I just found out we're on the Scarface tour for definite."

"Wow, that's fantastic. Does Matty know yet?"

"No. Vince was going to give him a ring later on."

"I knew it," she says, brushing her fringe off her forehead and widening her eyes at me. "You're probably going to think this is stupid but a friend of mine has been drawing up a star chart for Matty and she reckoned something amazing was just about to happen for him. I could get her to do one for you, if you like. You're Libran, aren't you?"

I don't bother correcting her.

"Thought so," she says, touching my knee with her hand. "You've got all the typical traits."

I feel my cock start to wither and I immediately stop listening to what she's saying. It's one of those things. You can be having a perfectly civilised conversation with someone and then they ask you what your star sign is and you instantly realise that you're talking to a moron. She might as well be talking about bigfoot or witchcraft or sacrificing virgins in the middle of Bodmin Moor.

". . . and I've just been given this book on reiki," she says, getting into her stride. "It's really interesting. It's all about the transfer of the universal life energy. Like a massage for your aura or something."

"Right," I say. "Sounds good. But . . . you know . . . Alison's mum bought me an electric foot-massager a couple of years ago and it's been in the cupboard under the stairs ever since so . . . maybe massage isn't really my thing."

She smiles at me. She doesn't seem to mind that I'm taking the piss.

"Seriously," she says, "you really ought to read it. It'll completely change the way you look at the world."

She's beginning to annoy me now. What's wrong with the way I look at the world? She's read half a crappy paperback by someone who once went on holiday to India for a week and she thinks that makes her an expert on the human condition. I think that's the main appeal of mysticism to people like Kate. A couple of health-food shop leaflets and a quick visit to the hocus-pocus library and you're instantly an expert on your subject compared to everyone else. It's a short cut. It means you get to feel superior and knowledgeable without actually having learned anything. Of any use. Whatsoever.

I let her finish up her tea but I don't bother offering her another cup. I thank her for sorting out the gig, tell her that I'm expecting a call from Alison and she finally takes this as her cue and gets up to leave. She offers to lend me her book on reiki so that I can be more informed about life-forces and my hidden self. I think about telling her that I'd rather chew off my own foot, but I don't want to hurt her feelings so I tell her to give it to me next time she sees me. I didn't know what else to do. It was the only way I could think of to get rid of her.

The phone hasn't stopped ringing all afternoon: a woman from BT offering to extend my Friends and Family package—I didn't even know I *had* a Friends and Family package—a man from Barclaycard ringing to see if I want an extension on my credit limit—very nice of them considering I already owe over two thousand pounds—and a quick call from Ike congratulating me about coming on the tour. Odd, really. He sounded quite magnanimous. I wonder if he had anything to do with it. Probably decided he quite fancied the idea of having a whipping-boy on tour with him after all. Wait until he sees us play, though. Wait until he meets Vince. Vince will sort him right out. Must remember to tell Matty not to make friends with him, though. Matty's terrible like that. He's so trusting. He'll meet Ike and he'll share a couple of beers with him and before you know it Ike will be his brand-new, best-ever mate.

Maybe we could get him a tattoo: *Must not make friends with Ike*. We could have it inked across his forehead in backwards writing. Bit harsh. Maybe we could just write *Ike is a cunt* across the top of his drumheads to remind him what's what.

I think I must have dozed off. The last thing I remember is an Alsatian having his piles removed by a cute-looking nurse on *Pet Rescue* and now it's almost eight o'clock. I check the answerphone to see if Alison called me while I was asleep. Nothing.

Maybe I should nip down to the shops and buy myself something to eat. My hangover stomach seems to have settled down a bit and I'm suddenly starving hungry. I decide to risk it. I'll just record a new answerphone message in case Alison calls me while I'm out.

"Hi, if that's you I've gone to Budgens."

Shit, maybe I shouldn't say I've gone to Budgens. Sounds like I have no life. Who am I trying to kid? Alison already knows I have no life. Try again anyway.

"Hi, if that's you I've gone to the pub . . . with Vince . . . and with Matty . . . and some new friends that you don't know."

That's no good either. She knows I don't ever go out with anyone apart from Vince and Matty. I know, I'll pretend I'm doing something cultural, that'll impress her.

"Hi, if that's you I've gone to the opening of Kate's new art exhibition . . . I probably won't stay very long . . . I definitely won't be late . . . in fact I'm probably already back . . . but, if not, leave a message . . . or a number where I can call you . . . your hotel or something . . . bye."

I grab my wallet, dash down to Budgens and end up shopping in a bit of a rush. I try to buy ingredients for Thai green curry but for some reason I end up forgetting about the rice. And the fish sauce. And the lime leaves. And the green curry paste. I flick the answerphone button as soon as I get back. Someone called but they didn't bother leaving a message. It was an international number. Bollocks.

I make myself some kind of messy sub-student food involving peppers and curry powder and a wok full of tinned tomatoes and eat it flicking between the news and an episode of *The Sopranos* that I've already seen. She doesn't call back. I study my Bruges brochures for a while, listen to a spot of Leonard Cohen with the lights out, think about having a wank over one of Alison's old copies of *Vogue* but decide against it. I can't seem to settle. I really want to talk to her. I want to know how she is. I want to tell her all about Ike and the tour and Kate turning out to be a New Age loon and I really need to ask her advice vis-à-vis me and flared trousers. I want to tell her that I miss her. I want to tell her that the flat feels empty without her.

I try her mobile one more time but it still doesn't seem to have been switched over. It's the same every time I call. It takes ages for anyone to answer and then all I get is a bonkers recorded message in Flemish. I give up. It's way past midnight. I might as well go to bed.

23

"So, she didn't call you until this morning?"

"No, she called me last night but I was out."

"Where did you go?"

"Yeah, why weren't we invited?"

"I didn't go anywhere. I was at Budgens. I was out buying two-for-one lager and replacement Toilet Duck."

"And she didn't bother leaving you a message?"

"No. I said on the answerphone that I was going to Kate's art exhibition and for some reason it sent her into a bit of a strop."

"Why?"

"I don't know."

"Probably because you lied to her."

"Well, I didn't want her to think I was just moping around the flat on my own."

"But that's what you were doing."

"Yeah, but that's not the point. The point is she tried to phone me back later and I was engaged for three hours."

"Who to?"

"No one. I was on-line. I was just about to go to bed but I don't get the chance to use Alison's computer very often because I always end up deleting something important or messing up her favourites folder and, you know, once you log on, well, it's addictive, isn't it?"

"What were you looking at?"

"Oh, nothing much, music sites mainly."

"What, for three hours?"

"Well, yeah, that and the Kentucky Fried Chicken website."

"The KFC website? Are you mental?"

"Probably, but I was watching this advert for bargain buckets the other day and I couldn't help noticing that there was a web address given at the bottom of the screen."

"So what? Doesn't mean you have to go and look at it, does it?"

"I couldn't help myself. It just kept eating away at me. I had to know what was on it. I had to understand what kind of a person would bother to log on to a fried chicken website. I mean, why would you do it? What could you possibly expect to find?"

"Naked chicks?"

"No."

"Naked chickens?"

"No."

"The Colonel's secret recipe?"

"No. They keep it locked away in some kind of a vault. In Louisville. It's over sixty years old. The Colonel came up with it way back in 1939."

"You don't say."

"Yeah, it's true. Plus, if you live in the States, you can use the automatic store locator and order yourself a bucket of hot wings over the Net whenever you want."

"Wow," says Matty excitedly. "Delivery hot wings. How cool is that?"

"Jesus," says Vince, lowering his head into his hands. "You finally get the place to yourself and you spend the whole night looking at deep-fried chicken thighs when you could have been looking at porn. You're a very sick man."

• • •

This is not strictly true. I did look at some porn. It's almost impossible not to. Type in the Great Wall of China and—one way or another—your search engine always finds a way of directing you to Asian Babes. I couldn't seem to find anything good, though, especially not if you want to download it for free. The best I could come up with was a dodgy mpeg involving an irate pig and a man with a giant scrotum and a site called "One Dollar for Seven Days of Lesbians."

"Sounds like a bargain," says Vince thoughtfully. "Just make sure you remember to erase it from your Internet history before Alison gets back from Bruges."

"Right," I say, "good idea. I'll make sure I do it as soon as I get home."

We stub out our cigarettes, crank up the PA and prepare ourselves for another quick run-through of the set. It's hot down here. We've spent the last five hours rehearsing in a John McCarthy–style basement with no windows and no ventilation, and we're all beginning to feel a bit claustrophobic. Everyone is sweating. Vince has a steady trickle of salt droplets skidding down his temples to his cheeks and Matty's T-shirt is practically soaked through. It's a good thing, though: it helps wash away the stink of the mould.

The final run-through takes just over an hour, and by the end of it Vince seems almost satisfied. He's a perfectionist. If we screw up part of a song or hit a couple of bum notes he always makes us go back to the beginning and play the whole thing over again instead of just working on the section we messed up. He's always been the same. Vince was always the leader. He chose what we should wear and how we should wear it. How we should cut our hair; what brand of cigarettes we ought to smoke.

He decided where we should rehearse and for how long, and only when he was completely satisfied that we'd got it right would he let us move on to something else. We've done it, though. We've made it to the end. We've played through the entire set without a single fuck-up.

"Not bad," says Vince, unplugging his amp and winding a length of guitar cable round his arm. "There's still a fair bit of work to do but a couple more months and we should be almost ready."

We breathe a sigh of relief. I don't know about Matty but another hour down here and I'd probably have ended up having a stroke.

We're recovering in the local beer garden with a couple of pints of well-chilled lager and we're deep in discussion about touring and transport and trousers.

"No way."

"Why not?"

"What are you thinking of? Why would we want to dress in bell-bottoms and surgeons' overalls?"

"It'll look interesting."

"No it won't, it'll look stupid."

"Well, we've got to find some way of making an impact," says Vince, rolling down his sleeves. "We need to distinguish ourselves from Scarface, don't we? You got the four of them ponced up in leather trousers, army boots and Che Gue-fucking-vara T-shirts and then you got us—"

"In giant flares and surgeons' overalls?"

"Yeah, why not?"

"Because we'll look ridiculous."

"Well," says Vince triumphantly, "that's where you're missing the whole point. We're rock stars. We're meant to look ridiculous."

• • •

"So," I say, attempting to get things back on track, "how much do you think it's all going to cost?"

"Well," says Vince, "there's the thousand dollars for the buy-on fee, then there's the cost of hotels and van hire . . . add to that the wages we're all going to lose while we're off work and I reckon we're probably looking at the best part of three grand."

"What about a roadie for the gear?"

"Can't afford it. We'll just have to hump the stuff ourselves."

"What about sound and monitors?"

"Well, we can't afford to take our own so we'll have to find out how much Scarface's sound guy is gonna want to take care of us."

"Yeah, but he's bound to screw us over, isn't he? He's bound to make us sound shit compared to Scarface."

"You got a better idea?"

"No," I say, "I haven't. I'll give their tour manager a ring tomorrow and find out how much he's going to want."

I help myself to one of Matty's pork scratchings—I try to find one that doesn't have any hair coming out of the top of it—and we move swiftly on to the subject of accommodation.

"Looks like it's going to have to be bed-and-breakfasts," says Vince, crossing out another set of zeros on his beer-mat. "I mean, there's no way we can afford to lay out for proper hotels, but if we share a room in a B&B and spend a couple of nights in the van we can probably just about swing it."

"Great," I say, draining the beer at the bottom of my glass and nodding at Matty. "Remember to pack your earplugs, then. Vince snores like a rhino full of snot when he's pissed."

"I do not."

"Yeah you do. We shared a room on the last Agent Orange tour and I hardly slept a wink for the whole three weeks."

"Yeah, well, at least I change my socks once in a while. You wore the same pair for the whole tour. They were crisper than a packet of cheese-and-onion kettle chips by the end of it."

"Well, at least I don't spend all morning fiddling about with my hair. I mean, how many toiletry products can one bloke take away with him?"

"What about you? I've seen you poncing about in front of the mirror with your tub of Black and White. I bet you spend hours in the bathroom trying to give yourself one of them shark's-fin haircuts when no one's looking."

"Don't be ridiculous. Of course I don't."

"Christ almighty," says Matty, getting up to buy another round of drinks, "you two are worse than a married couple. It's going to be like going on tour with my mum and dad."

It's starting to get late. I promised Kostas I'd put in a couple of extra hours at the video shop before closing time, so I leave the guys soaking up the last rays of evening sunshine and head off to work. I've no idea how I'm going to contribute my share of the money. I know Vince has some savings from his plumbing job and Matty always seems to earn pretty good money for his DJing, but it's hard enough for me to come up with my share of the rent, let alone find a spare thousand pounds for the tour. I suppose I could always see if Alison would lend it to me—I know she would if I asked—but I feel like I've taken too much off her already. It looks like I'll just have to find a way of raising the money by myself.

24

I stroll north down Ferme Park Road and rest at the lip of Crouch Hill to admire the view for a moment. The sky is celebrating. The horizon is swigging tequila over Alexandra Palace to signal the day's end, and it suddenly feels all wrong. It doesn't suit my mood. I don't like sunsets anyway. They're gaudy. Burnt orange, blood red, labia pink, and bell-end purple all mixed together with a dollop of crimson and a splash of tutti-frutti mauve. It's horrible. It clashes. Why didn't someone force God to sit down and watch a couple of episodes of *Changing Rooms* before he set about butchering our sunsets like a colour-blind Umpa Lumpa. Why didn't they persuade him that he might be better off starting with something easy, like grass, for instance. Even God couldn't manage to fuck up grass.

After careful consideration—the time it's taken me to walk from the pub to the clock tower—I've decided that it's supremely selfish of Alison to desert me during the summer. It would be okay if it was winter because in the winter it's freezing cold and therefore perfectly reasonable to stay in your flat at all times. No one need know that you spent the whole of Saturday night trimming your toenails with the blunt utensils from your Swiss Army knife and sniffing the cheesy stink off the scissors.

No one would ever guess that you spent the whole of Christmas on your own, chewing the hard end of a Bernard Matthews turkey roast and watching repeats of *Morecambe and Wise* with a piece of damp tinsel wrapped round your head.

The summer is different, though. A bloke needs to have a girlfriend in the summer: someone to go on holiday with; someone to go up to the lido with; someone to walk up to Alexandra Palace and watch the tasteless city sunsets with.

(It should also be noted that girlfriends come in very useful for helping you choose swimming trunks that don't make you look like a child molester. I thought my navy-blue sixth-form Speedos were fine. The material was a little worn in places and they were a tad on the small side but otherwise they seemed perfectly good. Apparently not.)

It's almost nine o'clock and the entire population of Crouch End seems to be outside: people unwinding with bottles of Chinese beer in front of the World Café, girls tumbling out of newly opened cocktail bars with skimpy clothes stuck to their hot skin, and lines of tactile couples wandering out of Oddbins, loaded down with wine and Pimms and bottles of ice-cold lemonade. Everyone seems to be enjoying themselves; relishing the one week in every year when Crouch End actually begins to feel like a village.

People (estate agents mostly) often describe Crouch End as having a villagey atmosphere, but it's not really true. Most of the time it looks like any other tatty suburban town centre: small Boots, grotty Woolworths, a couple of bakers serving up bread and birthday cakes and sugary torpedo-shaped buns, and a handful of homeless teenagers selling *The Big Issue* and begging for spare change next to the building-society cashpoints. It's quite ugly, really: double-decker engines breathing petrol fumes across the dirty pavements, a dozen crappy hairdressers perfecting bubble perms and Essex-girl highlights; cheap lingerie shops selling push-up bras and genuine nylon knickers; and a slew of interior design shops peddling overpriced junk to people who wish they could afford to live down the road in Islington.

Except for tonight. Tonight the air is bathtub warm and filled with chatter and the whole place feels relaxed and friendly and open: Indian restaurants filling the leafy streets with the scent of hot smoke and cardamom, overfed cats spreading their legs and bellies to the warm pavements and a handful of tiny cafés with their polished picture windows gaping wide open to the breeze.

It's always like this in London. One sun-scorched evening and the whole city takes on the expression of a child who's been allowed to stay up late for the very first time.

It's another slow night in the video shop: a couple of nervous teenagers trawling the shelves for hardcore—Kostas sends them home with a copy of *Confessions of a Window Cleaner*—a girl looking for a copy of *Die Hard 3*—Kostas packs her off to Blockbuster—and a bloke in a leather waistcoat looking for some Dogme '95.

I work through the evening on autopilot. I tidy the stockroom, help Kostas lock up the shop and call in at the 7-Eleven for some beers and a cheese-and-potato pasty on my way home. It's humid outside. The breeze has dropped to almost nothing and the air feels thick and moist, like hot fog.

There's a small pile of letters waiting in the communal entrance hall when I get home and I pick them up, grab the local paper and shuffle up the three flights of narrow stairs to the flat. I'm trying to be quiet but every second stair always manages to sound like it's in pain no matter how gently I tread on it. I know Mr. Dunn (our downstairs neighbour) will come out and give me a bollocking in the morning, but there's not much I can do about it now. He's a miserable man. I can hear him snoring through the floorboards every night while I'm watching the TV. I can smell the fat from his Sunday pork and the gills from his Monday fish and I hear him arguing with his shrewish, gammy-eyed wife every morning before she goes off to work. And he's always shouting at his dog. His nasty, snappy, smelly Scottie dog. "Naughty boy, Robbie," he says, "naughty boy."

All day long.

The post is mainly bills. A red one from British Gas, a black one from British Telecom, and a small brown paper parcel decorated with glitter that turns out to be from Kate. It's a pamphlet on reiki. It has a note pinned to it. *Dear Danny*, it says, *really cool that you seemed so interested in this. Matty thinks it's all a load of rubbish. Give me a ring some time and let me know what you think . . . xx Kate*.

And then I find it. Tucked into the folds of a takeaway pizza menu. A postcard. From Alison. It's a picture of two fat men in traditional Belgian dress and they're drinking giant flagons of beer and slapping each other's podgy thighs with their outstretched hands. I turn it over to read the message.

Weather is here, wish you were lovely.
Miss you loads, Alison xxx.

Just over a week and she'll be home. I suddenly can't wait to see her.

25

Alison is coming home tomorrow. I like the sound of that. I think I'll say it again. Alison is coming home. *Tomorrow*.

I've done everything right this time. I've booked a posh restaurant for Saturday night, blagged the whole weekend off from Kostas and filled the fridge with six different flavours of Bacardi Breezer. Maybe I should have one now, just to see whether they're okay. I've never tried the watermelon one before and I'm quite keen to see what it tastes like. Ugh. Disgusting. Disgusting in a pleasantly sickly, mildly alcoholic sort of way. I wonder if the cranberry one is any better. Hmmm. Not bad. Not bad at all. Maybe if I mix them both together.

Anyway, it's going to be a top weekend. Kostas told me about this swanky restaurant in the West End that all the celebs go to, and we're going to take taxis everywhere and go on to a late bar and I'm going to pay for everything on my credit card. Well, why not? I mean, if that nice bloke at Barclaycard is willing to put up my credit limit by another two hundred quid, then why not make use of it? Come to think of it, it's easier getting credit now that I'm in debt than it ever was when I was solvent. Honestly. I get new offers every day: leaflets from Access and Goldfish and Amex and glossy ten-page catalogues from Egg. They all say exactly the same thing:

Dear sir, we hear you are very badly in debt and a loser. We would like to offer you one of our platinum cards so that you can plunge yourself still deeper into destitution and penury. How's about it? Best wishes, your friendly neighbourhood bailiffs.

PS: We hear you own a very nice Blaupunkt stereo (with turntable) and a vintage Stratocaster guitar. How would you feel about us coming to collect them in the middle of the night and selling them off at auction for a fraction of their real worth? Just an idea xxx.

Still, bankruptcy is a way off yet: I've got just enough left for some flowers and a haircut and a packet of Featherlite condoms.

Why did I come in here? What possessed me? I knew this was a bad idea. I knew I should have stayed in Crouch End and gone to Hair on the Hill. This place is way too trendy. Everyone's listening to Arab Strap and reading *Dazed and Confused* and I'm beginning to wish I'd stuck with my regular barber, Mr. George.

"Hello, my name is Patio and I'll be your hairdresser this afternoon."

"Right, good, nice one. Hello."

"You look a little tense, yeah, how about a nice vodka and cranberry juice to help you chill?"

I hate that. I hate it when people tell you that you look tense. Because I'm not tense. I mean I wasn't, but I am now. The very act of Patio suggesting that I am tense has made me tense. Still, a barber's that serves drinks while you get your hair trimmed can't be all bad, can it?

• • •

"Is everything okay?" says Patio cautiously. "You've gone a bit pale."

"No . . . I'm fine. Wow . . . interesting haircut . . . looking good."

"You *sure*?"

"Oh, yes. Absolutely."

"Good."

"Fine, then."

"Okay, fine."

I'm lying. It looks terrible. Mr. George would never have done the whole haircut with a Bic razor. I mean, what is he doing? Why is he slicing into my hair with the edge of the blade like that? Why did I say yes when he suggested I go a bit shorter on top? That's it. I've had enough. I look like a toilet brush. I'm going to say something. I am.

"Urhuumm."

"*Sorry?*"

"Urhuumm," I say again.

"Is something wrong?"

"Well . . . er . . . I was just wondering . . . I mean, obviously you're only halfway through and it's not going to look like this when it's finished . . . is it?"

"You don't like what I'm doing?"

"No, it's not that . . . the thing is I usually don't have it quite so short."

"Well, what d'you want me to do, stick it back on for you?"

"No, obviously not. I was just thinking that maybe now might be a good time to stop cutting. Maybe now might be a good time to think about moving on to the drying phase of the haircut."

"Stop cutting?"

"Yes."

"And leave it like this?"

"Yes."

"All ragged like this?"

"Well—"

"Because I think you look loads better already," he says, pushing the remains of my fringe into a jaunty sideways spike. "And you want to make a good impression, don't you? When your girlfriend comes home."

"Yeah," I say, imagining Alison spotting me on the platform and being too embarrassed to get off the train. "I suppose it looks a bit better than it did."

"Of course it does," he says, running his comb over my head like he's searching for nits. "I don't know where you usually get it done but it looked like you'd been letting the family dog have a chew on it or something."

"Okay then," I say, finishing off my second Sea Breeze and thinking about ordering myself another. "Maybe you're right. I could use a bit of an image change now you mention it. I'm sure it'll look okay when it's finished."

"Of course it will," he says, rubbing his hands together and juicing up his electric clippers. "And now we've come this far, how's about we take you a little bit shorter on the sides?"

I walk up Dean Street with an itchy neck, a near-naked scalp and a much lighter wallet in my trousers. Fifty quid. *Fifty sodding quid* for a lousy haircut, a painful head massage, and a couple of piss-weak cocktails that I thought I was getting for free. Still, no point in moaning about it now; I'm determined not to let anything spoil this weekend. I'll just go for a quick look at the second-hand guitars in Denmark Street and then I'll buy some flowers and head back to the flat to make a start on the tidying up.

• • •

There are two types of tidy in this world: me tidy and Alison tidy. Me tidy involves doing the washing up, pouring a splash of bleach down the bog and piling the week's newspapers into a heap on the coffee table. Alison tidy is something completely different. I've never been able to work out exactly what she does. It's weird. It doesn't seem to involve that much extra cleaning, it's more to do with putting everything back in its proper place: the way she arranges the cushions on the sofa, the way she arranges the pillows on the bed, the way she puts everything away in the kitchen cupboards and hangs up all the mugs on their shiny silver hooks. I know she's got some anal kind of arrangement involving the storage jars on the kitchen shelf but I can never remember exactly how it's supposed to go. Is it spaghetti then lentils or lentils *then* spaghetti? Maybe the spaghetti's not meant to go up there at all. Maybe it should go in the cupboard with the rice. Yeah, that looks better. That makes much more sense.

The other thing about Alison is that she's always throwing things away: the newspapers (before I've had a chance to read them), the TV guide (before I've had a chance to find out what's on TV), and any packet of out-of-date food that she suspects I might be particularly looking forward to. She also has a habit of throwing away my Studiospares catalogues and my back issues of Q. And my copies of *Sound on Sound*. And my clothes. And my plectrums. And any piece of soft furnishing that we've had for longer than six months. I can't keep up with it. She must have spent a fortune on throws and lampshades and cushions, and the thing is I quite liked the cushions we had when we first moved in here. Must remember not to tell her that, though. When I said I preferred the last bedroom lampshade to the one she'd just lugged all the way home from Habitat it sent her into a bit of a rage.

There. I've done it. I've cleaned the place from top to bottom. I've even changed all the sheets and swept underneath the cracked bit of lino on the kitchen floor that gets all the bits of cheese stuck in it. It looks good. It looks like a hotel. A cheap one. In Torquay.

I arrange the flowers as artfully as I can—which is not very artful at all on account of cutting them way too short for the vase—and put them on the chest of drawers in the bedroom. I'm knackered. I keep thinking that there's something else that I'm meant to do but I can't remember what it is. Maybe I should have another one of Alison's Bacardi Breezers to perk myself up. Maybe I should make some green curry and see if there's anything on the telly about clitorises. Maybe I should get an early night; I've got to be up by midday, I've got to make sure I'm at Waterloo by half four.

26

Today is starting out very well indeed. I managed to trump the shower by jumping out a millisecond before the water turned cold and I narrowly avoided answering another tedious phone call from Kate. She's been trying to get hold of me all week to find out what I thought of the pamphlet she sent me, and it's becoming increasingly difficult to shake her off. It's my own fault—the longer I go without telling her that I couldn't give a toss whether my moon was rising in Mercury or setting in Sainsbury's carpark, the more she thinks I might be into it. Still, not to worry, much more important things to consider: like what I should wear when I go to pick up Alison from Waterloo this afternoon.

Try on all six of my clothes, take them all off, put them all on again and have a look under the bed to see if there's anything that I've missed. I'm not really sure what I'm looking for. Something clean, obviously; something that looks like I've made an effort but doesn't make me look too gay. Something slightly scruffy but still suitably hard. Actually, everything I put on makes me look hard now on account of my excellent number two haircut. I've decided that I quite like it, except for the fact that it's exposed a couple of grey hairs at the sides. When did that happen, then? When did I start getting grey hairs at the sides? Maybe I could try dyeing them. Maybe I should see if Alison still has that box of L'Oréal Born Blonde in the bathroom. Maybe I should put my underpants on my head and see if it makes me look anything like David Ginola.

Spend a quality moment in front of the bathroom mirror wearing my underpants on my head and telling myself that I'm "*worth it*" in an *'Allo 'Allo* French accent before deciding that I look a complete cunt and going back to the wardrobe to put on my Brownies T-shirt and my navy-blue hooded top. Perfect. Why didn't I think of that straight away? Never fails to please.

For once the traffic in central London is fairly clear and I arrive at Waterloo Station with time to spare. Alison's train isn't due for another half an hour so I buy myself a stale chicken tikka sandwich, pop into W.H. Smith's to read through the latest issue of *Sound on Sound* and spend a few minutes checking out the columns of horny Parisian women pouring off the Eurostars on to the dusty platform. They look incredible: tight skirts, high heels, skinny waists and tiny, low-cut T-shirts clinging to their snobby, "no chance, mate" tits.

I have a thing about Parisian women. Ever since a gang of long-haired Gallic super-sluts came to visit our school on a language exchange scheme in the summer of 1986. They were fantastic. They smoked Gitanes. They thought we were all wankers. They kept the entire fifth form—including half of the teachers—in a permanent ball-aching lather for the whole two weeks they were there. Especially Colette. She looked like a cross between Sylvia Kristel in *Emmanuelle II* and O from *The Story of O*. I wonder if Alison has learnt any French while she's been in Bruges. I wonder if she fancies renting *The Story of O*. I wonder if she'll notice that I've had a haircut.

• • •

"You've had your hair cut."

"I know. D'you like it?"

"Yeah, you look cute."

"*Cute?*"

"Yeah, you look about twelve. It's cute."

"Not hard?"

"No."

"Not even a *bit*?"

"No . . . not really."

"What about if I go like this?"

"Nope. Now you just look like you've got a bad case of wind."

I relax my eyebrows, unsnarl my lip and go into a bit of a sulk. That does it. I'm definitely going to have Patio killed. He's definitely going to the top of my list.

"Hey," she says, attempting to cheer me up, "I've bought you a present."

"Wow," I say, pulling off the wrapping paper and taking a look inside, "the European Parliament building made entirely out of chocolate fondant icing. You really shouldn't have."

We've been home less than three and a half minutes and Alison has already scored a hat trick.

"But *why*?"

"Why what?"

"Why would you want to put the spaghetti in the cupboard?"

"Er . . . to go with the *rice*?"

"But it's got its own jar. It goes on the shelf."

"Yeah, right, I forgot."

"Okay, but look, it looks much better out, doesn't it?"

"Yeah, I see what you mean," I say, stepping back and rubbing my chin. "It looks great. Really sets off the lentils."

• • •

"And what's this?"

"Oh, nothing, it's from Kate. It's just some pile of old nonsense about reiki or something."

"I can see that, but what's it doing here?"

"Kate posted it to me. She came over to organise this gig we're doing at her art colle—"

"Kate came over *here*?"

"Yeah. Why?"

"No reason. Was Matty with her?"

"No, er . . . she was on her own."

"Right."

"*Danny*."

"What? What is it?"

"Have you been using my computer while I've been away?"

"Er . . . *yes*?"

"I thought so."

"Why? What's wrong with it? I haven't broken it, have I?"

"No."

"Shit, I didn't spill Bombay Mix into the keyboard again, did I?"

"No."

"Well, what then? Why have you got that look?"

"What look?"

"That look. The one you get whenever I start discussing the NHS with your dad."

"Well, it's just that I can't decide what's worse. The fact that you spent forty-six and a half minutes looking at the Kentucky Fried Chicken website last Thursday night or the fact that you spent two and a half hours trying to download 'One Dollar for Seven Days of Lesbians.'"

• • •

Shit. I knew there was something else I was meant to do before she came home.

Alison lights up a post-coital cigarette, passes it over to me and curls up against my arm with her head on my chest.

"Better?" I say, reaching down to stroke her hair off her face.

"Mmmmn," she says, "much."

This feel good. It's taken us a couple of hours to get completely relaxed with one another again, but two cups of tea, three Bacardi Breezers, and one fantastic shag later and we're both completely cured.

"I felt like I was going on a date," she says, pulling the sheet up to her breasts and sliding on to her back.

"Really?" I say, running my hand across her stomach. "How so?"

"Well, you know, I was nervous about seeing you, I suppose."

"How could you have been nervous?"

"Well, not nervous, then, *excited*. I mean, it's weird, I spent the whole morning deciding what I was going to wear. And look at you—I bet you just picked up the first thing you could find and drove straight over to meet me."

I shrug my shoulders and pass her the cigarette.

"Hey," she says, "you're starting to get a couple of grey hairs at the side."

"Am I?" I say. "I hadn't noticed."

"Yeah," she says, climbing on top of me and kissing my chest. "I like it. Makes you look sexy."

"Hmmmn," I say, "maybe you should go away to Bruges more often."

"Hmmmn," she says, "maybe you should spend more time trying to download 'One Dollar for Seven Days of Lesbians.'"

• • •

We have sweaty, tangled, welcome-home sex one more time for good measure and then Alison curls up next to me and falls asleep. She really is spectacularly good looking: giant Jaggeresque mouth that would look ridiculous on anyone else, cute lopsided nose covered in a crop of rust-coloured freckles, and that incredible fifties porn-star body that still makes me want to jump her the second she comes through the door.

There's a thin frown running across her forehead, and I reach over and trace my fingers along the length of its crease. She looks vulnerable when she's asleep; it's the only time she does. I think she worries that the world might get the better of her while she hasn't got her eye on it; that it might find a way to do her down while she sleeps. It makes me feel insanely protective. I want to burn her laptop and set fire to her mobile phone, and I don't want the outside world to be able to get anywhere near her.

And those eyes. Those gorgeous, flinty, sexy, ink-blot-blue eyes that always seem to know exactly what I'm thinking.

"What are you thinking?" she says, opening her eyes and curling her arm round my waist.

"Nothing much," I say. "I was just wondering if you were asleep, that's all."

She looks up at me and smiles.

"I missed you too," she says. "I missed you too."

27

"Why didn't you tell me about it before?"

"Because I wanted it to be a surprise?"

"But you should have said something on the phone."

"I thought you'd be happy about it."

"I am."

"Well, it doesn't sound like it to me."

This evening is starting out very badly indeed. We're buckled into the back of a death-trap minicab heading west through Camden into town and I've just told Alison all about the band going out on tour with Scarface. I didn't mean to. I meant to tell her over dinner. After they'd lit the candles. After we'd ordered our food. I meant to wait until we were halfway through our first bottle of house red wine.

"So how long is it going to be for?"

"Two weeks," I say, reaching into my pocket for the tour dates. "It's going to be brilliant. We're playing at some really big venues: Manchester Apollo, Glasgow Barrowlands, The Royal Court in Liverpool, and we get to finish the whole thing off back down here in London."

"I see," she says, turning her face to look out of the window.

"At the Shepherd's Bush Empire," I say with a small flourish.

"I see," she says again.

I don't know what's wrong with her. I thought she'd be excited about it. I thought she'd be pleased that something was finally beginning to happen. She's been like this all day. Ever since I asked her how her job was going in Bruges. Ever since I asked her how tall Didier was. Maybe I should have waited until the end of *CD:UK* before I started quizzing her about the pillow mints.

"I *am* pleased for you," she says, reaching into her bag for her lip salve and dabbing it on to her mouth. "Honestly. It's amazing news, Danny. Well done."

"Thanks," I say. "I mean, we haven't got a particularly good slot or anything but, you know, it could mean a lot of exposure for us. Vince thinks it's the best chance we've got of finding ourselves a record deal by the end of the year."

"That's great," she says, turning back to the window. "That's really great."

The moment we arrive at the restaurant I realise that I've screwed up. It's all wrong. It's tacky and noisy and cramped and even if we ditch the starters and stick to pasta and mineral water I know it's still going to cost me a small fortune. I feel totally out of place: everyone is done up in shirts and jewellery and bespoke designer suits, and I'm the only bloke in the whole gaff who isn't wearing a Rolex and a girlfriend half his age.

I watch Alison adding up the Essex-style ambience: the brick-shaped bouncers by the door, the ice-cream-shaped waitresses at the tables, and the gold tasselled rope strung across the entrance to the members-only bar.

"This is lovely, Danny," she says, shooting me a market trader wink. "Very classy and not at all vulgar."

"Sorry," I say. "Kostas recommended it. I didn't realise it would be quite so flash."

"Don't be stupid," she says, putting her arm through mine. "It'll be fun. We can play spot the boob job and guess which children's TV presenter has just snorted coke in the bogs."

"You sure?"

"Definitely."

She starts to laugh. She's just spotted a low-league soap actress with "tits" written across her chest in glitter and "arse" written across the seat of her jeans in Braille.

"How do you know it says arse?" I say, taking our reservation number out of my wallet.

"Educated guess," she says. "Educated guess."

According to an eighteen-year-old death camp commandant called Tamara, we're late for our booking.

"I'm afraid you're late for your booking, Mr. McQueen."

"Are we?"

"Yes. It says here that you booked a table for eight o'clock."

I look at my watch. It's just gone ten past.

"But it's only ten past."

"Exactly."

"What do you mean, *exactly*? We're only ten minutes late. That's nothing."

"Well, we operate a very strict shift system here at Food. We have three sittings per night and if you arrive late it compromises the rest of the evening's diners. You should have been told that when you booked."

"But it's only ten minutes."

"Exactly."

"Six hundred seconds."

"Exactly."

"Less than a quarter of an hour."

"I'm sorry," she says, examining her table plan and shooting me the kind of look that indicates that she isn't sorry at all, "there's really not much I can do. We've already given away your table. Our next available booking isn't until . . . let me see . . . eleven fifteen."

"*Eleven fifteen?* That's three hours away. What are we supposed to do until then? I'm starving. I've only had a couple of slices of Marmite toast all day."

"Well, if you like you could always wait at the bar."

"For *three* hours?"

"Sorry, it's the best I can do."

*

The rest of the West End is officially full—even the restaurants in Chinatown are turning people away—and the only place we can find a table is in a Spaghetti House full of tourists near Piccadilly Circus.

"Sorry about that," I say. "I should have known better than to take a recommendation from Kostas."

"That's okay," she says. "I didn't fancy eating there anyway. I'd only have got drunk and ended up writing 'penis' across your trousers in Braille."

"You don't mind, then?"

"No, and let's face it, it could have been worse. We could have ended up at an Angus Steak House."

"Or a Bernie Inn."

"Or a Harvester."

"Or a McDonald's."

"I suppose we're lucky, then," I say, looking down at the sticky plastic menu and wondering what to have.

"Yeah," she says, "we certainly are."

• • •

Alison looks fantastic tonight, completely out of place with the rest of the customers. She's wearing a posh silk dress with a deep slit up the side and she's got a giant purple flower pinned into her hair that makes her look a bit Hawaiian. Everyone is staring at her: the waiters, the barman and the door girl, and the funny little bloke in the kitchen who looks like he's just about to do something gross to our mixed green salad. Actually, there's a small chance he might just be looking at me. Alison insisted I made a bit of an effort when she found out I was taking her somewhere expensive, so I'm wearing the trousers I wore to my nan's funeral last year: they're almost ten per cent wool and they itch like a bastard. It's not right, though, she deserves to be somewhere better than this. She deserves someone better than me.

"So what are you going to have?" I say, trying not to look like I'm scratching the edge of my left buttock with my spoon.

"The works," she says. "Prawn cocktail, spaghetti Bolognese, Black Forest gateau, and a bottle of the house Chianti. But only if it comes in one of those wicker basket thingies. What about you?"

"Half a ripe avocado, steak and chips and a generous helping of Death by Chocolate, 'the ladies' *favourite.*'"

"Excellent choice," she says. "Excellent choice."

This meal is going far better than I'd anticipated. We've only had to wait twenty-five minutes for our starters and I've managed to keep Alison highly entertained with a whole series of interesting facts from the KFC website and some astonishing details about the bloke who invented Thousand Island dressing.

"Yeah," I say, as I watch her slip another ketchup-coated prawn in her mouth, "he came from this part of upstate New York where there are, erm . . . lots of islands."

"I see."

"Apparently he was the same man who invented the Waldorf salad."

"Wow, busy guy."

"Exactly," I say, pointing my fork in the air for extra emphasis. "I bet that ponce Oliver has never invented his own salad dressing."

"No," she says, "probably not."

"So, how are you getting on with the whole mayonnaise on the chips issue?" I ask, attempting to keep up the culinary theme.

"Not bad," she says. "I quite like it, actually. It's a bit sickly at first but you sort of get used to it after a while."

"Right," I say. "I bet old Didier likes a bit of mayonnaise on his chips of a teatime."

"*Danny*."

"Sorry, sorry. I know, he's five foot nothing with a club foot and a huge hairy mole on his upper lip."

"Exactly."

"So I shouldn't be jealous about him taking my girlfriend out for expensive dinners, then?"

"No."

"You'd rather be drinking cheap Chianti at the Spaghetti House with me?"

"Yes."

"*You're sure?*"

"No question, and anyway, it's me who should be jealous. You're the one about to go on tour with a rock band. You're the one who's going to be boozing it up every night and taking class A drugs and sleeping with groupies and—"

"Yeah, right. Me, Vince, and Matty head to toe in a bed-and-breakfast bunk bed. We're bound to be inundated with offers."

"Well, you never know."

"I do. I'm certain. The nearest I'm going to get to an illicit sexual encounter is waking up with one of Vince's sweaty socks stuck to my head. And anyway, why would I want to waste my time with a bunch of greasy teenage groupies when I've got a gorgeous girlfriend like you to come home to?"

Good answer.

After a quality moment working out how many coffee beans we can stuff into our amaretto glasses before they overflow, we decide to pay up and take a walk down to the embankment to look at the London Eye. It's a clear night. The river is dark and oily and still and you can see the wheel's reflection turning through the water like a giant metal Polo mint. There's a light breeze coming off the water and I wrap my denim jacket round Alison's shoulders to keep her warm. It feels good. It feels fresher than it has for days.

"Sorry about earlier," she says, sitting down next to me on one of the graffiti-covered benches. "I *am* pleased about the tour. You must be excited about it."

"Thanks," I say, shielding a match from the wind and lighting us both a cigarette. "So why were you being so dismissive about it before?"

"I'm not sure. I think it's because you seemed so full of yourself. You were going on and on about it the whole way up here in the cab, and the thing is you've hardly asked me anything about what I've been up to in Bruges."

"I have."

"No. You haven't. You asked me how tall Didier was and if he was keen on mints. You didn't ask me anything about my job or the city or where I was working or anything."

"Right, you're right, I'm sorry. Er . . . how are you finding the job?"

"It's okay, I suppose."

"Just okay?"

"Well, it's much more corporate than I thought it would be.

They're pretty set in their ways. I suggested they redesign their company website to tie in with the product launch but they wouldn't hear of it. I don't know, I suppose I thought it would be a bit more creative, that's all."

"Right," I say. "Bummer."

"And it's long hours," she says, picking at some loose flakes of paint on the bench. "They agreed to let me have the afternoon off yesterday but some evenings I haven't left the office until gone nine."

"Well, sod that," I say. "Tell them they're working you too hard. I mean, you're in charge, aren't you? You're overseeing the whole project."

"That's the problem," she says gently. "And the thing is . . . well, I was thinking . . . it might be better if I came home on Saturday mornings in future."

"You're *kidding*?"

"I know it's a pain," she says, "but there's a ton of stuff to get in place before the campaign starts, and I'm not sure I'll always be able to get away early enough. I'll just have to see how it goes."

We take a short pause.

"Well then," I say, scuffing my foot on the pavement and trying not to sound as disappointed as I feel, "I suppose it's not for very long. And it's all good experience, isn't it? If you make a success of things in Bruges it probably means you can get something much better when you come back to London at the end of the year."

"Just more of the same, really."

"Yeah, but it's good money, though, isn't it?" I say, trying to sound encouraging.

"Yes," she says, "it is."

"And we need it, don't we? Just until the band thing takes off."

"Yes," she says, turning her head and gazing back out over the river. "I suppose we do."

28

I'm knackered. I don't usually have much trouble getting off to sleep but I did last night. I tried everything: watching a programme about plate tectonics on *The Learning Zone*, flicking through my *Virgin Encyclopaedia of Rock and Pop*, eating half a packet of Alison's Nytol Extra and washing it down with some medium-sweet cooking sherry, but nothing did any good. I ended up falling asleep on the sofa at around 6:30 this morning and waking up just in time for the one o'clock news. I feel like shit. I feel achy. I feel jet-lagged and cranky. And anxious.

Three things: firstly, Alison and I didn't have sex again the whole weekend. Secondly, I thought she seemed a bit distant and withdrawn. Thirdly, she wanted to go to the cinema yesterday afternoon instead of going out for a late lunch at Banners and spending some quality time discussing the pros and cons of flared trousers. Fourthly—

"I thought you said there was only three things."

"Okay, okay, I meant four, then, I meant to say four."

"Well, you should say what you mean. You shouldn't give a bloke the expectation that he's only going to have to sort out three problems for you when he is, in fact, being asked to sort out four."

"Actually there's five, now I come to think about it."

"*Five?*"

"Yeah, five."

"Well, that's no good, that's nearly half a dozen. That's significantly more than three. Significantly more than a few. I'd have to say that we are now entering into the realms of many."

"Can I carry on now?"

"Yes," says Vince, tinkering with a piece of feta cheese in his salad, "you can carry on."

"So, *fourthly*," I say, narrowing my eyes at him in case he tries to interrupt me again, "she was wearing a new dress."

"A new dress?"

"Yeah, *brand* new."

"Nice, was it?"

"Yes, very. So nice you could practically see her whole body through it. It was all tight and see-through. But that's not even the worst of it. The worst of it is I'd never seen her wearing it before."

"So what?"

"Well, it's obvious, isn't it? It means she must have bought it while she was away in Bruges."

"So? They do have dress shops in Bruges, don't they?"

"Yes, of course they do, but what was she doing buying herself a sexy dress while she was away? Who was she buying it for? Who was she trying to impress? Why did she wait until she was just about to make the train journey back before she decided to go upstairs and put it on?"

"Hmmnn," says Vince. "That *is* a bit suspect."

"Exactly," I say, stuffing some curly fries into my tuna melt and taking a bite. "Ezaggglee."

"So, what's the other one?" says Vince, tucking into his third portion of pita bread.

"How d'you mean?"

"Five, you said. 'Come to think of it,' there were *five* things that were bothering you."

"Well," I say, "the last one's not strictly to do with Alison. It's more to do with my mum."

"Your mum?"

"Yeah. Alison found an old message from my mum that I'd forgotten to wipe off the answerphone and she guessed that I probably hadn't bothered to call her back yet."

"So now you've got to submit yourself to an hour and a half of top-quality earache."

"Exactly. Alison won't stop giving me grief about it unless I do."

"Still on the antidepressants, is she?"

"Who, *Alison*?"

"No, you plank. Your *mum*. Still knocking back the Jelly Tots, is she?"

"Yeah," I say, "I think she probably is."

I'm just about to launch back into a detailed description of the low-cut nature of Alison's brand-new dress when I spot Matty coming into the café with Kate. He seems amused by something. Very amused.

"What's so funny?"

"Baldy, *baaaldeey*."

"I am *not* bald."

"Yeah you are, *baaaldeey*, you look like you've been scalped."

"What's this, then?" I say, bending my head towards him over the table. "I'll tell you what it is, shall I? It's *hair*. I clearly have hair. I am not bald. At all."

"Oh yeah? So what did you chop it all off for? Must be because you *thought* you were going bald."

Look at him. Look at him with his baggy trousers and his tight T-shirt and his stupid beady necklace tied round his neck. Just because he still has a hairline that starts halfway down his forehead he thinks it's okay to sit there and take the piss out of me and my number two haircut. Well, it's not on.

"I am *not* going bald," I say firmly. "I am not now, nor have I ever been, suffering from alopecia or premature male-pattern baldness. I simply had a nasty scissor incident with a vindictive hairdresser called Patio."

"Patio?" says Matty thoughtfully. "Isn't that something you make out of chicken livers?"

"Well, I like it," says Kate. "I think it really suits you."

"What are you eating there, Vince?"

"What does it look like I'm eating?"

"Well, it looks like a salad, but that must mean . . ."

"That I'm on a diet?"

"Right."

"Something wrong with that, is there? All right for you lot to spend all day worrying about the size of your minuscule arses and the teaspoonful of cellulite round your knees but it's not okay for a bloke to take pride in his appearance once in a while?"

"Well, no. I think it's good that you're trying to eat more healthily. I have a gluten allergy myself so I understand all about listening to the needs of your own body. I could lend you a pamphlet, if you like."

"That's not it. I'm not trying to eat more healthily, I'm just trying to get myself back down to Iggy Pop weight before we go on tour."

"I see."

"Soon as it's over I'm straight back on the chips."

"Right."

"Back on the meat and two veg."

"Right."

"Back on the bacon, back on the eggs, back on the sausage, mushrooms, kidneys, grilled black pudding, and fried bread. So, Kate," says Vince sadistically, "how's that no meat, no wheat, no milk, vegan thing working out for you, then?"

"Good," she says, trying not to lick her lips. "As a matter of fact I've never felt better in my life."

Kate and Matty head over to the counter to order themselves some drinks and I have a quiet word with Vince while they're out of earshot.

"Calm down, Vince," I say. "I mean, she might be a bit of a loon but there are times when I've even thought about going veggie myself."

"Well, she winds me up," says Vince, "the way she thinks it's okay to lecture everybody all the time. And that whole gluten allergy thing, what's that all about? Matty says she was reading some poncy article about wheat intolerance and she suddenly decided that she didn't like bread. Apparently it aggravated her negative energies. And there's something else," he says, lowering his voice and leaning in over his olives. "Something you might want to think about."

"What?"

"Well," he says, rubbing his lips together, "I just think you want to be a bit careful around her at the moment."

"Why? What do you mean?"

He's just about to start telling me when he spots Kate and Matty heading back towards us with their drinks.

"I'll tell you later," he says under his breath. "I'll tell you later."

• • •

"So," says Matty, stretching his muscle-bound arms over his head and yawning, "how's everyone getting on with raising money for the tour?"

"Not bad," says Vince. "I think my savings are gonna cover most of it and my uncle's offered me a few extra jobs to make up the change."

"Cool, cool, me too. I reckon I'm pretty much sorted. A couple more nights on the turntables and I'll be nearly there."

"What about you?" says Kate, looking straight at me.

"Er . . . well, you know, haven't had much time to think about it really, what with Alison being home and everything."

"Are you going to do some extra work at the video shop?"

"No, I don't think so, there's only so much work Kostas can give me."

"Well, what about Alison, can't she lend you the money?"

"No . . . I mean, I haven't asked her. I don't want to if I can help it."

"Don't worry, mate," says Vince, "I'm sure we can work something out between us."

"Cheers," I say, "I'm sure I'll come up with it somehow."

"Woah," says Kate, "hang on a minute, I've just had a fantastic idea."

"You have?"

"Yeah. I think I know a way you might be able to make yourself some extra cash."

"You do?"

"Yes. They're always having trouble finding models for the life drawing classes at my art college and I reckon you'd be perfect. It pays quite well, I think, around fifty quid a throw."

"Really? Do you think they'd have me? I mean, don't you have to look like . . . I don't know, Johnny Depp or something?"

"No, of course not. They've got a class this afternoon. I think they might still be looking for someone to fill in."

"Right," I say, wondering why Vince is kicking me under the table.

"Tell you what," she says, "I'll give my tutor a quick ring and find out what's going on. If they're still short for today, shall I tell them I've found someone?"

"Yeah . . . erm . . . okay then. Why not?"

"Cool. I'll just pop outside and use my phone."

Vince rolls his eyes and lowers his head into his hands.

"You plank," he mutters underneath his breath. "You complete and utter plank."

"Okay," says Kate excitedly, "you're on. If we head off now we can just about make it for the three o'clock class."

"Right," I say, "and am I all right in what I'm wearing?"

"What do you mean?"

"Well, I don't know, should I bring a change of clothes or something?"

"I don't think so," says Kate. "There's not really much point."

"I'm okay as I am, then?"

"Yeah, I mean, *of course*. Come on, we'll be late."

Why is he laughing? Why is Vince pissing himself? What's so fucking funny all of a sudden?

29

"*Naked?* What do you mean I'm supposed to pose naked? You must be fucking joking."

Oh God. Oh *God*. This cannot be happening. What am I going to do? Why didn't Vince say something in the café? He knew they'd be expecting me to get my kit off? What a bastard. What a complete and utter bastard.

"Are you all right in there, Mr. McQueen? I think we're almost ready for you out here."

"Fine," I croak, "I'm absolutely fine."

"Okay then. Whenever you're ready."

I am *not* fine. I am very bloody far from fine. I am stark naked bar my socks and I'm hiding in the art room stationery cupboard with a box of horsehair paintbrushes digging into the gaps of my goose-pimpled ribs. It's cold in here. So cold that my knob has shrunk. More than usual. It looks like it does when I've just come out of the sea. I have no knob. I have micro-penis. It's the size of a wrinkled windfall acorn.

What if I get an erection? Fucking hell. What if I get an *erection*? I mean, it's not like being on the beach, is it? I can't just lay on my front or cover it over with a towel. What if one of the students is really good looking? What if she starts sucking the end of her pencil in a sexy manner. What if I catch her looking at my knob? What if I catch her sniggering at my shrivelled-up, pint-sized, laughable, Lilliputian knob?

Maybe I should try mustering up a bit of quarteri so it looks bigger. Good idea. Need to think of something midly erotic but not too juicy. Somewhere between waking up in the middle of Destiny's Child and wanking into a basket of dead kittens. Maybe I should try thinking about those French women on the train. No good. Too stimulating. Ugly French women, then. French women with hairy backs. French women with hairy backs and hare-lips. No, that's no good either. It's not working. I mean it *is* working. Too well. I think I'm even turned on by *ugly* French women. Shit.

"Erhemm . . . are you still in there?"

"Yes . . . I'll be out in just a second."

"Everything all right?"

"No problem, none at all. Be right with you."

"There's really no need to be embarrassed, Mr. McQueen. Just try imagining you're at the doctor's surgery."

"Right, good, no problem. I'm not embarrassed. At all."

"Okay then."

"Okay then."

"And don't worry. I won't let any of the students in until you've got yourself completely comfortable."

I ease myself out of the cupboard with my sweatshirt held round my waist and inch towards the low wooden plinth in the centre of the room. So far so good. The art tutor must be fifty if she's a day and there's something about her manner that makes me feel less nervous. Less like I'm about to be viewed naked by a troupe of trendy teenage art school students and more like I'm about to be examined by a vet. I wonder if she'd mind moving the easels a bit further away from the plinth. I wonder if she'd mind turning off a couple of the overhead strip lights before we start.

"Now then," she says, peering at me over the top of her glasses, "if you'd just like to remove the last of your clothes I'll ask the students to come back in and take their seats. Adopt any pose that feels natural to you. Any pose at all.

"Now . . . Mr. McQueen, when I said *any* pose at all, I probably meant any pose except that one."

"Why? What's wrong with it?"

"Well, cross-legged with your hands in your lap wasn't exactly what I had in mind. How shall I put this? It rather ruins the line. Why don't we try you lying on your side with your head on one arm. That's it . . . lovely . . . very good. No, no, don't move now. Keep that arm by your side. Good. That's excellent. Stay exactly where you are."

This is excruciating. This is worse than being picked last for games. Worse than getting myself trapped in Vivian Ducksford's swimsuit elastic when I was trying to finger her for chips. Worse than my mum turning up to sports day in her clay-stained pottery smock and her furry Minnie Mouse slippers. I can't look. I can't look at them. Keep your eyes on the easels, McQueen. Don't look at the students. Don't look them in the eyes. Bollocks. I've looked. I couldn't help myself. I can see that girl's nipples poking through her shirt. I can see that bloke checking out my arse. He likes my arse. He definitely likes my arse. He probably fancies me. Shit, now the girl with the nice nipples is telling her mate that she thinks I'm gay. Maybe I am. Maybe I am gay.

Maybe I'm giving off some kind of closet homosexual-type vibe that I didn't know I had and it's encouraging him to pay particular attention to my arse. Or maybe he's just having trouble capturing the dimensions of that week-old bum boil near the top of my left leg.

This isn't bad. Not bad at all. What a great way to earn a living. Lying here stark naked in all my glory while horny fine-art students attempt to immortalise me in thirty-six different colours of chalk. This is my dream job. It's definitely bringing out the exhibitionist in me. Maybe I should phone up the pictures editor of *For Women* and see how much they'd be prepared to pay me. I mean, a bloke with my experience, I could earn a fortune. I could earn the tour money in no time.

This is boring. I have never been so bored in my entire life. Not since Vince spent a whole weekend smoking banana skins and attempting to convince me of the merits of *Dark Side of the Moon*. Not since he started telling me about the time he bumped into Kevin Rowland in the frozen-food section of his local branch of Waitrose.

"Danny, did I ever tell you about the time I bumped into Kevin Rowland in the frozen-food section of my local Waitrose?"

"Yes, Vince, you did, about a hundred thousand million friggin' times."

I'm beginning to get uncomfortable. I have dead-leg. And dead-arm. And I have an odd tingling sensation in my right calf muscle that probably means I'm going to end up with a life-threatening deep-vein thrombosis. Why isn't anyone looking at me any more? It's the strangest thing. Even though they're staring straight at me, none of them seems to be paying me the slightest bit of attention. I'm not even sure they realise that I'm naked. I don't even *feel* naked. I'm pretty sure I could jump up off this plinth, grab hold of my nuts and start twirling my knob around like a sideways helicopter blade and no one would even raise an eyebrow. Maybe I will. Maybe I'll do it now and see what happens. Maybe I'll leap up, twirl my knob and see if I can get my knees to bend backwards like that toss-wipe off of Riverdance.

"Mr. McQueen . . . Mr. Mc*Queen* . . ."

"Sorry, sorry, I was miles away. Is it time to put my clothes back on now?"

"Yes, Mr. McQueen, I think it is."

The students wait outside while I get dressed and I take the opportunity to look at some of their drawings before the tutor lets them back in. Well, what's the point? What's the point of that, then? It's just a green blob. A green blob with a set of random pencil squiggles running through the middle of it. It looks nothing like me. And look at this one. He's done me square. He's come over all Cubist and drawn me as a naked square. I have a square arm. And a square knob. And a rectangular arsehole. And a revolting rhombus-shaped bum boil.

Hold on, though, this one's more like it. Excellent. Pretty accurate, I'd say. I look like a cross between Russell Crowe in *Gladiator* and Mark Wahlberg in *Boogie Nights*. Maybe I should see if they want to sell it. I wonder how much they'd want. Perhaps I could send it to Alison in Bruges. I could have her put it up in her room for when Didier comes round to visit. Maybe I'll ask the tutor if I can have it.

• • •

"Um . . . if you don't mind me asking," I say, trying not to look too pleased with myself, "who did this one?"

"Yes, I see what you mean, it is rather good, isn't it? Excellent use of light and shading."

"Exactly, and . . . well, I was just wondering. Do any of your students ever sell any of their work?"

"Not usually. But I'm sure you'll be able to hold on to this one for a while."

"How come?"

"Well, your friend sketched it. The girl with the red hair. What's her name now . . . ?"

"*Kate?!*"

"Yes, that's right, of course, Kate. She's in the sculpture department, isn't she? Didn't you notice her? She was over at the back there, just next to the door."

Shit. I didn't even realise Kate would be taking the class. I had no idea she was there. Why has she drawn a picture of me that makes me look like an extra from a King Dong movie? What does it mean? What if she fancies me? What if this whole thing was a convoluted ploy to get into the pockets of my baggy khaki combat trousers? This is not good. This is probably quite bad. I've a nagging feeling this might be very bad indeed.

30

"Hey, Danny, what d'you think of my drawing? Do you like it?"

"Yes . . . it's very good, it's, er . . it's great, definitely my favourite one."

"Cool. I was hoping you'd like it."

Well, what was I supposed to say? She was gazing up at me with her squishy brown eyes and tugging at my sleeve like a distemper-ridden puppy, and the thing is she really wanted me to like it. And I do. I do like it. And now she wants to walk me home.

"Hey, I'm heading back your way," she says brightly. "Do you mind if I walk with you?"

"No," I say, "I don't mind at all."

I know what you're thinking. You're thinking that I'm asking for trouble. But I'm not. I have a plan. I have everything under control. I'm going to ask her up to the flat for a cup of herbal ant's milk, or whatever it is that she drinks, and I'm going to sit her down and get a few things straight. I'm going to start by telling her that I don't fancy her. I'll tell her that I'm flattered by her attention but that I'm strictly a one-woman bloke. I'll remind her that she's my best mate's girlfriend. I'll remind her that I'm a meat-eating, leather-wearing, short-haired daytime television addict with no prospects and inordinately hairy toes. That ought to do it.

We're halfway down Stroud Green Road—somewhere between my favourite Indian greengrocer's and the late night Tesco's Metro—when I suddenly realise that I have no idea what I'm doing. What if I've got it wrong? What if she doesn't fancy me at all? What if she's just being flirty and bohemian? Maybe it's normal for artistic types like Kate to while away their afternoons sketching naked pictures of their friends. Maybe I'm just being uptight. And why would she fancy *me* anyway? Why would she fancy me when she's already going out with someone like Matty? He's taller than I am; he can drink more beer than I can; he can eat whatever he likes without keeping an emergency packet of antacids hidden under his pillow; and he can play fourteen different rhythms at once.

He can wear a beady choker round his neck without looking like a girl; he can wear a tight T-shirt with a cigarette packet stuffed into the sleeve without looking like a complete git; he has all the best-looking waitresses in North London desperate to take him home and get into his Calvin Klein underpants and he doesn't even know it. He doesn't even try to pull them. Bastard. Maybe I should go back to the flat and have a quick snog of his girlfriend. That would show him.

What am I talking about? What am I saying? Why am I even thinking these things? I would rather snog a dog's arsehole than get off with Kate. I feel dizzy. I wonder if this is what a panic attack feels like. I'm having a panic attack. I am. When did this happen? When did I become the sort of bloke who gets off with other blokes' girlfriends and has panic attacks in the middle of the street?

• • •

"—you were so cool this afternoon, Danny. Most men would have been nervous getting their clothes off in front of all those people, but you seemed really comfortable with it . . . woah, are you feeling all right, you look like you're about to throw up or something?"

"Yes . . . no . . . I'm fine," I say, wiping a trickle of sweat off my palms. "Kate?"

"Yes?"

"Do you mind if I borrow your mobile phone for a second? I've suddenly remembered that there's someone I have to call."

I leave Kate standing in the middle of the pavement, nip into the greengrocer's, crouch down behind a pyramid of fist-sized oranges and a tower of freeze-dried popadums and dial Vince's number as quickly as I can.

"Vince, *Vince*, are you there? . . . If you're there pick up the phone . . . I'm in big trouble . . . you've got to help me . . . Kate's just seen me naked and now she's gone mad . . . she's a sex addict . . . she's lost the plot . . . Vince . . . this is serious . . . I'm not joking . . . I think she might fancy me."

I'm just about to give up hope and start planning my escape through the rear entrance of the shop when the receiver picks up with a deeply satisfying click. It's a bad connection but I can just make out Vince hooting to himself at the other end of the line: he seems amused by something; he seems to be saying something about pies.

"Vince, not now, okay, I know you're on a bit of a big gay diet and it's making you obsess about Fray Bentos but now is not a good time to be talking to me about pies."

"Not pies, you wanker," he says, bellowing through the static, "*surprise!* Surprise fucking surprise."

"You *knew*?!" I say, standing up and banging my head on a giant tin of tamarind paste.

"Of course I knew. It's pretty bleedin' obvious, Danny. You'd have to be blind not to have clocked it. Alison spotted it straight away. Why d'you think she's always had it in for Kate?"

"You're kidding me."

"No, I'm serious. It was great. Whenever they were in the same room it was like watching a couple of cats fighting over their favourite piss bush."

"You're comparing me to a piss bush?"

"No, not exactly . . . well, yes, in a manner of speaking."

"Why the hell didn't you *tell* me?"

"Dunno. I was sort of having a sweepstake with myself on how long it would take you to twig. I was going to tell you about it in the café this afternoon. I suppose I never thought it would come to anything. How was I to know you were going start stripping your keks off and waving your knob about front of her face?"

"Vince?"

"I think I'm in trouble."

"Don't worry," he says seriously. "Here's what I reckon you should do . . ."

I'm not entirely sure that Vince is right on this one. He thinks I should ignore the whole situation. He thinks it's just a crush. He thinks I should be as unfriendly to her as I can without being overtly rude and that I shouldn't—under any circumstances—invite her up to my flat for a cup of coffee.

"Kate? Do you want to come up to the flat for a cup of coffee?"
"Yeah, nice one, I wouldn't mind. Thanks."

I have no idea why I did that. I have no idea why I just asked Kate to come up to the flat. I don't know what came over me. I suddenly felt compelled to get things sorted out. I couldn't stand the tension. I couldn't stand the thought of seeing her all the time and bumping into her with Matty and not having things out in the open. It would be like living in a haunted house and never bothering to go down to the basement. It would be like having a perfect, pus-filled scab and not bothering to pick the crusty lid off the top.

Good job I've worked out what I'm going to say, though. It would be a bit crap if I hadn't worked out what I was going to say.

"What music do you like, Kate?"

"Music?"

"Yeah. Do you fancy listening to a record? Shall I put a CD on or something?"

"Yeah, all right . . . I'll choose something if you like."

"Okay, good idea."

She's taken her time but she's finally gone with *Midnight Vultures* by Beck. This seems an innocuous enough choice: better than Barry White, better than Smokey Robinson, better than my collection of Azerbaijani love songs or Alison's double album of Sinatra's greatest hits.

"This is such a great opening track," she says, sliding the CD into the tray and easing it shut.

"Is it?"

"Yeah, 'Sexx Laws,' it's so cool, it makes me feel really loose."

"Right," I croak. "I know exactly what you mean."

Okay then, this is it. I'm going to break the ice. I'm going to ask her if there's something she wants to tell me. I'm going to ask her if there's something that she thinks we should sort out. I'm going to tell her that I have no feelings for her other than friendship. I wonder if I should tell her that I don't even like her very much. I wonder if I should tell her that she's possibly one of the most irritating people that I've ever met in my entire li—

"*Kate!* Get off me. What do you think you're *doing*!?"

"What? What is it? What did I do wrong? I thought this was what you wanted."

"*No!*"

"But you looked like you were just about to . . . you did . . . you were just . . . but you were taking so long to make up your mind . . . I've wanted to kiss you for so long, Danny. I know that you've wanted it too."

"No, no I *haven't*. What are you talking about?"

"Come on, I've known you felt the same way ever since you invited me up here to talk about the gig . . . you know, that afternoon you spent the whole afternoon looking down my dress."

"No, Kate, this is wrong, this is all wrong."

"I know. It's hard, you're still with Alison and I'm still with Matty, but we can sort everything out, Danny. It's karma. We were meant to be together."

Kate reaches out with her hand and starts massaging her along my thigh. I feel nauseous. My heart is beating out of my rib cage. I can't believe I let her come up here. I can't believe I didn't follow Vince's advice.

"Look, Kate," I say, pushing her hand away and jumping up off the sofa, "that's *not* what I meant. I meant *this*, you and me, it's all wrong. You've got everything arseways up. I only asked you up here so we could sort things out."

"We will, Danny, we will."

"No. We won't. Because I don't fancy you, Kate. At all. Not one little bit."

"Oh yeah? So that's why you always kiss me on the lips every time you see me, is it? That's why you had a stiffy when you noticed me in the street the other day. That's why you invited me up to your flat and spent all afternoon staring at my tits."

"I wasn't staring. I was in a trance. You were going on and on abut all that star sign, bigfoot nonsense and it sent me into a bit of a trance."

"Look," she says, standing up and walking towards me, "I understand, *trust* me. I do. I know it's going to be difficult . . . come on, you couldn't wait to get naked in front of me, could you? You were gagging for it. And you were staring at me the whole time I was drawing you, you were totally getting off on it, I could tell."

"No I wasn't," I say, backing into the stereo and knocking the volume down to zero. "I wasn't looking at you at all. I was looking at the girl in the blue shirt. The one with the hard nippl—I mean, I didn't even know you were there."

"Well, I'm here now," she says, coming over to me and pushing her hand into my crotch. "I'm here now."

"Kate, stop doing that, stop crying . . . urghh, that's a colossal bit of snot you've got there, Kate . . . wow. Should I get you a hanky or something?"

"Shut up, Danny."

"Look, I didn't mean it . . . honestly. You're a very attractive woman . . . just not to me."

"You said I was ugly."

"Well, no, I mean, yes, I did, but I didn't mean it."

"You said you'd rather snog a dog."

"Well—"

"You said you'd rather have sex with a diseased sheep. You said I was stupid and annoying and—"

"A nut job?"

"Yes. Thanks for reminding me. Thanks for reminding me that you think I'm a complete crank."

I fetch a handful of bog roll from the bathroom and offer it to her to wipe up the snot. I didn't mean to be quite so harsh, but what was I supposed to do? She had her hand on my knob. She had her fingers on my fly. It was an emergency.

"I feel so stupid," she says, dabbing her eyes with the Andrex. "I was so sure."

"I'm sorry," I say. "I didn't mean to give you the wrong idea."

"Like hell you didn't. You've been leading me on ever since Alison went away."

"No I haven't. I had no idea. Why would I think you fancied me when you're already going out with someone like Matty?"

"I know," she says, grabbing another piece of tissue. "I suppose that would seem pretty unlikely."

"It *would?*"

"Yeah. I mean, he's way better looking than you are."

"Thanks, thanks very much."

"And he's fantastic in the sack."

"Good . . . good . . ."

"But I don't know. He's just so . . . well, he's just so dopey sometimes. And you're like this really bright, funny guy, you're really sexy and vulnerable and you've just seemed so miserable since Alison walked out on you."

"What are you talking about? Alison hasn't walked out on me."

"Well, it can't be long, can it?" she says scornfully. "Why else would she go off and find herself a job in Belgium? The two of you are obviously in trouble. You've got to face it, Danny, she couldn't care less whether you get a record deal or not. She just wants out."

"Look, Kate, I think it might be better if you left now."

"Fine, I'll go. But I bet you I'm right. I bet you two won't still be together by the end of the year."

"Get out, Kate. I mean it, you've said enough now."

"Okay, but you've missed your chance, Danny. You've totally missed your chance. Don't come crying to me when she leaves you."

"I'd rather come crying to a rabid squirrel."

"Fuck you."

"Well, that's very nice, I'm sure. Very Taurus or whatever."

"I'm a Pisces, you moron."

"And there's something you should know," she says, turning her blotchy face to stare at me from the doorway. "I was being generous. With your drawing. *Very* bloody generous."

I shut the door behind her, turn the stereo back up to ten, and light myself a well-earned cigarette. I think that went rather well.

Considering.

31

What am I talking about? I couldn't have handled that any worse if I'd tried. I feel like a total git. Maybe I should give Vince a call and tell him what's happened. Maybe I should have a beer to calm me down first. Maybe I should take a quick shower. I'll feel better after a shower. I'll feel much better once I've washed the sickly stink of Kate's patchouli oil off my skin.

"Have you had a drink?"

"Yeah, I've had two bottles of beer."

"Have you listened to a record?"

"Yeah, I've listened to 'Wave of Mutilation' thirteen times."

"Have you tried thinking about Kate naked and knocking one off?"

"*No!*"

"Only joking, mate, only joking."

"Vince, I'm serious, I've tried everything. I've showered and shaved and shat and I've smoked my way through two whole packets of fags and—"

"You're still not feeling any better?"

"No. I still feel like a complete cunt."

"Well, what do you want me to do about it? I told you she was trouble, didn't I?"

"Yes."

"I told you to stay away from her, didn't I?"

"Yes."

"I told you that under no circumstances *whatsoever* should you walk her home and invite her up to your flat for a nice cup of tea."

"Yes, Vince. You did."

"So what more do you want me to do? I offer you the benefit of all my years of hard-earned wisdom regarding women and you toss it in the bin like a week-old kebab wrapper coated in lard."

"I know, I should have listened to you."

"Too right you should."

"I should have done what you said."

"Too right you should."

"Okay, I admit it, you're a guru. You're a godlike genius who knows everything there is to know about women and bass amps and girls. Now, are you coming up the pub with me or what?"

"Not sure."

"I'll buy the drinks."

"Not sure."

"I'll get the crisps in."

"Not sure."

"I'll let you tell me all about that time you bumped into Kevin Rowland in your local branch of Waitrose."

"Hmmnn . . . yeah, all right then, but I want to finish watching this programme on the history of Stax records first."

"Can't you tape it?"

"No."

"Why not?"

"Because I don't want to."

"Come on, Vince, this is important."

"No. I'm sorry, but a programme should be viewed at the time of its originally intended broadcast. Watching it back on video isn't the same."

"Are you serious?"

"Yes, mate, I am."

"Well, how long is this programme on for?"

"Another hour."

"An *hour*? But it's nearly eight already."

"Look, do you want me to come out with you or don't you?"

Nine o'clock. What am I supposed to do for entertainment until then? Sixty minutes, a whole hour. I need more beer. I need someone to talk to. I need to spend a whole series of related and interconnected quality moments talking about *me*.

What if Kate was right? What if Alison really has had enough of me? What if this whole record deal thing really is just her way of breaking it to me gently? What if taking her to the Spaghetti House and eating half her prawn cocktail was the final straw? What if she was wearing a brand-new dress to go back to Bruges because she knew Didier would be picking her up from the station? What if she's decided to stay in Bruges on Friday nights so she can spend more time seeing *him*? Perhaps I should listen to "Wave of Mutilation" again and see if it makes me feel any better.

Well, that wasn't much good. It only used up two minutes and three seconds and I've still got almost forty-nine minutes left before I can go to the pub and meet Vince. Maybe I should listen to a bit of Joy Division to see if I'm developing any suicidal tendencies. Maybe I should listen to a bit of Radiohead to cheer myself up. Maybe I should give Rufus a bell and see if Alison has mentioned anything suspicious about her Friday night activities to him. No good. I'm too agitated. He's bound to realise something's up.

Right then. There's only one thing for it. I've decided to embrace it. I've decided to stare it down. I sometimes favour this approach at times of acute anxiety. After all, why waste your limited energy on trying to make yourself feel better when you have a golden opportunity to make yourself feel immeasurably worse?

This might be the ideal moment to give my mum a quick call.

32

There's a small porcelain figurine that lives on the sitting-room sideboard in my mum's house, and for some reason it's this that I think of as I begin to dial her number. I think it's meant to be a likeness of Judy Garland in *A Star Is Born*, but I always thought it looked more like our alcoholic next-door neighbour, Melvin Hatt. I can picture it now—the face is round and pale and puffy like a clown's, and the hands are so badly chipped that Judy only has three fingers left on her right hand. I don't know why she keeps it. I don't know why she keeps any of that stuff: the posters, the diaries, the piles of old newspaper clippings and videos and the boxes of film books and music scores that are still gathering dust at the bottom of her MFI wardrobes.

Perhaps things would have been different if she'd remarried and had some more kids; perhaps things would have been better if she'd gone off to drama school like she'd wanted when she finished her O-levels, instead of shagging my dad on the back seat of his Hillman Imp and getting herself pregnant with me. Perhaps she wishes she hadn't chased after a fat man with a famous name and a chronically diseased aorta. Perhaps she wishes she'd had a son who looked like he was actually going to make something of his life instead of having to make do with a serial waster like me.

• • •

"Hey, Mum, it's me, Danny."

"Is that you, Steve?"

"Yes, I just said so, didn't I?"

"Well, I wasn't sure, it's been so long since I've heard your voice."

"Sorry. I've been meaning to phone you back. I've just been really busy."

"Well, I've been worried about you. I was wondering how you were coping."

"Coping?"

"Since Anna left you."

"Mum, her name's Alison. We've been together for five years, she cooked Christmas dinner for you two years running. You *know* her name is Alison."

"All right, there's no need to get yourself all worked up. I was just wondering how you were getting along since she left you, that's all."

"She hasn't left me."

"Hasn't she? I thought you said she'd moved abroad."

"She hasn't moved abroad, she's home at weekends. And it's only for six months. I told you."

"Oh, I thought you said she'd moved abroad."

What's the point? This is worse than talking to Kate. She's purposely trying to wind me up. I bet she's not even dressed yet. I bet she's still in her dressing gown.

"So, Mum," I say, attempting to change the subject, "how's things going with you?"

The line goes quiet. She knows I'm not really expecting an answer. I'm expecting a sound. My mum communicates best when she's not using actual words, and she has this weird ability to make her voice sound like a bent, rheumatic shrug. It's a cross between a grunt and a whine and a sigh, and it means "What kind of a question is that?" "How *can* I be?," it says, "What kind of life do I have stuck out here in the suburbs with my clippings and my curlers and my *Great Escape* posters and my cats?"

"Neurghggh," she says after a while.

"That bad?" I say.

"Neurghggh," she says again.

If I want to keep this conversation on anything approaching an even keel it's probably best that I steer our conversation away from my floundering music career. She's never forgiven me for dropping out of school before I took my A-levels, and she still counts the fact that I didn't grow up to look like a chisel-jawed matinée idol as an act of wilful disobedience on my part.

"But you were such a beautiful child," she used to say. "You looked like a young Paul Newman. I don't know what went wrong. I knew I should have stopped you masturbating so much in your teens. I knew I should have told you it was bad for your skin."

If only she knew. If only she knew.

Sod it, I can't resist it. I'm going to tell her about the tour.

"Hey, Mum," I say. "I thought you'd want to know. I've just had some good news, about the band."

"Oh, really? Are you going to be on *Top of the Pops*?"

"No."

"Are you going to be on *CD:UK*?"

"No."

"Are you going to be on the Lottery show with Dale Winton? Lovely man, Dale Winton, don't you think so? Don't you think Dale Winton is a lovely man?"

"No, Mum, I'm not going to be on the Lottery show with Dale Winton. Not yet."

"Oh," she says disappointedly.

"But it's still good news, though," I say, trying to pep her up. "We're going on tour again in a few weeks. We're supporting a really big band. I think it might be the break we've been looking for."

"Well . . . that sounds promising. How much are they going to pay you?"

"Um . . . nothing."

"*Nothing*? How can they pay you nothing? What kind of an organisation makes you perform for no money?"

"No, Mum, you see it doesn't work like that. I've told you before. It's more about doing the right gigs and getting ourselves some decent exposure and—"

"Well, I don't understand it. It doesn't make any sense. A man of your age. Playing in a band. For no money. You want to try getting yourself a job on one of those cruise ships. I've heard you can make good money playing on a cruise ship. I thought about doing it myself once. I had a very good voice when I was your age."

"Yes, I know," I say, hoping that she's not going to launch into her "married too young, got pregnant too early" speech. "I know you did, Mum, but how many times do I have to tell you? I'm not going to get a job on a cruise ship."

"Of course, your cousin Jason is working in the films now, as a director."

"I know," I say, resigned to what's coming next, "you told me all about it the last time I called you."

"Did I?"

"Yes, you did. You told me all about his job and his car and his six-bedroom house in Barnes and all about his air-hostess girlfriend called Elaine."

"I always hoped you'd do something like that one day."

"What, date an air hostess?"

"No, darling, work in film. He was quite interested to see what you were up to, as a matter of fact. He's always on the lookout for bits and pieces of incidental music for his soundtracks."

"*Really?*"

"Yes, and he's buying himself a second home, you know, in Malaga."

"I bet he is."

"Your aunt's so proud of him, Steve. He's sending her on a cruise. To the Caribbean."

"Oh yeah?"

"Yes, and he's paying for her to have a brand-new kitchen put in."

"Is he?"

"Yes. It's got a slide-out larder."

"You don't say."

"And a halogen hob."

"Really?"

"And a fridge that makes its own ice."

That's it, I've had enough. I promised myself I wasn't going to tell her about this, but enough is enough.

"Mum, have you any idea what kind of films Jason makes?"

"No," she says, "I'm not sure. It's art-house stuff, isn't it?"

"No, Mum, it's not art house, it's porn. Jason makes hardcore porn films."

"Are you sure?"

"Yeah. We got a bunch of them offered to us at the video shop a couple of months ago."

"Well, well, well," she says, lowering her voice and taking it all in. "The little so-and-so. I knew it. I always said he was a little sod. Didn't I? Didn't I always say he was a little sod? Just wait till I tell your aunt."

"Listen, Mum," I say when she finally stops cackling to herself. "I ought to be getting off. I'm meeting Vince for a drink and I don't want to be late. I was just checking in to see if you were Okay, that's all."

"Oh. I see."

"Mum, don't start."

"No, if you don't want to talk to me, I understand. Why would you want to waste your time? You're young. You've got your own life to lead."

"It's not that, I'm happy to talk to you. It's just that I'm in a bit of a hurry. I'll give you a call next week. Maybe me and Alison could pick you up in the car and take you to see a film or something. I think *North by Northwest* is still showing up at the Phoenix."

She pauses for a second and I hear her take a short puff on her cigarette.

"*North by Northwest?*" she says, tapping her fingers on the side of the phone.

"Yeah."

"With Cary Grant?"

"Yeah."

"The one where they try to kill him with a crop plane and he ends up fighting for his life on the edge of Mount Rushmore?"

"Yeah."

"Neurghggh . . ." she says. "I don't think so. I don't really like leaving the cats."

I know when I'm beaten. I put down the phone, pick up my jacket and head off down the pub to catch up with Vince.

33

"Yees . . . excellent, four pounds, the last point at which we could go home empty handed."

"Fuck, the next question's cookery. We don't know anything about cookery."

"I do."

"No you don't."

"I do . . . shit . . . the timer's running out . . . quick, push the phone-a-friend button."

"Arse."

"Arse."

"Shall we put in another quid?"

"How much have we spent?"

"Nine quid."

"How much have we won?"

"Two quid."

"Okay, let's have another quick go."

"Right then, fastest finger first: 'Starting with the earliest, put these Dexy's Midnight Runners songs in the order they were first released.'"

"Unbelievable. Unbelievable. Fuck me, this never happens . . . I can't believe it."

"Vince, stop freaking out and get on with it. We're running out of time."

"Right then, okay, okay . . . ahh . . . shit . . . well, 'Dance Stance' obviously, A, then 'Geno,' D, then 'Come On Eileen,' B, then 'Jackie Wilson Said . . .' that's it, that's *it*, press it . . . press the buttons . . . ADBC . . . *ADBC!*"

"I'm pressing it, I'm pressing it."

"Got it, got it. Nice one. All three lifelines intact. Shooting, my friend, shooting."

"Right, it's a question about tropical fish."

"We don't know anything about tropical fish."

"I do."

"No you don't."

"Yeah I do . . . shit . . . the timer's running out . . . quick, press the phone-a-friend button."

"Arse."

"Arse."

"Shall we put another quid in?"

"How much have we spent?"

"Ten pounds."

"How much have we won?"

"Two pounds."

"Fancy a go on the Addams Family pinball?"

"Yeah, go on then. Why not."

This is great. This is really helping. We've spent the last hour and a half shovelling pound coins into the *Who Wants to Be a Millionaire?* quiz machine and we're about to spend the last half hour before closing time stuffing fifty-pence pieces into my favourite pinball machine of all time. I'm going to get multi-ball any second. I'm a wizard. I am deaf, dumb, and fucking blind. Get in there . . . come on . . . get in there . . . here comes Thing, look out for Cousin It . . . get up the ramp, get in the hole, get in the bloody *hole*. What do you mean, tilt? No way tilt. I never touched you. I never even touched the fucking sides.

Bastard.

"Well, it's obvious, isn't it? The flippers are duff."

"No they're not."

"Yes they are, look, completely unresponsive, completely fucked."

"No, mate, it's you. You've obviously lost your touch. Step away from the machine. Make room for the master . . . woah . . . *multi-ball* . . . check it out, check it out . . . *extra* multi-ball . . . oi, look at this, mate, six balls, six fucking balls at once . . . yeees, get in there, get in there. *Lovely!* . . . quick . . . give us another quid, I might be on for top score here."

"We've run out, Vince."

"Well, go and get some change . . ."

"What shall I buy?"

"I don't know . . . does it matter? . . . just get some fucking crisps or something."

"What flavour?"

"*Danny* . . . I'm running out of time here . . . just get us some fucking change, will you."

"Sorry, mate."

"That's all right, mate."

"Do you fancy another pint?"

"Yeah, go on then, why not."

That's the great thing about Vince and me. We don't even need to talk. We don't need to "express our feelings." We don't need to sit here all night talking about women and our careers and our rapidly deteriorating mental health. We can just be ourselves. We can play a game of pinball and drink a pint of beer and while away the hours discussing the pros and cons of mini-disc recording and it makes us happy. It's the small stuff. Sometimes the pleasure is in the small stuff.

"Vince?"

"Yeah?"

"Can you stop going on about the new StudioSpares catalogue for *one* second and let me get this Kate thing off my chest."

"I thought you'd decided that you didn't want to talk about it."

"Yeah, well, I think I do now."

"I thought you said you'd rather forget all about it."

"I've been trying, but it's nagging at me."

"Come on," he says with a sigh, "let's hear it then."

"Okay. Firstly, do you think she'll tell Matty what happened?"

"No."

"Do you think *I* should tell Matty what happened?"

"No."

"Do you think I should tell *Alison* what happened?"

"Not in this lifetime . . . *no*."

"Do you think I led her on a bit?"

"'Course you did."

"Should I feel guilty about it?"

"No."

"Not even a bit?"

"No."

"I think I was a bit flattered."

"'Course you were. Who wouldn't be?"

"That she fancied me more than Matty."

"I hear what you're saying."

"What do you think it was?"

"You what?"

"That she fancied about me."

"Who knows? There's no accounting for taste with some people."

"Do you think it was my haircut?"

"No."

"Do you think it was my hooded top?"

"No."

"Do you think it's my charismatic, existential, 'man alone' demeanour?"

"No, mate, I don't. I reckon it's probably the fact that you let her witter on about flying saucers for six hours straight without feeling the need to give her a swift clout round the head."

"Maybe it's my passing resemblance to Phil Daniels in *Quadrophenia*."

"Danny."

"Maybe she was awestruck by my naked male form."

"*Danny.*"

"What?"

"Leave it now."

"But maybe she was—"

"*Leave it.*"

"But what if she was—"

"I'm warning you . . . leave it."

"Okay. Perhaps you're right. Maybe we should move on to the things she said about Alison."

"You hesitated, you definitely hesitated."

"I didn't."

"Yes you did. I definitely sensed some hesitation."

"I was swallowing my beer."

"So that's it, then? You think she's having an affair?"

"No. I said no. Did I or did I not answer 'no' when asked if I thought Alison was having an affair?"

"But you hesitated."

"I didn't."

"You did."

"I was swallowing my fucking *beer*."

"But Vince, you were the one who suggested it in the first place."

"What are you talking about?"

"That time in All Bar One. Before she went away. 'Maybe she's having an affair,' you said. You did. I remember. You definitely said it."

"I was winding you up."

"Why would you wind me up about a thing like that?"

"Dunno. It amused me. It amuses me to wind you up."

"So you don't think she's having an affair, then?"

"No, Christ almighty, for the last time, Danny, I *don't* think Alison is having an affair."

"Okay then."

"Okay."

"So why not?"

"Why what?"

"Why don't you think she'd have an affair?"

"Fuck me . . . I don't know. I don't reckon Alison's the type, that's all."

"Are you saying my girlfriend isn't *attractive* enough to have an affair?"

"That's not what I meant."

"You think she's just a bit fed up with me, then, do you?"

"Mate, she's been going out with you for five years. Of course she's fucking fed up with you."

"I can't believe it."

"*What now?* What can't you believe?"

"I can't believe what you just said."

"All right then . . . maybe she's not fed up with you, maybe she just wishes—"

"I mean, I can't believe it, I can't believe you don't think Alison is attractive enough to be having an affair."

"That's it. I've had enough. I'm going back on the quiz machine."

"Yees, excellent . . . four pounds . . . the last point at which we could go home empty handed."

"Fuck, it's a question on rowing. We don't know anything about rowing."

"I do."

"No you don't."

"I do . . . shit . . . the timer's running out . . . quick, push the phone-a-friend button."

"Arse."

"Arse."

"Shall we put in another quid?"

"How much have we spent?"

"Eleven quid."

"How much have we won?"

"Two quid."

"Maybe we should think about calling it a night."

"Yeah, maybe we should think about calling it a night."

"Maybe we should have one more go."

"Yeah, good idea. I was hoping you were going to say that."

34

I know it's hard to believe but these last two weeks have been full of good things: band rehearsals are going exceptionally well, I've written a brilliant new song—provisionally entitled "Get Off Me You Loony"—and, despite all my fears, there's been no detectable fall-out from my recent débâcle with Kate. Things are beginning to look up on the money front, as well. Kostas is giving me two extra shifts a week, Sheila is paying me (in Mr. Kipling's cakes mostly) to keep her garden in good shape, and after some protracted negotiations involving myself, my cousin Jason, and my mum, I am now proud to announce that I am singularly responsible for creating the entire musical soundtrack to *Gang Bang Lavatory Lust 3 (The Poo Chute Years)*.

It was great. Me and Matty spent the whole of last weekend looping bits of the *Shaft* soundtrack on to his sampler and knitting them back together so that they were in perfect time with the on-screen humping. It was a bit tricky at first, what with all the speeding up and slowing down, but Matty proved particularly useful in making sure that everything was right on the beat. We spent all of Monday night editing the final mix and, in what I consider to be something of a masterstroke, we ended up splicing some top-quality BBC sound effects onto the finished version right at the last minute. These included: various cats shagging, various football crowds cheering, trains going through tunnels, waves lapping against sandy shorelines and—I'm particularly fond of this one—the sound of a praying mantis feasting on the remains of its partner's recently severed head. All in all I'd say we added a potent sense of ironic, postmodern gravitas to the ambiance of the finished film.

I'm not entirely sure that my cousin Jason saw it the same way. In fact, he said the praying mantis sample made him feel sick. Still, he's not got much choice really: either he pays me five hundred pounds for all the hard work I've done this week or I give my mum the go-ahead to have a deeply incriminating conversation with my aunt.

That'll show him. I'd like to see him try to fob his mother off with a fridge that makes its own ice after that.

And there's more good news: Sheila has lent me a book of top-ten chess moves so that I can give Rufus a run for his money next time we play, and Matty phoned up yesterday afternoon to say that we'd been given a small mention in the local press. Okay, it was just the *North London Herald*. A free paper. That no one reads. But it was quite a big piece. It took me a while to find a copy, but when I finally managed to salvage one from the communal dustbins outside Sheila's house I was quite impressed by the extent of the coverage: a whole page, with photos, dedicated to the upcoming Scarface tour.

Our bit was right at the bottom of the page: after the bit about Scarface being nominated for a Brit award, after the bit about Ike running into Julia Roberts at a film première, after the bit about ticket sales being quite poor because Scarface are still largely unknown in this country, after the bit about Ike sending his mother on a holiday of a lifetime to the Azores:

. . . and some late news just in, pop pickers, UK rock band Scarface will be supported on their September tour by some local boys from Crouch End: an unknown, unsigned, six-piece skiffle group called Daktari.

Okay, so we're not a skiffle band; Okay, so they got our name wrong; Okay, so the whole gist of the piece was that the tour might turn out to be a pile of claggy old man's underpants, but still, as Matty so rightly pointed out: "It's a start, man, it's a start."

And you can't argue with that, can you? It is, by anyone's definition of events, most definitely a start.

For some reason I'm also feeling much less anxious about Alison than I was a couple of weeks ago. We've decided to limit our phone conversations to three times a week so there's less chance of screw-ups and, loath as I am to admit it, I find I'm not missing her quite as much as I was. I'm enjoying having the flat to myself. I'm enjoying having Vince and Matty round to play poker until five o'clock in the morning. I'm enjoying playing my guitar in front of the TV and eating my dinner in my underpants, and I'm particularly enjoying the opportunity to record heartfelt works of lyrical genius into my mini-disc recorder in the middle of the night.

Still, at least I've stopped asking everybody I know whether they think she's having an affair. It hardly even crosses my mind now. I hardly give it a second's thought.

"Now, Daniel, you look a little off colour this afternoon. You're not still worried that Alison might be sleeping with that Belgian fellow, are you?"

"No, Sheila, not at all. Not in the slightest. In fact I can honestly say it's the furthest thing from my mind at the moment."

"Are you sure?"

"Yes, absolutely."

"Good. I'm very glad to hear it."

"Sheila?"

"Yes, dear?"

"You know when you were in Antwerp before the war . . ."

"Yes."

"Well . . . um . . . what did you think of the Belgian men? Did you think they were more or *less* attractive than English men?"

"Well, it's hard to say, dear. What kind of English men did you have in mind?"

"I don't know, men in their late twenties, dark-haired ones, average height, average build, men like, well, say *me* for instance?"

"Daniel?"

"Yes?"

"I really don't think you have anything much to worry about. You're a very handsome young man. Especially now that you've had your hair cut. I know it's dreadfully old-fashioned of me to say so, but I do like a man to have tidy hair. Now, those John Woo films Kostas ordered for me, I especially enjoyed *Violent Tradition* and I was wondering if you could reserve me a copy of *Bullet in the Head*."

"No problem, Sheila," I say, oddly encouraged by her support for my new haircut. "I'll just go and fetch the order sheets for you."

The order sheets aren't in their usual place so I nip into the stockroom to ask Kostas where he thinks he might have hidden them. Kostas is on the phone. He's tutting and sighing and shouting down the line in a rapid stream of phlegm-filled Greek, and I have absolutely no idea what he's saying. He sounds like he might be arguing with someone, but he could just as easily be discussing the finer points of last night's episode of *EastEnders*.

"Danny," he says when he finally puts down the phone, "I have some very good newses for you."

"Wow, what is it, Kostas, have the distributors come across a Telly Savalas film that you've never seen before?"

"No. And there is no need to be rudes, my friend. It just so happens that I have some good ideas to save you money."

"Go on."

"Well," he says, hitching his belt up with both hands, "as full-time manager of the bands I decide is up to me to help you out with the tours."

"Honestly, Kostas," I say, putting the kettle on to make us some coffee, "you don't need to, you've helped us out loads already."

"Yes, but now I can help you some more. I speak to my cousin Charalambos just now and he say to me he has one very nice van you can use for the tours."

"A van?"

"Yes, is a very nice van, very good condition, lot of rooms to store your equipments, and he say to me that you can have it for two weeks for fifty pounds only."

"Fifty pounds? Wow, that would be great. That would save us about three hundred quid. I mean, we were going to rent one. Cheers, Kostas, that's fantastic. When can we go and have a look at it?"

"Well, my cousin is using it for the rest of the summers but he say is okay for you to collect it the weekend before you go."

"Okay, great, but you're sure it's big enough?"

"Definitely is big enough. Very comfortable seats in front and the whole of the backs is empty to store your guitars and amps and drums kits."

"Okay, that sounds perfect. How old is it?"

"He only have it for two years. Shall I tell him you think is okay?"

"Yeah, all right, why not? It would really help us out."

"Okay. I call him back right away and tell him you accept his offer."

I leave Kostas to his phone call, finish up the rest of Sheila's order and head off to the flat to ring Alison. This is very good news. What with all the extra shifts and the porn money this means we've probably got most of the cash we're going to need for the tour. Maybe we'll end up having more than we need. Maybe we'll be able to afford some decent accommodation and a few stage lights to make us look good. We might even have enough to pay for our own sound man at the London gig.

What did I tell you? There's no doubt about it. The last two weeks have definitely been full of good things.

35

"Hey, Alison, it's me."

"Hey, how you doing?"

"I'm good, how are you?"

"Good."

"How's the job going?"

"The same, you know . . . busy but dull."

"How's the apartment?"

"It's nice. I mean, it's not as swanky as the hotel or anything but it's right near where I work so—"

"How's Didier?"

"He's fine, Danny."

"Still a midget, is he?"

"Yeah. In fact he's probably shrunk since the last time you asked me about him."

"Good, good."

"So, how about you? What's been going on with you?"

"Oh, you know . . . nothing much."

"Right."

"Kostas has given me a few more shifts at the video shop."

"Right."

"And we've been rehearsing quite a lot."

"Have you?"

"Yeah, it's going really well. I've written a whole bunch of new songs."

"Good."

"And we've had a write-up in the *North London Herald.*"

"That's nice."

"Don't you want to know what it said?"

"What did it say?"

"It said we were a six-piece skiffle group called Daktari . . . *don't* laugh, it's not funny."

"Sorry . . . I'm sorry. But it is a bit, isn't it?"

"Yeah. You're right. It is."

"So."

"So?"

"So what else have you been up to?"

"That's it really; rehearsing, writing, working up at the shop, trying to organise a van for the tour—"

"Have you found one yet?"

"Yeah. Kostas has found us a cheap one that we can rent off his cousin for fifty quid."

"That's good of him."

"Yeah. Kostas is a top bloke."

"How's Sheila doing?"

"She's fine. She taught me the Nimzovich opening and the King's Indian Defence and the next time I see Rufus he's going to be very sorry he agreed to a rematch."

"You reckon?"

"Yes I do. He better not think I'm going to take it easy on him just because he's schizo."

She knows I don't mean it. She hates it when people patronise her brother. It drives her crazy that people can't see how bright he is.

"All right then," she says, sniggering. "I'll be sure to let him know next time I speak to him. And thanks for checking in on him last week. I know you've been busy."

"Yeah. No problem."

"Cool."

"Cool."

"So, Danny . . . have you seen anything of Kate this week?"

"No, absolutely not, not at all . . . *why?*"

"No reason. I just wondered if she'd stopped bombarding you with books about reiki yet."

"Oh yeah, she's totally stopped bothering me with all that. I told her I thought it was all bollocks so she's sort of . . . given up on me."

"Okay. Well, look, I suppose I should be getting off. I'll see you on Saturday morning."

"What time shall I come and pick you up?"

"I'm not sure. Can I give you a ring Friday and let you know?"

"Yeah, of course, no problem."

"Good luck at the gig tomorrow."

"Cheers. It should be good. Matty reckons it's almost sold out."

"Well, I hope it goes okay. I wish I could be there."

"Yeah. I wish you could too."

"Love you."

"You too."

"See you Saturday."

"Yeah. See you Saturday."

It's the weirdest thing. I look forward to speaking to her all day but when I'm talking to her I almost feel like I can't wait to get off the phone. It's no good without the facial expressions. It's no good without the sexy crinkle of her mouth and the admonishing curve of her eyebrow, and one way or another I never seem to end up saying what I mean. It's not like we end up arguing or anything, it's just that I can't seem to make a proper connection over the phone. It feels stilted. And uncomfortable. And strained. I can never work out what she's thinking. I can't tell if she's happy to hear from me or if she's genuinely interested in what I've been up to or if she's just asking questions out of a sense of duty.

It's the weirdest thing. While we're talking there's a part of me that can't wait for the conversation to end. As soon as I've put down the phone, all I want to do is call her straight back.

36

It's the afternoon of our warm-up gig at Kate's art college and everyone—including me—is in fine spirits. The sun is shining, the venue is already sold out (they're selling tequila for fifty pence a shot all night), and we've just heard that there's half a chance we might even get paid. It's going to be brilliant. We haven't gigged together for almost six months now and I can't wait for us to get back on-stage and play the new songs in front of a crowd. I'm not even that bothered about running into Kate. I've decided to play it cool. I've decided to act like nothing happened: chances are she'll be way more embarrassed than I will.

Vince turns up right on time. We load our equipment into his white Transit van, tie the door closed with a length of green string and pack Vince off to the gig with me and Matty following behind in a minicab. I'm excited. I'm looking forward to the whole routine: setting up the gear, running through the sound check, arguing about the set list and soaking up the anticipation from the crowd when it's time for us to go on. It's a great feeling. It's like going into battle. The moment you walk on that stage you've got precisely three minutes and seven seconds (me and Vince have done extensive research on the exact timing) before the audience decides whether they like you or not. It's all in the first few seconds. The first few moments. The entire fight is won or lost before you've finished the coda to your very first song.

As soon as we arrive at the whitewashed union building I feel my heart sink a little. The venue is tiny—about the size of my flat—and there's barely enough room onstage for Matty's drum kit, let alone the whole band.

It's a crummy set-up: the stage is less than a foot high, the monitors are held together by what looks like infant-school papier-mâché, the microphones stink from the pools of band spittle that have collected in them over the years, and the PA looks like it was borrowed from a pre-war Russian dance hall.

The sound guy waves at us from behind his desk and shoots us a clumsy smile. He's barely out of short trousers and he clearly has no idea what he's doing.

"Hey, guys," he says nervously, "won't be too long now. I'll just switch on the PA and we can get started."

All three of us suspect what's coming next and we manage to cover our ears just in time. It starts off innocently enough—a low rumbling and a couple of muted speaker pops—but within seconds the PA is yowling like a newly castrated dog and letting off a volley of feedback spikes loud enough to split teeth. Short Trousers Boy looks startled; he isn't sure what to do: he's pressing random buttons and fiddling about with insert leads and he's just beginning to show visible signs of panic when Vince strolls over to the sound desk and pulls down the main fader. Matty shakes his head in disgust. Another know-nothing student who doesn't know his arse from his elbow. What's new?

Venue restrictions mean we can only make noise for fifteen minutes or so, and we're barely halfway through our first song when the power cuts out and we're forced to call it a day. It sounds awful on stage. It always does in places like this. Vince is having trouble hearing his vocals, I'm having trouble hearing my guitar, and Matty's monitor is so fucked he's having trouble hearing anything at all. Short Trousers Boy tries to convince us that it will sound better when the place is full, but Vince and I both know that it's highly unlikely.

There's not much else to be done. We give our gear a final once-over, make our excuses and leave as quickly as we can. There's four hours to kill before we go on. We might as well go and get pissed.

"No. We are not going to go and get pissed."

"Why not? You heard it up there, it's a shambles. What's the point? At least if we're wankered we won't notice."

"No, I'm serious. This is the last chance we've got to play in front of an audience before the tour. It doesn't matter how it sounds, it's about the playing, it's about the songs. It's about having some fucking pride in yourself when you're up there."

"Yeah, well, I was only saying . . ."

"No you weren't, Danny. You're a defeatist little fucker and I'm not having it. You go up there tonight and you give it a hundred per cent or you don't bother doing it at all."

"Okay, keep your hair on."

"I mean it, mate."

"Yeah, all right, chill out. I know you do."

For want of anything better to do we make our way to the student cafeteria and load ourselves up with chocolate and mugs of sugary tea. I'm a little taken aback. I know Vince can be pretty demanding sometimes but I'd almost forgotten how seriously he takes the whole gigging experience. He sees it like some kind of moral contract: as soon as someone buys a ticket to see you play you're duty bound to perform to the absolute limit of your abilities. It's part of the deal; anything less is as good as nothing at all.

"Sorry, Vince," I say, screwing up my Toffee Crisp wrapper and flicking it into the ashtray. "I didn't mean it. I suppose I'm just a bit out of practice or something. It's been a long time."

"Yeah, it has. But I'm serious, mate, we can't keep looking for excuses as to why things don't happen for us. There's no point in blaming everybody else. I'm telling you, if we go on like that, it definitely ain't going to happen."

"No," I say gloomily, "I suppose you're right."

It's forty minutes to show time and the place is beginning to fill up nicely. Vince and Matty are nursing a warm pint of lager over by the bar, the students are getting pissed on cheap tequila and milling about in front of the stage, and I'm taking my ritual tour of the crowd to try and ease my nerves. I like to see who I'm going to be playing to. I like to wander round the venue and get the full measure of them. I like to eavesdrop on their conversations and queue up behind them at the bar, and I like to try and suss out what kind of music they're into. Mostly I just like to see if any of them are talking about the band.

It doesn't look good. The tiny room is populated by arty girls with lesbian haircuts and spiky rubber backpacks, and a smattering of earnest-looking blokes wearing ironic tank tops and second-hand National Health glasses held together with sticking plaster. No one's talking about us. Everyone is talking about Tracey Emin. They're going to hate us. They're going to bottle us. We're going to need six feet of chicken wire to protect us. It's going to be that scene from *The Blues Brothers*—the one I have vivid recurrent nightmares about—all over again.

"They're going to hate us, Vince," I say, dashing over to the bar and ordering myself a pint.

"No they're not."

"They are, look at them, they probably listen to . . . to . . . *jazz*."

"You're just nervous. Finish your pint and forget about it."

"I'm not nervous."

"Yeah you are, you're always nervous before a gig. Have you been for your dump yet?"

"What dump, what do you mean? Since when did I have to take a dump before a gig?"

"Come off it, you do it every time. Ten minutes before we go on. You pretend that you're going outside for a fag but you're really heading off to the bogs to lay some top-quality cable."

"I am not. Fucking hell, Vince, that's totally untrue."

"It's nothing to be embarrassed about," says Vince, tugging on his roll-up. "Matty here has the occasional bit of gyp with his piles and you like to stretch your ring before a gig. You've got a bit of a nervous stomach. It's no big deal."

"Excuse *me*, I do not have piles."

"Yeah you do, Matty."

"Yeah . . . he's right, I do."

"Look, I do not have a nervous stomach, Vince. That's bullshit. I've got an iron constitution."

"Okay, mate, whatever you say."

"Vince?"

"Yeah?"

"How long till we go on?"

"Ten minutes."

"I think I might just nip outside for a quick fag."

"All right then, don't be too long."

"Vince?"

"Yeah?"

"You didn't happen to notice which way the bogs were, did you?"

"Yes, mate, they're over the back on the left-hand side by the door."

That was amazing. That was quite possibly one of the best gigs we've ever done. It was exhilarating. I have no idea what the sound guy did in between sound check and us going on but it sounded brilliant up there. He's a genius. He's an artist. With a bit of help he could even make a band like Toploader sound good. Maybe we should get him to do sound for us at the Shepherd's Bush Empire. Maybe I'll grab him later and see whether he's free.

And they loved us. They fucking loved us. They moshed up and down and cheered in between songs, and a couple of them sweated right through the armholes of their ironic tank tops. I can't believe it. I can't believe we went down so well. Four blokes have already asked me if we've got a record out, two women have asked Matty if he wants to sleep with them, and four people have asked Vince for a copy of our demo CD and an autograph. An *actual* autograph. He hasn't done that for years, not since our Agent Orange days, not since some long-sighted ginger groupie called Linda mistook him for Miles Hunt from the Wonder Stuff.

"That was great," I say, wiping the sweat off my face and stacking my amp in the corner of the stage.

"Yeah, it was," says Vince. "I told you it would be."

"You were fucking excellent tonight, Vince, you totally had them."

"Yeah, well," he says, "we were all good. I thought we sounded pretty tight, as it goes."

"*Tight?* Sod that, we were ace. We were kicking, we were . . . I don't know . . . we were . . . we were *proper.*"

"Proper?"

"Yeah, we were proper, we were a proper band up there tonight. Like we were meant to be up there."

"Yeah, well, there's still a lot of work to do before we're ready for the tour. The new songs still need a bit of shaping up and I want to make sure my voice is in slightly better nick before we kick off."

"Fuck that," I say, waving at the barman and ordering us some more drinks, "the new songs went down really well, and your vocals sounded brilliant . . . the best they've sounded for months . . . it was like being on stage with . . . I don't know . . . Neil Young or something. You were totally on top of it."

"Yeah, well, we're getting there. Matty was very good tonight, I thought."

"Yeah, he was, he was shit hot. Where is the little bastard? Let's find him and go and get smashed somewhere."

"Hold up, Danny, you might want to leave it for a bit."

"Why?"

"He's not on his own."

"Who's he with?"

"Who d'you think?"

Bollocks. I knew it was too good to last.

37

Kate and Matty are sitting together at a small table over by the jukebox. She doesn't miss a beat. She clocks me as soon as I glance over, shoots me the kind of look that would melt motorway tarmac and turns round to Matty and snogs him as flamboyantly as she can. I'm not sure what she's trying to do. She's wearing tons of makeup and a skirt that looks like a cross between a belt and a hankie, and if I didn't know better I'd say that she was trying to make me jealous. Vince is not impressed.

"Soppy tart," he says, rolling some liquorice papers between his fingers and shaking his head. "What does she think she's playing at?"

"I don't know," I say, trying not to catch her eye. "What more do I have to do to convince her that I don't fancy her?"

"Come on then," he says, "let's get over there and break the ice."

"No way," I say. "I'm staying right where I am."

"Don't be a plank," he says. "You're going to have to talk to her some time, you might as well get it over with."

We light our fags, pick up our pint glasses and head over to join Kate and Matty at their table. Kate gives us another dirty look and Matty leaps straight out of his chair to slap us both on the back.

"Wow," he says excitedly, "how good was that, man, how good was that? It was a wicked gig, wasn't it? Wasn't it a wicked gig? Kate thought it was mega, didn't you, Kate?"

Kate looks up and holds my gaze for a long second before speaking. She takes a sip of her drink, rubs her hand across Matty's arm, leans in close to his face and directs her answer back at him.

"Yeah," she says gently, "it was great. You looked fantastic up there tonight, really sexy."

We sit down, nod our heads and neck our beers in silence. Matty is gabbing on about how good the gig was and how we're all going to be rich and famous by this time next year, and Kate is fiddling about with her hair and checking her watch every couple of minutes. By the looks of things she's planning on making a quick exit. That suits me fine; the sooner she's out of here the better.

"Who fancies another beer, then?" says Matty, reaching into his pocket for a tenner.

"Good idea. I'll come over and give you a hand if you like."

I know he's only trying to help but I still wish Vince hadn't left me alone with her like this. The way she's looking at me is sort of giving me the creeps. It's like she can't quite decide whether she wants to shag me senseless or see me burnt at the stake.

"How are you, Danny?" she says when the guys are safely out of earshot.

"Fine," I say, "absolutely fine, very good, never felt better . . . very good indeed . . . how are you?"

She doesn't answer.

"You didn't waste any time telling Vince, then?" she says, tugging firmly on her cigarette.

"What do you mean? I haven't said a word."

"Oh yeah, so that's why he was shooting me all those negative vibes just now, was it?"

"He wasn't. You're imagining things."

"What, like I imagined you fancying me, you mean?"

"Yeah, I mean no . . . I mean . . . listen, Kate, we both said some things we didn't mean the other day, but I think we should just put it behind us and get on with things . . . for Matty's sake."

She takes a deep slug of her vodka and Coke and gives off a thin laugh.

"What?" I say. "What is it? You haven't told him what happened, have you?"

"No," she says, "of course I haven't."

"Good."

"But I might."

I look directly at her to see if she means it and I'm pretty sure that she does. She's smiling at me. She's tapping her fag on the edge of the table and spilling tubes of pale grey ash on to the carpet, and she clearly feels like she's just played her trump card.

"Why?" I say, trying not to sound agitated. "Why would you want to tell him?"

She shrugs her shoulders.

"Dunno," she says blithely. "I mean, I haven't made up my mind whether I want to stay with him or not yet, but if we're going to split up, I think it's only fair that he knows."

"*Knows?* Knows what? There's nothing to know. Nothing happened."

"I'm sorry, Danny, that's just the way I am. I believe in being honest with people. Someone like you wouldn't understand."

I can't believe what she's saying. I can't believe she's being such a bitch. I can't believe she's attempting to occupy the moral high ground like this, and I'm just about to give her what for when I hear Vince coughing behind me to announce that he's on his way back.

"Everything all right?" he says, sitting back down and handing out the drinks.

"Yeah," I say, "everything's just fine."

We make idle chitchat for the next twenty minutes or so but it isn't long before Kate is feigning a headache and asking Matty to take her home. He doesn't want to go. He wants to stay here and celebrate, but there's something about the way she speaks to him that makes him get up and leave. It pisses me off. It's not right. He should be staying put and getting wasted with us.

"What a cow," says Vince after they've gone. "Did you see the way she was pushing him around?"

"Yeah," I say, "I did. And that's not even the worst of it."

"Oh yeah, how do you work that one out?"

"She's thinking about telling Matty about what happened."

"Yeah, well, don't worry. She won't do it yet."

"How come?"

"Because she's enjoying herself too much. I know what her sort are like. She's totally getting off on the drama of the whole thing."

"But what if he blames me? What if he blames me for splitting them up and drops out of the tour?"

"Don't worry about it, Danny. I'm telling you, she won't think about rocking the boat until after the tour's finished."

"How do you know?"

"She's hedging her bets, mate. She wants to see what's going to happen. She ain't going to dump him while there's still a chance he might end up being successful."

"You reckon?"

"Yes, mate, I do."

• • •

"Vince, you know on this tour?"

"Yeah."

"Well, there's probably going to be lots of women around, aren't there?"

"Yeah, I'd say so. Why?"

"Well, maybe it's time we sorted him out."

"Who?"

"Matty. Maybe it's time we showed him what he's been missing."

"Fix him up, you mean?"

"Yeah, help him realise that he can do better than someone like Kate. You could even say that we have a moral obligation—"

"—to show him the error of his ways?"

"Exactly."

"I don't know, mate, you've seen what he's like. He makes Lassie look disloyal."

"Yeah, but think about it. You're going to need someone to go out on the pull with, aren't you?"

"Yes, mate, you're right there."

"And I'm going to have to amuse myself one way or another, aren't I?"

"Yes, mate, you are."

"So let's have a bet on it, then."

"On what?"

"On how many women we can get Matty to sleep with over the duration of the tour."

"Isn't that a bit out of order?"

"I don't see why."

"No, good point, neither do I."

"Right then, I'm saying four. What about you?"

"Well, that depends. Are we counting blow-jobs or just full-on penetration?"

"Yeah, okay then, I see what you mean . . . I say we count noshing but not hand-jobs."

"Okay then."

"Okay."

"So what's your best bet, then?"

"Ten."

"*Ten?* In fourteen days?"

"Yeah. Once we point him in the right direction I reckon he'll be like a dog in a bone factory."

"Right then. Twenty quid says he only manages six."

"You're on."

"You're on."

"Done."

"Done."

"Fancy going to that late bar on Green Lanes for a couple more jars, then?"

"I thought you'd never ask."

38

Midnight.

I love this place. You have to order food if you want to drink late but you can quite happily nurse a single plate of hummus all night and the waiters will still be bringing you cups of cloudy ouzo and beakers of ice-cold beer when the sun comes up. It's one of the things I'm going to miss when the drinking laws are changed. It's one of life's great challenges: finding the perfect spot for a satisfying after-hours drink while everybody else is safely tucked up in bed or taking the last Tube home. Somewhere where you don't have to listen to loud music and watch teenage girls puking Malibu on to their boyfriends' trainers; somewhere where you don't have to take your seat next to a group of sunken-faced, purple-nosed alcoholics and spend all night inhaling the fumes from their pickled, whisky-soaked tongues.

I like drinking late. I like the whole illicit nature of the thing. It's part of the thrill. It's like having to queue up outside a rancid urinal for thirty minutes just so you can snort a contaminated line of coke from the edge of a piss-soaked cistern. If they let you snort it off a bone-china plate balanced on the damp crack of a bent copper's arse it wouldn't be the same.

• • •

"No, it would be much better."

"Better?"

"Yeah. I wouldn't mind snorting it off a cop's arse. Obviously I'd rather snort it off Kylie Minogue's arse but as long as it was the copper's job to hand me a sheet of Kleenex Balsam to wipe me nose with afterwards I think I could definitely go for it."

Vince launches into a detailed discourse on the pros and cons of coppers' arses vis-à-vis the snorting of cocaine and I set about ordering us another round of ouzo. And some more beer. And a couple of Metaxa chasers. And a giant plate of runny hummus.

12:30 A.M.

"That was good stuff tonight, wasn't it?" says Vince, tossing back the last of his wine. "Reminded me a bit of the old days."

"Yeah," I say, topping up our glasses. "We had some great times, didn't we?"

"Yeah. Remember that time when you tried to crowd-surf at the Leadmill and the crowd just split apart underneath you—"

"—and I fell straight on to the floor and hit my head?"

"Yeah. Fuck me, I laughed so much I thought I was going to have a heart attack."

"Remember that time in Spain—"

"When we did that rock festival—"

"Yeah. We ended up driving all the way to Barcelona and back in three days."

"How did we do that, then?"

"Three cheese pasties and a packet of speed, if I remember rightly."

"Shit. We were nutters in them days, weren't we?"

"Yes, mate, I suppose we were."

"We thought we were going to be massive, didn't we?"

"Yeah, we were going to be bigger than U2."

"Do you miss it?"

"What, the drugs and the pasties?"

"No, the optimism. Do you miss the optimism we had in those days?"

"Yes, mate. I suppose I do."

1 A.M.

"You're a top bloke, Vince."

"Yeah, well, you have your good points."

"No, I mean it, Vince, you're a top bloke . . . you changed my fuckin' life . . . hey, shall we get some more hummus?"

"How?"

"We can order some. They'll serve us all night if we want . . . they make great fucking hummus in here, though, don't they . . . don't they make great fucking hummus in this place?"

"No, you plank, how did I change your life?"

"I don't know," I say, shrugging my shoulders. "You just did."

"How did I?"

"Because."

"Because what?"

"Because I had this stupid bloody name and this barmy bloody mother who thought I was going to grow up to be Burt Lancaster or something . . . and I wasn't . . . I mean, was I . . . I was crap . . . at everything. Crap at school, crap at making friends, crap at getting into girls' swimming costumes and, I don't know . . . you gave me something, I suppose."

"What? What did I give you?"

"Something I could be good at. Getting in Code Red was the best thing that ever happened to me."

"You daft bastard."

"I know. Shall we get some more zambuccas?"

"Yeah, come on then, why not."

"And some more hummus. Don't forget the hummus."

1:30 A.M.

"I'm sorry about earlier, Danny."

"What about?"

"You know, when I started giving you grief at sound check and that."

"Forget about it."

"No, I mean it, I was bang out of order. I don't know what gets into me."

"Yeah, well, we all lose it sometimes, don't we . . . fuck me, isn't zambucca supposed to taste like liquorice or something? This tastes like lemons. It does . . . have a bang on it . . . it definitely tastes like lemons."

"Yeah, it does, it does taste like lemons."

"So what was it, then . . . was it your time of the month or something?"

"No . . . I just got to thinking . . . what would we do if we gave it all up?"

"At the end of the year?"

"Yeah. I mean, I'm not sure I could take the slap, Danny. What would I be? Ten years' hard graft and what would I have to show for it? Nothing. Just another sad fucker who thought he was going to turn into Kevin Rowland one day, but what am I really? Nothing."

"You are, Vince. You're better than Rowland . . . Rowland is nothing compared to you, he's an impostor, he's—"

"Don't say that, Danny, it's not funny."

"Sorry, sorry, . . . shhh . . . oops . . . shhhh . . . didn't mean it, Vince."

"Yeah, well, like I was saying . . . I suppose it just wound me up when you said you weren't arsed about playing properly, because this is it, isn't it? This is our last chance. If we fuck this up then they were right all along."

"Who?"

"Them ones that said we wouldn't amount to anything."

"Which ones are they, then?"

"All of 'em, every single one of 'em. Everyone we've ever known in our entire lives except for you and me."

2 A.M.

"Is this the hummus?"

"No, it's the taramasalata."

"Which one's that, then?"

"The one with the fish eggs."

"Isn't that the one with the yoghurt?"

"No, that's Torremolinos."

"Isn't that on the Costa Brava?"

"Exactly."

"And you know what else?"

"What?"

"It's completely different for you."

"How?"

"Well, you've got someone, haven't you? If you give up the music at least you've got Alison to go home to. What have I got?"

"You've got your record collection."

"Exactly."

"And your Transit van."

"Exactly."

"And I could always let you borrow my *Virgin Encyclopaedia of Rock and Pop*."

"I'm serious, Danny. It makes a difference having someone. I've been pretty miserable since Liz left me, as it goes."

"Have you?"

"Yes, mate, I have."

"Well, let me tell you, it's not nearly as good as it seems."

"What isn't?"

"Having a long-term girlfriend. It's a very tricky business. It's racked with difficulties."

"Is it?"

"Oh yes. I mean, take Alison, for instance. She pretends that she loves me but secretly she hates me a bit."

"No she doesn't."

"She does, Vince, she resents me. She's lost all respect."

"Bollocks."

"I'm serious."

"You're a wanker."

"Don't call me a wanker."

"Shut up."

"You shut up."

"Alison loves you, you mad fuck . . . she just wants what's best for you, that's all."

"No she doesn't. She hates me. She hates me on account of the prawn cocktail incident. She hates me because I can never afford to pay my share of the rent. She hates me because I've decided to go out on tour with you and Matty instead of buying myself a suit and jacket and getting myself a proper job."

"Rubbish."

"It's true. I can't seem to make her happy, Vince. When I told her about the tour she went all quiet on me."

"No she didn't."

"She did. I mean, I thought she'd be happy about it . . . but she just went all quiet on me . . . she hardly even talks to me any more."

"Of course she does."

"No . . . she doesn't . . . there's all these long silences on the phone and she never asks me how rehearsals are going or if I've come to any decision vis-à-vis me and flared trousers, and the thing is, she's probably too busy thinking about him."

"*Who?*"

"Didier."

"Who the fuck's Didier?"

"The one she's having the *affair* with."

"She's not *having* an affair."

"Of course she is!"

"That's it . . . I've had enough . . . I'm going to hit you now."

"Don't . . . don't hit me. You're my mate . . . you're my best friend . . . hey, watch what you're doing . . . look out, you're going to spill the zambuccas . . . you're going to knock over the hummus—"

"I told you before . . . it's not hummus, it's *taramasalata*."

"O*w* . . . fuck me . . . that really hurt . . . you shit-bag . . . I'm going to have a bruise."

"Yeah, well, you deserved it."

"How, how did I deserve it?"

"Because you're a moaning, self-absorbed little git."

"What . . . *ow* . . . did you just hit me? . . . Why does my face hurt? . . . Why is my face hurting?"

"Because I just hit you."

"Why? I'm nice. I'm a *nice* guy."

"Because you piss me off."

"Vince . . . what . . . why do I piss you off?"

"Because that's the thing about you, Danny. You have absolutely no idea how lucky you are."

39

I'm a lucky man. I am. Vince said so, so it must be true. No matter that I've borne the entire weight of my mother's unfulfilled ambitions from the age of five and a half, no matter that I have a black eye and the kind of hangover that is making me want to kill myself, no matter that my girlfriend rang me from Bruges last night and told me that she didn't want picking up from Waterloo this afternoon.

Why doesn't she want picking up? Why doesn't she want me to come and meet her? In what sense is she doing me a favour by getting a taxi instead? I wanted to pick her up. I like picking her up. It makes me feel important. It makes me feel useful.

"But you are very usefuls here, Danny."

"Very nice of you to say so, Kostas, but frankly, if I'm pushed, I'd rather be fetching my girlfriend from the station than spending the afternoon reorganising the stockroom with you."

"I am hurt, Danny," says Kostas, puckering his lips and holding out his heavy arms. "I am very hurts that you don't wants to spend your afternoons here taking stocks with me."

"Very funny, Kostas," I say, rubbing my eye with the back of my hand. "Very bloody funny."

• • •

My eye is even more tender than it looks. It does look great, though. I have a purple-black bruise that runs from the edge of my right cheek all the way up to my brow bone, and the white of my eye is bloodshot and badly discoloured around the iris. Kostas was quite impressed. Maybe that's because I told him I'd fought off a gang of knife-wielding muggers who were intent on nabbing my boxed set of *Godfathers 1* and *2* instead of admitting to a smack in the head with a hummus fork from my so-called best friend.

Maybe I should get some rare steak to put on it. I wonder if that even works. I quite like the idea of it, though. I quite like the idea of Alison coming through the door and finding me with a pound of raw steak strapped to the side of my head. I wonder if it would give her the horn. Maybe I should try the mugger story on her and see if she buys it.

"Danny, shit, what happened to you?"

"Vince hit me on the side of the head with a hummus fork."

"Why?"

"I don't know. Something to do with me being a self-absorbed, moaning little git."

"Right . . . well, you want to get that turkey slice off your eye. It stinks. It'll probably end up getting infected or something."

"It's not a turkey slice."

"What is it, then?"

"It's an escalope."

"With breadcrumbs?"

"Yeah."

"Aren't you meant to use steak?"

"Yeah, but it was four pounds a pound. Escalopes were much cheaper."

"Right, that makes total sense."

"Don't you think it suits me, though?" I say, taking the turkey off my head and offering my profile to Alison.

"*Suits you?*"

"The bruise. Don't you think it looks . . . sort of cool?"

"No, I think you look like a football hooligan."

"Excellent."

"Listen, chuck me my bag and I'll try dabbing a bit of concealer on it. I'm not going out with you looking like that."

"Out? Where are we going?"

"Don't say you've forgotten. We're going over to Ruth's. I haven't seen Ruth and Shelley since I went to Bruges and you said you'd come over with me."

"*Did I?*"

"Yes, Danny, you did."

Great. Exactly what I need right now. A night in watching weepies with Alison's poncy girl mates.

Ordinarily I wouldn't go along to one of Alison's girls' nights unless you told me they were going to dance around stark naked, covered in butter. And even then I still might turn it down. But this is different. I only have two days with Alison every fortnight and I want to spend as much time with her as I can. Even if it does mean having to put up with Ruth. Even if it does mean having to drink white wine and Bacardi Breezers and sit through Shelley's holiday video of that time she went to Fuerteventura with her sister and had a "real laugh."

"Does anyone want to see my holiday video?"

"Which one?"

"The Canaries, Fuerteventura. I went with my sister in December. We went on a glass-bottom boat. We had a real laugh."

"Yeah, great, we'd love to see it . . . wouldn't we, Danny?"

"Yeah, fantastic, put it on."

• • •

We've been at Ruth's flat less than half an hour and I'm already bored out of my mind. I had big plans for this evening. I was going to get Matty to phone Vince and tell him that I'd had a brain haemorrhage in the middle of the night. I was going to tell him I was in hospital fighting for my life and see if he bothered to come down with any flowers for me. I wonder what he would have brought. Carnations probably. That's typical. I bet the bastard wouldn't have sprung for roses even if he'd thought I was dying from a subdural haematoma caused by a vicious blow to the head.

I wonder what I'll die of in the end. I hope it's something cool. A gunshot wound or something. Or a disease that no one has ever heard of. I can see it now, a sexy *ER*-style nurse mopping my brow with a damp swab dipped in rubbing alcohol and a room full of high-level medical types standing round my bed and rubbing their chins in confusion.

"I've never seen anything like this in my life, Dougal."

"Nor I, Cedric. This goes against every medical convention we've ever seen."

"Just so. I mean, who would have thought it, a man of his age dying of 'turning into Christopher Walken' disease."

"Terrible stuff, Dougal, terrible stuff. There's only the hair left to go now. As soon as the hair turns thick and lustrous and black we'll know he hasn't long left."

"I think it's almost time. Perhaps you should call in his wife."

"And his six children."

"All boys."

"He sold over ten million records, you know."

"So I've heard. Apparently his mother was very proud."

Arse. Not much chance of dying of Christopher Walken disease. Much more chance of dying from chronic video-induced boredom.

"Hey, does anyone fancy watching my hen-night video after we've finished with this?"

"Yeah, why not, it's been ages since we last watched it."

"You don't mind, do you, Danny?"

"No, fantastic," I say, wondering if it's possible to commit suicide with the edge of a broken Pringle. "What a treat."

Still, it might not be that bad. I know what girls are like when they go out on the piss. They're worse than men. They're probably going to get drunk, put on sexy outfits and run around making fools of themselves.

Well, this isn't much good, it's just a tape of them going out for dinner at some rubbish pizza restaurant. I wonder if the whole tape is going to be this boring. I wonder if any of them are going to dress up in French maid outfits any time soon. I wonder if Shelley and her bridesmaids are going to get naked at some point. I wonder who that weird bloke with the wire-rimmed spectacles is.

"Hi. Danny, isn't it . . . I'm Ruth's partner, Bob. Thought you might want saving from the girls. Would you like to come next door and take a look at my brand-new Mac? It's got a thirty-eight-gig hard drive."

Bob? Where the fuck did he come from? I didn't even know he was here. Good idea, though. Loath as I am to tear myself away from Shelley's drunken attempts to chat up a fat Italian wine-waiter, something tells me I might be able to have some top-quality amusement with Ruth's partner Bob and his brand-new Mac.

"So it's *free* then, is it?"

"Well, no, not exactly free, but *one* dollar—I mean, come on, Bob, that sounds like a bargain to me."

"Okay then, why not."

"That's the spirit, Bob. If they're going to spend all night sipping white wine and watching home-made chick flicks I think it's only fair that you and I get to drink beer, talk about gadgets and watch some peculiarly poor-quality porn."

"Right, then, I'll just go and fetch my credit card. And how about a quick snifter of Scotch while we're at it? I think I've got a bottle of Glenmorangie somewhere."

"Good thinking, Bob. That sounds like just the ticket."

"I'm quite drunk."

"You don't say."

"Sorry, Alison."

"That's all right. I shouldn't have made you come."

"You didn't make me. I wanted to come."

"No you didn't."

"No, you're right. I didn't. But I had a great time, though."

"What did you make of Bob?"

"Great bloke. I'm thinking of making him my new best friend. Instead of Vince."

"You weren't corrupting him, were you?"

"Me?"

"Yeah, you."

"Nonsense. We were having a very nice time. We were chatting about Palm Pilots and having a nice, civilised drink."

"So, you weren't getting him pissed and making him download filth from the Internet?"

"No. Not at all."

"You're sure?"

"Sure I'm sure."

"Okay then, because Ruth already thinks you're a bad influence and I don't want her phoning up tomorrow and telling me that you've turned her boyfriend into a sad, lonely pervert like you."

"Excuse me, Alison, but I'll thank you not to slag off my new best friend."

"He told you about his stockbroking firm getting free tickets to Formula One, didn't he?"

"No. He absolutely did not."

"Yeah he did."

"Yeah . . . all right then . . . he did."

"Thought so."

Damn it. How does she do that? How come she can always tell what I've been up to? I love that about her, actually. I love that she knows me so well. It's one of the twenty thousand things I miss about her when she's away.

"Alison?"

"Yeah?"

"I really missed you last week."

"Did you?"

"Yeah, I did, I missed you a lot. I know I didn't say so on the phone or anything but that's the weird thing about you being in Bruges."

"What is?"

"Well . . . I don't know. It's a bit of a paradox, actually."

"Is it?"

"Yes. Because . . . it's very strange . . . the thing is . . . I mean, it's very peculiar . . . I only seem to realise how much I've missed you when you come back."

"Thanks very much."

"No problem. Alison?"

"Yeah?"

"I think I might have to go to sleep now."

"Okay then."

"Goodnight then."

"Goodnight."

40

When I wake up Alison is nowhere to be found. She's probably just gone shopping or popped out for breakfast but I wish she'd left me a note to say where she was going. I was planning on taking her out to lunch. I thought we could walk up to the funfair at Alexandra Palace and have a quick go on the dodgems or maybe drive up to Hampstead Heath and lie about in the sun for the afternoon. It's my own fault. I shouldn't have got drunk again last night. I shouldn't have kept her up all night with my snoring. I shouldn't have taken the piss out of Shelley's holiday video and spent the last half of the evening squinting at out-of-focus lesbians with Ruth's partner, Bob.

Still, one good thing has come out of it: the whole Bob encounter has left me feeling much brighter about my career prospects. So what if the band doesn't get signed by the end of the year? So what if we decide to give it all up? Getting a proper job doesn't have to be that bad, does it? Maybe I could get a Mac with a zillion-gigabob hard drive. Maybe I could get a Palm Pilot and join a private members' club in the City. I wouldn't have to get pissed in Green Lanes with Vince any more. I wouldn't have to put up with Kostas lecturing me on the reasons why Telly Savalas never won an Oscar—he was cheated, obviously—and I wouldn't have to suffer the crunch of Sheila's garden snails under my feet or eat my way through twenty packets of fondant fancies every week.

I wonder how long it takes to become a stockbroker anyway. Or a lawyer maybe. I wonder if you're more likely to get on the course if you've paid close attention to *Ally McBeal* over the years. Good idea. Maybe I should ask Alison for a summary of the last four hundred episodes. Maybe I could devote my life to saving people from the electric chair and specialise in a bit of sexual harassment law on the side.

The shower and I are mid-wrestle—it's just spat a stream of freezing-cold water straight at my head—when I hear the front door slam shut. Alison must be back.

"Hi," I say, wrapping a towel round my waist and wandering into the kitchen. "I was just wondering where you'd got to."

"I went over to Camden to catch up with Rufus," she says, throwing her handbag on the table and flicking the kettle on for some tea.

"Really?" I say, slightly hurt that she didn't ask me to come with her. "How was he?"

"Good," she says. "He's looking really well. He still needs badgering to go to his hospital appointments on time, but he seems better than he has in ages."

"So," I say, wondering if she fancies coming out for lunch, "have you eaten? Did the two of you go out for breakfast or something?"

"Yeah," she says, "we went to one of the cafés on Parkway . . . and then we went shopping . . . round the lock."

"You didn't see anything you liked, then?" I say, wondering why she isn't carrying any bags.

"No," she says, "there wasn't much about."

"Well," I say, wondering why she looks so edgy, "I thought you might fancy doing something this afternoon. If you're still hungry we could go to Banners for lunch. We could go up to Hampstead Heath afterwards, if you like. We could get a kite or something."

"It's not very windy out."

"I know, but it'll still be fun. We can crash our kite into some kids' kites and make them cry."

"Okay," she says. "Just give me a couple of minutes to get changed."

Alison heads off to the bedroom and (if I lean over sideways and stand on one leg) I can just see her getting changed from the kitchen doorway. I can see her taking off her leather jacket and changing into the Snoopy T-shirt I bought her when we first started going out. I can see her fixing her lipstick and searching around for her trainers, and I'm just about to enjoy a quality moment watching her squeeze into her short denim skirt when I notice her fish something out of her handbag. It's a piece of paper. A small piece of paper folded into a tight, neat square.

I watch her as she opens it out and sits down on the bed. I watch as her lips move slowly as she starts reading from it. I watch as she folds it back up and packs it carefully into her suitcase between her clothes. I wonder what it is. I wonder if I should ask her. I wonder if it's Didier's phone number or something. What if that's it? What if she went out on her own this morning so that she could phone Didier while I wasn't around? Maybe I should ask Rufus. Maybe I should call Vince up and ask him what he thinks. Shit, I can't. I'm still not talking to him.

"So, how long is this feud between you and Vince going to last?"

"Not very long," I say, pulling the kite we've just bought out of its polythene wrapper and struggling to put it together.

"We've got a rehearsal on Monday so we'll have to have made up by then."

"Maybe you should give him a ring."

"No way. Look what he did to my eye."

"Come off it, Danny, you love that bruise. You went to the bathroom to wash the concealer off as soon as we got over to Ruth's."

"That's because it looked ridiculous. I looked like Quentin Crisp."

"You looked fine. You just wanted everyone to see you'd been in a fight, that's all."

"No I didn't."

"Yes you did."

"Yeah, you're right, I did."

"So what was it all about, then?" says Alison, finishing off the kite and handing it back to me.

"All what?"

"Your fight with Vince?"

"I don't know. We were both pretty hammered and I said something disparaging about Kevin Rowland and he just sort of lost it and clocked me one."

"It wasn't anything to do with me, was it?"

"You? No. Why would it have had anything to do with you?"

"I don't know. I just thought this whole ultimatum thing might have been causing trouble between the two of you."

"No, not really," I say, throwing the kite into the air and watching it crash unceremoniously into the ground. "He sort of agrees with you, actually."

"Does he?"

"Yeah. I suppose he thinks we should put a time limit on things as well."

"Look," she says, leaning over and giving me a kiss on the shoulder, "let's just get to the end of the year and see where we're at. Okay?"

"Okay," I say. "Good idea. Alison?"

"Yeah?"

"Are you any good at getting kites down from fifty-foot sycamore trees?"

"This is never going to work."

"What isn't?"

"This."

"The *band?*"

"No, the kite. It's not windy enough. You'll never make it fly."

"I bet I will."

"You can't, Danny. What are you going to do? Blow on it?"

"Come on," I say, picking the kite off the floor and grabbing Alison's hand.

"Where are we going?"

"See that hill?"

"Yeah."

"We're going right to the very top of it."

"And then what?"

"And then we're going to run down as fast as we can with the kite trailing behind us."

"That won't work."

"Yes it will," I say. "It'll definitely work. I'll make this bastard fly if it's the last thing I ever do."

We hang out on Hampstead Heath for the rest of the afternoon. We sip bottles of ice-cold beer by the lake, snog like sweaty teenagers in the rough grass, and wander back to the car feeling sunburnt and tired and warm. I don't know what I was worrying about—Alison wouldn't cheat on me in a million years. Vince is right, it's just not her. If she'd met someone else she'd tell me. If she was pissed off at me for going on tour she'd let me know. I'm just being crap. The fact that she's away all the time is making me paranoid. I bet if I asked her what that bit of paper was she'd tell me straight away. I bet it was something really innocent, like a Eurostar timetable or something.

"Alison?"

"Yeah?"

"You know when you were getting ready to come out this afternoon?"

"Yeah."

"Well, er, what was that bit of paper you put in your suitcase?"

"What bit of paper?"

"You know, you had it in your handbag. You were reading it while you were getting changed."

"Oh . . . I don't know. It was nothing . . . a Eurostar timetable, I think . . . why?"

"No reason. I was just wondering."

41

"It wasn't a Eurostar timetable, then?"

"No. It was a list of dates."

"Dates?"

"Yeah. A list of dates stretching from Christmas all the way to the middle of next summer."

"Weekly or monthly?"

"Bimonthly."

"Well, it was probably hair appointments or something."

"I don't think so."

"Maybe it's her periods or something like that."

"Vince, since when did women start having bimonthly periods?"

"Well, I don't know, do I? I still think you're a sad fucker for looking in her suitcase, though."

"What would you have done?"

"I would have asked her about it. I wouldn't have gone sneaking around behind her back."

"Yeah, well . . . I couldn't help myself."

"No, mate, I don't suppose you could."

Vince and I have officially made up. I apologised for being a moaning, self-absorbed git and he apologised for hitting me on the side of the head with his hummus fork. Apparently his girlfriendless status has been getting him down more that I'd appreciated. Apparently I go on about Didier—and the Belgians in general—more than I'd realised. As it turned out Matty was the most upset out of all three of us. He couldn't believe he'd missed out on such a top-quality ruck.

"So, how did the rest of the weekend go?" says Vince, ordering himself some more tea and tucking into his baked beans on toast.

"All right, I suppose. I didn't fuck up any more restaurant bookings or anything."

"You just hung out at the flat and went up to Hampstead Heath?"

"Yeah. Alison said we should stop trying to make the weekends feel special and just try to behave like we usually do when we're at home together."

"You spent Saturday night watching *Blind Date* and ordering a takeaway curry, then?"

"No. We spent Saturday night getting pissed with Ruth's partner Bob."

"Bob?"

"Yeah. If you hadn't made up with me I was planning on promoting him to the status of new best friend."

"What about me?"

"What *about* you?"

"Well," says Matty, "surely if anyone is going to be promoted to new best friend it should be me."

"Not necessarily," I say, pouring some extra salt on my bacon.

"What do you mean, not necessarily?"

"What I say. I mean, think about it. Can *you* get Formula One tickets and introduce me to Elizabeth Hurley?"

"No . . . I can't."

"Do you have a million-gigabob computer and a cupboard full of twenty-five-year-old malt whisky?"

"No . . . I don't."

"Do you belong to a private members' club in the City and drive a Saab convertible with central locking and tinted windows?"

"No. I don't."

"Well, then, on what grounds do you think I should promote you to new best friend?"

"Dunno," he says quietly. "Let me think about it for a minute."

The three of us get on with our breakfasts in silence and I can almost see Matty's brain ticking over while he eats. He nearly thinks of something a couple of times but then he stops, shakes his head and goes back to buttering his toast. It's at least five minutes before he decides that he's cracked it.

"Right, then," he says, pointing his butter knife straight at me. "I've got it. This is good. This is definitely going to do it."

"Go on, then, I'm all ears."

"Well, Bob might be mates with Mika Hakkinen but I bet he can't do my trick."

"What trick?"

"The one where I put a condom up my nose, pull it out of my mouth and run it backwards and forwards through my sinuses like a giant piece of dental floss."

I mull this over for a while and then I say:

"No, Matty. You're right there. I don't think Bob *would* know how to do that."

"So I'm in, then, am I?"

"Yeah," I say, laughing. "You're in. Had Vince refused to apologise over the infamous hummus fork incident you would rightfully have been promoted to the position of brand-new best friend."

"Wicked."

"Good, then."

"Excellent."

"That's settled, then."

"Mega."

"Matty?"

"Yes, Danny?"

"You do realise you're not *actually* being promoted to new best friend, don't you?"

"Yeah, 'course, but if Vince gets killed in a nasty road accident or something, something where his guts are splattered all over the place and all his limbs are hanging off . . . it's definitely going to be me that gets promoted and not Bob?"

"Yes, Matty. It's definitely going to be you and not Bob."

"Okay then."

"Okay."

"But . . . I was wondering, though," he says, chewing thoughtfully on one of his chips, "what about if he's only brain damaged?"

"Brain damaged?"

"Yeah. What if Vince isn't actually dead? What if he's just brain damaged?"

"Well, then, I suppose it would depend on how bad it was."

"Really bad," says Matty enthusiastically.

"Coma?"

"Yeah."

"Dribbling?"

"Yeah."

"Loss of bowel function . . . loss of speech . . . failure to recognise Kevin Rowland in a hastily organised band line-up?"

"Yeah."

"Hmmn," I say. "It would be a pretty close call but, on balance, I'd reckon I'd still promote you to the position of new best friend."

"Excellent," says Matty, tucking into his fried egg and pouring extra vinegar on his chips. "Hear that, Vince? I'm going to be Danny's new best friend after you've had your coma."

"Ain't never gonna happen," says Vince, reaching over and nicking one of Matty's sausages.

"Why not?"

"Wouldn't matter how fucked up I got. I'd always be able to pick Kevin Rowland out of a band line-up."

"Arse," says Matty, putting down his fork and pushing his plate away. "That's just typical of you, Vince. I knew you'd find a way of stopping me becoming Danny's best friend."

We spend the rest of the afternoon rehearsing and arguing about the running order of the set list and (as is the way of things) hanging out with Vince and Matty for a few hours cheers me right up. I've decided not to worry about Didier any more. I've decided not to worry about Alison's mystery timetable. I've decided not to think about Saab convertibles and ways of saving people from the death penalty and methods of turning myself into Ruth's partner Bob.

I'll give the band everything I've got for the rest of this year and worry about the consequences later. If we fail, I'll find myself a half-decent job and get on with it. If we make it, Alison will regain her respect for me overnight. It's going to be okay. There's only two weeks left until the first gig and I have a strange feeling that something good is going to come out of it all.

"It's sounding good, isn't it, Vince?" I say as we pack up our gear to go home.

"Yes, Danny. It is."

"Everything to play for, then?"

"Yes, mate," he says. "Everything to play for."

42

These last two weeks have been full of very bad things. My credit card has gone belly up, the shelves I tried to put up in the bathroom have fallen down, my haircut is growing out in what can only be described as a wilfully perverse manner, and I'm badly in need of a decent night's sleep. It's Vince's fault. He's been phoning me at all hours of the day and night. He's turned into hyper Vince. He won't leave me alone. He wants to discuss trousers and set lists and the most direct routing between major British cities, and he especially wants to discuss the collection of top-notch compilation tapes that he's putting together for the tour.

He's made a different tape for each journey: tape A (for the drive between London and Wolverhampton), tape B (for the drive between Wolverhampton and Cambridge), tape C (for the drive between Cambridge and Nottingham) and an extra-special tape (tape X) for the journey between Aylesbury city centre and London, Shepherd's Bush.

He calls me every day. He calls me at home and he calls me at the video shop and yesterday he called me at two o'clock in the morning to ask me which version of "Hard Rain" I thought he should include on our Birmingham-to-Bristol tape. He was most put out when I said that I wasn't all that arsed. He accused me of not giving my full attention to his problems. He accused me of being a closet Roxy Music fan. He said that everyone knows the Dylan version is infinitely superior to the Brian Ferry version, and when I pointed out that if this was the case then why was he phoning me up in the middle of the night to ask which one to include on the tape, he slammed the phone down in a full-on strop.

It's difficult to come to terms with: Vince in a state of high excitement, whilst a rare and beautiful thing, is enough to stretch the firmest of friendships to its limits.

It was a similar story when we went shopping for gig clothes in Camden last weekend. Vince was totally on one. He was rushing round the stalls like a bull terrier with worms; picking up flares and T-shirts and armfuls of crushed-velvet trousers, and he wouldn't take no for an answer when me and Matty refused to crouch down behind the Chinese noodle stand and try them on. He claims that he's doing us a favour. He claims that he has a duty to share his innate sense of style with lesser mortals like me and Matty. Just because he once got beaten up for wearing a Bri-Nylon blouse in the middle of Leytonstone High Road during his short-lived Morrissey period, he thinks he has a moral obligation to introduce us to our camp sides.

And that's not even the worst of it. Among other things: Bob has failed to come through with the six tickets to the Monaco Grand Prix that I asked him for; Ike's tour manager has left a message on my answerphone saying that we might not get any sound checks on this tour; and Rufus beat me at five successive games of chess when I called round to see him yesterday afternoon. He slaughtered me. He saw through my Sicilian defence in two moves. He saw through my Nimzovich opening in one. It's no good. I'm going to have to buy myself a new book. *The Boy's Own Annual of Classic Chess Moves* that Sheila gave me had half of its pages missing: I probably shouldn't have tried to make up the rest of the moves on my own.

Still, at least my mum has been looking out for me this week. She's been most helpful and not at all bordering on mad. How nice of her to start sending me a selection of job applications that she's clipped out of the local evening paper and underlined with six different colours of felt-tip pen.

MUSICIANS WANTED TO WORK ON RUSSIAN CRUISE SHIPS.
MUST BE AU FAIT WITH CHRIS DE BURGH SONGS AND SIMILAR.
MUST BE COMFORTABLE WEARING FRILLY VISCOSE SHIRT AND CLIP-ON BOW TIE.
MUST BE PREPARED TO SERVICE/ENTERTAIN LONELY,
SINGLE WOMEN OF A CERTAIN AGE.
NOW BOOKING FOR SUMMER SEASON.
PORTS TO INCLUDE: HELSINKI, VLADIVOSTOK AND A
THREE-NIGHT STOPOVER IN SUNNY MURMANSK.
FREE VODKA, PROSTITUTES, AND AS MUCH PICKLED CABBAGE AS YOU CAN EAT.

Cheers, Mum.

Thanks a lot.

Of course, this all pales into insignificance when you consider what happened to Sheila last weekend. There she was, innocently cleaning some rubbish out of her kitchen cupboards, stretching over to clear a stubborn pile of muffin crumbs from underneath the cooker hood, when all of a sudden her stepladder gave way beneath her and she ended up falling over and damaging her hip. It's not broken but it still means that she's going to be laid up for the next couple of weeks or so. I went round to see her the day after she'd done it and she was looking pretty sorry for herself.

"How stupid of me, Daniel," she said, sitting up in bed and tucking into the packet of Eccles cakes that I'd brought her.

"You see, I still think I can do all those tricky little things like climbing up ladders and cleaning out the kitchen cupboards and I can't."

"You should have called me," I said. "I would have come over and helped you."

"Yes, well, I would have, Daniel, but I don't like to bother you too often if I can help it."

"Why not?"

"It makes me cross."

"*Cross?* Why does it make you cross?"

"Having to ask for people's help all the time. You don't know what it's like. You're much too young to understand."

"No, Sheila," I said, helping myself to a biscuit, "I think I know what you mean."

"I'm sorry, Daniel," she said firmly, "but I don't really think that you do."

She was right, of course.

We ended up having a really nice afternoon. I told Sheila all about my concerns over Alison's mystery timetable and Sheila told me all about her obsession with martial-arts movies and the years she spent living in the Far East. It turns out Sheila has had an amazing life. She's lived all over the world: India, China, Malaysia, and Japan, and she spent ten years running an English-language school with her husband in Hong Kong after the war.

"Of course, we didn't make very much money, Daniel, but it really was a lovely way to live. We saw so many interesting things. You see that small vase over there on the mantelpiece? That was given to me by the son of a Mongolian warlord."

"Wow," I say, going over to the fireplace to take a closer look. "It's beautiful, Sheila."

"Yes, it is. I received quite a lot of presents when I was teaching. I dare say I was something of a catch in those days. If I hadn't been happily married . . ."

"You might have run off with the son of a Mongolian warlord?"

"Well . . ." She laughs, forcing some colour back into her parched cheeks. "You never know."

"I'm a bit jealous, Sheila," I say, helping myself to a fondant fancy and watching her bony fingers struggle with her hot teacup.

"Are you, my dear? What on earth for?"

"Well, because you've really lived, Sheila."

"Of course I have, Daniel. What else is life for?"

She seemed a little better the last couple of times I saw her. Her daughter is coming up from Cornwall to look after her this weekend, and with a bit of luck she'll be up and about before we head off for our first gig in Wolverhampton on Monday. It makes you wonder, though. I mean, who would have thought it? She speaks five different languages (including Mandarin), she's lived in ten different countries (including Tibet), she's had fifteen proposals of marriage (including one from a genuine Mongolian warlord) and she still gets ignored at the supermarket checkout when she's queuing up to pay for her tinned sardines. Maybe I should see if Alison fancies setting up a language school in Tibet. Maybe I should be looking to Sheila as an example of how to live my life instead of wondering about ways to turn myself into Ruth's partner Bob.

Maybe I should have one more go at trying to make myself rich and famous before I think about applying for a job on a Russian cruise ship.

• • •

"Danny, it's me."

"Hey, I'm glad it's you. There's something important that I need to ask you about."

"Really?"

"Yes. Now, given the *choice*, would you rather live in Tibet or Murmansk?"

"Um . . . neither, really."

"Come on, if you had to choose?"

"Well . . . Tibet, I guess."

"Good. I was hoping you'd say that. Vince reckoned Murmansk but he was only saying that to be perverse."

"Danny, listen, I've got something to tell you."

My heart misses a beat. I hate it when people say that. It's always bad news. It can only mean one of two things: a) she's decided to leave me or b) she's just found out that she's got a brain tumour.

"What is it?" I say, opting for brain tumour option over the leaving me option. "You're not ill or anything, are you?"

"No, it's nothing like that."

"*Shit* . . . what is it, then . . . ?"

"It's about this weekend. I've got to work. I won't be able to make it back to London before you go away."

"You're kidding?" I say, half relieved about the brain tumour/leaving me news and half put out that she won't be coming home to see me off.

"No," she says softly. "I can't help it, Danny, they want me to put in a couple of extra days on this project that I'm doing. We've got a presentation that needs finalising by Monday morning and I can't really say no."

"But that means I won't get to see you before the tour."

"I'm really sorry, Danny. I'll be back for the last night at Shepherd's Bush."

"But I was looking forward to seeing you."

"I know. Me too. But there's nothing much I can do."

What did I tell you? These last two weeks have definitely been full of very bad things.

43

"You're not serious."

"Yes I am."

"But you can't."

"Why can't I?"

"Because we've got things to do."

"What things?"

"Rehearsals."

"Vince, we're as rehearsed as we're ever going to be. We've played through the set a million and two times."

"Well, what about collecting the van from Kostas's cousin tomorrow morning?"

"You'll have to go and pick it up with Matty. I've made up my mind, Vince. I'm going to Bruges."

I have made up my mind. I'm going to Bruges. If Alison can't come home to see me before the tour starts then what's to stop me getting on a train and going out to Belgium to see her?

Vince thinks I should let her know that I'm coming but I think it'll be much better if I turn up unannounced. I can see her now, slumped in front of the TV watching a late-night Belgian quiz show; sucking down a warm bottle of beer and tucking into some cold *moules et frites*; jaw dropping in amazement as I burst through the door with champagne and roses and an extra pot of garlic mayonnaise to sweep her off her feet. It's going to be great. It's going to be a top weekend. I'm going to get the 11:20 Eurostar from Waterloo first thing tomorrow morning. Shit, it's nearly three a.m., I'd better get some sleep.

I overslept. Not too badly, but enough so as I narrowly missed the 11:20 train. And the 12:20 train. And the train that goes at twenty past one. Still, here I am, happily ensconced in my second-class carriage, loaded up with newspapers, guidebooks and an extra-long chicken tikka baguette and the latest scintillating issues of *Ultimate Gigger* and *Sound on Sound* neatly propped up in front of me.

I have a table all to myself. I have loads of room. I can put my feet on the chair opposite and fling my possessions all over the place, and I have to say this travelling by train idea is turning out to be rather enjoyable. I might go and get myself a beer in a minute. And a bar of Yorkie maybe. And one of those giant beefburgers that's been blasted in the microwave until it's grey and rubbery and hot enough to burn a hole right through your tongue.

I am squashed. And deaf. I might very well be exhibiting the early signs of chronic claustrophobia. Where did they all come from? Who said they could all get on at Ashford International? Why have they brought babies with them? Why did the two women with the twins think it would be a good idea to come over here and sit down next to me?

I have baby puke on my shoulder. I can smell loose baby faeces over the stink of my Mega-Big-One burger wrapper. The toddler in the blue dungarees is eating my copy of *Sound on Sound*. The one in the red is trying to stick his hand in his own poo. I wonder if infanticide is legal in Belgium. I wonder if there's some odd legal loophole that says it's okay to throw evil twins out of train windows so long as you're travelling through long, dark tunnels at speeds in excess of a hundred miles an hour.

This is much better. I've packed up my things and moved up to first class. I have a big comfy seat and a much bigger table and a jolly-looking woman is just about to come through the carriage with a selection of hot drinks and buns. I'm going to have the cream tea. I am looking forward to it very much. I'm going to watch the French countryside slip past my window, ponder on the horrors of the trenches—and war in general—and stuff my hole with some top-quality cake. I wonder, should I have the cherry—or the strawberry-flavoured jam? Or maybe the raspberry? As long as it doesn't have any pips.

I have been thrown out of first class. I was in the middle of discussing the jam/pip situation with the cream-bun lady when a shifty-looking bastard in a grey-and-green uniform swept through the carriage and demanded to see my ticket. Apparently it's not good enough to say that you've lost it. Apparently being on the run from mutant killer twins is not a good enough excuse. Apparently you're not allowed to take your scone back to second class with you, even though you've already buttered it up and taken a great big bite.

At last. I've arrived. I've changed trains at Brussels, smoked a fag on the platform while we swapped drivers in Ghent, read and reread my 1997 guidebook to Belgium, and now I'm in the back of a black-and-white taxicab heading straight for the centre of Bruges.

Well, this is very nice. What a nice-looking city. All those archways and courtyards and cobbled canalside streets. All those squares and churches and quaint little chocolate shops. All those funny-looking blokes on bikes who think it's okay to have odd facial hair arrangements involving short, pointy beards and no moustaches. I quite like the clock tower, though. According to my guidebook it's over eighty-three feet high. Reminds me a bit of the one in Crouch End.

The taxi driver drops me off in the middle of the Grote Market and I spend a couple of minutes taking in the atmosphere and shopping for flowers and wine. After lengthy consideration—the time it takes to drive a Belgian shopkeeper round the bend—I choose half a dozen brick-coloured roses and a bottle of top-quality champagne. And some chocolates. And a Hercule Poirot fruitcake. Don't ask me why.

So this is it, then. This is where she lives. Number 13 Sint-Jacobsstraat: next to a lace shop; above an all-you-can-eat fondue restaurant; opposite a pavement café with red-and-white checked cloths on the tables and bunches of wind-dried hams hanging in the window. I can't believe it. I mean, how weird is that? Alison. With her own apartment. That I've never seen. I can't wait to see her face when she realises it's me. I bet she'll be really glad to see me. I bet she's had a rotten day, what with being bossed about by a midget and having to go to work on a Saturday. Here goes, then. I'm going to ring the bell. I'm going to give Alison the surprise of her life.

For some reason I never considered the possibility that she wouldn't be in. I considered the possibility of finding her *in flagrante* with a midget; I considered the possibility of finding her slumped out over the sofa looking miserable and pining for me, but I never considered the possibility that she wouldn't be there. I wonder where she is? I've tried her mobile phone but I only got her voice mail and I don't want to leave a message in case it spoils the surprise. It's almost seven o'clock. Maybe she's working late again. I'll just have to sit in the café across the road and drink beer and read about famous Belgians until she turns up.

According to my guidebook there are 242 famous Belgians. This is rubbish. I've never heard of any of them. If I've never heard of any of them then how can they be famous? Fred Deburghgraeve. Who's he? Who's Flory Van Donk when he's at home? You don't know either? Of course you don't. No one does. By my reckoning there have only been four famous Belgians in the entire history of the world: Jean-Claude Van Damme (short actor/martial artist); Django Reinhardt (jazz guitarist/musical virtuoso); King Leopold II (homicidal tyrant/loony), and a gentleman by the name of Adolphe Sax who invented the saxophone. Fancy that. I bet Alison will be fascinated when I tell her. And not at all bored. I wonder if she knows who Django Reinhardt is. I wonder if she knows much about the Belgian Congo. I wonder if she knows that Jean-Claude Van Damme used to work as a pizza delivery boy before he found fame and fortune in such timeless Hollywood classics as *Bloodsport*, *Timecop*, and *Universal Soldier*. I wonder if that's an apparition or if that really is Alison coming towards me on a bike.

Alison is coming towards me on a bike. It is, it's definitely her. She's freewheeling down the cobbles on a bottle-green bone-shaker and the worst thing about it is she's not alone. There are six of them: three men and three women; all laughing and joking and smiling and talking and not a single mole-ridden midget among them. It looks like they're all going out to dinner. It looks like they're heading into that swanky candlelit Flemish bistro at the top of the street.

Right. This is it, then. This is the moment I've been waiting for. Now is the perfect time to run out of the café, bottle of champagne in hand, bunch of flowers held aloft, and scoop my gorgeous girlfriend into my arms and shout "*Tadahh.*"

I don't, though. I close up my guidebook, pay the waitress for my tumblerful of Trappist beer and spend a quality moment selecting the perfect vantage spot from where I can spy on all six of them without being seen.

The problem with hiding behind a wrought-iron lamppost is that it doesn't afford you quite the level of camouflage you might expect. In fact it's completely crap. I have to stand sideways on. I have to strain my neck in a most peculiar fashion if I want to see what Alison and her posh mates are up to, and it may be my imagination but I have the distinct impression that people are beginning to look at me funny. I have the feeling that I might be rather conspicuous. Perhaps I should move to the lace shop over the road. I'll probably get a much better view from the lace shop over the road.

44

As soon as I get to the lace shop over the road I have the overwhelming urge to run away. It hits me in the gut like a low punch, and it's all I can do not to turn on my heels and scarper. I can just make out Alison through the restaurant window. She's sat at a large wooden table at the back of the room and she's surrounded by half a dozen people, none of whom I know. The table in front of them is loaded down with empty glasses: wineglasses, beer glasses, and towers of tiny shot glasses that the waiter is just about to fill to the brim with schnapps. Alison likes places like this. Places you can order a steak rare enough to make your hair curl.

It looks to me like they're celebrating. The girls are throwing their arms up to raise a toast and a slick-looking bloke in a beige shirt is topping up their glasses and trying to look down the front of their skimpy summer dresses. I want to punch his face in. I want to punch him for wearing beige and ogling my girlfriend's breasts, but mostly I just want to run away.

I wonder if that's Didier. I wonder why Alison said he was a club-footed midget when in fact he's very tall with no obvious signs of physical deformity. At least he's not very good looking. He might have a square jaw and blond hair and a super-wide chest but he has none of my boyish charm. I wonder how much his suit cost. I wonder if it was more than a hundred pounds.

I pick up my denim jacket and sneak across the cobbles to take a closer look. I need to see Alison's face. I need to see the look in her eyes and the curve of her mouth and the way that she's holding her hands. Alison taps her fingers when she's nervous or bored. She taps her fingers and hums gently under her breath and she seems to drift off to some distant place of her own.

She doesn't look bored. She looks like she's enjoying herself. She looks like she knows these people and likes these people and she doesn't look like she's missing me at all. It's not what I expected. I didn't expect her to have friends to hang out with and things to go out and celebrate, and for some inexplicable reason I didn't expect her to be living any kind of a life. Without me.

I should go in there. I should go in there right now. I should swing the door open, march across the restaurant and rescue her from the clutches of the evil Belgian warlord who's just put his hand on her bare, tanned shoulder.

But I don't. I turn round.

And go home.

For some reason the return journey seems much faster than the one going out. Maybe it's the six brandy miniatures that I drank at Bruges station. Maybe it's the Cointreau on ice that I sucked down in Ghent. Perhaps it's the whole bottle of champagne that I finished off all by myself, and maybe it's the fact that I hit my head on the plastic tray table when I dozed off in the middle of the Channel Tunnel. Still, at least I managed to make one person happy. The cream-bun lady thought the orange roses were lovely. She was less keen on the Hercule Poirot cake.

• • •

I crawl home from Waterloo at two o'clock in the morning; tired, drunk, and depressed beyond belief. The answerphone is flashing wildly: four messages. None of them from Alison. All of them from Vince. He wants me to call him as soon as I get home. If not sooner.

I take off some of my clothes, lift my bottle of non-duty-free whisky out of its creased carrier bag and head for the bedroom via the bog. Fuck him. He probably just wants me to help out with another insane compilation tape crisis. It can wait until Monday. I don't even plan to get *up* until Monday. I plan to spend as much of the next twenty-four hours as is humanly possible getting drunk, feeling sorry for myself and watching daytime television in bed. It doesn't even have to be *Columbo*. It doesn't even have to be *Supermarket Sweep*. It could even be repeat episodes of the bastard *Naked Chef*.

Right now I couldn't care less.

45

It's Monday morning, the sun is shining and today is the first day of the tour. I should be excited. I am excited. I just wish I didn't feel like a giant bag of crap. I wish I hadn't spent the whole of yesterday getting pissed, eating stale cereal and putting a pillow over my head every time Vince left me another irate message on the answerphone.

I did speak to Alison, though. She called me late last night. I didn't say anything about coming out to see her in Bruges but I did make her suffer by being rude and short-tempered on the phone. She wanted to know what was wrong with me. She wanted to know why I was giving her such a hard time. I didn't say much. I made up some bollocks about being anxious about the gigs and being disappointed about her not coming home this weekend, but I don't think she really believed me.

She sounded genuinely sorry that she hadn't been able to get away. She said she was looking forward to seeing me. She wished me luck. She didn't say anything about riding around Bruges on a bike or going out to dinner in sexy low-cut dresses, and even though I asked her a whole series of complex and deeply probing questions, she completely failed to mention getting drunk with rich, tall Belgian men in expensive Flemish restaurants.

She didn't even laugh at my famous Belgians jokes. She said that there were loads of famous Belgians. She proceeded to name about ten. I said that since they were only fashion designers—people who have a GCSE in sewing—they didn't really count. She got a bit cross. I think she was intimating that she thinks I'm vaguely xenophobic. How mad is that?

"Where the fuck have you been?"

"Belgium."

"I thought you was coming home last night."

"Yeah, well . . . um, I did."

"Then why the hell didn't you call me when you got in? I left you fifteen fuckin' messages."

"It was late. I thought it could probably wait until this morning."

"No, mate, it couldn't. It needed sorting out last night. It's too late now."

"Too late for what?"

"Too late to get ourselves another van."

I put my rucksack down on the pavement and turn round to look at the heap of rusty metal parked up in front of Vince's flat. It's not what we were expecting. It's a converted kebab van. It has "Charalambos' mobile Ockacbasi" written down the side in loopy red letters, and it still has its long wooden serving hatch nailed to the left-hand side instead of a window. It has a picture of a cheeseburger on the bonnet. And a drawing of a shish kebab on the door.

"It's a kebab van," I say, unable to do anything but state the obvious.

"No shit," says Vince, lighting himself a cigarette.

"Well, what are we going to do? Have you spoken to Kostas?

Did he *know* this was the van we were getting? I mean, what did he say?"

"He said, and I quote, 'What is wrongs with van? This is very nice vans. Why you don't like my cousin Charalambos's van?'"

"And what did you say?"

"I said, 'Kostas, it's a mobile kebab van. It's not what we was after. It's still got its electric doner kebab wheel in the front. It's got no windows and no radio and it's got pictures of flame-grilled burgers all over the piss-poor bodywork that look like they were stencilled on by an epileptic cat.'"

"And what did he say?"

"He said for fifty quids what did you expect?"

"Christ almighty," I say, taking in the yellow vinyl seats and the giant furry dice in the window. "We're going to look like a right bunch of prats turning up to gigs in the back of that."

"Yes, mate, we are."

"Does it go? I mean, is it even going to make it up the motorway?"

"Yeah, it goes. Just about."

"Well then," I say. "I suppose we haven't got much choice. It's too late to rent anything else now and, besides, we've already allocated all the spare money."

"We could always paint it," says Matty, trying to be helpful.

"What do you mean?"

"We could paint out the burgers and the kebabs and write the name of the band over the top. Maybe we could come up with a name for the tour and stencil that underneath it."

"A name for the tour?"

"Yeah, you know. We could call the tour something. Something that sums up the band. Something that sums up what the music's all about."

"Any ideas?"

"Well . . . yeah . . . what about the Curly Fries Tour?"

"The *Curly Fries* Tour? Are you mad?"

"No. I mean . . . well . . . we all *like* curly fries, don't we? And the good thing about it is we'd only have to paint the word 'curly' because, look, it's got the word fries painted on it already."

I shake my head in amazement and Vince lowers his head into his hands.

"Why not?" he says finally.

"Vince, you're not serious?"

"No. Fuck it. Why the hell not? I've got a tin of silver spray paint in the garage. Let's paint the bastard. I'll just go and fetch it."

"Wow. Mega. Fantastic. Can I have the first go?"

"Yes, Matty," I say, "I don't see why not."

And so it was that on the last T-shirt warm morning of the year, the three of us set off on tour in a rust-ridden, mobile kebab van with "Dakota: The Curly Fries Tour" painted down the side in giant silver letters. Matty made a grand job of it. He painted stars and stripes and spliffs and drum kits and three gangly stick men to represent the three of us. It looked like we were on our way to San Francisco instead of Wolverhampton. It looked shiny in the early autumn sunshine. It looked like we were a proper band. Almost.

And off we went. Me and Matty loaded the gear into the back of the van and Vince loaded the first of his compilation tapes into the cassette machine and pressed Play. We crossed our fingers. The engine started. The rough edges of London slipped away behind us and the opening bars to *Pistolero* (our favourite Frank Black and the Catholics album) began rattling through the tiny mono speaker. We waited for the buzz of the guitars. We waited for Frank Black's righteous voice to kick in. And then we all started to sing along.

We left the ground and we floated above this town that
never got better.
We got drowned in the sea of love and I know that it's
gonna get wetter.
We're like bad harmony, we're like bad harmony,
We're a couple of wannabees who do not know what
they are doing.
We're like bad harmony. We're like bad harmony,
We are good company going down the road to ruin . . .

We were loud and proud and—apart from Vince—hideously out of tune, and it was definitely one of the most perfect moments I can ever remember.

46

DAY ONE

Drive:	London—Wolverhampton (138 miles)
Venue:	Wolverhampton Civic Hall (capacity 3,000)
Sound check:	6:45–7:15
Doors open:	7:30
Onstage:	8:00–8:30
Hotel:	The Grand (bed and breakfast)
Check out:	9 a.m. SHARP
Hot water:	6 a.m.–6:10 a.m. only (bring own soap and towels)
Breakfast:	Full English, 7:30–8:00

Despite our worst fears, the kebab van handles like a dream. It's a bit shaky round tight corners, a bit noisy when you get above fifty-five but, all in all, it more than does the job. We take it easy. We stop off at a variety of service stations for coffee and cigarettes and bumper packets of wine gums, and we spend a whole series of quality moments selecting our mechanically recovered meat products of the day.

Vince favours the traditional pork pie; I opt for the novelty of mini Scotch eggs filled with chopped egg and cheese; and Matty plumps for a steak-and-potato Ginsters which he foolishly decides to microwave.

"It's gone all soggy."

"How long did it say to cook it for?"

"A minute."

"How long *did* you cook it for?"

"Three minutes."

"Well then, that will probably be the seat of your soggy pastry problems right there."

"Can I have some of your pork pie?"

"No, mate. You can't. There are valuable life lessons to be learnt on this tour and I think we can safely say that over-microwaving your steak-and-potato Ginsters is just the first of many."

"Why didn't you warn me?"

"Well, Matty. That's just it. You have to learn these kind of things for yourself."

We arrive in Wolverhampton in good time for sound check but it takes us longer to find the Civic Hall than we'd hoped. We get lost. We end up taking a mildly interesting—and not altogether intentional—detour to Dudley Castle. Vince's 1982 Collins road atlas is a bit out of date. Traffic on the A459 is a bit busy. Still, if we hadn't got lost we wouldn't have had so much time to admire the beautiful Staffordshire countryside and run around all those Iron Age hilltop forts pretending to be Vikings. We wouldn't have been able to stop off in Moseley for a quick half of bitter and stock up on fresh supplies of tube socks and underpants and soap. Vince insisted. He reckons four pairs each isn't quite enough to cover the whole two weeks.

• • •

The first thing I notice as we drive our customised kebab van up to the stage door is the size of Scarface's trucks. They're huge. Two giant articulated lorries with blue lightning flashes stencilled down the sides stuffed with sound gear and lighting gear and boxes full of spare leather trousers. And then there's Scarface's bus: a sleek silver people carrier with a video system fitted in the front, personal PlayStations drilled into the backs of the seats, and charcoal-tinted windows to shield them from the prying eyes of their fans. It's impressive. It's extravagant. It's demoralising in the extreme.

Inside the venue things are even worse. The whole place is fizzing with pre-gig activity: harassed tour managers shouting into state-of-the-art mobile phones, grouchy sound engineers plugging in leads and humping giant speaker stacks across the floor, lighting designers bathing the stage in various puke-making shades of magenta and lime, assorted back-line technicians stringing guitars and setting up drum kits, fearless lighting technicians hanging off fifty-foot trusses that look moments away from collapse, and a troupe of chubby-faced caterers laying out platters of sausage rolls and sandwiches for the crew.

And there's Ike Kavanagh, right in the middle of it: slouched at a long trestle table, poring over the day's tabloids and tucking into a slap-up three-course dinner with wine. My stomach starts to rumble. I'm suddenly aware that all I've eaten in the last twenty-four hours is cereal, wine gums, and a packet of novelty Scotch eggs.

"What do you think they're eating?" says Matty, eyeing up the smoked-salmon sandwiches.

"Roast beef and Yorkshire pudding, by the looks of it."

"Do you think we'll be allowed to have any?"

"No, Matty. I don't."

"Do you think they'll mind if we nick a doughnut?"

"Yes, Matty, I think they will."

"How do you know?"

"Because it says so on the sign. Food for Scarface personnel only. Not to be eaten by low-life support bands who couldn't afford to pay the tenner a head for the catering."

"Right then."

"Right."

"So what do we do for food?"

"Easy. We wait until Scarface are onstage and then we sneak into their dressing room and eat their rider."

"Gotcha."

I'm pretty sure that Ike has seen us come in but he doesn't bother coming over to say hello. He watches us load our gear in from the van. He watches us stack it up next to the stage and he watches us pack it all up and move it to the other side of the room after the stage manager screams at us for getting in the way. He finishes his meal. He lights up a thick white joint; sticks it between his pale lips and disappears back to his five-star hotel with the rest of his band. Everyone ignores us. It's at least half an hour before anyone bothers to come over and tell us what to do.

It's a very close call. We finish setting up our gear moments before the venue opens its doors and it's clear that we won't have time to do anything approaching a proper sound check. We make sure that the amps are working and the tuners are working and we attempt to butter up the sound guy by offering him a wine gum but I'm not sure that it does us any good. It's always like this on the first night of a tour, he says. We'll definitely get more time to sort things out tomorrow.

We don't bet on it. We pick up our set list, grab our guitars and head up to the dressing room to steady our nerves.

• • •

"Whoa, look at this," says Matty excitedly. "This dressing room is great, isn't it?"

It certainly is. It's the biggest dressing room I've ever been in. It's got chairs and mirrors and showers and a sink and there's even a crate of beer and soft drinks stacked up in a cardboard box by the door. And a bottle of Jack Daniel's. And some bottled water. And some cans of cola-flavoured drink. No sandwiches, though. Not even fish pastes.

It's a little too clean, though. It's definitely too clean. It's not like we're vandals or anything but something about the brand spanking newness of the place is making me feel more nervous than I already do. Maybe if I wrote the name of the band on the wall in Magic Marker. Maybe if I ground a couple of cigarettes into the carpet. Maybe if Matty rolled up his sleeves, unzipped his jeans and took a long satisfying piss in the sink.

"Sorry, guys," he says, smiling at us. "Couldn't hold it. The bogs are miles away."

This is very bad news. There's only ten minutes left before we go on and I still haven't been for my pre-gig shit.

It's almost time. The three of us stand at the side of the stage waiting for the lights to go down and, despite my closely timed, semi-liquid pre-gig shit I'm still feeling nauseous with stage fright. It's huge out there. It's almost a quarter full. It's almost three-quarters empty. The audience look bored. And restless.

"Right then," says Vince, stretching his arms and pouring himself a generous Jack and Coke, "I don't want any fuck-ups. I want everyone giving it a hundred per cent. It's going to sound crap out there tonight so you're just gonna have to rely on what you can hear in your own heads. Got it?"

"Got it."

"Right then. There go the house lights. Let's get on with it."

And off we go.

"Jesus, Danny, where were you?"

"I know, I know. I'm sorry. I lost it."

"Too right you did. You were all over the shop."

"I'm sorry, Vince, I'll be better tomorrow. First-night nerves or something."

"Yeah, well, you'd better be. Me and Matty were on our own up there and it's not on. Snap out of it. Whatever the fuck it is that's wrong with you . . . just snap the fuck out of it."

I don't blame Vince for being pissed off with me. He's actually taking it pretty well considering how badly I messed up. I played like shit tonight. I couldn't concentrate. All I could hear was the feedback from the monitors and the boom from the PA and the whole of the two front rows calling out for Scarface in between songs. All I could see was the sound man reading his paper behind the desk. And the punters walking off to buy more drinks midway through our set. And the row of skinny, teenage, white-faced Goth girls at the front. The ones with the sad panda eyes. The ones with *fuck me Ike* written along their arms in bright red ink.

I screwed up. I should have been thinking about the set. I should have been thinking about the songs and the gig and my responsibility to Matty and Vince. I should have been thinking about the band.

But all I could think about was Alison.

47

The dressing room, 8:45 p.m.: post-gig debriefing.

As is his way on such occasions, Vince decides to give me the benefit of the doubt. He vents his disappointment by kicking the dressing-room door halfway off its hinges and hands me a single night's grace. If I fuck up tomorrow he's unlikely to talk to me for the rest of the tour, but for now he's doing what he can to make me feel better. He offers me the bottle of Jack Daniel's. He tells me it doesn't matter when I know that it does. He says that we'll make sure things sound better onstage tomorrow when we know full well that they won't. We discuss changing the set list around and getting a bit more communication going between the three of us on stage. Vince reckons it might have been having so much room onstage that put me off.

I take it all in. I listen to what he's saying. I wipe the sweat off my neck with a threadbare towel and I sit down and take a long, hot swig of the bourbon. It makes me feel better. It makes me feel like talking. For some reason it makes me tell Vince and Matty all about my abortive day trip to Bruges and the difficulties of spying on people from behind wrought-iron lampposts. Perhaps it was a mistake. It's all Vince can do to stop himself punching my lights out there and then.

• • •

"You toss-wipe," he says, throwing his towel at the mirror and watching it slide on to the floor. "You wanker, you week-old, unwashed jizz-rag. Why didn't you go into the restaurant? Why didn't you let her know you was there? You should have told her you were coming. I told you. Didn't I? Didn't I say that you should have let on to her that you was coming?"

"Yes. You did. I'm an idiot. I shouldn't have tried to surprise her."

"Rubbish," says Vince, tugging on his roll-up. "It weren't nothing to do with surprising her. The reason you never let on you was coming is because you're the type of sad bastard who enjoys hiding behind lampposts and spying on your girlfriend. Serves you right."

"Do you think she's with him now?" I say, tipping up the bottle of Jack Daniel's and pouring a trickle of warm alcohol into my mouth.

"Yeah. I do," says Vince. "I bet she's fucking him. I bet he's putting it in her *right* now. I bet he's got it—"

"*Fuck* off, Vince," I say, standing up and heading towards him with the bottle.

"Well, what d'you expect me to say? I thought we had all this shit worked out before we left. I thought we settled all this over the hummus."

"Yeah, well, maybe we didn't."

Vince pushes his chair to the wall and gets up to meet me. He holds his face centimetres away from mine. I'm not sure which one of us wants to punch the other one more.

"I'm telling you," he says quietly, "you screw this up for me and Matty now and I'll fucking kill you."

"I'd like to see you try."

Shit. That didn't come out right. That came out all wrong. How come my voice goes all high and shrill like that when I'm angry? How come when Vince gets angry he becomes abnormally centred and composed?

"You and Alison will be all right," he says, shoving his index finger into my chest. "The two of you will work things out. In the meantime you've got a job to do here. If you don't want to do it, fine, tell me now. Tell me right now and we can all stop wasting each other's fucking time and go home."

"I don't want to go home, Vince."

"Don't you? Well, I do. I'd love to go home. I'd love to go home right now. I'd like to get back on that motorway, drive all the way back down to London, sit down in my comfy bleedin' armchair and spend the rest of my life in front of the telly watching mindless, fucked-up rubbish about clitorises and incest, and most of all I'd like to stop driving my useless fucking arse round the length and breadth of the country in a clapped-out kebab van pretending that I've still got half a chance in hell of making it."

"So why the fuck don't you, then?"

"Because we agreed, Danny," he says, narrowing his eyes in disgust. "We agreed to give it one last go. We made a deal. It's up to you now. If you want to call it a day just say so. For once in your sodding life make a fucking decision and stick to it."

We take a short pause. Vince turns his back on me and pours himself a drink. Matty fiddles with his necklace and scuffs at the floor with his trainer. I try to imagine that my veins are filled with warm milk instead of nitroglycerine.

"Okay then," I say, trying to slow my heart down by taking deep breaths. "You're right. We've got a job to do. Let's get on with it."

"You're sure?"

"Yeah. I'm sure."

"Right then. That's it. You've made up your mind. I don't want to hear another fuckin' word about it."

• • •

It takes a while for both of us to calm down, but after a couple of minutes and half a bottle of Jack Daniel's I'm almost able to focus my eyes again. Matty is still scuffing the floor. He hates confrontation almost as much as I do, and the pair of us almost coming to blows like this has made him violently uncomfortable. He desperately wants to make things better. He wants to sort things out. I think a small part of him is worried that Vince is going to take a pop at him now that he's decided not to hit me.

"Hey," he says, "sounds like Scarface have just gone on."

"So what?"

"Well . . . none of us fancies going to watch them, do we?"

"No."

"So?"

"So?"

"So why don't we go off to their dressing room and eat their rider like you said?"

"Nice one. Good idea. I'm starving."

And off we go.

Scarface's dressing room is ten times the size of ours. It's got sofas. And a series of anterooms. And a stainless-steel power shower. And a Jacuzzi.

"Where do you think the grub is, then?" says Matty, rubbing his hands together.

"Dunno. Must be through there in one of the other rooms."

"What do you reckon they'll have? Do you think they'll have M&Ms with all the brown ones taken out? Do you think they'll have quails' eggs and caviare and slices of arctic roll?"

"No, mate, I don't. I think they'll have cheese."

"Cheese?"

"Yeah. Fifteen different types of cheese."

• • •

It turns out that Scarface are uncommonly keen on cheese. Presumably the catering ladies bring out more food after the band comes offstage but right now all there is to eat is ten different types of cracker and fifteen different types of cheese.

"Arse. I hate cheese," says Matty sadly.

"What about Cracker Barrel?" says Vince. "Everyone likes a nice bit of Cracker Barrel."

"Not me," says Matty. "I don't like none of it."

We work as carefully as we can. We cut the Brie in half and chop bits off the Stilton and Vince digs about in the Bel Paese with the back of a spoon. Matty has a sniff of the Camembert and says he's going to be sick.

"It smells like girls' pants," he says, turning up his nose and fanning his hand in front of his face.

"How would you know?" says Vince.

"What do you mean, how would I know? I've smelt loads of girls' pants. I lost my virginity when I was thirteen, remember."

"Yeah, but how many girls have you actually slept with? I mean recently? How many girls have you slept with since you've been going out with Kate?"

"None. Woah, what do you mean, Vince? I wouldn't cheat on Kate. What would I want to cheat on Kate for?"

"It's your duty," says Vince, spreading a bit of Dairylea on a cream cracker and swallowing it down in one bite. "You owe it to her to cheat on her."

"Do I?"

"Yes, you do."

"Wow. How come?"

"You're serious about her, right?"

"Yeah, I suppose."

"Well then, it makes sense that you ought to cheat on her now, before you get married or start living together or having kids or anything like that."

"Wow. Kids."

"Exactly."

"I don't know, Vince, I'm not really sure."

"I'm telling you," Vince says, breaking off a square of feta and popping it into his mouth, "now's the time. Now's the time to get it out of your system. That way you'll be more likely to stay faithful to her once you get hitched."

"You reckon?"

"Yes, mate. I do. Definitely. Sow your oats now and you won't want to cheat on her later on. She'll be grateful."

"Will she?"

"Yeah."

"She won't be cross or nothing?"

"No."

Matty tucks into a buttered water biscuit and mulls this over for a while. I can almost hear his brain ticking over as he thinks.

"Maybe you're right," he says, munching distractedly on a slice of Camembert. "Maybe I should try it. I've been thinking lately that I ought to start trying more new things."

"Good thinking, Matty," says Vince, patting him on the back. "It's about time you started broadening your horizons a bit."

"Well . . . maybe just the one, then. Just to prove to myself how much I love Kate."

Matty sneaks off to take a piss in Scarface's Jacuzzi and Vince and I are left alone.

"You bastard," I say, breaking the silence and attempting to get back onside.

"Yeah, well, I ain't going to force him. I'm just pointing him in the right direction, that's all."

"Yeah, but you know what he's like, he'll do anything you tell him to. He looks up to you."

"Does he?"

"Yeah, he does."

"Well, he shouldn't," says Vince miserably.

"Why shouldn't he?"

"Because I'm a git. I'm a first-degree arsehole with a lousy temper who treats his best mates like shit."

"I'm sorry about screwing up the gig, Vince," I say, offering him a swig of my beer.

"Yeah, well," he says, taking the bottle from me, "I'm sorry things are still dodgy between you and Alison."

"I'll get a grip tomorrow, I promise."

"Yeah, mate," he says quietly, "me too."

"Okay then. Good. No one would even know we'd been here."

I'm not sure this is entirely true. It looks like Scarface's cheese plate has been attacked by a troupe of giant mice who've just come off a week-long hunger strike. I'm not sure that sticking the Brie back together with a forkful of creamy Philadelphia has really done the job. Sod it. Who cares? It's been a rough day and none of us can face trawling round the back streets of Wolverhampton looking for cold meat pies and kebabs. It's time to go. Scarface are midway through their final encore and none of us wants to get caught red-handed with a pocketful of cheese.

We head back to the van and load up our gear as quickly as we can. We crack open the remains of the booze, plug one of Vince's compilation tapes into the cassette player, and drive off across town in search of tonight's luxury B&B. It's a perfect end to the day: Wolverhampton's grey concrete skyline slipping away in the distance and "Please Please Please Let Me Get What I Want" by the Smiths oozing out of the speakers just as we hit the ring road.

"I like this song, as it goes," says Vince thoughtfully.

"Yeah," I say. "I like it too."

48

DAY TWO

Drive:	Wolverhampton—Cambridge (115 miles)
Venue:	Corn Exchange (capacity 1,500)
Sound check:	6:45–7:15
Doors open:	7:30
Onstage:	8:00–8:30
Hotel:	To be announced (possibly back of kebab van)

Last night's B&B was supremely awful. For one thing it was locked up when we got there. We had to ring the bell for ages. We had to bash the knocker and shout through the letterbox and it wasn't until we started throwing handfuls of grit and garden stones at the top-floor window that anybody bothered to come down to let us in.

The owner looked like a bit of a weirdo. He was wearing paisley pyjamas and velvet leopard-print slippers, and for some reason he had a dirty white bandage wrapped right round the top of his head.

At first I thought he was planning to butcher us with an axe or strangle us with his bandage but it turned out he was quite glad to see us. He showed us to our room and called us his "boys." He wanted to know if we fancied some cocoa, and he was most put out when we told him that we didn't.

It was quite hard to get rid of him. It was only Vince asking him what time we should come down for breakfast in the morning that made him stop fiddling with his bollocks through the slit in his pyjama pants and get up off Matty's bed and leave. It was only then that we put down our bags and took stock of the room. The kind of room that's frequented by travelling salesman called Warren and middle-aged prostitutes called Keith. The kind of room that has mould on the carpet and damp patches on the ceiling and crusty, yellow cum stains on the sheets.

"Is this what I think it is?" says Matty, pulling back the sheet on the one double bed.

"Jesus, yeah, it is," says Vince. "Help me get them curtains down. We'll pull 'em off the window and sleep on top of them instead."

And so we did. Me and Vince lying fully clothed on top of the filthy chintz curtains and Matty near naked on a pile of dusty blankets on the floor. I didn't sleep a wink all night. I was too worried about catching nits. Or VD. Or TB. Or a particularly virulent head cold. It didn't seem to bother Vince, though. As soon as we switched out the lights he was snoring like a walrus full of fish. And so was Matty. Who also grinds his teeth. Loudly.

Today is going to be a much better day than yesterday. It has to be. No matter that we were forced out of our room at 7:30 this morning by an overzealous cleaning lady with a yellow feather duster and a mop. No matter that the full English breakfast neglected to include bacon or mushrooms or toast. Or black pudding. At least there was a tasty starter of tinned tomato juice and half a sugared grapefruit. At least Mad Bandage Man only spent twenty minutes asking us how we like our eggs and telling us why he's never seen the need to leave Wolverhampton. He likes it here. He likes the Midlands. He also likes wearing a bandage on his head to keep out all the microwaves.

I never thought I'd be quite this relieved to see the inside of a mobile kebab van.

Vince has made plans for the rest of the day. He thinks it's vital to map out our spare time so we don't get bored. That's one of the crap things about being in a support band: you get slung out of your bed-and-breakfast at the crack of dawn and you've got ten long hours left to kill before you can head up to the next venue and do your sound check.

Vince thinks we should try and make the best of it. He thinks we should take the opportunity to look at some prime English heritage sites as we travel up and down the country, and he's particularly keen to stop off at Hadrian's Wall on our way up to Scotland at the weekend. Matty is quite keen to stop off in Ashby de la Zouch. He doesn't know why. He just likes the sound of it.

The first thing we do is stop off at the nearest service station for a quick wash and brush-up. The B&B showers were freezing cold and carpeted with deep-pile pubic hair, and we all feel much better after we've cleaned up in the service station urinals and spent a quality moment perusing the contents of the petrol station shop.

"Wow, look at this," says Matty excitedly. "Can we buy this?"

"How much is it?"

"Five pounds fifty."

"What is it?"

"It's a cricket kit."

"Is it?"

"Yeah, look. It's got a ball and stumps and a little plastic bat and we could go and have a bit of a knockabout, couldn't we? After lunch."

"Okay then. You're on. You buy the cricket kit, Danny can go pay for the petrol, and I'll get me map out and find us somewhere good to stop for grub."

Vince rubs his stomach, lights a cigarette and stifles a small belch. All three of us are full to the brim with pub lunch. We can barely move. Vince found this great little place just outside Leamington Spa that does real ale and real cider and giant Yorkshire puddings filled to the top with tinned chicken curry. They were excellent. And not at all stodgy. And there's quite a trick to eating them right. For a start, you have to make sure you eat a substantial portion of the tinned chicken curry before you think about tackling the sides of your giant Yorkshire pudding. It's a very tricky business. If you're not careful and you make the mistake of eating the sides too soon the curry has a tendency to leak out over the top. It's a bit like breaching a dam. Only with curry. Instead of water. As Matty found out.

"Shit. My pudding's burst."

"That's because you ate the sides first."

"But my curry's gone all over the table."

"So I see."

"Can I have some of yours, Danny?"

"No you can't."

"Why not?"

"Because I'm enjoying it."

"Vince, why didn't you tell me not to eat the sides first?"

"Like I said, Matty. You have to learn these kind of things for yourself."

"Can we go and play cricket now, then?" he says miserably.

"Come on then," says Vince. "I don't see why not."

We set up our kiddies' cricket set in the fields opposite the pub and spend a couple of quality hours pretending that we're playing for the world cup at Lords. It's a very close match. Matty is Zimbabwe, I'm Pakistan, and Vince is the West Indies.

"Why do I have to be Zimbabwe?"

"Because you do."

"But they're rubbish. Why can't I be England or Australia?"

"Because we said."

"Why can't I be something cool like Sri Lanka or something?"

"I told you. The barman from the Moby Dick already bagsied it."

"Well, can I have a go at batting yet? I've been fielding for ages."

"In a minute, Matty. In a minute."

It's a top afternoon and I manage to score three hundred and fifty runs before the barman from the Moby Dick finally bowls me out LBW. It definitely wasn't LBW, though. That was definitely a deeply suspect call on Matty's part. If I didn't know better I'd say he only declared me out so that he could have a quick go at batting.

The West Indies win the cup. Vince is 384 not out. He scores sixteen sixes in a row. He belts up and down the length of our makeshift pitch like a pissed hare on roller skates and he knocks our plastic crimson-coloured ball halfway to Saffron Walden and back.

Gary Sobers, eat your heart out.

• • •

"How you feeling, Matty?" I say, examining the grass stains on my jeans and tucking into the remains of a cheese-and-pickle sandwich in the back of the van.

"Knackered. I'm totally knackered."

"Sorry you didn't get to bowl, Matty."

"Or bat," he says emphatically. "I didn't get to bat either."

"Yeah, well, never mind that now," says Vince. "I've got an idea. How's about we have a quick kip before we carry on down to Cambridge. Forty winks. Sleep off some of the beer. Get ourselves psyched up for tonight's gig. What do you say?"

"Nice one . . . mega . . . very good idea."

"Right then," says Vince, parking up outside the Corn Exchange and switching off the engine. "Who wants to bet me that we don't get to sound-check tonight either?"

"I do," says Matty, putting up his hand.

"You bet that we *do* get one?"

"Er . . . *yeah*?"

"Right then. Ten quid says you're wrong."

We spend Matty's tenner on a bottle of vodka and a carton of cranberry juice and neck the lot in the dressing room right after we come offstage. We weren't bad tonight. Much better than yesterday. An afternoon of top-quality bonding has really helped with my concentration onstage. I was good. I played really well. The sound man still isn't doing us any favours and Vince is still having a bit of trouble pitching his voice over all the feedback but I could tell that some of the crowd were really getting into it. A few of them even clapped. A couple of them were almost moshing.

"So, what do you think we should do now?" says Matty, rubbing his hands together.

"How do you mean?"

"Well, should we go and see Scarface do their set or should we go back to their dressing room and nick all their cheese again?"

We don't hesitate. We speak as one. We can almost smell it now. Ten different types of cracker and fifteen different types of cheese.

I can't wait to tell Alison what a great time I'm having.

49

"I'm having a great time."

"Are you?"

"Yes."

"What have you been up to?"

"You know, loads of stuff. Playing cricket, eating pies, running away from loonies with bandages on their heads; fighting with Vince, taking the piss out of Matty . . . stealing all of Scarface's cheese."

"I see."

"It's quite dangerous, actually."

"Is it?"

"Yeah, they'd probably chuck us off the tour if they found out."

"Right. Sounds fascinating."

"Yes, well, it's not all cricket and cheese, you know. We *have* been doing the gigs as well."

"I'm very glad to hear it. How have they been going?"

"Not bad. The first night was a bit dodgy but tonight was pretty amazing."

"Have the crowds been okay?"

"They've been fantastic. We've had them moshing up and down and clapping their hands and all sorts."

"Good. I'm pleased it's going well."

"Yeah, it is."

"Good."

"Good . . . Alison?"

"Yes?"

"Did I tell you that I'm having a great time yet?"

"Yes, Danny, you did."

The line goes quiet for a moment. I feed another pound coin into the call-box to make sure I don't run out of money and wait patiently for Alison to pick up the threads of our conversation. She doesn't say anything. I wonder if she's still pissed off with me over the famous Belgians incident. I wonder if she's upset that I'm managing to have such a good time without her. I wonder why she sounds like she hates my fucking guts.

"So," she says finally, "have you managed to catch up with Ike yet?"

"Um . . . no. Not really."

"Why not?"

"Well, I don't know. He's very busy. The whole of Scarface had to be helicoptered up to *Top of the Pops* and back before the gig tonight and they're always doing interviews before they go on-stage and 'meet and greets' when they come off and besides . . . we're sort of avoiding them."

"Why?"

"I told you, on account of the *cheese*."

"The *cheese*?"

"Come on, Alison," I say, getting agitated, "keep up. At least pretend that you're interested in what I'm saying to you."

"I'm trying to, Danny, but, you know . . . it all sounds like such an incredible whirlwind. You're doing so many crazy, spurof-the-moment, rock-and-roll things it's hard for me to keep track."

"There's no need to be sarcastic."

"Yeah, well, you started it."

"Yeah. You're right. I probably did."

There's fifty pence left on the call and I'm wondering if there's any point feeding more money into the meter. She clearly doesn't want to talk to me. She's clearly not interested in what I have to say. I'm beginning to wish I hadn't bothered. I'm beginning to wish I hadn't badgered Vince to drive round Cambridge for the best part of forty-five minutes looking for the last phone box on earth that was still making outgoing calls.

"So," I say, feeding a circumspect twenty-pence piece into the phone and kicking at a piece of broken glass with my foot, "are you still coming back for the London gig or what?"

"Of course I am," she says. "What kind of a question is that? You know I wouldn't miss it. Not for anything."

"Yeah . . . I know. I just thought . . ."

"What did you think, Danny, that I couldn't be bothered?"

"Dunno. I just thought—"

"I mean, how long is this going to go on for?" she says crossly. "How long are you going to be pissed off at me for not coming home last weekend? I said I was sorry. I've apologised a hundred more times than you deserve and . . . fuck it, Danny, I've got responsibilities too."

"I know you have. I didn't mean—"

"I can't just drop everything and jump on a train every time you want me to come back to London and hold your hand."

"What do you mean?" I say, getting angry. "I just wanted to see you, that's all. I *really* wanted to see you."

"No you didn't, Danny," she spits.

"I did. What are you talking about?"

"If you'd wanted to see me you would have done."

"How?"

"You could have come over here."

"To *Bruges?*"

"Yes, Danny, to Bruges. It's not that far away. It's not the Arctic fucking Circle."

"But you were *working.*"

"Not the whole time. I had the evenings free."

"Well how was I to know?"

"You weren't . . . it just would have been nice if you'd asked me, that's all."

"Alison?"

"Yes."

"I'm not having that great a time."

"I know," she says. "I didn't think you were."

I pocket the rest of my change, slam the receiver into the coin meter with as much force as I can muster and head back across the road to the van. Matty and Vince are leant up against a low wall, chatting and drinking and smoking cigarettes, and they both go quiet when they see me coming.

"How was that, then?" says Vince, offering me a drag on his roll-up.

"Fine," I lie. "She sends her love."

"Everything's okay, then?"

"Yeah. Everything's fine."

"It's okay if you want to talk about it or something."

"No, Vince. I don't think I do."

He knows better than to ask me again.

"Right then," he says. "I thought it would be a good idea if we made do for tonight. Save ourselves some money, kip down in the back of the van and spend the extra cash on a better B&B tomorrow."

"Sounds great."

"You don't mind, then?"

"No," I say. "I don't mind at all."

We make ourselves as comfortable as we can. Vince unties a couple of moth-eaten sleeping bags that we bought after the bed-and-breakfast cum-sheets fiasco, and we move some of the gear into the front seats and spread them out in the back of the van. No one says very much. We park up next to a streetlight and play a couple of hands of poker, but none of us is really in the mood.

Vince brings out the bottle of Jack Daniel's that we saved from the gig and we pass it round in silence. I can hear the sizzle from Matty's cigarette as he pushes it into his empty beer bottle. I can hear gangs of pissed-up students staggering out of the pubs and making their way back home. A couple of them bang their hands on the sides of the van and try rocking it off the kerb as they walk past us. And then it all goes quiet again.

"Anybody mind if I put on some music?" I say, searching through the piles of tapes on the floor.

"No, mate," says Vince, "you go right ahead."

I know exactly what I'm looking for. Grandaddy, *Under the Western Freeway*.

"Everything Beautiful Is Far Away."

50

DAY EIGHT

Drive:	Newcastle—Glasgow (148 miles)
Venue:	Barrowlands (capacity 1,900)
Sound check:	6:45–7:15
Doors open:	7:15
Onstage:	7:45–8:15
Hotel:	THE GLASGOW HILTON!
Check out:	MIDDAY!
Hot water:	CONSTANT!
Breakfast:	Full English, SERVED IN ROOM!
Amenities:	INDOOR POOL! SWEDISH SAUNA! PAY-PER-VIEW MOVIES! HOTEL PORN!

So much has happened in the last five days that I'm not quite sure where to begin. For a start, we've finally made friends with Scarface. Everyone except for Ike. It turns out his own band hate him almost as much as we do—on account of him taking sole credit for writing all their songs and keeping the rest of them on a crappy wage—and they're quite happy to have some new faces to hang out and get pissed with.

They're not a bad bunch. In fact, when we told them that we didn't have any food on our rider and that we were sleeping in the back of our kebab van most nights they went out of their way to try to help us. They said we were welcome to come backstage and eat their crackers any time we wanted. They've been really generous. They've got more champagne than they know what to do with. And spirits. And Jammy Dodgers. And chicken wings. And pharmaceutical-grade cocaine.

Even better than that, their tour manager, Malcolm, has managed to score us rooms in some of their top-notch hotels. The band have a personal travel agent that negotiates them special room rates, so now we're spending every other night in the lap of luxury: one night in the mobile kebab van, the next night in a super, swanky five-star on the cheap.

But that's not even the best of it. The best of it is that Matty has become a brand-new man. He's taken to after-gig slutting like a cat to its very first litter box. He's incredible. You ought to see him go. He's slept with four different girls already and, the way things are going, it looks like Vince is definitely on to win our bet. It's all Scarface's fault. Thanks to Malcolm combing the front two rows for groupies every night and inviting them all backstage after the gig, there's a distinct surfeit of girls. The ones that Ike doesn't want get passed on to the rest of his band. The ones the band don't want get passed on down the line to us. When I say *us*, of course, I really just mean Matty. I'm completely out of commission and Vince doesn't seem to be having very much luck. Matty has a theory about this. He thinks it's because Vince spends too much time talking to them.

"Of course," says Matty, mulling over his lavish room service breakfast (he got drunk last night and ticked everything on the order form, including the prunes), "the main thing I've realised is that they don't want a lot of chat. They just want to get down to business. That's where you're going wrong, Vince. You don't want to start talking to them about *Too-Rye-Aye* being great and *Astral Weeks* being seventeen different types of shite. You don't want to start bothering them about your views on transitional shoes, and you definitely don't want to be asking them what they think about the philosophical implications of quantus physics."

"*Quantum* physics, Matty. It's quantum, not quantus."

"Right, whatever. The thing is, it's best to play it cool. Tell them they've got a nice dress on or something."

"A nice dress?"

"Yeah, or nice eyes maybe."

"*Really?*"

"Yeah. Or sometimes you don't even have to bother. Ritchie from Scarface just says 'Do you fancy coming to the toilets and giving me a quick blow-job?' Just like that. No hello, no preamble, no how d'you do. Nothing."

"So what you're saying is that I should play it thick?"

"Yes, well . . . no, not exactly *thick*."

"You reckon I should treat every girl I meet like she's a bag of chopped mince, then, do you?"

"No, 'course not, I didn't say that."

"Okay then. What exactly are you saying? Where *precisely* is it that you think I'm going wrong?"

"Well," says Matty cunningly, "that's just it, Vince. You have to learn these sorts of things for yourself."

That did it. He's on a mission now. He's definitely on a mission.

"Phwoar . . . Vince . . . steady on . . . you smell like a poodle at a pet parlour."

"Yeah, well, you know, you have to make the effort, don't you."

"Is it for the groupies or the journalist?"

"What do you think?"

"Well, I don't know. Maybe if you shag the journalist we'll get a better review."

"I ain't going to shag the journalist, Danny. No one is."

"How do you mean? I thought Scarface were lining him up with a couple of women."

"Yeah, well, they always do that. Doesn't do him any good, though."

"Why not?"

"He can't get it up."

"Can't he?"

"No, he's well known for it. All the bands line him up with girls to boost his ego and that, but Malcolm reckons he's impotent."

"Maybe he just doesn't fancy the girls."

"No, mate, he does. Cries his eyes out apparently."

"Wow. Poor sod."

"Yeah. Poor sod."

"Vince?"

"Yeah?"

"Do you reckon the fact that he can't get it up is likely to make him give us a better or worse review?"

"Don't know, mate. All I know is that I haven't got laid for five months myself and if I don't manage it tonight I'm hanging up me lead singer badge and going home for good."

"Hey, don't worry, Vince. I'm sure it'll happen for you soon. You just need to relax a bit more."

"Matty, did anyone give *you* permission to speak?"

"No, Vince. They didn't."

"Well then?"

"Right. Sorry. I'll shut up."

• • •

Tonight's gig is the best one yet. We've been doing the odd local radio interview here and there and we've managed a couple of half-decent write-ups in the local press, and word seems to be getting round that we might be worth turning up early for. The crowds are definitely beginning to get into it. They're cheering more and moshing more and a lot of them seem to be talking about us in the crowd. I know. I've checked. All we need now is to convince the sound man to start giving us a break and we might actually be on to something.

"Malcolm," I say, as we stand at the side of the stage waiting for Scarface to go on, "do you think you could have a quick word with the sound guy again? I know he's not going to make us sound as good as Scarface but, you know, if you could just get him to turn us up a bit and sort out all the feedback problems we've been having."

"I'll see what I can do, Danny. I promise. I'll have another word."

"Really?"

"Yeah," he says uneasily. "But . . . it's not that simple."

"Why not?"

"Well," he says, taking his Maglite out of his pocket and signalling the stage manager to bring down the house lights, "do I have to spell it out for you?"

"*Ike?*"

"I didn't say that."

"It is, isn't it? Ike's put the word out that he wants us sounding like shit up there."

"Yeah, well," he says cautiously, "you didn't hear it from me."

It's a big night back in the dressing room; we're exactly halfway through the tour and everyone is clearly on for a bit of a bender.

It's a fairly typical scene. Ritchie from Scarface is cutting out lines of cocaine on the buffet table, Malcolm is handing round plastic beakers of champagne spiked with vodka, Matty is sitting in the corner chatting to the music journalist, and Vince is messing with his hair and changing into his best pulling shirt.

A few groupies have already made their way to the dressing room courtesy of the special backstage passes Malcolm has given them. The passes have numbers scratched on the back in red ink. Malcolm has already graded them. And marked them out of ten.

The party starts to move up a gear. The whole of Scarface are lining up for their groupies and their nostrilfuls of coke but I don't bother joining the queue. I need to get out of here. I need to get some fresh air. I need to take a walk and clear my head, and most of all I need to come up with a way to stop Ike from screwing us over onstage.

It takes me a good half hour to walk back to the hotel, and by the time I arrive at the bar everyone is already three-quarters cut. Ritchie is playing the theme tune from *Rocky 4* on the hotel piano and the rest of Scarface are sat around drinking tequila slammers and picking their way through a plate of dried-up sandwiches and crisps. Vince is nowhere to be seen, and I'm hoping that maybe he's finally got lucky. Matty is off his tits. He's clearly had a bang or two on Scarface's drugs and he's sitting at their table nursing a pint while Ike sips measures of ten-quid-a-throw whisky and dishes out words of wisdom to his doting entourage: the time he bent a low-league supermodel over the back of a toilet seat and fucked her up the arse; the time he told a fat teenage groupie that she was ugly but that he was going to do her a favour and screw her anyway; the time he stuffed a rotten banana down his pissed drummer's underpants so that he woke up the next morning thinking he'd shat himself. Everyone thinks he's hilarious. Obviously.

As I get closer to Scarface's table I can tell that Ike is pretty fucked up. His pupils are badly blown and he's having trouble focusing as he watches me cross the room. He has an idea. Something is amusing him. His molten, rubber face struggles to support the beginnings of a smile, and he decides to turn his attention to Matty. He wants to chat. He has some extra-special words of wisdom. Just for him.

"Listen up, Matthew," he drawls, topping his glass up with Scotch. "I might not bother to talk to you for the rest of this tour so pay close attention."

"Right. Wow. Okay."

"It's simple, this music-business game."

"Is it?"

"Yeah, dude, it is. One rule. All the girls have to want to *shag* you and all the blokes have to want to *be* you. Easy as that."

"Right . . . cool," says Matty, nodding gently over his pint glass. "I see what you mean."

"That's where you're going wrong with this little band of yours."

"Is it?"

"Yeah. You care about the music too much. Especially your fucking singer, what's his name, Gordon, is it? Anyway, he's got it all wrong. It's all about the look. The look is everything, man. It's five per cent talent, ten per cent slog, eighty per cent image, and ten per cent luck. You wanna remember that. Now then, how's about you be a good boy and run over to the bar and fetch me another little drink?"

I can't stand it. I can't stand to see him humiliating Matty like this. Something snaps. Maybe it's because he picked on me in school for all those years; maybe it's the injustice of him making it big instead of me. Maybe it's because he's a coked-up, witless little fuck who can't even add up to a hundred.

I move quickly. I step into Matty's seat and make a grab for Ike's wrist as he reaches over for his cigarettes.

"You're wrong," I say, picking up his soft-pack of Marlboro and helping myself.

"I don't think I am, dude," he says, trying (and failing) to meet my gaze.

"Yeah you are," I say carefully. "It's all about talent. Sad thing is, you haven't got any. That's why you're paying your sound guy to screw us over night after night."

"Bullshit, man," he says, grinning at me. "You're just crap. You sound like shit coz you play like shit."

"That's not true," I say, leaning across the table and exhaling a thick stream of smoke past his face. "You're scared, Ike. You took us on tour because you were too scared to take anyone else. You thought we'd be a soft touch. You didn't think we'd be any kind of competition."

Ike snorts and fumbles to light a cigarette with his shaky fingers.

"But that wasn't the way it worked out, was it? Turns out that we're ten times the band you are and you're so threatened by it you go out of your way to have us fucked over. You're a coward, Ike. A miserable fucking coward. Always were, always will be."

And then I get up. And walk away. I don't know what came over me. I've never done anything like that in my life. Perhaps the whole Bruges débâcle has affected me more than I thought. Perhaps this would be a good time to celebrate my newfound courage with a hotel sandwich and a well-earned drink. Perhaps this would be a good time to go back up to the room and call my girlfriend.

51

"Hey, it's me."

"*Danny?*"

"Yeah, sorry. I didn't wake you up, did I?"

"No, it's okay," she says. "I'm really glad you called."

She sounds sleepy. She sounds sexy and husky and very far away, and I think the fact that she was just about to go to bed has caught her slightly off guard. She doesn't seem as cross with me as she was. She asks me how things are going with the band and I ask her how things are going with her job, and even though there's a part of both of us that is still treading on eggshells, we have a better conversation than we've managed for days.

Maybe it's because we avoid talking about anything sensitive. Maybe it's because I summon up my last morsel of pride and avoid mentioning anything to do with Didier. I stick to the basics. I tell her all about the contents of our well-pillaged minibar. I tell her about the flat-screen television on the wall and the miniature speakerphone in the loo, and I tell her all about Ike screwing us over onstage. She sounds sympathetic. She says we should splash out and organise our own sound man for the London show. She says that she's looking forward to seeing me.

I tell her that I'm missing her too.

• • •

As soon as I put down the phone to Alison I hear a volley of swearing from the corridor. It's Vince. He's forgotten his key. Again.

"Sorry, Danny," he says after I let him in. "It's them fucking bits of plastic. I can never seem to keep track of 'em."

"Don't worry about it," I say, handing him a can of beer and flicking the telly on. "Where've you been anyway?"

"Oh, you know. Here and there."

"Out on the shag?"

"No. Not as such."

"What d'you mean, not *as such*?"

"What I say. Not as such."

Vince opens his beer and I wait for him to explain himself. He looks knackered. He looks troubled. He looks every inch of his thirty-three and a half years.

"What is it with me, eh?" he says after a while. "How come I can't get me end away any more? I'm not a bad-looking bloke, am I? I used to do all right. I was pulling all the time in our Agent Orange days. Wasn't I? Wasn't I always pulling in our Agent Orange days?"

"Yeah, Vince. You were."

"So what's wrong with me now, then? It's my hair, isn't it? It's because I'm losing my hair."

"Vince, you're not losing your hair."

"Of course I am, you soft bastard. Look."

"What? There's nothing to look at."

"Exactly."

"No, I mean it, it's fine. I'm telling you, Vince, there's nothing wrong with your fucking hair. There never has been."

"Well," he says, draining his first beer and opening another, "that's even worse, then."

"How? How can it be worse?"

"Because it means it's something more serious. Something fundamental. If it's not my hair then it must mean she just thought I was a prat."

"Vince?"

"Yeah."

"You want to tell me what happened?"

"Not particularly, no."

"You're going to, though, right?"

"Absolutely."

"A *spiteful hand-job*?"

"Yeah. Nearly had the end of me knob off, she did. I feel like I've got sunburn of the knob. It don't make no sense—Matty's busy getting himself a knicker collection to rival Tom Jones's and all I'm getting is a toothy snog and a spiteful bleedin' hand-job."

"How old was she?"

"I don't know. What difference does it make?"

"How *old* was she?"

"I dunno. I *dunno*."

"Vince?"

"Twenty-three."

"Twenty-three?"

"Eighteen."

"Eighteen?"

"Seventeen, then, she was seventeen. She was seventeen years old with skinny tits and long hair and a bum like a bagful of conkers. What you gonna do, have me arrested?"

"'Course not."

"Good, because the last thing I need is you coming over all moral majority on me."

"So," I say, watching Vince pace round the room, "where is she now, then?"

"I took her home, didn't I?"

"Did you?"

"Yeah. How sad is that? I got her a minicab but the bloke looked sort of dodgy so I got in the cab with her and saw her home. Just to make sure. You know. I didn't want nothing to happen to her."

"Far, was it?"

"Yes, mate, it was. It was very fucking far. It was halfway to bleedin' Edinburgh."

"Grateful, was she?"

"Not particularly, no. She said I was boring."

"Boring?"

"Yeah. She said I was less fun than her rheumatic granddad and was there any way I could sort it out for her to shag one or two of Scarface at Monday night's gig in Leeds. She said I owed her one."

"How come?"

"Well," he says gloomily, "turns out she only done me the spiteful in the first place coz she thought I might introduce her to Ike."

Vince slumps down on the bed and tucks into his second beer. He stares at the floor and tugs hard on his cigarette, and by the way he's pummelling his temples with his fingertips, I can tell that he's trying to make some sense out of it all.

"Still," he says, taking some tobacco out of his pocket and starting on another roll-up, "it's my own fault. I mean, it's rubbish, isn't it, it's sad, a bloke like me, running around smelling of poodles and trying to get off with sarcastic teenagers half my age?"

"Yeah," I say, opening a packet of peanuts, "I suppose it is."

"I should be married or something, shouldn't I? I should be thinking about having some kids or something like that; before

I'm too old to play football with them; before I'm too old to teach them how to play the guitar. Before I'm too old to pick the little fuckers up."

"Did you ever think about having kids with Liz?" I say, offering Vince a peanut.

"Yeah," he says, "I did. I even asked her to marry me once. I did the whole palaver—flowers, candles, 1998 Argos catalogue so she could choose herself a ring—"

"What did she say?"

"She said she wasn't ready, she said she had a whole lot more living to do before she settled down with someone like me. She said I had a pessimistic nature. Said I was the worst kind of person to live with because I was always looking on the worst possible side of everything."

"Wow, Vince," I say, offering him another peanut, "I never realised."

"Yeah, well, I didn't like to say. I was pretty crushed, as it goes. I mean, how could she say that? To me? How could she say I've got a pessimistic nature when she knows 'Come On Eileen' is one of my top-five favourite songs of all time?"

We while away the next couple of hours listening to music and mulling over the multitude of ways in which our lives have gone wrong. We get depressed. We switch to listing the ways in which our lives have gone well. All I can think of is Alison. All Vince can think of is that he hasn't become an alcoholic.

It's almost 5:30. The sun is coming up and we're both running out of things to say, and I'm just about to call it a night and crash when Matty comes staggering through the door like a newly born foal.

"Out of my way," he says ominously, "I'm going to puke my ring."

He's as good as his word. He belts through the bathroom door, trips over the rubber mat, falls to his knees and throws up a night's worth of alcohol and cheese.

"Are you all right in there, Matt?"

"*Eughghghgh*," he says grimly.

"*Eughghghgh*," he says again.

"Do you think we should go in there?" I say, hoping that he's not going to choke on his own vomit.

"No," says Vince. "Leave him to it. He'll feel better once he's got it all up."

Vince fetches a couple of Panadol and a glass of water and we both sit in silence waiting for him to come out. I can tell Vince is feeling guilty. We both are. We shouldn't have encouraged him to get so wasted every night. We shouldn't have encouraged him to cheat on Kate. I should have made him come back up to the room with me instead of leaving him down there after my showdown with Ike.

"How you feeling?" I say when he finally emerges from the bathroom.

"Not very well," he says, sitting down next to Vince and taking a sip of the water. "I think I had one too many Drambuies and Coke."

"I don't think it was the Drambuies that fucked you, Matty."

"Wasn't it?"

"No. It was probably the coke."

"I feel a bit fed up, Vince."

"Do you?"

"Yeah, I do. I don't know why."

"It's the drugs, Matty," says Vince, helping him to his feet. "They make you depressed."

"Do they?"

"Yeah. Soon as you stop taking them they do. It's a mug's

game, mate. You want to be careful. You don't want to end up a sad cokehead like Ike, do you?"

"No, I don't."

"There you go, then."

"Vince?"

"Yeah."

"Why didn't you warn me?"

"Like I said, Matty. You have to learn these sorts of things for yourself."

And then Matty pukes up again. All over Vince's favourite transitional shoes.

52

By week two of the tour the gloss is beginning to wear thin. It's a two-hundred-mile drive down to Leeds, there's a distinct smell of autumn in the air, and while none of us is brave enough to say it out loud, all three of us are beginning to wonder why we've come.

No one is saying very much. Vince has taken to playing a lot of Nick Cave, I've taken to studying the 1982 *Collins Road Atlas of Britain*, and Matty is slowly gearing up for an apology about last night. It feels like we're extras from *The Wizard of Oz*. None of us knows where the Emerald City is, but we're all pretty sure it's going to be crap when we get there.

"Sorry about last night, guys," says Matty from the back of the van.

"Don't worry about it, mate."

"No, I mean it. Thanks for looking after me and that. Thanks for letting me sleep in the bathroom all night and helping me out when I was going through my downer."

"No problem, Matty," says Vince. "So, what did it feel like, then?"

"What did what feel like?"

"Being depressed."

"Dunno. It was strange. I've never had it before. I kind of liked it in a weird sort of way."

"Don't worry, mate," says Vince ominously. "There's plenty more where that came from."

"Right. That's good to know. And Vince?"

"Yeah?"

"I'm really sorry about puking up on your shoes."

"No sweat, Matty, they came up lovely."

"Did they?"

"Yeah. Nice bit of shower gel and a quick scrub with your toothbrush and they came up good as new."

"Cool. I was a bit worried there for a minute. I thought I might have ruined them for good."

"So, how, are you feeling now?" I say, offering Matty some of my Tizer.

"Yeah, better, you know. Not sick, anyway."

"Sounds like you had quite a night. Did you find yourself any more groupies to sleep with?"

"Not really," he says, finishing my drink and screwing up the empty can, "and to be honest, Danny, I'm thinking of putting a stop to all that."

"How come?"

"On account of Claire," he says wistfully.

"Claire?"

"Yeah, Claire from Newcastle. The one with the brown eyes and the hair with the sparkly clips in it."

"Are you trying to tell me you've fallen for one of them?"

"I'm not sure. But, well, the thing is she's really nice. She's much nicer to me than Kate is."

"That's not the way it works, Matty. You're not supposed to fall for them, you're supposed to love 'em and leave 'em. It's the rules."

"I know. But I like her, Vince. I think I might just stop off and give her a quick call after we get down to Leeds. I think I might want to see her again or something. I've been thinking that I might want to finish things with Kate when we get back to London."

Vince and I exchange glances. This wasn't the way it was supposed to happen. It probably means that our bet is null and void.

It cheers us right up.

"So, Matty," I say, "you never finished telling us about last night. What happened with you and Ike after I went up to the room?"

"Nothing, really. After you gave him what for he decided to moan his arse off at me all night. He's a twat. He spent the whole time complaining about how hard his life was. How hard it is being famous and that. Pissed me right off."

"Leave it out, Matty," says Vince from the front of the van, "nothing pisses you off."

"Well, that did. I mean, he's going on and on about how hard it is losing his privacy and how hard it is having to live up to everyone's expectations all the time, and I just thought . . ."

"What did you think?"

"Well, I just thought . . . what a load of old hooey. You know, if you don't want your private jet, give it to me. If you don't want your house in Hollywood, give it to me. If you don't want everyone following you about and giving you money and sending you stuff for free . . ."

"Give it to you?"

"Yeah. Give it to me. Coz it's nonsense, isn't it?"

"Is it?"

"Yeah, it is. It's selfish. I've wanted to be in a famous band since I was six years old. Ever since my dad showed me a tape of Keith Moon blowing up his drum kit and wrecking Pete Townshend's ears. I've dreamt about it for years. I've spent all this time wondering what it would be like if I finally got to be a drummer in a famous band and there's Ike stoned off his nuts, chucking his weight around and telling me that it's not even worth it when you get there."

"And that pisses you off, does it?"

"Yeah. It does. Because it's not even true. It's great being famous. I can tell. I'd be totally mega at it. I wouldn't moan about it one bit. And the way I see it, he should be grateful he's got it in the first place."

"Grateful?"

"Yeah. Because he's crap, isn't he? He can't sing, he can't play, he doesn't even write any of his own songs, and the thing is he should make up his mind. He should shit or get off the pot. Because that's the thing, isn't it, if you don't like it you can always stop. Can't you? It's like me with all them groupies I've been shagging. If you don't like it you can always call it a day."

We can't believe what we're hearing. We can't believe this is Matty talking. Vince doesn't waste any time. He pulls the kebab van over on to the hard shoulder and reaches over to shake Matty by the hand.

"I'm proud of you, grasshopper," he says turning round to congratulate him. "You have studied from the master and you learnt well. It may almost be time to send you out into the big bad world on your own."

"Wow, do you mean it, Vince?"

"Yes, Matty, I do. A couple more years and we'll make a full-blown cynic out of you yet."

"Cool. Nice one. Thanks very much."

• • •

I'm just about to join in with the mutual congratulations when something suddenly dawns on me.

"Hold on, Matty," I say, "what was that last bit you said about Ike?"

"What bit?"

"That bit about him not writing any of his own songs?"

"Oh yeah, didn't I tell you? That journalist bloke told me, the one with no knob. Apparently his record company send him down to this château in the south of France twice a year. It's like a factory or something. All these fat old blokes in cardigans sit around drinking Beaujolais and writing his poncy songs for him."

"You're kidding."

"No, it's true. No Knob's going to expose the whole thing in his review. He really liked us, though. He thought we were ace. He thought we were one of the best bands he'd seen in ages. He thought we were a million zillion times better than Scarface. Maybe it's because I let him get off with that girl who was after me all night. She was really good looking. She did him a deal. She said if he didn't manage to get it up he didn't have to pay her . . . Hey, does anyone fancy stopping at the next service station to see if they've got curly fries?"

Against all the odds; it turns out that we do.

53

It's the last day of the tour. I should be excited. I *am* excited. I'm probably more excited than I've ever been in my life. Our gig review came out yesterday afternoon and it turns out that No Knob was as good as his word. He completely slated Scarface. It was brutal. He couldn't actually come out and say that Ike doesn't write his own songs but the implication was obvious to everyone who read it.

It was fantastic. You should have seen Ike's face when I showed it to him. He looked like his dog had just died. Maybe I shouldn't have stuck it up in his dressing room. Maybe I shouldn't have underlined the bit about him being a talentless phoney with rubbish trousers. Maybe I shouldn't have drawn a circle round the final two paragraphs. The ones about us. The ones that said we were the next big thing.

It's official, then. I am a "uniquely talented guitar genius." And Matty is the son of Keith Moon. And Vince is the reincarnation of Jeff Buckley with a dash of Kevin Rowland (I know, I couldn't believe it either) thrown in. And that's not all. It gets better. According to the review we're all in our mid-twenties. According to No Knob it's a crime we're not signed. According to Kostas, three different record labels have rung up to speak to him already and four different managers have called round. To the video shop. In Crouch End. How mad is that?

I've never seen Vince look so happy. I never knew he could smile like that. It's sort of sickening, to tell you the truth. You can see his teeth. You can see his gums. When he throws back his head and lets out one of his Sid James–style cackles you can almost see the back of his red furry tongue. I think he should stop it. I think he should get a grip. You wouldn't catch me and Matty getting above ourselves and loosing our decorum like that.

"Oi, what do you pair of tossers think you're doing?"

"We're mooning Milton Keynes, Vince."

"Why?"

"Dunno. We just felt like it."

"Well, stop it. Put your arses away and sit back down. Jesus Christ, one half-decent review and you think you're in the fucking Monkees."

"We are."

"Aren't we?"

"No. We're not. We've been here before, remember. And besides, a bunch of record companies coming down to the gig ain't going to do us much good if we still sound like a bag of spanners when we get up onstage."

Vince is right. And we do. We sound rotten. Despite my showdown with Ike we're still being screwed over big time, and unless we can find our own sound man for tonight's gig we're unlikely to impress anyone very much.

"Right," I say, pulling up my *Dawson's Creek* boxer shorts and sitting back down, "let's stop off at the next services. I've still got the number of that kid who did sound for us at Kate's art college. With a bit of luck we can convince him to come down to the Empire and sort us out."

"Any luck?"

I shake my head. I've tried everyone I can think of but no one seems to know where he is. Kate thinks he might have gone away for the weekend. His flatmate reckons he might be staying with his girlfriend in Shoreditch. No one has her number. We don't know what else to do.

"Shit," says Vince, crushing his empty cigarette packet into the ashtray, "we should have sorted this out last week. I said so, didn't I? Didn't I say we should have sorted all this out last week?"

"Yes, Vince. You did."

"So why didn't we, then?"

"Dunno."

"Dunno."

"Because we're wankers, that's why. Because we always leave things to the last sodding minute. We never think ahead. We never make a plan and stick to it. Fuck it. I'm going for a slash."

We make a few more calls, drink a few more coffees, spend a series of quality moments discussing who would play each of us in a short movie about our lives, but there's still no good news. It's getting late. We decide to call it a day and carry on down to London. Vince wants to make sure we're on time for our sound check. Just in case Ike has a change of heart. Just in case we can convince the sound man to start acting like a half-decent human being and give us the sniff of a break.

It's six o'clock by the time we arrive at the Shepherd's Bush Empire and people are already queuing up outside the venue. I can't believe we've made it. I can't believe the kebab van has pulled us through the whole tour. It's filthy. It smells. Its guts are stuffed with newspapers and burger wrappers and bundles of empty beer cans and bags of ten-day-old sport socks as stiff as wood.

Most of the silver paint has peeled off in the rain. You can just about make out the stick men and the stars, but you can't read the name of the band any more. The name of the band has all but washed away.

Upstairs in the dressing room our spirits are temporarily lifted. There are good-luck messages from all of our friends: a home-made Bruce Lee card from Sheila, a plate of stuffed vine leaves from Mrs. Kostas, a bottle of champagne from Alison, and a handwritten note from my mum. She wishes me luck. She hopes the gig goes well. She wants to know if I've heard back from any of the Russian cruise ships yet.

And then Scarface's tour manager knocks on the door. And ruins everything.

"All right, boys?" he says, sitting himself down and helping himself to one of our vine leaves.

"Not bad," we say, wondering what he wants.

"I suppose you've heard about Scottie, then?"

"The sound guy?"

"Yeah. He got hit by a lighting truss when we were packing down yesterday. Broke his arm in three places."

"I take it he's not going to be doing the gig tonight, then?" says Vince, attempting to look concerned.

"No," says Malcolm, wiping a dribble of grease off his chin. "We had to get someone else. He did a few dates on our American tour so he knows most of Scarface's set already. Bit of a bastard for you lot, though."

"How do you work that out?" I say, wondering how things could possibly get any worse.

"Well, Ike's a bit jittery. He wants to have a super-long sound check to make sure everything's okay. I doubt you lot will even get up onstage."

"You do surprise me," says Vince.

"Yeah, well. Sorry, guys. That's the way the cookie crumbles. Not much else I can do for you, I'm afraid."

We're fucked. This is the worst possible outcome. We won't get a chance to check our amps or get a feel for the venue. We won't even get to play through a song. I can feel my stomach churning. I can feel my nightly pre-gig nerves kicking in. I can feel Vince prodding me sharply in the ribs with his elbow.

"Come on, then," he says, "let's get ourselves down there."

"What for?" I say gloomily. "You heard him. We aren't even going to be allowed up onstage before the gig."

"Yeah, well, I've got an idea, haven't I."

"What are you going to do?"

"Well," he says, taking his wallet out of his pocket, "we've still got three hundred quid left in the kitty, haven't we?"

"Yeah. So what?"

"So let's get down there and offer it to the new sound man to sort us out. See what he says."

"Do you think it'll do us any good?"

"I don't know, mate," he says, shrugging his shoulders, "but the way things are going I reckon it's our only chance."

By the time we get downstairs Scarface are just finishing up their last song. Ike has jumped down off the stage to have a chat with the new sound man and it's pretty obvious that he's talking to him about us. I can see the sound man nodding his head. I can see Ike handing him a brown paper envelope stuffed with cash. I can see flecks of white spittle glinting on Ike's lips as he smiles and walks towards us and waves. And then I notice something. And my jaw drops. And I'm convinced that there might actually be a God.

"It can't be."

"It can."

"It isn't."

"It is."

"Is it?"

"You're right, mate, it is."

"*No way*. Wow, Vince Parker and Danny McQueen. I had no idea Dakota was you lot. Stroll on, who would have thought it? How long has it been now?"

"A good couple of years, I reckon."

"What about you, Dan? Must be six years or something?"

"More like ten, I'd say."

"Ten years? Blimey. Only seems like yesterday, don't it?"

"Yeah, it does."

"Fuck. Where was it we used to rehearse in them days? Somewhere down Stratford way, weren't it? What did they call it, that place? Fucking dump."

"Broken Lives."

"That's it. Broken fucking Lives. Shit, takes me right back, that does."

"It's good to see you again, Woolfy."

"Yeah, too right. It's good to see you lot an' all."

It takes us less than five minutes to sort things out. Woolfy waves away our offers of money and promises to make us sound better than we have in our lives. It turns out Woolfy is one of the most sought-after sound engineers in the country these days. He's even done monitors for U2. He doesn't think very much of Ike, though. He reckons Ike is the most miserable git he's ever had to work for. It'll be his pleasure, he says. To help us get our own back.

We can't help smiling when he tells us what he's going to do.

54

Almost everyone I know is out there: Kostas and Mrs. Kostas, Ruth and Ruth's partner, Bob, Kate and Shelley and Allen and No Knob and any distant acquaintance whose name was even vaguely legible in my 1990 Musicians Union diary that I could phone up and persuade/beg/convince to come down.

The record companies have all turned up. I know. I've checked. I've read and reread the guest list, checked and double-checked with Kostas, and I've even trudged all the way down to the box office and back—twice—to make sure that they've definitely come in. The box-office lady was very helpful. And not at all rude. Even though the queue was very long. And she didn't really have a lot of time to talk to me.

And somewhere out there is Alison. The woman I love. The woman that I haven't seen for the longest two weeks of my life. Who hasn't seen me for a month.

"Can you see her anywhere?" says Matty, peering into the crowd over my shoulder.

"No," I say, "I can't."

"Don't worry, mate," says Vince. "She said she'd be cutting it pretty fine, didn't she. I'm sure she's out there somewhere."

"Yeah," I say. "I know she is."

There's half an hour left before show time and Vince suggests we go back up to the dressing room for some peace and quiet. He likes to gather his thoughts before a gig and he's insisted that no one comes backstage to bother us before we go on.

We sit in silence. We creak and fidget on the sofas, slurp up the foam from our beers, try on the crushed-velvet bell-bottoms that Vince has chosen specially for our last night and conspire to hide our nerves. In less than an hour it will all be over. All three of us will know where we stand. It's unlikely we'll carry on if we screw this one up. I doubt we'll get a chance this big again.

"Right then," says Vince, rubbing his hands together. "There's ten minutes left. Better get off for your pre-gig shit."

"No, you're all right," I say. "I don't think I'm going to bother."

"Come off it, Danny. I don't want you haring offstage in the middle of the gig with a nuclear dose of the squits."

"No, I mean it. I don't think I'm going to bother."

Vince and Matty exchange worried glances.

"Honestly," I say, picking up my guitar and giving it a quick tune. "I don't even feel that nervous. I reckon I'm going to be all right."

Vince gives me one last chance to change my mind, and at five minutes to eight we make our way through the warren of breeze-block corridors and take our places at the side of the stage. I lean my head round the curtain to take a final look at the crowd. It's rammed out there. Even in the balconies. It's easily three-quarters full. I wonder why they've all come so early. I wonder if it's got anything to do with us. I wonder if that's the sound of people cheering as the lights go down or if it's just my imagination. Too late. It's time. Vince shoots me a quick wink and we walk out on to the stage, plug our guitars into our amps, and wait for what seems like a lifetime for Matty to begin the first count.

"One, two, three, four . . ."

Go.

It's difficult to convey what it feels like when everything goes right onstage. It's effortless. It feels like everything in the room is connected: the band, the instruments, the amps, and the crowd, even the plaster on the walls. My mind never wandered for a second. There was no place left for it to go.

We sounded brilliant up there tonight. I could tell by the reaction of the crowd. We carried the whole audience with us. From the first to the last. From beginning to end. From the opening click to the last dying chord, and we never dropped the pace for a second.

We don't say a word as we walk off the stage. We know we don't need to.

"*Hic*, woopah, *woopahhhh! Mega. Hic hic*. MEGAAAHHH! *Hic. Woopah!*"

Matty is so excited that he has the hiccups. He's sat in the middle of the dressing-room floor with a towel wrapped round his head, a stuffed vine leaf sticking out of his mouth, and a magnum of champagne clutched under his sweat-soaked armpit. He hiccups and yells and hiccups and woopahs and bursts the cork out of its tight green neck with a hugely satisfying pop.

"Here you go, then, here you go," he says, pouring the champagne into cups and passing it round. "I love you guys, I do. *Hic*. You were brilliant tonight. Both of you, *hic*. Completely brilliant. Especially Vince. And especially Danny. And especially, *hic*, most especially, *Meeee! Woopahhhh. Hic.* I am great. Hands up who thinks I'm great. Hands up who thinks I'm the best. *Hic.* Hands up who thinks I'm the best fucking drummer in the best fucking band in the whole of the *whole* fucking worl—"

"Excuse me, guys, not disturbing you, am I? Is it okay if I come in and have a quick chat with the three of you?"

His name is Colin Drapper. He's from Diablo Records. He's their top A 'n' R man. He's their *only* A 'n' R man. He wants to know if any other companies have spoken to us yet. He wants to know if we can call in to his office early next week. He thinks I'm a talented songwriter. He thinks Vince is a bit of a star. He has a very important proposition for all three of us. He wants to offer us a deal.

I can't quite believe it. I can't seem to take it all in. I may be mistaken but I think I might want to go for that shit now.

55

The dressing room fills up quickly. Matty is deep in conversation with Kate, Kostas is deep in conversation with Ruth's partner Bob, and if I'm not mistaken Vince is deep in conversation with his ex-girlfriend Liz. What a dark horse. He never even told me he was inviting her. I wonder if he knows where Alison is. I wonder if she's on her way up yet.

And then I spot her. Walking through the door with a half-drunk beer in her hand. Smiling at me. Waving. Winding through the crowd like an elegantly stoned cat.

She looks stunning. She's wearing low-slung jeans that cling to her hips, a low-cut T-shirt that clings to her breasts, and a giant purple flower pinned tightly in her hair. I can't wait to talk to her. I can't wait to tell her what's happened. I can't wait to see the look on her face.

"Hey," I say, handing her a cup of warm champagne.

"Hey," she says, kissing me on the cheek.

"Come over here and sit down," I say. "I've got something important to tell you."

"So that's it really," I say, lighting us both a cigarette. "We're seeing him first thing next week."

"And you think he's going to offer you a deal?"

"Yeah. They're only a small label so I don't suppose they've got very much money or anything, but if we put out a couple of EPs with Diablo we stand a pretty good chance of being picked up by a major later on."

"How long would it take?" she says, fiddling with the label on her drink.

"How long would what take?" I say, wondering what she means.

"You know, recording the EPs, putting them out, getting picked up by a bigger record company."

"Well, that sort of depends," I say. "The Diablo guy thinks we need to develop our sound a bit more. He thinks we should ditch some of the samples, Pare it right down, you know, get back to the basic instruments."

"Right."

"He thinks Vince has got a wicked voice, though," I say, wondering why she looks unconvinced. "And he thinks I'm a top-quality songwriter."

"Right."

"So, what do you think, then?" I say, attempting to gee her along.

"About what?"

"About everything I've just said. It's great, isn't it? It means we don't have to give up after all. A record deal or a job, that's what you said, wasn't it?"

"Danny, I didn't really—"

"Okay, so it's not like I'll be bringing in much money yet, but we'll be all right, won't we? For the next year or so? I can carry on working at the video shop while we're getting things sorted out, you'll get another top-notch job when you come back to London, so—"

"So nothing changes, then?"

"Alison, what do you mean? Of course it does. Everything changes. Did you hear what I just said? We're going to get a record deal. An *actual* record deal."

"Yeah," she says. "I heard you." And then she says she needs to take a piss.

Alison has been gone a long time and I'm beginning to wonder where she's got to. I've been making polite conversation about hard drives and soft drives and weekend breaks in Marrakech for almost an hour now, and it feels like my head is about to explode. No one wants to talk about anything interesting; like the width of James Caan's shoulders in *The Godfather* or how long Nick Cave has been dyeing his hair.

It's my own fault. I shouldn't have got myself stuck with Ruth's partner Bob. He must be the most boring man on the planet. I'm considering poking him in the eye. I'm so desperate for someone else to talk to that I'm even considering striking up a conversation with Ruth.

"Hey, Ruth," I say, interrupting Bob's fascinating discourse on the single European currency, "you didn't happen to notice where Alison went, did you?"

"Yes," she says, smiling at me strangely. "I've just seen her. She's outside in the corridor."

Alison is outside in the corridor. She's sitting on the floor with her arms wrapped round her knees, staring lazily into space.

"I wondered where you'd got to," I say, sitting down next to her and trying to catch her eye.

"Well, now you've found me," she says, looking at the floor.

"You seemed a bit quiet."

"Did I?"

"Yeah, before. You didn't even say what you thought of the gig."

"I thought it was good."

"*Good?*"

"Yeah. I thought it was okay."

"What do you mean?" I say, getting agitated. "It was more than okay, wasn't it? Vince reckons it was the best gig we've ever done."

She sighs and rolls her eyes at the ceiling.

"What is it?" I say, trying to work out what she's thinking. "Are you saying that you thought we were crap?"

"No, of course not. You weren't crap."

"Well, what then? Are you saying you didn't think we were very good?"

"I don't know, Danny," she says, pushing her hair off her face. "I mean, there are dozens of bands at your level, aren't there?"

"Yeah, I suppose. So what?"

"Well, they're all doing the same thing, aren't they? Trudging round the country for years on end, doing no-mark gigs and pointless tours . . . and every so often one of them gets offered a poxy little deal. It was bound to happen to you sooner or later."

I'm speechless. She carries on.

"It won't come to anything, Danny," she says, standing up. "It never does. You'll put out your EP and slog your guts out on one toilet tour after another and before you know it you'll be right back where you started."

I want to ask her what makes her such an expert on the music business all of a sudden, but I find I'm still having trouble getting my jaw to move.

"It's a waste of time," she says, taking a small swig of her beer. "I'm not sure I can put up with it any more."

"Put up with what?"

"With this. I'm not sure I can sit around and watch you waste your life like this."

"What do you mean?" I say angrily. "How am I wasting my life?"

"It's a fantasy, Danny. It always has been. The only reason you keep doing it year after year is because you're too shit scared to do anything else."

That's it. That did it. That was the final straw.

"Why don't you say it, Alison?" I say, standing up and slamming my hand into the wall. "Why don't you stop fucking around and say what you mean?"

"What are you talking about?" she says, trying not to cry. "I don't know what you want me to say."

"Tell me what you think, what you've always thought. Tell me to my face that you think I'm a loser."

"Okay then," she says, staring straight at me. "You're right, Danny. Maybe I do."

I don't say another word. I watch as she goes back into the dressing room to look for Ruth and Bob and I stand by the door and watch them leave. She turns to look at me when she reaches the end of the corridor. And then she walks away.

56

The after-show party continues back at Scarface's hotel. I convince Matty and Vince that Alison wasn't feeling well and the three of us decide to get royally wasted. It doesn't take us very long. By one o'clock in the morning we're splayed out over the hotel armchairs in a semi-catatonic stupor, and Vince is suggesting we all get rooms.

"Yeah, come on," he says, topping up our glasses with whisky, "let's get one each. We've still got the rest of the kitty money left, haven't we? I reckon we should spunk it on some rooms."

I know what he's thinking. He's thinking that he might be able to persuade Liz to stay the night. He's thinking that he might be able to persuade her to have hotel sex with him.

"No," he says thoughtfully, "it's not that. I mean, it *is* that, yeah, but I was actually thinking more of you and Matty, as it goes."

"Were you?"

"Yeah. Of course I was. I mean, Alison ain't going to be too happy if you roll home pissed out of your skull at four o'clock in the morning, is she, and as for Matty . . ."

"What about Matty?"

"Well, he's going to need somewhere safe to kip, isn't he? After he's given Kate the big heave-ho."

• • •

It's decided, then. We get rooms. We get three single rooms and another bottle of Scotch and we stay up for four more hours getting drunk. I have a wonderful time. I get pissed with Woolfy and talk over old times. I get pissed with Scarface and commiserate with them over the terrible feedback problems they were having all the way through tonight's gig. I don't think about Alison once. She doesn't even cross my mind. I'm not even thinking about phoning her up. And I'm certainly not planning on ordering myself a minicab and going back home to the flat.

"Wait up, Danny. Where are you going?"

"Home, Matty," I say decisively. "It's definitely time to go home."

"But you can't."

"Oh yes I can."

"But *Dan*—"

"Look, you see that cab outside?"

"Yeah."

"The one with eight doors?"

"Er—"

"Well, as soon as this bastard revolving door stops revolving I'm getting in it."

"But it's not a revolving door, Danny."

"Isn't it?" I say, amazed.

"No, it's not."

"Well then, never mind that now. It's time I was getting off. Lots of things to be getting on with. Plenty of things to be sorting out."

"But you can't go," he says, tugging at my shoulder. "I need you to stay."

"Just watch me," I say, lurching towards the door.

"No," he says urgently, "I mean it, Danny. I'm in ten different flavours of shit. Please, I really need your help."

"Right, then," I say, sitting down next to Matty and attempting to sober up. "Let me get this straight. Claire is texting you from Newcastle every five minutes, Kate is demanding to know what's going on, you've got two teenage groupies chasing you round the hotel lobby, and there's another one that you slept with in Birmingham waiting for you upstairs outside your room."

"Yeah," says Matty, scratching his head. "And I don't know what to do. I mean, I didn't ask her to come down or nothing. I think she must have got the wrong idea."

"Matty?"

"Yes."

"Did you explain to her that it was a one-night stand when you slept with her?"

"No."

"Did you tell any of them that it was a one-night stand?"

"No. I didn't want to upset none of them. I sort of said they could come and visit me in London some time but . . . you know, I was just being nice. I didn't mean now. I didn't mean *today*."

"Hard luck, mate," I say, trying to stand up. "I'm still going home."

"Please, Danny," he says as I crumble back into my chair. "Just go upstairs and distract her. Just for a second. Just until I can get into my room with Kate. I don't want her finding out like this. I want to tell her myself. Come on, Danny. I'll owe you a big one."

"Why can't you ask Vince?" I say, realising that it's hopeless.

"I can't," he says. "Vince has already gone upstairs with Liz."

Well, what was I supposed to do? He's my mate. He'd have done the same for me.

"Hey, Matty," I say, waving the cab driver away and staggering towards the lift. "How will I know it's her? How will I know I've got the right one?"

"Easy," he says, toasting me with his bottle of vodka. "Her name's Elodi. She's got a funny accent. I think she might be French or something."

"*French!*"

"Yeah. Didn't I tell you? She's from Paris. That's in France, isn't it? Anyway, you'll definitely know it's her. She's got dark brown hair and light green eyes and bazookas the size of Wales."

God help me.

I'd like to tell you that I didn't end up sleeping with Elodi last night. But I did.

I'd like to say the sex was crap. But it wasn't. Not at all.

I'd like to say it didn't mean anything. And I can. Because it didn't. At least not to me.

She leaves first thing in the morning and I make sure I do the decent thing. I get up and walk her to the lift. I make sure she's got enough money to get home and I tell her that I won't be seeing her again. She doesn't seem to mind. She's not quite as beautiful as I thought she was last night but she's still pretty attractive. Especially compared to me. I've never felt uglier in my life.

The lift door closes and I crawl back to my room on all fours. I'm not very well. My head feels like a china pot that's been shattered into a thousand pieces and stuck back together with flour-and-water glue. By a chimpanzee. With no thumbs. I'm having trouble seeing. I'm having trouble opening my eyes. That's why I don't notice her at first. Until I'm almost outside Matty's room. Until I'm almost next to her. Arms folded. Lips pursed. A look of vindictive delight on her overly made-up face.

"Kate," I say pathetically, "it's not what it looks like."

"Isn't it?"

"No, not exactly. I mean, it almost is . . . but not quite."

I have the distinct feeling that my brain is haemorrhaging. My face is filling up with blood. Of all the people to catch me at a moment like this, Kate has to be the worst possible candidate.

She can't believe her good fortune. She can't believe she has a chance to pay me back for rejecting her. She has other grievances as well. She blames me for Matty breaking up with her last night; she holds me personally responsible for his behaviour on tour. She still believes in honesty at all costs, she says. She doesn't want to get drawn into my lies.

"Look, Kate," I say, getting desperate, "I know you believe in all this karmic bollocks, but please . . . don't tell Alison about this."

"Why not?" she says.

"Because it'll only hurt her. It was a mistake. It was just a drunken fuck."

"Yeah, I know, it didn't mean anything, right?"

"No. It didn't."

"That's crap, Danny. You're going to have to come up with something way better than that. Give me one good reason why I shouldn't call Alison and tell her everything right now."

"Because I love her, Kate."

"Yeah," she says, walking towards the lift, "that's the sad thing, Danny. I think you probably do."

57

Guilt is a funny thing. There are moments when you don't feel anything at all. There are moments when you almost feel elated. There are moments when you're stoic and moments when you're calm and moments when you remember what you've done.

I've just remembered what I've done. It's exactly the same. Every time. I could be listening to a record or reading a book but it always hits me in the same way. It lurches through my stomach like curdled milk. It fills up my chest like a city. It scuttles through my head like a bucket full of wasps and escapes through my mouth with a groan. It's audible. My guilt is audible. I'm pretty sure I'll be hearing it for the rest of my life.

I know precisely why I did it. It wasn't because I was drunk. It was because she was sexy and beautiful and careless and young and she had no way of knowing what I'm like. She hadn't made up her mind yet. It was wonderful. For one night it meant that I hadn't either.

The problem is, Alison is right. I am scared. I've been scared my whole life. Scared of doing badly, scared of doing well, scared of making a move without Vince being there to guide me, and scared of running out of places to hide. So I did what I've always done. I entered a race I couldn't win. What safer place is there than that?

I don't blame her for not getting excited. There's not much to be excited about. Diablo were the only record company to contact us after the gig on Saturday and it turns out they're even less well funded than I thought. It would be a small miracle if we ended up making any money. It's unlikely we'd ever make a bean. It's just another way of putting off the inevitable. Another reason to blame the world when it doesn't work out.

It's getting late. Alison went back to Ruth and Bob's last night and I still haven't been able to get hold of her. I wonder if Kate's told her what happened yet. I wonder if Ruth's told her how many times I've phoned. I just want to hear her voice, that's all. I'm pretty sure things will be all right again if I can just hear her voice.

"Danny, it's me. Something awful has happened."

58

The drive to the police station seems to take forever but it probably takes less than half an hour. Alison is sat in the waiting room, slumped down on one of the hard wooden benches with a cup of cold tea in her hand. She looks fragile. And tired. Like her frustration has drained every last drop of her strength.

"How long have they had him in there?" I say, sitting down next to her.

"Hours," she says angrily. "They won't even let me see him. They're saying he's been violent and abusive but they're lying. Rufus wouldn't hurt a fly."

Alison's brother has been arrested. He was picked up for causing a bit of a ruckus outside a theme pub in Camden Town, and at first they just thought that he was drunk. It took them two hours to work out that he might be schizophrenic. Two more to work out what to do. And then they phoned Alison. And now they want him sectioned.

"He doesn't need to be sectioned," she says scornfully. "He just needs to be taken home. He probably missed his last hospital appointment, he's probably been neglecting his medication this week. It's a balancing act, Danny," she says bitterly. "It doesn't always work."

She looks upset. She's worried about him being alone in the holding cell. She's worried he'll become depressed and she's worried that he's frightened and she doesn't know why no one will take any notice of her. They've been waiting for the police surgeon to come down and assess him for hours, and Alison doubts anyone will arrive until morning now. She doesn't want him to spend all night alone in there. She just wants to be allowed to take him home.

"Where's Ruth and Bob?" I say, wondering if I should put my arm round her.

"They've gone," she says. "I told them to go. Ruth just started getting upset and Bob got abusive with the duty sergeant. I think they ended up doing more harm than good."

"I'm glad you called me," I say, wrapping my arm round her shoulder.

"I'm glad you came," she says, leaning into my chest.

The duty sergeant is a wretched, humourless human being. He's chewing on a pen lid and slurping on a cup of coffee, and at first he has no interest in what I have to say. I can see how someone like Bob would have annoyed him. With his cut-glass accent and his Hugo Boss suit, and I bet it wasn't long before he was waving his tiny fists about and threatening him with his job. He was equally unimpressed by Ruth and Alison. He probably wrote them off as hysterics the moment they walked in the door. I doubt he has much time for women; men like him never do.

I sit down in his stark white office and close my eyes for a split second. I stifle my initial response. My body is resorting to its usual fight-or-flight mechanism and my brain is saying, "Danny, run away." But I don't. I stay right where I am.

I consider appealing to his compassionate side for a moment, but I doubt that he actually has one. I do the only thing you can do when you're faced with an irrational human being who's relishing the power that they hold over you. I flatter him. I make him feel important. I convince him he's the far better brain.

It takes me a good twenty minutes to press all his buttons, but they're not very difficult to find. I thank him for picking Rufus up. I recognise he was only doing his job. I explain a little of Rufus's history and I tell him that he's never been violent in his life. I persuade him that the holding cell could be far better used. I convince him Rufus is no kind of threat. I remind him that it's almost pub chucking-out time and I suggest that his efforts might be far better used somewhere else. Why doesn't he save himself the trouble? I say. Why doesn't he give Rufus back to us?

He ums and ahs and grimaces for a while, and he informs me that my "wife's" friends were skating on very thin ice. He agrees to release Rufus into our custody if we promise to take full responsibility for him. We thank him profusely. We agree to have him seen by a doctor first thing in the morning.

And then we take him home.

"How is he now?" I say as she comes out of the spare room and shuts the door.

"He's sleeping," she says. "He's exhausted. I just spoke to Mum and Dad and they're going to come down to fetch him tomorrow morning. They'll take him back up to Lincoln to stay with them for a while."

"That's a good idea," I say. "It'll probably do him the world of good."

She gets up and walks over to the kitchen and comes back with two large glasses of wine. She sits down next to me on the sofa and rests her head carefully on my shoulder.

"Thanks, Danny," she says quietly. "I don't know what I'd have done without you tonight. I knew you'd know what to do."

"*You did?*" I say, wondering whether I've heard her right.

"Yes," she says. "You were fantastic. You handled it brilliantly."

"That's okay," I say, putting my arm round her, "it wasn't that difficult in the end."

"Yes," she says, "it was. It was all about staying calm. Bob went leaping in feet first and I was too angry to think straight. But you sorted it, Danny. You got him out. I couldn't have done it without you."

I pull away and take a big gulp of my wine. It's making me uncomfortable, her being so nice to me like this.

"I'm sorry about what I said last night," she says, wondering why I've pulled away. "I didn't mean any of it, you know."

"That's okay," I say, fiddling with the TV remote control. "You were right. It's unlikely the record deal will come to anything much."

"No," she says, "that's not what I meant. You have to let me explain."

"So," I say, scratching my ear, "you didn't think we were rubbish, then?"

"No," she says, "I thought you were incredible. It was so unexpected, seeing you perform up there on that giant stage; with all those people jumping up and down and getting into the songs and clapping and cheering and, shit, Danny . . . I don't even know how to say this—"

"What is it?" I say, urging her on. "What is it you're trying to say?"

She knits her fingers together and hums quietly under her breath.

"I know it's awful of me," she says slowly, "but I was . . . well, I was just incredibly jealous."

"*Jealous?*"

"Yes."

"Of *me?*"

"Yes. Of you. I've never been more jealous in my life."

"Why?" I say, shaking my head in disbelief. "Why would you be jealous of me?"

She takes a sip of her wine before she answers.

"Because you looked so happy up there, like it was everything you'd ever wanted to do. And I was envious of it, I suppose. Envious of your self-belief. I can't believe you've had the guts to pursue it all these years, that you've had the courage to see it through."

"But . . . I thought you said I was running away, I thought you said I was wasting my time."

"No," she says gently, "I've never thought you were wasting your time. I think you realised early on that you were good at something and you've followed your ambition ever since. It wasn't because you were trying to live up to your mum's expectations and it wasn't because you were too scared to do anything else. It's because you're good at it, Danny. Much better than I ever realised."

"Shit," I say, draining my glass, "I don't know what to say. I thought you wanted me to be more like Ruth's partner, Bob."

"No," she says, relaxing slightly, "I don't want you to be anything like Bob."

"Well, what about Didier, then? I thought you wanted me to be more like him."

"*Didier?* You must be joking," she says, grimacing at the thought. "He's an arsehole, a complete lech. He makes the whole office go out to dinner with him every time we complete a new part of the project and then he spends all night ordering schnapps and telling crap jokes and trying to wrap his podgy arms round all the women. He's a wanker, Danny. No one in the office can stand him."

"Wow," I say, pouring us some more wine. "So you're not having an affair with him, then? You've not been having a bit of Belgian leg-over action while you've been off on your holidays in Bruges?"

"You're serious, aren't you?" she says, turning round and narrowing her eyes at me. "You honestly thought there was a chance I might be sleeping with him?"

"Well," I say, feeling ashamed of myself, "I didn't know what to think. I mean, what about all those sexy dresses? What about the mystery timetable that I found in your bag?"

"What sexy dresses? *What* mystery timetable?"

"You know, that *one*. That dress you wore to go back to Bruges that time. The one with the low-cut bits and the see-through bits and . . ."

She starts to smile.

"I was trying to make you realise what you were missing, I suppose. You were so preoccupied with the band when I came home that you barely seemed to register that I'd been away. I wasn't even sure that you were missing me. You seemed more interested in discussing your flared trousers than finding out about what I was getting up to in Bruges."

"Right," I say. "You're right. I suppose I was a bit preoccupied now you mention it. But what about the timetable, then, what was that all about?"

She takes a deep breath before she answers.

"You know that morning I told you I'd been out shopping with Rufus? Well, that wasn't all I did. I went up to the university afterwards. They were having an open day."

"I don't understand," I say, still confused. "Why would you want to visit the university?"

"Because . . . I've been thinking about going back to college, to study creative writing or journalism or something. So you were right in a way, it was a timetable. It was a list of course dates."

She stops for a moment to gauge my reaction and then she carries on.

"I've been thinking about it for a while," she says, taking a prospectus out of her bag and showing it to me. "I mean, I've always loved writing, ever since I was a kid, and I just thought . . . well, this is my last chance, isn't it? If I leave it any longer it'll be too late."

"Too late for what?"

"Too late to change. In a couple of years we might want to have kids and we'll probably have a mortgage and then I'll be stuck, won't I? Stuck in a career that I hate for the rest of my life."

"I didn't know you hated what you were doing," I say, genuinely surprised. "I mean, I knew you weren't all that happy but I never realised you hated it."

"No, Danny, of course you didn't. You weren't paying any attention. You never do. I didn't say you weren't still a selfish fucker."

Her smile belies the harshness of her words. And then she says she has a confession to make.

"The thing is," she says uneasily, "I think I gave you the ultimatum because part of me hoped you'd fail. I suppose I thought it might be your turn to take a proper job for a while. Your turn to take some responsibility for once."

"I thought you liked it. I thought you liked being the responsible one."

"No," she says, shaking her head, "not really. I just don't

know how to do anything else. I'm not like you, Danny, I'm not any good at taking risks. I think it might be something to do with growing up with Rufus, seeing the chaos he's had to go through over the years. It makes me want to be in control . . . it makes me want to feel safe. I'm sorry, Danny. It's not fair. I should have been straight with you. I should have told you what I wanted from the start."

I can't bear to hear her apologising to me like this. I can't stand to see the look on her face. She's gazing up at me with those giant blue eyes and she's asking me to forgive her but I can't. Because my body is full of sour milk and insects. And there's the weight of a city pressing on my chest. And I open my mouth. And I let out a groan. Because I've suddenly remembered what I've done.

"I've got a confession too," I say suddenly. "I've got something I have to tell you. I'm sorry, Alison. It's pretty bad."

She smiles, suggesting it can't be quite as bad as I think it is. "I know, you nutcase," she says, laughing at me. "The thing is I already know."

"You do?" I say, wondering why she's being so calm about it. "You mean Kate's already told you what happened?"

"Kate? No. What's Kate got to do with anything? I saw you for myself. I saw you hiding behind that lamppost. With your flowers and your wine and your ridiculous Hercule Poirot cake. I know you came to Bruges, Danny. Can you believe it? I saw you and I didn't even come out and say anything. I wanted to see what you'd do. I wanted to know if you'd ever get round to telling me. It's ridiculous, isn't it? I've been punishing you for it ever since.

"This is crazy," she says, tapping her fingers on the edge of the table. "The two of us are just as bad as each other."

"Not quite," I say sadly, "not quite."

59

She can tell. I know she can. She can tell from the look on my face. She doesn't want to believe it and she's hoping that she's made a mistake but deep down I think she already knows. She pulls away. She moves to the corner of the sofa and tucks her knees tightly into her chest. Because she thinks I'm about to hurt her.

And she's right.

"This isn't about you coming to Bruges, is it?" she says finally.

"No," I say, "I wish it was."

"What, then? What's wrong?"

"I'm sorry," I say bitterly, "I didn't mean it to happen . . . it was a mistake . . . it was after we'd argued at the gig. I was angry about what you said and—"

"Tell me," she says quietly. "Just tell me what you've done."

"I'm sorry, Alison. I slept with someone else."

In the split second it took for the words to leave my lips our whole world changed. She asked for everything back: the trust, the affection, the comfort and the love and the right to touch her skin. I lean towards her. I put down my wineglass and reach out for her hand and she pulls it away like a snapped elastic band.

"Don't," she says. "I don't want you to touch me."

I try to make things better but I'm not sure there's any way that I can. I apologise until I'm sick of the sound of my own voice. I promise her it will never happen again. I answer all her questions and fill in all the gaps and try to find some explanation for why it happened. I tell her that I was drunk. That I never intended to sleep with anyone. That I wouldn't have planned to hurt her like this for anything in the world.

"It didn't mean anything," I say, wringing my hands, "I swear to you. It was a mistake."

"Did you know her?" she says. "Was she someone you knew?"

"No. I'd only just met her. I don't even know where she lives."

"Did she stay the whole night? Did you have breakfast with her?"

"No. I mean we didn't have breakfast, of course we didn't."

"But she did stay the night?"

"No, it was a couple of hours. It was dawn before I even went up to the room."

I'm making things worse. I can see her wince with every new detail even though part of her is desperate to know. I try again. I try to make her understand.

"Look," I say, "I know I've done a terrible thing to you and there's no reason on earth why you should forgive me but it was a stupid mistake. It was only a one-night stand. I swear to you. That's all it was."

She starts to cry. Fat tears ooze over her lashes on to her cheeks and she makes no attempt to wipe them away.

"You don't get it, do you?" she says scornfully. "Don't you see, it's worse that it was a one-night stand. It makes things even worse."

"How? I don't understand. How does it make things worse?"

She turns away. She can't bear to look at my face.

"Because it does," she says. "It means our relationship was worth so little to you that you were prepared to sacrifice it for one meaningless fuck. How do you think that makes me feel? If you'd loved her . . . if you'd even liked her a little bit . . . I don't know, Danny . . . it just makes things worse."

We talk long into the night but I'm not sure it does any good. Both of us are exhausted and the longer it goes on the more we seem to be repeating ourselves.

"I'm sorry," I say, wondering whether she's still listening, "I'd never have done it . . . I'd never have done it if I'd known."

"If you'd known what?"

"If I'd known how you felt . . . about the band, about your job, about wanting to go back to college . . ."

"You're just making excuses," she says, rubbing her eyes with the back of her hand. "It doesn't make any sense. I'd never have done that to you."

"But I'm telling the truth. I thought we were finished. I was confused . . . I really thought you wanted to leave me."

"So it's my fault, then, is it? I forced you to get pissed and fuck a groupie behind my back?"

"No, of course not."

"But that's what you're saying, isn't it? Even now, even after everything that's happened, you still can't take responsibility for what's going on, can you?"

"No. That's not what I meant. I'm not trying to blame anyone. I've never hated myself more than I do right at this moment, but you've got to believe me . . . I was hurt. You said some pretty harsh things that night."

"So that's it, then, you did it out of spite?"

"No," I say hopelessly. "It wasn't out of spite . . . I was . . . I wasn't thinking straight . . . I thought we were over . . . I thought you didn't care about me any more and . . . I don't know, Alison . . . I was devastated."

"Well," she says coldly, "at least you know how it feels."

It's almost daylight when she picks up her wineglass and walks towards the bedroom door. We've both been silent for a long time. Neither of us could think of anything else to say. I watch her cross the room: her face streaked with makeup and salt, her legs creased red from sitting still for so long. She looks like she's been kicked. And she has. And there's absolutely nothing I can do about it.

"Alison," I say, standing up and walking towards her, "is there any way we can get through this? I'll do anything, I don't care what it is."

"No," she says, closing the door on me, "I'm not sure that there is."

60

I'm waiting for Vince in one of the greasy spoons on Park Road and the scent of hot pig fat is filling up my nostrils and making me heave. I order tea and a couple of slices of dry white toast; wash down a couple of aspirin with a slug of Pepto-Bismol and try to work out how I'm going to tell him. It's been three days since the gig at Shepherd's Bush and I still haven't managed a decent night's sleep. I'm tired and regretful and completely talked out and I'm not sure if I'll be able to find the words.

Vince is oblivious. He strolls in, orders himself breakfast A with extra fried bread, nicks one of my Marlboro Lights and sits down opposite me with a wide grin on his face.

He's looking particularly dapper this afternoon: two-tone, suede leather belt; purple wide-collared shirt with snow-covered Matterhorns on the front and a giant pair of charity-shop glasses that he picked up from the local Oxfam for a pound. He looks slightly demented: part rock star, part retard, part cheapskate Eastern Bloc pimp.

"You look like shit," he says, unbuttoning his shirt and rolling up his sleeves.

"Thanks very much," I say, pushing away my toast and taking a small mouthful of tea. "You look like an Austrian bag lady."

"Well, you've got to make the effort," he says, straightening the collar on his shirt. "I mean, now that we've got ourselves a deal. Now that we're full-time recording *artistes*. So what's up, then? You sounded pretty wound up over the phone."

"Vince," I say, putting down my tea, "there's something I've got to tell you."

Vince wipes a piece of fried bread round the pool of egg yolk that's spilled out on to his plate. It repulses me and makes me feel hungry at the same time.

"Well, then," he says mid-wipe, "I think you should just get on and do it."

"You don't think I should try and get her to stay?"

"Look, Danny," he says, already resigned to the situation, "I don't see what else you can do. If this is the only way of saving your and Alison's relationship then I think you should bite the bullet and go. And anyway," he says, pausing to put some bread in his mouth, "it doesn't sound like she's gonna give you another chance if you don't."

I feel like shit. Vince has invested more than a decade in this band. In me. Why should I be ruining the best chance he's ever had just because my relationship with Alison is in crisis?

"Maybe I'll have a word with her," I say, taking a small bite of my toast. "See if she might change her mind."

"No, mate," he says, "I don't think you should. Alison is right. It'll do you both good to get away. I'll give Matty a ring this afternoon. Let him know what's been going on."

"You don't have to do that, Vince," I say glumly. "I'd rather he heard it from me."

Vince stares down at his plate and starts digging into a piece of bacon like it's still alive. I always knew he was a great friend but

I never realised quite how selfless he is until this second. He hasn't even asked me why I did it. I doubt the question even crossed his mind. He hasn't given me a moment's grief for being stupid because he knows right away there's no point. He doesn't try to persuade me to stay. Even though he knows it's going to fuck everything up for him if I go.

"Cheer up, you wanker," he says, noticing the look on my face, "you never know, we might even make it without you. You was always a shit guitarist anyway. We'll get someone better. Someone who looks good in flared trousers. Someone who doesn't cack his fucking pants every time he has to get up on-stage."

I smile. I can't help smiling.

"And anyway," he says, getting serious again, "at the end of the day, Alison is more important than the poxy band, ain't she?"

"Is she?" I say, wondering if I've heard him right.

"Yeah," he says, "she is. I realised that the other night when I had cheap and nasty hotel reunion sex with Liz."

"You're not back together with her, are you?"

"No," he snorts, "no chance. But we did end up having a nice little chat. And I'll tell you what, mate, she's a right miserable sod. Made me realise that I never really liked her all that much in the first place. I mean, all that stuff about me having a pessimistic nature and that, I don't even think that it's true. I reckon I'm a pretty optimistic bloke, as it goes. It was just that I was always being negative around her."

"Because you never loved her that much, you mean?"

"Yeah, that and because she's got fucking lousy taste in shoes.

"And anyway," he says, pushing his plate away and wiping his mouth with his serviette, "it's like I said before. When you think about it, Danny, you're a very lucky bloke. I've never had anything close to what you and Alison have got. You've found someone you love, someone you want to have a go at sharing your life with. And you can't say fairer than that, can you?"

The waitress collects our plates and deposits a clean ashtray with the bill. We smoke another couple of cigarettes in silence. Neither of us is quite sure what to say.

"It probably would have been shit anyway," I say, stubbing out my cigarette and watching it smoulder in the ashtray. "I mean, we'd probably have ended up hating each other, wouldn't we? Or we'd all have become cokeheads like Ike. It would have fucked us up in the end, wouldn't it? The fame and the money and that? It would definitely have fucked us both up?"

"No, mate," says Vince, pocketing the last of his change. "I ain't gonna lie to you. I think it would have been great."

We stand outside the café for a long while, both of us wondering where to go now. Vince doesn't fancy going for a drink that much and I decide I'm going to head on back to the flat.

"Hey, Vince," I say as he turns round to walk away. "Do you think I'm doing the right thing?"

"Danny," he says, turning back to face me for a second, "I think you already know the answer to that question."

And he's right, of course. I already do.

61

Winter has been especially greedy this year. By mid-November it's eaten almost every leaf. The skies have been pissing down sheets of pin-sharp rain for the best part of a month now and I'm almost glad to be leaving. The flat looks bare. Like a body stripped of its clothes. Four years of memories packed into a dozen cardboard boxes. The flesh of our relationship reduced to bones.

But Vince is right. I'm a very lucky man. No matter that I'm moving to Belgium at the end of the week; no matter that I'm leaving all my friends. The important thing is that Alison wants to work things out, and that she's agreed to give me another chance. I know she's not that happy about renewing her contract in Belgium but I don't think I gave her much choice. The only way she was prepared to stay with me was if we both got away from London for a while. Away from all the distractions. Somewhere quiet. Somewhere she could learn to trust me all over again.

I should be grateful. I've even managed to find myself a job. I'm going to edit music for a brand-new Internet company based on an industrial estate in Ghent. It's going to be excellent. And not at all boring. Because Belgian music is very up and coming these days. Apparently.

• • •

I think Kostas is more upset about me leaving than he's letting on. He's genuinely sad to see me go. He gave me a boxed set of Telly Savalas films as a parting gift to remember him by, and told me I'd been like the son he never had. The errant one. The clumsy one. The one he would happily have swapped for a couple of half-decent donkeys and a few bald hectares in Larnaca given the chance.

He doesn't really see what all the fuss is about. A man is supposed to cheat on his wife. It's expected. It's inevitable. He's never heard such nonsense in all his life. A woman telling the mans what's to do. A man who isn't kings of his own castle. And then he went home to Mrs. Kostas. Who he's never cheated on in his life. But he could. If he wanted to. If he thought he could get away with it. If he thought Mrs. Kostas would let him live.

I think Sheila was the most upset out of everyone. She couldn't quite believe what I'd done. I went round to see her just after it happened and she knew immediately that something was wrong.

"Now, Daniel," she said, searching around for her glasses, "you don't seem your usual self today, you seem a little off colour to me. Am I right?"

I knew there was no point in lying to her so I said, "Yeah, Sheila, you're right."

"Oh, Daniel," she said after I'd told her, "what a shame. What a dreadful shame."

She did her best to cheer me up, which is good of her considering she's got problems of her own. She hasn't recovered from her fall quite as well as she'd hoped and she's still having some trouble getting around. She only manages to come up to the video shop once a week these days so I've been dropping films off at her house as regularly as I can. I don't mind. Now that I'm not rehearsing any more I've got plenty of free time.

"So when are you off, Daniel?" she says, offering me a plate of biscuits. "It must be fairly soon."

"Yes, Sheila," I say gloomily. "I'm driving down to Bruges at the end of next week."

"Well then," she says firmly, "I'm sure everything will work out for the best."

We spend the next half hour chatting about her daughter and her grandson, but I'm not paying as much attention as I should. She pretends not to notice at first but she instinctively knows my mind is somewhere else. She opens up her giant biscuit tin, offers me another custard cream and taps me sharply on the hand.

"Now, Daniel," she says, "I don't want you to worry. These things have a way of sorting themselves out. If she truly loves you she'll forgive you in time. We all make mistakes in our lives one way or another. It's the way we behave afterwards that counts."

"You're right," I say, kissing her on the cheek and making her giggle. "Thanks, Sheila, I'm sure that you're right."

"Of course I am," she says ruefully. "Just wait until you get to be my age. Then you'll know what's what."

We chat a while longer but she's beginning to look tired so I make my excuses and get up to go.

"Hey, Sheila, I almost forgot," I say, reaching into my carrier bag. "I've got you that video you ordered last week."

"Has it got plenty of fighting bits in it?" she says seriously.

"Yes, Sheila," I say, "it's got quite a lot of them, I think."

"Good," she says. "Because it's quite important, you see. I like the fighting bits the best."

I finish up some more packing back at the flat and head up to the pub to catch up with Vince and Matty for a quick drink. I've seen a fair bit of them since I left the band but things aren't quite the same between us as they were. They've decided to push on without me. They're even considering pressing on with signing the deal. As soon as they can find themselves a new guitarist. As soon as they've taught him all the songs.

"So, how's the packing going?" says Vince, tucking into his pint. "Still got you wrapping her knickers between three different layers of tissue paper, has she?"

"Very funny, Vince," I say, sitting down and opening my crisps. "And where were you anyway? You said you were going to come up and give me a hand."

"Yeah, well, sorry about that, mate. I've been pretty busy, as it goes."

"How are the auditions going?" I say, changing the subject and letting him off the hook. "Have you managed to find someone decent yet?"

"No, mate," says Vince, "we haven't. You should see the sort of blokes that have replied to the ad. Useless. Every man-jack of 'em. Bald, fat, crusty wankers. They got no idea, most of them. No idea at all."

"Yeah," says Matty, nodding into his vodka and Red Bull, "but Greg's going to help us find someone good now, isn't he? He said he had a couple of really cool people in mind."

"Greg?" I say. "Who's Greg?"

Vince shoots Matty a quick look before he answers.

"Yeah, well, I was going to tell you about that, Danny. He's some sort of a manager or something. Nothing big, you know, just some bloke that Diablo put us in touch with."

"Yeah," says Matty enthusiastically, "he's a really great guy, he knows everyone in the whole music business, doesn't he, Vince? He manages some really mega bands. He reckons he can get us on another support tour no problem and maybe even a few dates in the US. He reckons we're not far off getting features in the music press, doesn't he? And a couple of big-cheese labels have already been asking questions about us and—"

"*Matty*."

"*Ow!* . . . sorry, Vince. I forgot."

Vince and Matty exchange another private look and Matty carries on.

"I mean, yeah, it's probably all bullshit, Danny. Coz managers are like that, aren't they? All talk and that."

"Exactly," says Vince, removing his boot from Matty's shin. "Chances are it won't come to nothing. We haven't even agreed to let him manage us yet."

I'm not stupid. I can see exactly what's going on. There's clearly some real interest developing about the band within the industry and Vince is doing his best to spare my feelings. He doesn't want me to know that things are going as well as they are. He doesn't want me feeling any worse than I already do.

"'Ere," says Vince, coming back from the bar with more drinks, "have you heard about Matty moving in with Claire?"

"Is this true?" I say, turning round and slapping Matty on the back. "Are you really planning on moving in with her?"

"Yeah," says Matty bashfully. "I am. She's coming down from Newcastle in a couple of weeks and we're gonna get a flat together and that."

"How did Kate take it?"

"I don't think she gives a toss," he says, shrugging his shoulders. "She's more pissed off that she didn't manage to ruin things between you and Alison. She still can't stand the fact that you managed to get in there before her."

"Well," I say, not wanting to dig over old ground, "I'm dead pleased for you, Matty. I hope it all works out."

"Thanks," he says anxiously, "I hope so too. But Vince says I've got to be especially careful. On account of the language barrier."

"The *language* barrier?"

"Yeah. Apparently it can put quite a strain on a relationship when you both speak different languages."

"Matty, what are you on about? Claire's English."

"Yeah, but she's a Geordie, though, isn't she? And they've got a whole different language, haven't they? Vince reckons it's a bit like Welsh."

"*Welsh?*"

"Yeah, except you never get to hear it, because they only use it with each other. In private. Like a secret communication sort of thing."

"Matty's planning on learning," says Vince, shooting me a grin. "I said I'd get him a book."

I give Vince the nod and join in.

"So, Matty," I say, "have you had a good look at her toes yet?"

"Her *toes?*"

"Yeah, they have webbed toes, don't they, your Geordies. Like the Man from Atlantis. One in five of them, I heard it was."

Matty stares into his drink for a moment. And then he starts to laugh.

"Yeah, right," he says, shaking his head, "that's a good one. Webbed toes. Fuck me, you're having me on again, aren't you?"

We don't say anything. Matty begins to look worried.

"You are, yeah? Aren't you? I mean, you *are* joking, right?"

"Yes, mate," I say. "We are. We are most definitely having you on."

"Cool," he says, looking relieved. "I thought so. Now then, Vince, where did you say I could get hold of that book?"

62

It's first thing in the morning and I'm woken by the irritating cheep of my brand-new mobile phone. It was Alison's idea that I get one—probably so she could keep track of me—but it's Kostas that calls me the most. He's immensely keen on text messaging, for some reason, and ever since I told him I was leaving he's been sending me useless bits of information on a regular basis. It's an odd mixture of stuff: meatball recipes, video reviews, the odd weather report—usually from Cyprus—and sometimes he just likes to call me to make sure that I'm up.

I can't be bothered to read it. Most of the time I can't even understand what he's trying to say. He's learnt every single abbreviation in the *Mobile User's Handbook*, and it takes me longer to work out the words than it does for Kostas to write the message in the first place. Sod it. There it goes again. I suppose I might as well see what he wants.

DNY URGNT SHLA TKN 2 HSPTL
CUM RGHT AWY
C U THR LUV KSTS.

I jump in the car and drive over to the hospital as quickly as I can. Kostas is pretty easy to find. He's sitting in the A & E waiting room, wedged between a snoring drunk and a heavily pregnant woman, and it's obvious he's been crying. I'm a little taken aback to see it: this strong, solid bear of a man, blinking back the tears from his eyes and dabbing at his cheeks with one of the pregnant lady's tissues. I can feel my throat begin to tighten. I know what he's going to say. I'm already too late.

Kostas sees me coming and stands up to give me a hug. His heavy arms wrap themselves around my shoulders and he sniffs a little before he speaks.

"She is gone," he says simply. "I am very sads, Danny. She is already gone."

I flop down opposite him on one of the cracked plastic seats and listen quietly while he fills me in. She had a heart attack, he says, she was brought in by ambulance late last night. She never even managed to regain consciousness. They tried everything that they possibly could.

Kostas offers me a spare tissue and I find myself pulling it apart in my hand. I can't believe it. I can't seem to take it all in. I'm sad and angry in equal measure, but the thing that's bothering me most is the fact that she died alone. Sheila liked company. She made every effort to seek it out. She loved to while away her afternoons chatting to me and Kostas at the video counter, she loved pottering in and out of all the Broadway shops. She spent every lunch-time drinking tea in her favourite café just so she could be around other people. Someone ought to have been with her. Someone she knew. No one should have to die alone.

Kostas goes to the bathroom to wash his face and I search out one of the nurses who looked after Sheila when she was brought in. She does her best, she tells me the standard things: Sheila wasn't in any pain, she wouldn't have known what was happening to her. It was a blessing, she says, she passed away very peacefully in the end.

I take it all in. I nod and smile and try to be polite but I'm not entirely sure that it's true. I'm grateful that she wasn't in any pain but I doubt that her death was peaceful; I don't think it ever really is. I imagine she fought it, I imagine she clung to life as hard as she possibly could. That would have been Sheila's way. She wouldn't have given up without a fight.

The waiting room begins to fill with new faces and the two of us sit for a while, watching them, trying to work out what to do next. There's no point hanging around in the hospital, but for some reason neither of us wants to leave. Kostas suggests we walk up to the cafeteria for a drink; he thinks we could both use a cup of coffee before we head home.

"I'm going to miss her very much," says Kostas, staring into his steaming paper cup.

"Yeah," I say, "I'm going to miss her too."

"She was a very great lady."

"Yeah, Kostas," I say, "she really was. Remember when she first came into the shop, remember when she asked for a copy of *Enter the Dragon*? You'd already fished out a copy of *Driving Miss Daisy*, hadn't you? Do you remember the look on her face?"

Kostas shakes his head. I thought this story would make him feel a little better but it seems to have made him even more sad.

"I don't know, Danny," he says, shaking his head miserably, "maybe it was all too much for her."

"What do you mean? She loved coming to visit us, it was a really important part of her day."

"Yes, I know, but maybe there is something more we could have done."

"Come on, Kostas," I say, attempting to cheer him up, "we both kept a good eye on her, didn't we? I looked after her garden, you used to pop round with hot meals from Mrs. Kostas, and you heard what the nurses said, they're sure she wasn't in any pain."

"But Danny," he says sombrely, "I feel terrible. Maybe it is our faults that she is dead."

I stare down at my vending-machine coffee and watch the thick bubbles of milk powder struggle to reach the surface. Maybe Kostas is right. I could see she was looking tired when I went to visit her the other day. Maybe I should have phoned her daughter. Maybe I should have called the doctor and asked him to come round and check on her. I feel guilty, like I've let her down. I can't believe she spent the whole afternoon feeding me biscuits and trying to cheer me up when she was obviously feeling unwell.

Kostas nods his head.

"All these things are true, Danny," he says gravely, "but I am afraid is much worse than that. I really think maybe her deaths had something to do with us."

I'm not sure what he means. I'm about to tell him he's being daft but I can tell by his expression that he's serious. He seems uncomfortable. He seems genuinely worried about something.

"What is it, Kostas?" I say, urging him on. "What is it that's bothering you?"

"Well," he says, rubbing his chin, "she had a heart attacks, didn't she?"

"Yes, she did. But I suppose that's just the way things are. She was an old lady. The nurse said it could have happened at any time."

"Yes," he says, shifting uneasily in his seat, "but didn't you hear what that doctor said? He said Sheila had her heart attacks in front of the television, while she was watching a Kostas video."

"You're *kidding*?"

"No," he says, lifting his hand to his forehead, "I am afraid is true, right in the middle of *Fist of Fury*. Just as Bruce Lee is taking revenge on his most deadly of rivals. Is a terrible thing, Danny. Her next-doors neighbour heard her knocking over the giant biscuits tin when she dropped her remotes control. What? . . . Why are you smiling? . . . Danny, this is not some kind of a funny jokes . . ."

He's right, I know he's right, but somehow I can't seem to help myself. I think it would have made her smile too. Given the choice, I'm pretty sure that's exactly the way she would have wanted to go.

My first instinct when I get home is to pour myself a large drink. The journey back from the hospital has left me feeling drained and depressed and there's something about the piles of cardboard boxes and the blankness of the bare plaster walls that makes me feel even worse.

Everything is changing. In another week I'll be leaving this place for good, and the truth is I'm going to miss it. I'm going to miss Vince phoning me at all hours of the day and night. I'm going to miss Kostas badgering me to get up and come into work. I'm going to miss Matty and the shop and my endless battles with the shower and everything about being in the band. And I'm going to miss Sheila. More than I realised. In her own way I think she believed in me more than anybody else.

I lift a cold bottle of beer out of the fridge, but something makes me put it back. I suddenly want to speak to Alison. I want to pick up the phone and speak to someone I love. In the end it doesn't matter what I'm giving up here. This isn't about what I want any more: this is about the two of us.

I lift the receiver and dial Alison's number by heart. I count the rings until she answers and wait for the intense familiarity of her voice. Sheila once told me she was married for almost fifty years. And I hope that means something. I hope that means she never felt truly alone.

• • •

"Hey, it's me."

"Hi. How's the packing going?"

"Fine, it's going fine. But listen . . . I've got something to tell you . . . I've got some sad news."

I finish the call and gather my thoughts for a moment. It was good to speak to her. Our conversations have felt pretty strained over the last few weeks, but she seemed a little more open this time. I could feel her coming back. I could sense the tenderness in her voice when I told her about Sheila, and it's the first time I've felt she still cares. That's the kind of person she is, she couldn't stop herself. Even though she's a long way from forgiving me, her instinct was still to reach out. It's a good sign. I suppose I've got Sheila to thank in a way.

Alison said something else as well. Something that made a lot of sense. She said given how much I'm going to miss Sheila I should make a proper effort to keep in touch with my mum while I'm away. Maybe she's right. Maybe this would be a good time to give her a quick call.

"Hey, Mum, it's me."

"Steve, I was just thinking about you. I'm so glad that you phoned. I was wondering if I'd get to see you before you left."

"Of course you will," I say. "I thought I might drive over tomorrow afternoon if that's okay?"

"Good," she says, "because I've got some very interesting job adverts for you to look at."

"That'll be nice," I say. "I'll look forward to it."

63

Sheila's funeral is something of a triumph. The small congregation is filled out with people that she'd befriended on her travels round Crouch End over the years, and several members of her family stand up and make touching speeches about her life. It makes all the difference. I remember what it was like at my grandmother's funeral; all the speeches were left to the vicar, someone she'd never even met. He made all these well-meaning comments about how nice she was and what a kind lady she'd been, and the thing is it wasn't really true. She'd always been a bit of a battle-axe. It made everyone feel uncomfortable. I remember thinking that it might have been better if he'd told the truth.

Today is very different. Sheila is instantly recognisable in their words. They talk about her intelligence and her humour and her unbowed lust for life, and her grandson even mentions her devotion to Bruce Lee and her love of Mr. Kipling's cakes.

Kostas can't quite believe it. His wide shoulders heave up and down with silent laughter when they mention Sheila's frequent visits to his shop, and I notice Mrs. Kostas take hold of his hand and give it a quick squeeze. I just wish Alison could have been here. It's a shame she couldn't get the time off work. Still, at least I know she's thinking of me. Because she called me this morning and said that she was.

• • •

Everyone heads back to Sheila's house for tea and sandwiches after the service and I'm glad to see that everything is much the same. The hallway is full of flowers and cards, but I can still sense Sheila everywhere I turn: smiling out from the photos on the mantelpiece, nodding approval at the selection of cakes. I'm not sure she would have approved of the paper doilies, though. I think she would have thought they were a little fussy.

I park myself on one of the wobbly kitchen chairs that are dotted about the living room, and it's not long before Sheila's daughter comes to find me. Her name is Grace; she's about fifty years old with dyed blond hair and a familiar sense of mischief in her eyes.

"You must be Danny," she says, reaching over to give me a hug. "I just wanted to thank you for everything you've done."

"That's okay," I say, a little taken aback by her display of affection. "I didn't do anything very much."

"Oh yes you did," she says emphatically. "My mother spoke about you all the time. You brought her a lot of happiness over the years, you know. She said you were quite a young man."

"Yes, well," I say, beginning to get embarrassed, "and she was quite a lady."

"Yes," says her daughter, "she most certainly was."

I warm to Grace straight away. She's a nice person: direct and open and honest like her mother, and she shares her same sense of adventure as well. She spent twenty years working as an interpreter in Japan after she left university, and she's run a small hotel in Cornwall with her husband for the last ten.

"I kept asking her to come down and live with us," she says, shaking her head and offering me an extra bourbon, "but she wouldn't hear of it. She was very independent, you know. Couldn't bear the idea of leaving London. I think she would have found living on the coast awfully dreary."

"I'm sure you're right," I say. "Sheila always liked to be at the centre of things."

Grace thanks me for doing her mother's shopping and helping out with the garden from time to time and I tell her all about Sheila's latest obsession with John Woo. It seems to make her happy. I notice that she giggles in much the same way Sheila used to when I tell her how many videos she used to order from the shop.

"I know," she says fondly. "Mum was incorrigible. She tried to get me to learn t'ai chi when we were living in Hong Kong. I wasn't very good at it, though, I'm afraid. She was very disappointed with me when I gave up."

"I'm sure she was," I say. "Mothers can be like that sometimes."

"Look," she says, tapping me sharply on the arm, "I'm supposed to tell you about this later but I don't see why I shouldn't just give it to you now. Stay where you are, Daniel. I won't be long."

Grace disappears to the bedroom and comes back moments later with a small piece of pottery tucked carefully underneath her arm. I immediately recognise what it is.

"Wow," I say, "it's the vase. From the Mongolian warlord."

"Yes," she says, "it's beautiful, isn't it? Sheila wanted you to have it."

"I can't," I say, turning the delicate porcelain over in my hand. "I think you should hold on to it yourself."

"No," she says. "My mother was quite insistent. We spoke about it the last time I came to visit. Give this to Daniel, she said. And make sure he makes proper use of it."

"I don't understand," I say. "What did she want me to do?"

"Sell it, of course. It's worth quite a lot of money. It's not Ming or anything ridiculous like that, but it's still a valuable piece. Close to ten thousand pounds, I think. Maybe more."

I can't believe what she's saying. It's a wonder I don't drop it on the carpet there and then.

"But I can't," I say. "You must be joking. Surely this should go to you or your son?"

"Nonsense," she says. "Mum wanted you to have it. She's left plenty of other things to us. She was quite the collector, you know. Her cupboards are full of pieces like this. I think she had rather more suitors than she let on."

"But I don't understand," I say, shaking my head. "Why didn't she sell some of it? I'm sure she could have done with the money."

"I don't think she wanted to. I think it gave her more pleasure to know she was passing them on. Her needs were quite simple towards the end of her life, Daniel. I don't think she wanted for anything much."

I chat to Grace a while longer, spend fifteen minutes luring Kostas away from the finger buffet, and then we get ready to leave. Grace comes over to kiss us good-bye.

"Now," she says gently, "don't be tempted to hold on to it for years and years or anything like that. My mother left strict instruction that it should be sold. She said life wasn't to be wasted on looking backwards and that you should use it for something you needed."

"I don't know," I say, suddenly feeling guilty, "I'm not sure I'd ever be able to sell it."

"Well, it's up to you, of course, but I'm certain it would have made my mother happy to know she was helping you in some way."

"She didn't have much time for nostalgia, did she?" I say, kissing Grace on the cheek and tucking the vase into one of Sheila's Budgens bags. "I mean, she thought life was for living, didn't she, not for wrapping up and putting away."

"Of course she did," says Grace, opening the door for me. "What else is life for?"

I'm not saying that it was an easy decision to make but Alison came round to my way of thinking in the end. After I'd blackmailed her. For over a week. After I'd told her it was Sheila's dying wish. After I'd promised to give up watching *Columbo*, cut down on my drinking, buy myself some new underpants and throw away all my back issues of *Q* and *Sound on Sound*.

After I'd told her that I loved her. More than I've loved anyone else in my whole life.

Because ten grand is a lot of money, isn't it? And it would be a shame not to make proper use of it. It means we could support ourselves for a few months. Just while I see if the record deal comes to anything. And Alison could go back to college if she wanted to. She wouldn't have to worry about giving up her job. She wouldn't have to worry about paying the rent and sorting out the bills and supporting the two of us any more.

Because Sheila was right. If Alison loves me then she'll forgive me, won't she? In time. It doesn't matter where we decide to live.

I put down the phone from Alison and ring Vince up straight away. It takes him a full minute to stop cackling and then he says, "Jesus Christ, Danny. Thank fuck for that. I knew you had to come to your senses sooner or later. I was only joking, you know. I never thought you'd actually go and do it. I always had you down as a bit of a soft bastard, but even you wouldn't be dumb enough to give up the band over a bird."

64

"Alison, stop doing that, it's really annoying."

"What? What am I doing?"

"You're getting the lyrics wrong. 'Yesterday' is the most frequently played song of all time. It's been performed more than any other song in the entire history of popular music. And you're singing the words wrong. How do you do that? How do you always manage to get the wrong words?"

"Okay, calm down. I don't see what difference it makes."

"You don't see what *difference* it makes? Jesus, are you mad? Of course it makes a difference. How can you not know how it goes? How can you not know the words to 'Yesterday'? That's typical. It's a woman thing, isn't it? It's definitely a woman thing. I knew I should never have let you come."

"Don't take any notice," says Vince sagely. "He's always like this before he goes on. He'll be all right once he's been to the bogs."

"Yeah," says Matty, "he gets mega-nervous or something. He gets all full of adrenal glands and then he has to dash off to the crapper for a big old poo."

"Of course, he's much better than he used to be," says Vince, lighting himself a fag. "He used to do it every time we went onstage. At least he only does it before we do interviews now. And live radio. And festivals."

"Is this right, Danny?" she says, nudging me. "Are you really that nervous?"

"No," I say. "It's rubbish. I'm completely and utterly fine."

I am not fine. I am very fucking far from fine. We're sitting in the green room sipping beers and smoking cigarettes and it's less than ten minutes before we're due to go on. It's the first time we've done it. Our first live performance on national television. Our first time on Saturday morning telly. Our first time on *CD:UK*.

They've got it completely wrong, though. I'm not worried about the performance at all. I'm worried about Alison meeting Ant and Dec. I mean, what if one of them fancies her? What if they both want to shag her at the same time? What if they wait until I'm onstage and then one of them walks over to her and says: "Hi, has anyone ever told you, you look a little bit like Cat Deeley?"

Bastards.

"Did you enjoy it?" I say, opening us another bottle of champagne.

"Yeah," she says. "It was brilliant."

"They're definitely gay, though, aren't they? I mean, you only have to look at that dark one's hair."

"Give it a rest," she says, topping up our glasses. "I had a good time because of you. You were amazing. All three of you were. I thought you sounded great up there today."

"You don't think we've sold out, then?"

"Don't be stupid. Of course you haven't. How do you mean?"

"Well, I don't know, letting them use our single in that curly fries advert and everything. I mean, that's the only reason we got so high in the charts in the first place."

"Danny, I don't think it matters. It's not like there's a nauseating, fat-tongued celebrity chef in it or anything. At least it's just a picture of some chips."

"Yeah," I say, "you're probably right. I just don't want people getting fed up with us. I don't want us getting dropped before we've had a chance to make our second album. Not like Scarface. Not before Vince gets to record his duet with Kevin Rowland. Not before my mum gets to meet Dale Winton again."

"They won't," she says, sighing at me. "You've only just started. You've got your whole careers ahead of you yet."

"You're right," I say, knocking back the rest of my wine. "You're definitely right. Come on, then, let's go home."

Alison undresses quickly and gets into bed. She closes away her folders, packs away her revision notes and rolls over to switch out the bedside light. I can hear the soft shoop-shoop of her breathing as she starts to drift off to sleep. I wait for her to say it. It's one of those stupid codes we have: one of those things she does to let me know that she's not cross with me any more. And then she says it: quietly, sleepily, under her breath.

"Goodnight," she says. "Goodnight, Steve McQueen."

ACKNOWLEDGMENTS

For all their skill, advice, support, and encouragement a huge thank you to:

Hannah Griffiths, Carolyn Mays, Sheila Crowley, Emma Longhurst, David Brimble, Faye Brewster, Georgina Moore, Jason Hyde, Jo Chappell, Tony Fisher, Richard Priest, Jonathan Stewart, Geoff Wener, Andy Maclure . . . and my mum, Audrey.